dangerous VOWS

THE DIFFERENCE BETWEEN A PROMISE AND A VOW?
PROMISES WERE BROKEN.

KRIS BUTLER

Dark Confessions Series
Book Three

dangerous vows

KRIS BUTLER

CONTENTS

BLURB

Between the truth and lies, I'd found the dark confession I'd been too afraid to acknowledge. I was tired of hiding behind fear, the lies holding me back too much. It was time to drop the mask completely and embrace the reality that had been staring me in the face.

Except now, I was the one with the secret.

Faced with an unimaginable dilemma, I had to face what was at stake—the family I was creating versus the woman I'd always been.

Maybe it was time to step out of my own shadow and into the woman I was meant to be?

Vowing to myself to fight for what I wanted, I wouldn't let anything stand in my way this time—even myself.

But what if I wasn't enough? Could I overcome the pressures or would I lose everything?

FOREWORD

This is the 3rd book in the series and books 1 and 2 must be read first. This is a why choose novel, meaning the main female character doesn't have to choose between love interests. This is a dark contemporary mafia romance, medium burn with a slow build harem. The characters are adults with most being 30 and above. This story deals with depression and other themes that may be triggering such as child loss, rape, death, violence, and kidnapping. This is an adult romance and intended for readers 18+ due to language and content. This series does contain an MM relationship.

This book is dedicated to perseverance and not giving up on a dream. Sometimes, you just have to turn your head so you can see the full scope of what it's meant to be. Don't ever give up. You're worth it.

PROLOGUE

CAMI

NINE MONTHS AGO

Wiping the bar top, I glanced up when I heard footsteps approaching. My cousin eyed me, assessing my countenance as he made his way over. There was always so much more than met the eye with Atticus.

"Camilia, how are you doing this evening? Are you finding Illusion to your liking?"

Nodding, I smiled at the intimidating man, trying to remind myself he was nothing like his father. "Yes, I am, actually. It's the perfect transition for me from that seedy bar I've been at the past year. I really do love bartending, and it's the perfect job with graduate school. I like the changes you've made, and the clientele has all been polite," I babbled, unable to stop myself.

"Very good. If you have any trouble or see any strange men sniffing around, be sure to let me or Saxon know. I'm hoping the new renovations and club structure will be enough changes to deter them, but I can never be too careful with *that* family. The masks will go into effect tomorrow as well. You know the rules on those?"

"Yes, sir. They're fascinating, and I like the concept a lot."

"Thank you." He briefly lifted his lip, almost allowing himself to smile in pride. "I like the idea of exclusivity and anonymity, myself."

"I'm sure you do." I grinned, the corners of my lips lifting. I imagined being the boss of a crime family didn't lend a lot of anonymity.

"Now, cousin, I know you're not applying any of your psychology education on me?" Atticus had a slight teasing tilt to his voice, the only thing that calmed my racing heart for forgetting momentarily who I was speaking with.

"Never, sir."

"Good." He smiled wholly this time, my heart slowing at the gesture. "Outside of you, and a select few others, as far as all the other employees are concerned, the Mascros no longer have any association with Climax, and it's now under new management."

"Understood."

He started to leave, but stopped, turning back to ask me one more question. "You're going by your mother's maiden name now, correct?"

"Yes, I'm legally Camila Costa. Mason continues to flaunt his imagined status around like anyone cares that he's a third cousin, twice removed or whatever of Dayton's," I scoffed, rolling my eyes. My brother was a tool, and an absolute moocher, a complete parasite if I'd ever met one. Our father had died when I was a teenager, making us of zero importance to the Mascros, but Mason wouldn't hear it. When I glanced back at Atticus, I realized my mistake; his father's death was still recent. "Sorry, I spoke out of line." I dipped my eyes, worried I'd lose this job before it even started.

"No, you're fine. It's just odd hearing his name." He cleared his throat, and I looked up, catching him straightening his tie in a nervous gesture. "Well, I'll be off. You know how to reach me if there are any problems. I'll be around, but I'd like to stay a secret."

"You got it." I nodded, and he smiled briefly, tapping the bartop before he stalked off. I fell back into work, the hours passing by quickly as I filled drinks and flirted with the guests.

It was a few hours later when *he* appeared.

I'd been chatting up a couple at the end of the bar when he'd walked in, setting my pulse racing and my pussy throbbing. There was something about his devil-may-care looks that had me wanting to run and lick every inch of him. The tattoos on his hands made me yearn to see them on my body, his stubble beckoning me to have it rubbed against my lady bits. His smirk set my pulse racing, and his dark eyes were lit with mischief. He was the first man outside of Seb I'd found myself attracted to. The hidden danger running through him was my kryptonite.

"Excuse me, gorgeous, what does a fella have to do to get a drink served by you around here?"

I eyed him up and down slowly as I walked toward him, every ounce of my seductive charms oozing out of me as I leaned against the surface, batting my eyelashes. "I don't know. What are you willing to do?"

The man eyed me, and there was no question in his gaze about what he wanted. "How about you come back to my place and find out? That is… if you're available?"

Biting my lip, I thought it over. I was currently part of a triad with a woman and a man, the three of us in a polyamorous relationship. Being bi-sexual, I enjoyed being with them both together and separately. Part of our poly relationship agreement meant we were open to other relationships outside our threesome, as long as we disclosed it to one another. If it became more than just a sexual fling, then it was a discussion. So far, none of us had found anyone worth bringing into our nucleus, but we'd all dabbled a few times. It had just been a while for me.

"Clearly, I misread the signals, my apologies." He started to walk away, and panic clawed at my throat at the idea of him leaving.

"Wait! How do I know you're not a serial killer? A girl's gotta cover her bases."

"Fair, but it seemed more than that. If you're taken, then it's my loss."

"I am, well, sort of. I'm in an open relationship with a man and a woman."

"So, where does that leave me?"

"I just…" something held me back, despite the panic at him leaving, I couldn't find the words to give in to the invitation either.

"What she meant to say was yes." Lark cozied up to the bar, giving me a look, and I rolled my eyes at her snark but smiled.

"Can you just excuse us for a second? If you wait for me over at that table, I'll just be a minute." The dangerously devilish man looked at me oddly but nodded, moving over to the table I'd indicated. Once he was gone, I pulled Lark around to the end of the bar for some semblance of privacy.

"Why did you do that?" I hissed.

"Because I could tell you were into him, and it's been a while since you had any side dick. I figured if I made the decision for you, then you'd be more likely to go through with it. You're too all up in your head about things, especially since—"

Squishing her lips together, I shook my head, not wanting her to say it. Saying it made it real.

"Nope." Shaking my head, I took a deep breath and let go of her.

"Sorry, Cams, but that right there is why I think you should go. Let go, ride some well-aged dick, and then come home and tell Seb and me all about it." Lark wrapped her arms around me, pulling me into her, and I melted. Ninety percent of the time, I was a hardass, not taking shit from anyone and living my life the way I wanted. But in Lark's arms, I was a puddle of mush, malleable to her desires.

"You know I fucking love you, right?"

"Duh, I'm awesome." She leaned back, smiling, and I knew I wanted her in my life forever. Kissing her softly, I kept it short, not wanting to get in trouble for PDA while working on my first day. My cousin might be the owner, but it didn't mean the bar manager knew that. No, I had to do well at this job, and that meant staying off the radar.

"Okay, fine. But I'm pinging you my location the moment I get there and holding you to a sexy gabfest later."

"And I have just the outfit to wear for it," she cooed, making me seriously debate calling off the sexy man and just going home with my girlfriend. I bit my lip, indecision weighing on me.

"Nope, no turning back. Go, ride that bronco until his Viagra wears off."

Snorting, I shook my head, playfully slapping her arm. "He's not *that* old. Geez, Lark. He's what, maybe early 40's? I'm 30. Not that big of an age gap."

"Oooh, age-gap! Yes, go, and let me know if it still works the same." She giggled, pushing me toward him. I hadn't finished any of my closing duties, but with her blocking the way, I knew there was no way I was getting back there. Knowing her, she'd take care of it for me. She was sweet that way.

The man smiled when I approached, making my insides quiver, and I was glad she'd pushed me to do it. She was right. It was time.

"You ready, gorgeous?"

"I think the question is, are you? I might be more than you bargained for."

"Oh, I hope you are. I really hope you are." His smile held a gleam of something, but I dismissed it, too caught up in the attraction to notice.

CURRENT

The pain jolted me awake, and I blinked, trying to make sense of my surroundings. The fever dreams had become so real, it was hard to tell reality from the past. The pain was the only thing that clued me into my reality. The circumstances I found myself in were not ideal. In fact, they sucked.

What I wouldn't give to be home and in the arms of my lovers, laughing about the misadventures of flings. Though Darren had become more than a fling in the end, and I'd messed things up with the best things in my life. After our first night together, I woke up in his bed, breakfast scattered all around me as he wooed me with his wealth, attentiveness, and desire for me. Like a cat drawn to catnip, I ate up every morsel he gave me, always ready for more.

When I realized he was Darren Delgado, the sworn enemy of my family, I was already in too deep and half in love with him. My first mistake was not telling Lark and Seb just who he was, though they wouldn't have known the significance, since they still didn't know my family was connected to the criminal underworld. My second mistake was not telling Atticus, and my third was believing anything Darren told me was true and that I could change him and not lose everything in the process.

I'd been a fool, a pawn from the very beginning, an easy mark. Especially at that time, after the death of my mom. I'd been too broken to deal with my grief, shoving it aside, and forgetting everything that mattered.

I almost believed I deserved this.

The door swung open, the hinges squeaking as the heavy wood rattled with each push. I didn't bother looking up. I knew who it was. Who it always was.

"Oh, pet, you're not looking so swell. Perhaps a bath is in order. I can't have my girlfriend looking under the weather at the big show tonight. That would be a crime!"

He laughed at his joke, finding it hilarious, but I kept my head down, not wanting to bear his cold, dark eyes. The eyes I'd stared at so many times and thought I was different, that I was the one.

Now, all I saw was pity, my failure to outwit him glaringly obvious with each punishment he gave me.

Yanking my hair back, he practically spat in my face with how close he was. "It would be wise to play along, darling. Otherwise, people might get ideas, and I can't have them thinking bad things about me. If you want to live, if you want to keep your pretty girlfriend and boyfriend alive, then you better do as you're told. Or, I could always trade you out for, say, Loren? Or how about young Immy? She was meant to be my child bride, after all."

Gritting my teeth, I pulled every ounce of strength left in me to the surface, the lives of the people I cared about were in jeopardy, and I prayed I'd be enough to save them, or at least give them time to figure out his plan. I'd lost hope I'd make it out of this alive, but perhaps, I could do that for them.

It was all I had. I just prayed it was enough.

"Whatever you need, Darren, my love. I'm yours."

"There's my perfect little pet. Good girl. For your obedience, I'll let you shower in private, out of view of my men's eyes."

My body shivered, the thought of the cold water he'd sprayed me down with the other day, and the way his "men" had leered at me, licking their lips like they wanted a taste. I was surprised he hadn't offered me to them, my only hope was I meant enough to him he didn't want to share.

It was fleeting, but I held onto it tight.

The words my mama always told me flooded through me, giving me the strength to stand up, despite my body being weakened by malnourishment and abuse.

"A Costa woman has two weapons she can use—her body and her mind. Men will look at you for your body and crave you. They will fear you for your mind. Beckon them in like a Siren with your body, keeping your intelligence hidden, and you'll never be without a weapon. For beauty is dangerous, but intelligence, well, child, that's lethal."

Besides, I was a firm believer in the concept that a woman was only helpless when her nail polish was drying.

Darren just made his first mistake by underestimating me and using my loved ones as bait. Now, it was my turn to exploit him. I was a Costa woman, after all. It was time to be lethal.

ONE

SAX

S ix words. Six words were all it took to wreck my world and destroy my heart.

Her question echoed around my head, the inevitable turning point for our relationship that had begun to mean more to me than anything else. Fear unlike anything I'd felt before ran down my spine, and I involuntarily stiffened, drawing Spitfire's attention. She assessed me with her unwavering gaze, waiting for me to answer.

"I think it's time we had a talk. Come on, Atticus is waiting."

Loren searched my eyes, and I tried to convey it was okay, that I wasn't dangerous despite her question. The question that would undoubtedly change her opinion of me. I became laser-focused on her every detail, watching for any sign of fear, doubt, or even disgust, but I saw nothing.

It appeared Loren had found the one thing she could hide from me.

She eventually nodded, and the hopeful part of me sighed, praying it meant she'd hear us out, that she'd listen without jumping to conclusions. It had been running through me from the moment I'd realized I wanted her forever, and I needed to know whether or not she could take me as I was with all my buried scars and darkness. My life hadn't been pretty, but it was one I was proud of. And now, I just wanted her to never change how she looked at me. Loren made me feel like I was more than just the muscle, more than just the intimidating asshole I'd become known as.

Loren, my spitfire, made me feel like a worthy man.

Wrapping my arm around her, I sighed some more when she didn't pull away, but leaned into my touch, seeking it out as much as I had. As we walked through the cemetery, we were quiet, stepping around headstones and memorabilia left by loved ones. The morning air was crisp, the sound of birds the only thing you could hear as the morning dew clung to each tiny blade of grass.

If I hadn't gotten the notification that she was in danger, I'd have been more curious about why she was here or what she'd been doing. But from the moment Beau had texted, rage and fierce protectiveness had risen up in me, and it had only been Atticus insisting he'd come along that had held me back from riding my bike at full tilt to get to her.

When the SUV came into view, I slowed, not ready for this peace to end. Stopping a few feet away, I turned, clasping her forearms. "Everything in me is screaming to shut up, to keep quiet like I've been trained to do, but a newer part of me, the one you've awakened, is yelling a little louder at the moment. It's telling me I'd be a fool to get into that SUV without saying something, without trying to make a plea."

Loren observed me again, taking in every detail of my face and cataloging it away. She swallowed once and gave a slight nod for me to continue. I hadn't realized I'd been waiting for her permission, but once it registered, I caved.

"I'm not a good man, Spitfire. There are demons in my past, fuck in my present and future too. It's the way of life I live, the one I chose to live. I never dreamed of finding someone like you who'd make me feel differently about the choices I've made. But there you were, minding your own business and sauntering into my heart with your fire and grace, completely wrecking all the carefully laid plans I had for myself. My hands will never be clean, and the life I lead will always be danger-ous, but I need you in my life, want you in my life, and I'm hoping there's a way to do that."

"Why does it feel like you're already expecting me to run away?" she whispered, moving her hand to cup my cheek. "Despite my appearance, I've never been ignorant of the danger you possess. I'm discovering it isn't always easy to point out the good guys and bad guys. I'd like the chance to hear all the information before I decide anything, so maybe," she shrugged, smiling, "give me that opportunity before you go making declarations you might not be ready to make."

Her hand dropped, and she went to move away, but I stopped her, pulling her close to my body, leaning down to whisper into her ear.

"Oh, Spitfire, I never say anything I don't mean. I'd keep that in mind before you go dismissing my heartfelt confessions."

Loren's words had given me the one inch of space I needed to breathe, allowing me to insert myself into her life where it would be impossible for her to ignore me. And I planned to use it to my full advantage. Her breath hitched as my lips brushed against her ear. I breathed in her coconut shampoo, running my nose along her neck and cupping her ass in one hand. In case it was a while before I got to touch it again, I wanted to get in a good feel.

For memories, of course.

Stepping back, I watched as she attempted to regain her composure, her breathing ragged as she blinked open her eyes. As she watched me, I shifted the steel rod in my pants, ensuring she noticed before I turned around, lacing our fingers together. Loren didn't resist when I pulled her along, the door being opened as we neared, by Elijah, the guard standing sentinel.

Taking Loren's hand, I assisted her into the dark space, sliding in behind her once she was seated. The door shut, and I returned to my role as a silent enforcer while I waited for Atticus to assess the situation. When he looked at me, I filled him in.

"Spitfire has a question. I felt it best for you to answer."

"I see."

He sat back, crossing his ankle across his knee as he waited. Mas was the epitome of a mafia boss at that moment, and there was a part of me that wanted to slap him for using his intimidation tactics on her. But I knew the score, and this was the game he had to play for the moment until we knew how she would react. When she didn't say anything, he flicked his eyes to me.

"Go ahead, Spitfire, ask your question again."

She turned to me, nodding before she found her voice. "Oh, um, well, you see," she fumbled, twisting her hands in her lap. I didn't know if she'd become flabbergasted in Atticus' presence or if the interlude between us had been more than she'd bargained for. She took a few seconds to gather her composure, and of course, I attributed it to me.

"Yes, Mrs. Carter?" Mas asked again, probing her. She swallowed. Atticus wasn't doing her any favors by making it easier, either.

"I've been thinking, and while at first, I dismissed it as a funny joke, I can't help but wonder now. Are you," she paused, clearing her throat before looking him directly in the eyes. "Are you in the mafia?"

Atticus watched her, giving nothing away. He was waiting her out, using his silent intimidation technique on her, which pissed me off. Clenching my jaw, I was about to tell him where to shove it when he finally opened his mouth and spoke.

"Can I ask how you came to that conclusion?"

Spitfire rolled her eyes, no longer unnerved by his presence. Smiling, I relaxed back, brushing her pinky with mine, giving a tiny ounce of moral support. I couldn't help getting a kick out of her verbally squeezing Mas' balls a little bit.

"Hmm, well, there's the outrageous amount of wealth, which could be explained away by your businesses. But it was mostly the suited men, the blacked-out cars, and the way they defer to you both that made me the most suspicious, even if I didn't want to admit it. But I think it was the underlying feeling of danger and power you hold, along with the apparent stalker I didn't realize I had who's tried to intimidate, threaten, and now kidnap me, that made me finally face the fact that you're not just a businessman, but a dangerous one."

She let out a breath like she'd held it in to say all her words and now sat back, deflated like a balloon at getting them out. I felt her pinky wrap around mine, and I turned my head, leaning against the window as I covered the smile forming there with my fist. Spitfire had been right; it was wrong for me to underestimate her.

While she was brilliant, and perhaps a little scared about what our life meant, she wasn't running away from it. Maybe I should be more worried about that fact, but if it kept Loren in my life, I didn't give a flying fuck about the reason.

I tilted my head slightly to watch Atticus out of the corner of my eye. He wouldn't admit it, but I could tell he was pleased. He always was a sucker for an intelligent woman, something his mother had conveyed the power of when he was young. Mas didn't talk about her much, but the few things he shared were always treasured memories, held to the highest esteem. I couldn't help but wonder if all these years it wasn't Jaz's death that kept him from settling down, but instead the vow he made to himself to find someone worthy in every way that mattered.

And Loren, this woman, was exceptional in every way.

"It's interesting you brought this up now, Mrs. Carter. I've come to the realization that you and the young Mr. Franklin are becoming permanent fixtures in our lives, despite my hesitancy for that to occur. While it goes against everything in me to reveal my family's secret, our history, I knew the time was coming when we wouldn't be able to hide behind obscurity. It's part of the reason why I'd wanted to hold the fundraiser for the center. I wanted to show you that there were more sides to us than just the one the media portrays."

He paused, waiting to see if she'd ask anything, but when she stayed quiet, he continued.

"So to answer your question, Mrs. Carter, yes, my family is part of the criminal underground, or as you'd said, the mafia. But," he interjected, stopping the question about to jump off Loren's tongue, "I'd like for you to give me the chance to explain who we are as I'd planned. Can you give me that? I promise everything will be explained in detail, but I'd like to do it in a way that gives you the full picture and not like this, after an abduction attempt in a cemetery by a desperate man."

Loren assessed him, her pinky wrapping tighter around mine in the process. I could see her weighing the options, wanting answers now that she'd finally come to the conclusion she had, but wanting to respect his choice as well. I think she wanted to see some good in him, the battle she'd been having with him coming to a cease-fire.

She nodded after a minute, and the tension in the air between us in the small space seemed to lift.

"Thank you, Mrs. C—... *Loren*. I know in the past I haven't always shown you my best side, often pushing your buttons or creating unnecessary conflict. And while I've apologized to you, I'm glad that you didn't forgive me right away. While things haven't been easy in my life, almost everyone has bowed to me, giving in to what I wanted and allowing me to get away with my poor behavior. You reminded me that just because most people fear me doesn't mean I should always take advantage of it. I do want to make amends, and I hope some of my recent choices have shown you that I'm committed to changing your view of me."

"They have, and I do find myself wondering who you really are. There's the man who questions me in my office about my background, fiercely protecting his sister. There's the man who purposefully brings up things that make me uncomfortable, pushing my boundaries. There's the man who showed me a side of myself in a dark club when I didn't even know who I was. There's also the man who helped rescue my dog, helped Monroe get his son back, and made sure his sister had a normal teenage experience by picking out a dress to wear. I see all these aspects of you, and they all make me curious. I can't deny that." Loren's voice had been sure, and she held his eyes the whole time. There was a fierceness that showed through her confidence and strength of character.

"So, where does that leave us?" Atticus asked.

I was proud of him for putting himself out there and not fighting his feelings for once.

"Where do you want it to leave us?"

I turned into the window again, covering my smile. It was such a Mas question, and to hear Spitfire ask it had me chuckling as she'd so swiftly turned the tables on him. I hadn't put it together before, but they had similar qualities, and I wondered if that was what drew me to both of them. Loren had been dulled when I first met her, but with each encounter, I saw her fire spreading through her, coating her in armor.

If Loren at half strength was already someone to contend with, I couldn't wait to see her at full. She'd be an avenging angel, wiping out her foes with nothing more than a look or carefully placed word.

I, for one, couldn't wait to watch the world burn around her.

I thought I'd be the one fighting for her, but I'd been wrong. Loren didn't need me to fight her battles; she just needed me to remind her who she was.

It was something I'd be willing to do until I took my last breath on this earth. I could only hope it wasn't anytime soon.

TWO

LOREN

My breath was stuck in my throat as I waited. I'd meant everything I'd said, but I needed him to put himself out there and open the door himself. I wasn't going to assume anymore, not where Atticus was concerned. He used it to hide behind, and I understood now that I couldn't let him get away with it. In a way, he'd been hiding his whole life. He hid behind his title, in the same way I'd hidden behind my 'perfect Loren' mask.

And if I'd learned anything, it was that masks were only good for Halloween and Illusion.

Hiding kept the truth from being free, and that was a dangerous game to play. One I'd no longer willingly participate in. The truth might hurt, but I much preferred it to the patronizing idea that everything was okay.

Staring, I didn't falter as I held his eyes, waiting to see if he'd continue to step out from behind his carefully controlled world or stay in the dark in his perceived safety. He smiled, the gesture at such odds with the firm stance he typically held, and it shocked me more than I wanted to admit, sending heat through my body.

"You're not making this easy on me, *Bellezza*, are you?"

"Easy is for toddlers and fools, and you're no fool, Atticus. Plus, I think this is something you need to work for, or it will never have meaning."

He nodded, moving forward to brace his elbows on his knees, making him more approachable and open. Slowly, he reached out his hand toward me, picking up mine that sat on my knee. His thumb grazed across the back of my hand, the gesture soft and intimate. Keeping his gaze lowered, he finally spoke.

"What if I'm a fool who wants to believe in happiness even if it scares me?" Atticus whispered, peering up at the end. His umber eyes seared me, and my pulse jumped. Swallowing, I pushed forward the words that had lodged themselves in my throat, knowing how important it was to get this part right.

"I think a person is only a fool if they don't believe that happiness and love are two of the strongest emotions, and that should be scary, but not in the way you're thinking. Happiness isn't something to hide from, to avoid for fear of being hurt when it's gone. Love should be the thing you fight for, only feared by those who oppose you. Because when you find real love, real happiness, you'll do everything in your control to hold on to it, and that's true power. Love doesn't make you a fool, Atticus; it makes you brave."

I wanted to shake myself for using the L-word, but I meant everything I'd said. Happiness and love weren't fleeting emotions, nor were they cure-alls. But when you understood that love didn't magically fix something, it opened doors to experiencing everything it had to offer, like compassion, support, and safety.

I'd never really known real love, but I was starting to.

He squeezed my hand, returning it to my knee as he sat back, clearing his throat. "Well, I guess I'll have to take your word for it."

Rolling my eyes, I snuggled against Sax, ignoring Atticus. He'd retreated, scared, and I wasn't going to coax him out like a frightened animal. He'd had everyone do that for him already; now, he needed to do it for himself.

"Yeah, I guess you will, because until you believe it's worth it, nothing will truly change between us, no matter how many fancy dinners or grand gestures you make."

He scoffed, crossing his arms, some of his defenses rising. "Pfft, you told me to act, and now you're saying it doesn't matter? I think you're the scared one, Mrs. Carter."

Ah, so we were back to Mrs. Carter, were we? I lifted my eyes, not removing my hands from Sax, enjoying his arm around me.

"Actions can be just as empty as words if they don't have meaning. That may sound confusing, but it's simple to me. If I learned anything in the past year, it's that sometimes, actions are just a behavior, forged in us from the womb, and it's as common as blowing your nose. While I appreciate you throwing this benefit for the center and honoring Jude, I imagine it wasn't hard for you to do." He started to argue, but I lifted my eyebrow, giving him a look. His jaw tensed, but he backed down and waited, silently stewing.

"It wasn't. You picked up a phone and had everything sorted. Now, helping me with Barkley, and Monroe with Levi, *that* was meaningful. You inviting my friends to go dress shopping and to the benefit, also meaningful. Renting out the entire store, so Immy was safe, also meaningful. The little things, those gestures, they're the ones that meant something to me. That's what I want to see."

"Why does it feel like I'm being tested?"

"Do you often feel the need to prove yourself?"

"Stop doing that."

"Doing what?" I smiled this time, having too much fun poking the man who'd so effortlessly done it to me a week ago. Sax's hand flexed against my hip, but I wasn't sure if it was because he was encouraging me to continue, enjoying the show, or urging me to stop. Peeking up at him from the corner of my eye, I found him attempting to cover a smile, and I relaxed.

"That!" Atticus answered, pointing at me and then to Sax. "You're answering questions with a question and keep making eyes at Sax. I don't like it."

Sitting back more, I crossed my legs, feeling some

power surge through me. I hadn't meant to break him down, but now that I started, I quite enjoyed it.

"You don't like that you're not getting your way?"

He glared at me, his nostrils flaring a little, and I knew he was close to losing control. The part of me that liked pulling the strings and finding out what was underneath someone wanted to tug real hard. Pushing Atticus' buttons was addictive.

"You know what you're doing."

"Oh? I'm just trying to get to know you."

"No, you're trying to psychoanalyze me and use your mind juju crap on me. It won't work. I'm skilled in the art of intimidation and manipulation."

"And yet, you want me to trust you."

"Yes! Haven't I earned it?"

I sighed, tired of this conversation. It felt too similar to some of the gaslighting Brian had used, and I was now aware of it. Letting go of the seductive feel of power, I sat up, looking at him, showing my vulnerability.

"Atticus, I... it's hard for me to believe you because you are so skilled at getting what you want. It makes me feel like I did with my ex at times, and that's something I don't want in my life anymore. Maybe I'm projecting that onto you a little too much, but it also seems we keep doing this dance of forward and backward while going in a circle. I'm not trying to make it difficult, even if it is fun watching you squirm. I'm trying to protect myself just as much as you are, but I'm also trying to show this damaged heart of mine that I'm worthy of love and respect."

"I'm not trying to say you aren't. I'm wanting to show you those things, but you're making it really hard, and it just makes me want to run away." Sighing, he hung his head, taking some breaths. I looked up at Sax, who was no longer watching me, but his best friend.

"I wonder if I might offer a suggestion," Sax began, looking down at me when he noticed I was looking. "While I do find it entertaining to watch you two spar, I see the toll it's taking on you both, and that isn't the purpose of the tension. I'm not skilled in relationships, but maybe, you both need a do-over. Starting with the party, you both drop the walls, clean the slate, and get to know one another without any of the lies muddling it up. Maybe then you can see if you hate one another, or if that's just a cover for the sexual tension I feel. Before either of you knew who one another was in the club, you shared a moment, so maybe you need to get back to those versions of yourself before all the mistakes were made."

He sat back, and I stared at him, stunned. When he felt me, he tilted his head slightly, giving me a wink. "Not such a neanderthal after all, am I Spitfire?"

Laughing, I shook my head, the tension easing a little more in the enclosed space. Glancing back at Atticus, I found him watching his friend with some of the same curiosity I had.

"Did you learn that from Harry Potter too?" he asked, joking with his friend, offering him a smile.

Sax shrugged. He'd already used his words to lay some truth between us. Atticus met my eyes, and I could see the difference already. Leaning forward, I took his hand this time, and the gesture took him off guard for a second before he grasped it wholly.

"I think Sax is right. When I first met you, I did find you seductive and enchanting, especially that night at the club." An idea came to me at the thought, and I smiled. "Somewhere along the way, you became the person I could target my anger at, not that you didn't deserve it, but you're right. You have been making an effort, and I haven't wanted to admit how nice it's felt."

"Thank you for saying that, Loren. I have to confess that I let my jealousy and fear get the better of me, and I saw you as everything that was wrong. I hated that everyone in my family was falling for you, and yet, you were off-limits to me."

"Why was I off-limits?"

"For several reasons, but mostly, because I feared if I let myself get attached, then you'd be taken away or even killed. I didn't know if I could go through that pain again."

I sucked in a breath, realizing that there was more at play here than just a man scared of being hurt. He was scared of people dying. When I thought about it that way, I guess his actions weren't as bad. Brushing my thumb across his hand, I let out a breath.

"So, what do you say, then? We have a do-over and get to know each other on a real level and not the masks we present to people?"

"It goes against everything I've ever been taught, but the only word running through my head right now is yes."

"And you're okay with it not being just you? I don't know what the future holds, but I know I care about more than one person, and I no longer want to give up the people or things that make me happy."

"I'm going into this with my eyes open, knowing that you're not something I can own. I might not like the other guys being part of it, but I can accept it and possibly grow to like it over time. I won't ask you to give them up, though. I'm not stupid enough to be that egotistical and believe I can replace all of them. I'm not perfect, Loren, far from it, but I've been trying to deny how you make me feel, and all it's done is make matters worse. If there's a way to explore the chemistry we have, then I'll do it, even if I have to squint, so I don't see the others."

Smiling, I laughed a little at his response, imagining him squinting. At least he understood that. It was the one thing I knew I'd be firm on, my heart cared for them all now and I was unwilling to do without. I relaxed my shoulders as I thought about how to ask the next part.

"I know we have the benefit, and I'm to go as your date. But I was wondering," I paused, biting my lip as my eyes dropped, some nervousness rising to the surface. When his thumb brushed against my lip, pulling it free from my teeth, my breath caught at how close he'd moved to me. His hand cupped my jaw, not moving as he gazed into my eyes.

"Yes, *Bellezza*? Don't be scared to ask for what you want, remember?"

"Well, it seems that the club has been a good source of breaking the ice with both of you, and last time I was there, I didn't get to explore some of the other rooms. Maybe, we could go, the three of us, or all of us, hell, I don't really care, but I just thought." I shrugged one shoulder, not knowing what else to say.

"You thought what, *Lore*?"

Looking up, I found his heated gaze on me, searing every inch of skin they touched. I didn't miss how he enunciated my shortened name either, making a version all for himself full of affection.

"It would be a good way to get to know one another without any barriers."

The corner of his mouth lifted up, and I worried I'd never recover from it. If he ever discovered the effect his smile had on me, I'd be done for. There wouldn't be a barrier I could put in place that would keep me from giving in with that smile beaming at me.

"I think that's a marvelous idea. Besides, it would be nice to check in on the place. It's been a few weeks since we've been there."

Blinking, I tried to piece the information together, but my brain stuttered. When he sat back, a smug expression on his face, and the cool air hit me, the Atticus haze I'd been under cleared, and I connected the dots I'd been missing.

"You own the club?"

He eyed me, confused. "Yes, did you not know that?"

Shaking my head, I sat back, wondering what else I didn't know. I thought I was ready to learn everything, but maybe I wasn't. The benefit would be enlightening, at least.

When we pulled up to their building, I was stunned for a second when it didn't pull up to the curb but turned and went underground to a parking garage.

"Whoa. I never knew this was there."

"That's kind of the point."

"Right. Mafia." I nodded, like that explained everything.

Sax chuckled, the deep sound rumbling through me as he turned, placing his lips on my neck. I didn't know what his new obsession with my neck was, but I wasn't complaining. There were so many erogenous zones there I hadn't known about, and each time he breathed, smiled or licked me, I felt my toes curl up and my pussy throb with need. Squirming in my seat, I felt him smile into the crook again, not helping the matter.

When we stepped out of the vehicle, I watched Atticus, wanting to see if I could tell the difference in him now that I knew who he was and that we'd had this conversation. Weirdly, I was kind of glad when he was still just Atticus.

"I hope you don't mind us coming straight here. The fight is this evening and I need to check some things before we go. I guess I should've checked that you had everything you needed. I can send someone to pick up clothes, or run you back to your place if you'd prefer. I just thought you might not want to be alone after what happened."

His thoughtfulness at my well-being helped soften some of the annoyance I felt at his assumption. I looked down at what I wore and knew it wasn't exactly the appropriate fight attire, not if what I wore last time was the standard. Biting my lip in thought, a growl sounded, pulling me from my thoughts, and I glanced up to find Atticus standing close again.

"I really hate when you mistreat your lip as such, Bellezza."

Swallowing, I tried to find an answer to his statement, but nothing came to mind, and we stared at one another, lost. Sax interrupted us a moment later, breaking the heated standoff between us.

"I have some errands to run now. I can run you to your place or pick something up."

"Oh, um, yeah, that would be great. Is Immy going to the fight?"

Atticus looked at me strangely for a moment, like I'd just asked if he wanted to snuff cocaine. "I don't typically allow my seventeen-year-old sister to attend these types of events."

"I can understand that," I started, trying not to take

his tone for the scathing refute it was, "but was that just because it was at the underground place, or because of the context? Isn't tonight's fight at your new arena, Upswing?"

"Yes, but I hardly think it matters. Immy would never want to attend something like that."

"Have you asked her? You might be surprised at what she'd want to do. I think you've underestimated her, and in trying to protect her, have sheltered her too much. I'm not saying stop doing all you're doing," I added, seeing the argument on both Atticus and Sax's faces, "but, maybe, in controlled places, you should allow her to make her own decisions. I don't know how this all works, the mafia life and hierarchy, but I know teenage girls, and the more you restrict, the harder they push. Giving her some freedom and letting her be a part of this life, it might be more helpful than you think. It's just my opinion, but what do I know? I'm just a therapist."

I winked, before turning and walking back toward the garage, hoping the sexy muscled man would follow me. When I heard his heavy stomps a second later, I smiled, feeling like I'd just won something there.

THREE

NICCO

Glancing at my phone for what felt like the millionth time in the last twenty minutes, I was beginning to worry. He said he'd be here, and yet, it was past the time he said, and now I was sweating bullets, thinking it meant something had happened.

Shit. This would be so bad.

On the one hand, I felt proud of myself for being concerned about his well-being, but the other half of me was worried how much Loren would want to kill me, and well, that felt a bit selfish in the light of Jude being potentially kidnapped, so I tried to pull that thought back in.

Instead, I focused on the fact the little weasel had wormed himself into my life and I cared for him. Sighing, I glanced at my phone again to see if there were any new messages in the last five seconds, despite not feeling it vibrate.

When the random text had come through earlier, I'd been confused. When Jude's message followed, stating he needed help, I'd dropped everything and told him I'd be here for whatever it was. Based on the first text, I assumed they were connected. He'd agreed to meet me at this park across from the apartment building, but now I reconsidered the brilliance of that plan with how isolated I was.

Footsteps sounded down the path, and I looked over, relaxing when I spotted Jude. Getting up from the bench, I waited for him to reach me. He bent over, breathing heavily as he caught his breath. I started to ask him a question when he held up his finger, telling me to wait.

Hiding a smile, I cleared my throat, waiting for him to be ready.

"Sorry, I thought it would be quicker to jog, but I clearly didn't take into account my out of shapeness."

"No worries, kid." I chuckled, feeling immense relief he was here. "You know, I bet you could get Wells to give you some exercises or work out with you if you wanted. It might give you some muscles on that lanky frame of yours."

Jude screwed up his nose, but I caught the look on his face that said he was considering my idea. "So, um, thanks for not telling me to take a hike earlier. I panicked and didn't know what to do. For some reason, your number was stuck in my head, so I used it." He paused, beginning to fidget as he twisted his hands on the strap of his messenger bag.

"I'm glad you reached out. I know I haven't always been the most... receptive, but I am here for you, kid.

You're important to Loren and Immy, making you, by default, important to me." I paused, looking him over. "I've grown fond of your little quips and genuineness, and I don't find you annoying, so, winning." He snorted, shaking his head, but the nervousness he had a minute ago fell away. "So, you need help? I'm guessing it has to do with the other message?" I asked.

Jude nodded, pushing his shoulders back now. "That was my brother. He cornered me outside of Ignite."

"And that wasn't a good thing? Not the happy family reunion you wanted?"

He scoffed, shaking his head. "No. Cameron… I think he tried at first to be a good brother after our parents died. We were all each other had while living on the streets, but once we separated and entered the system, it was like he changed. When he turned 18, I didn't see him for a whole year. And when I did, it wasn't good then either. Each time he comes back into my life, it's followed by trouble. A few months back, he got me arrested, and I just don't want to lose everything now."

"Okay, understood. What can I do?" I asked, acknowledging what he'd revealed. I wanted Jude to know I took what he said seriously.

"I don't really know, but I figured you'd have a better idea than anything I'd try to do on my own."

"Why not tell Loren?"

"I'm not going to keep it from her. Just at the moment, I figured one of my new daddies might be able to help."

I stared at him, blinking. "What the fuck?" I choked out, laughing. "Kid, seriously."

Jude laughed so hard, he bent over at the waist again, clutching his stomach. When he finally stopped, he stood, wiping his eyes. "Sorry, sorry, it's just too funny, and it felt like a moment to laugh."

"I see why Loren likes you. You're good for each other. Okay, now that we got that part of the situation out of the way, what do you think your brother is involved with?"

Jude shuffled his feet, looking me over, and I could tell he was debating something, and I wondered if this would be the moment he asked the underlying question. He'd been around the mansion long enough and knew from his time on the streets the kinds of people that went bump in the night. If he didn't have some idea of who we were after the events that had transpired, then I'd be shocked.

"I know you and the others, you're not just family in the sense that you all share the same DNA. I think... I think you're *more*. And, I believe Cameron's gotten himself involved in something bigger than he intended this time. Part of me wants to tell him good luck and wipe my hands clean of him, but I know my parents wouldn't want that. He's my brother, and I *do* care for him. I just don't want him to ruin my life in the process. So, I figured, you could help me by being the bigger baddie or through the endless amount of connections

Imogen's brother seems to have. You could maybe, I don't know, find what he got himself into?"

"You're a smart kid." I studied him, debating what to do. "Okay, I'll look into it with the understanding that you're gonna tell Loren the second you see her. She deserves our honesty, and I'm not going to hide anything from her ever again."

"Does that mean you're going to tell her who you are, then? I think it's only fair if you give her the full scope. Lor, she's tougher than people think."

"You're right, kid. I want to; my hands are just tied to a degree. But that's between her and me. You just worry about being open yourself."

"Fine, I will, but if you want to stay at the top of my favorites, you're gonna have to try harder, you know."

Swiping at him, I laughed. "Listen here, kid," I countered, "I'll be your favorite if you want to keep seeing Immy. I'm *her* favorite."

"Um, you sure about that?" He chuckled, ducking my hand this time, and I shook my head at him.

"My question is, why am I not automatically your favorite? What do the others have? I need to take notes, apparently." We started to walk out of the park toward the condos as we talked.

"Hmm, well, let's see. At first, Wells was last, but he has the dogs now, which bumped him up. Sax, he's automatically up because he's scary as fuck. Oh shit," he cringed, looking over at me. I didn't understand what he was worried about until I realized he'd cussed. A laugh escaped me, and I shook my head, pushing him.

"Kid, you can cuss all you want. I'm not your dad, no matter how much you call me daddy," I paused, a sick feeling coming over me. "Oh gross, that sounds weird. Let's just scrub that last minute from our heads and move past that whole thing."

Jude cringed, nodding. "So, Sax, he's scary, so he'll be up there just because, but I'm also hoping someday he'll show me how to ride a motorcycle. Monroe, he's probably my favorite because I've been around him the most, and he's teaching me hockey, which I really love."

"What about Mas, or Atticus, I mean?"

"Oh, well, if he was to ask, he's at the top because that feels like it would be important to him, and also he's Immy's brother and scarier in a different way. But in reality, he's my least favorite of you all. He's too stuck up his own ass and doesn't listen to Immy or what she wants. I know she's been through some things, but she's stronger than I think any of you let her be."

"Hmm, you might be right about that. So, where does that leave me?"

"Well, I guess you're, like, tied with Wells for 3rd place. So, what are you going to do to win me over?" He wiggled his eyebrows, and I guffawed at his candor.

"You're funny, kid. And you know, I could teach you how to ride a motorcycle too. But Loren might kill me, so maybe I will leave that to Sax. Let him get in her bad graces for once. I swear, that man can't seem to do anything wrong where she's concerned. If Beautiful didn't have such a big heart, I'd worry he'd push me aside."

Jude looked over, some of his teasing attitude diminishing. "You know, it's kind of refreshing to see that someone like you doubts himself a bit when you have all the things you do going for yourself. I don't know; it makes me feel not as weird, I guess." He shrugged, and I sympathized with him. Jude had grown in the few months he'd been with Loren, but it didn't mean all of his insecurities went away.

"Ha! Yeah, I think it's something guys don't talk about. Maybe the super asshole ones, the real douche canoes; perhaps they never doubt themselves. But other than those few select ones, I think it's something we as humans struggle with. It's one of those traps you can fall into if you're not careful, the whole rat race of life. Someone will always be better than you, do more than you, look nicer than you. If you focus on being the best, then I guess that's your choice on how you want to spend your life. I can say from my experience, finding people and something that gives you a purpose is far more fulfilling than being on top. It doesn't mean I don't strive to do my best, because I do. I take pride in my art and the work I put out, but I quit stressing over who was doing what and whether or not they were better than me years ago."

We got to the front of the park, and I stopped, turning to Jude. He was deep in thought, and I realized how philosophical I'd just gotten. "You've got a good head on your shoulders, though, Jude. You've lived a life most kids your age haven't, and you seem to understand what's important. I think that's what Immy likes in you. You're not pretending to be someone you're not, and you know that life isn't a piece of cake. But you keep moving forward each day, sharing your light with those you deem worthy. I never realized how alike in that aspect you are to Loren, but I see it now."

"Really?" he asked, a small smile lifting on his face.

"Yeah, kid. I think you're both the type of people that are rare—true good souls. Life beat you up a little, made you lose some of your glimmer, hiding away your light. But together, you're both able to rub off the dust and shine. You're stronger together."

"Okay, you might be moving into second." He blushed, sincerity ringing through.

Rolling my eyes, I shoved his shoulder again in play. Just as we crossed the street to the side the doors were on, a motorcycle rode up, the sound familiar to my ears. I stopped, turning to see why Sax was here. Jude noticed and stopped himself. When I saw Beautiful on the back of the bike, I grinned wide, walking over. When I approached, I helped her off the bike as Sax eyed Jude and me curiously.

"Beautiful! What a pleasant surprise." I kissed her once she had the helmet off, hearing Jude gag in the back. Loren chuckled, pulling away before I could deepen it.

"Back in third." I heard him cough into his hand, and I narrowed my eyes at him before shrugging.

"Worth it."

Loren looked between us both, a curious look on her face as well.

"What are you two doing together?"

"Ah, well, it seems when in need, I'm the one Jude reached out to," I said smugly, making sure Sax heard. He chuckled, shaking his head and not caring. Looking back at Loren, I kissed her again before letting go of her. "He'll explain, but I gotta head out to finish getting things together for tonight's exhibition fight. You're coming, right?"

"Yeah, I'll be there. Wells asked me to be his support person, whatever that means." She shrugged one of her shoulders, but I caught the blush as she began to bite her lip.

"Ah, look at Crash asking for something for once. That's a big deal, Loren. He doesn't usually have anyone there to cheer him on, much less be in his corner." The information slipped free quickly, not even attempting to hold it back in an effort to keep me as her main concern. Something about the broody asshole made me want to make sure he did well, and that he believed he was capable of winning outside of just being good for the family.

"Wow, okay, so should I make sure to give him a good pep talk or something?"

"I think you being there is the only pep talk he'll need."

"I was wondering if I could come, Lo? I'd like to support Wells too."

"Of course, Jude. I think he'd like that. I'm sure Monroe is going. Is there, like, a sitting area or something?" she asked, turning to Sax and me.

"Yeah, we'll take care of it. Do you need a ride there?"

"That'd be great. I just have the rental, and I like to avoid driving it."

"Perfect. I'll message you and let you know what time." I kissed her again, flipping my finger up over my shoulder at Sax. I heard him chuckle while Jude mumbled, *"Fourth."*

Pulling back, I smiled at Beautiful before turning and narrowing my eyes at Jude. "Don't forget what we talked about. I'll look into some things, but you get none of it unless you've talked to Loren, got it?"

"Yeah, thanks, Nicco. I do appreciate it."

"No problem, kid." I squeezed his shoulder and turned to head in the other direction, happy my apartment was only a few blocks over. I heard Sax's motorcycle rev back up a second later and wasn't surprised when I found him waiting for me when I made it to the front of my condo. I'd been thinking about where to start on Jude's request and knew I'd need Sax to help me.

"What's going on?" He was leaning against his bike, arms crossed, his glare sharp. Chuckling to myself, I nodded toward my place.

"Might as well come on up. I have to change and grab some things. I'll fill you in on the way. I could use your help, actually."

He looked surprised by that, but nodded and followed me in. Once we were in the elevator, he stared at me, some things never changing with the old man.

"What do you know of Jude's brother?"

"He's trouble."

"Seems Jude thinks the same. His brother approached him today, saying he needed help. It smells fishy to me, and I'm glad Jude reached out."

"You think something else is going on, like Delgado?"

"I wouldn't be surprised at this point. Darren seems to know more than we do, and he's confronted her two times."

"Three," growled Sax.

Surprised, I turned, anxiety rising in me. "When?"

"Earlier today. He cornered her in the cemetery and had one of his goons try to chloroform her."

"What the fuck! And I'm just hearing about this now? Why?"

"Calm yourself, little Nic. I had guards on her. Beau stepped in and sent for us. She, um, she asked the question."

"What question?"

The elevator dinged, and we walked off, heading to my apartment.

"*The* question."

Eyes wide, I turned to him and opened the door, waiting until we were behind it to ask more.

"And?"

"And Mas told her some but said he planned to share more at the benefit and asked if she'd wait. Loren, being Loren, agreed. She didn't..." he trailed off, stunned.

"She didn't what?"

He looked up, a foreign emotion emitting from his eyes. "She didn't run away when she knew. She accepted it, she... accepted *me*."

I could tell how much it meant to Sax, and there was a massive part of me that sighed in relief as well. "If we were different people, I'd like, I don't know, hug you right now. But since we aren't those people, how about a beer and we figure out what Jude's brother is up to? It definitely seems too coincidental now, that while Delgado was cornering Loren, someone else was hitting up Jude. Smells like a setup."

"Beer sounds great. I'll start running some checks while you shower or whatever you need to do to primp for tonight," he teased.

"Fuck off, Sax. I'll just be ten minutes. Make yourself comfortable." He laughed at me as I made my way into my bedroom. I stopped, gripping the doorjamb. "And thanks for telling me. It feels like we're a unit now, more than just family, and it feels nice to be included and taken seriously. So, um, thanks."

He nodded, but I saw the corner of his lip tilt up. Loren was showing me a whole new side of myself and my brothers. She was one in a million, and now that she knew the truth and hadn't run off, I planned to make it known I was never letting her go.

My course had set off in a direction I would hold onto with everything I had, swiping whatever obstacles sprouted out of the way.

Nothing else mattered other than the life I could build with Loren. Nothing.

FOUR

LOREN

Jude, Monroe, and I walked into Upswing wide-eyed as we took everything in around us. We'd been taken around back and ushered through a door marked for staff.

"This place is insane," Jude whispered. I had his arm clutched in mine, and as I looked over to respond, I stopped, smiling at him.

His nose scrunched up, and he gave me a lopsided look. "What?"

"Nothing, just that you've grown a couple of inches since you came to live with me. Even in heels, you're taller than me now. I just hadn't realized it." I moved some of his hair off his forehead, and he blushed. "I think you need a haircut, too. We're gonna have to plan an excursion or something. Maybe we could have a Jude and Loren date? Go and take some photos, do those scooter things around downtown, and get you some longer pants and a haircut."

"Sure, Lor. That sounds great."

"Awesome. I know with how things have been changing lately that we've both been kind of occupied." He gave me a look I didn't want to necessarily decipher from my seventeen-year-old foster son, so I ignored it. "But I never want you to feel like you're second. It's you and me, JuJu. No matter what. That's the misfit penguin creed."

He laughed, trying to hide his blush, but I saw it and knew he appreciated my gushiness, even if he couldn't return it.

"Sounds good. I have spring break in a week as well, so it would be a good time to go. Most everyone else is going on college tours, so I'll be left in the city alone."

"Is that something you'd want to do? You can go to college if you're interested. I can help you with it all."

"Oh, well... I just never thought about it before. Even with going to Timber Creek, it didn't seem like the path I'd take."

"What did you have planned?"

He shrugged, looking embarrassed. "I honestly never thought about it. It was always about surviving. I hoped to get a job or figure out something with community college, but it felt too scary to hope. I didn't want to end up like my parents or Cameron, but in doing so, I kind of avoided it at all costs."

"Hey, it's okay. I'm here now, and we'll figure out a plan together. That should be part of our mission state-ment. Speaking of your brother, are you worried about what his visit might mean?"

Jude had told Monroe and me on the way over about his brother approaching him outside Ignite and how he'd used Nicco's number and asked for help. It had warmed something maternal in me to see him reaching out for help like that from one of my guys. We hadn't gotten to talk about it too much, though, and I wanted to know more on how he felt about it, anyway. I knew he wouldn't talk as openly with others around.

"I never know with Cameron. At one time, he was the only person I had, and I thought he was my hero, able to do no wrong. But when he left me, while I knew it was to find a way to help us both, it still felt like abandonment. And then when he did return, he was so messed up with drugs. He wasn't the brother I remembered. I miss the brother who made sure we had food when we lived on the streets and the one who played with me while Mom and Dad were at work, but I don't know this version of him. The brother who got me arrested because he was doing a drug deal and now wants to pull me into something. I know whatever he's involved with, it's not good, and nothing I do will change that. I care for him, but I've lived in enough crappy places now to know I don't want to mess this up." He looked over at me, worry on his face.

Bumping his shoulder, I gave him a smile. "Is that all I am? A place?" I teased. Immediately, I regretted it when his face fell, and panic rose as he tried to find a way to fix it.

"No, no, not at all. Sorry, I didn't mean for it to sound that way."

"Ssh, it's okay, Jude. I was teasing, and it wasn't the time for it. I know you don't think of me as just a place. In fact, I was waiting to tell you this once I knew more." I paused, taking a breath, and turned, taking his hands. "I've been looking into the steps to adopt you, and I have everything ready to submit. I just need to know if you want that. This isn't how I thought I'd tell you, but yeah." I shrugged my shoulder, dropping my eyes, unsure if I could handle his rejection. He was seventeen, so he wouldn't necessarily need a guardian soon.

His arms wrapped around me before I could look up, and I relaxed into his hug. "That's the most amazing offer I've ever been given, and I would love to be your true family. Yes, Lor, please."

It was the 'please' that killed me like I'd ever say no to him.

Monroe walked back over after talking with one of the guards to see where we needed to go and found us a hugging and crying mess.

"Um, wow, okay, I didn't realize sporting arenas were this emotional."

Laughing, we pulled apart, and I started to wipe my tears. A handkerchief appeared under my eyes, and I looked over, finding Atticus holding one out. Smiling, I took it, nodding thanks.

"Sorry, we got a bit emotional. We're all good." I noticed Immy standing back wearing a cute gray skirt and black shirt combo. I smiled, feeling validated that he'd brought her. "Oh, Immy! It's so good to see you." I hugged her, and she relaxed. I didn't know what was going on, but I'd make a note to check in later with her.

"Hey, Lor," she breathed into the hug.

Jude looked put together when we pulled back and gave Immy a hug as well, and then we awkwardly stood in a weird circle of five, all looking at one another. Monroe, thankfully, stepped in, helping to dispel the weird energy.

"Lo, I found out where Wells is if you want to go, and I'll stay with Jude," he offered.

Before I could answer, Atticus spoke up. "Jude can come with us if he's okay with that." I looked over at him, and he nodded. I think if Immy hadn't been there, his answer would've been different since he'd spent the least amount of time with Atticus, but I was happy he felt comfortable enough to go with him.

"Thank you, Atticus. I appreciate it."

"You're most welcome, Lore. Shall I see you after?"

Nodding before I could find the words, I grinned. "Yeah, I'm sure we'll be up there once we figure out what Wells needs as his support."

He picked up my hand, kissing it softly. "I look forward to it." Atticus' eyes heated as he said it, cementing me to the spot as liquid heat raced up my body. The dress I wore wasn't as revealing as last time, but it felt like my nipples were on display from that simple touch. He didn't wait for a reply, just lifted the corner of his mouth in a crooked smile and turned, expecting everyone else to follow.

"How did I not piece it together sooner? He screams mafia boss," I mumbled to myself.

"You say something, Lo?"

"Oh, nothing." I startled, coming back to my whereabouts. Jude and Immy followed Atticus, a trail of bodyguards behind them as they went. Monroe took my hand and pulled me in the other direction, and we walked in silence for a few minutes.

"Were my eyes deceiving me back there, or did it seem like things have changed between you and the dark and deadly one?"

Lifting my head, I cringed when I realized I hadn't talked to the others about it. "Shit, I kind of did agree to give him a clean slate, but I didn't really talk it through with anyone else. I told him about you all, but I forgot the reverse. I'm sorry. Do you want to stop whatever we're doing?"

I halted my steps, pulling him into a hallway as I waited for him to decide. He shook his head, smiling at me as he backed me up until my back hit the wall. Slowly, he brushed my hair back and cupped my face. "You could have a hundred men in your life, Lo, and I'd still be here. I don't particularly want you to have that many because it would mean my time with you would be limited, but I'm here. As long as you continue to let me take up a part of your heart, I'm going to be along for the ride. And honestly, even if you decide 'no, Monroe needs to go,' I'm still going to be here, hoping you reconsider."

He kissed me, pulling my face to his and my whole body liquified from the intensity of it combined with his words. Monroe pulled away a second later, winking, and I wondered if I'd even uncovered ten percent of everything that made Monroe, Monroe. Linking our fingers, he pulled me down the rest of the hallway, and I let him, in a bit of a haze myself. We came to a door with a guard standing outside of it. When he spotted us, he nodded, and I realized it was Beau.

"Oh, hey, Beau." I couldn't help the blush after the events from this morning and realized he saw me kissing Monroe after saying Sax was my boyfriend. Thankfully, I didn't spot any condemnation in his eyes as he pushed open the door for us. I stopped halfway through the door, tugging Monroe to stop. "I just wanted to say thanks, for you know, earlier. I can't remember in the hustle of everything if I did. I don't," I shuddered, "want to think about where I'd be right now if you hadn't been there." I kept conveniently blocking that part out of my head.

"Of course, ma'am. It was an honor. Like I mentioned earlier, I see the changes you're making, and I appreciate the help you're giving our young Ms. Immy. You always have a friend in me."

Smiling, I dropped some tension I'd been holding and let go of the door, it automatically closing behind me. Monroe watched me, a concerned look on his face.

"You doing okay?"

"Yeah." I nodded. "I just needed to let him know. It felt important." Monroe squeezed my hand, and we both headed into the room further. I'd been expecting a locker room, but this was beyond anything I'd imagined. It was more of a luxury suite as we stepped into the second area. The first part consisted of scales, a first aid cabinet, and a medical table. There was some physical training equipment as well that I now recognized.

But when we walked into the second part, it was decadent and comfortable. There was an expensive leather couch, two TVs on the wall. One showed the arena, and the other had music playing on it. A door led to a bathroom, and there was a bar area decked out with food and drinks.

The door that had been closed opened and steam rolled out of it as Wells walked out, sweat dripping down his body as he dabbed himself off. He was barefoot, only a pair of athletic shorts on, and man did he look sexy.

Wells stopped when he spotted us, a smile crossing his face. "You made it." I dropped Monroe's hand and walked over to Mr. Surly. I didn't hesitate, knowing I needed to do this for myself and him. Grabbing his face, I pulled him down into a kiss. Our tongues tangled, his hands settling at my waist, and I got lost in the kiss as it all became about him and me for a second. When I pulled back, he smirked, and it only made me want to kiss him more.

"Happy to see me, Kitten?"

"I am. How are you feeling?"

He looked over my shoulder, spotting Monroe. Wells squeezed my hips, dropping his lips down to my ear. "Give me just a second." My breath hitched as his lips grazed across the area, and I nodded as he stepped away to greet Monroe.

"Roe." Taking a page out of my book, Wells grabbed the man by the back of his neck, pulling his lips to him. It was a quick kiss, but it was powerful, and I knew it was Wells giving Monroe time to trust him. When he pulled back, I watched as they stared at one another, a world of feelings and history between them. The part of me awakening wanted to smash their heads together and watch what else would happen. Shifting my legs, Monroe caught me, giving me a smile before he addressed his friend.

"Wells. How are you feeling?"

"Better now that you're both here. Something about tonight feels different, and I was getting all in my head about it."

Surly walked over, grabbed my hand, and pulled me down onto the couch with him. Monroe sat on the other side, and I found myself wedged between the two, my mind running rampant with ideas. Swallowing, I crossed my legs, my red dress riding up some as I tried to focus on what Wells said.

"In your head? Why?"

He was tracing my palm with his fingers, looking at it in awe almost.

"I think because before, I didn't care if I lost, the pain feeling warranted. Now, I have people waiting for me and who I want to return to. It changes things because I care if I walk out of that ring again."

Something about his statement both broke my heart and made it swell. Brushing the back of my hand against his face, I leaned into him. "Oh, Surly. If you use it correctly, I think you'll find that motivation can be even more powerful than apathy. You didn't care before, and now you do, but it also gives you more of a reason to win."

"I want to hate your therapy mumbo jumbo, but that makes a lot of sense. I guess," he paused, "I guess I was letting the fear of not being enough stop me. Shit, I don't think I've ever been this insightful before a fight." He huffed out a laugh, the sound husky.

"What do you find helps you the most? That's what we're here for, right?"

I looked back at Monroe, and he nodded. His eyes were more dilated now, and I realized I was practically draped over Wells and my dress had moved up even higher.

"I can think of a few things, but I don't know if we have time," Wells purred. The sound rolling over me, and this time I shuddered from lust.

"Hmm, well, I don't know if this is good or not, but what if I know something that won't take too long and hopefully help you relax? I just don't know if it's a bad thing or not, like if it would make you too relaxed and then you mess up. I don't want to screw anything up for you."

"Oh, what did you have in mind, Kitten?" He pushed my hair back on the other side, and goosebumps rose to the surface.

Leaning forward, I daringly took his earlobe between my teeth before speaking. "I was thinking I could slide to my knees before you and help you relax that way."

His breath hissed, and he looked down at me. "Are you saying you want to blow me, Kitten?"

"Yeah, badly apparently." I giggled, and I felt Monroe move closer, the heat increasing as his hand moved up my leg, skirting under the hem that was still visible. His breath tickled my neck, and he nibbled my ear. Eyes closing, my breathing increased as I tried to remember what I was doing.

"Fuck, that's hot," Wells hissed. "And no, Kitten, I don't think it would hurt me at all. Might be my lucky charm, actually."

Opening my eyes, I found his seared into me, lust and want, pouring back. Slowly, I trailed my hand down his abs, the beautiful muscles and skin on display. I skimmed over his tattoo, the arrows beautiful against his ribs. Deciding to stay on the couch, I twisted, so I could lower myself and kiss above the hem.

It probably wasn't the best time, but something I learned in graduate school started to rise to the surface as I brushed my lips against his abs, tugging his shorts down. Perhaps my brain wanted to focus on logic instead of the fact I was about to see a new penis. I think a part of me would always freak out each time I did. When you'd only seen one for most of your life, anything new was a novelty.

So as Wells' cock freed itself, the girth bigger than I'd expected, I wrapped my hand around the base, my fingers barely touching. Pumping my hand up and down, I lowered to kiss the tip, and the class where we'd discussed the mentality of aggressive sports started to replay in my head, and an idea formed.

When Monroe's hands continued their traveling, brushing over the fabric of my panties, I almost jumped. When the tip of his finger touched my clit, all thoughts of school left me, and I gave in to the moment. Closing my eyes, I opened my mouth as I sucked Wells down. His hands gathered my hair into a ponytail, and he pulled a little as I started to bob.

Monroe heaved my knees up onto the couch, bringing my ass right in front of his face. As he explored my pussy, I sucked and licked the thick cock in my mouth, using my hand to help build friction. Wells tugged a little on my hair, and I moaned, the vibrations rolling over his dick.

"Fuck, Kitten. Shit, this is hot."

"I agree. Seeing your dick in her mouth has me about to explode," Monroe groaned.

When his tongue connected with my pussy a second

later, I moaned again. His fingers quickened their pace at the new angle, and he worked in tandem with his tongue to flick against my clit. The whole thing had me on edge, and I found myself on the precipice of an orgasm. Deciding it was only fair to share the pain, I pulled back, licking the tip of Wells and then tucking him back in his shorts.

Monroe didn't stop, though, and even when I tried to pull away, he kept me braced to his mouth, increasing his tempo, and I found myself falling over the edge, crying out as I came.

"Fuck, Kitten. I want to be mad at you for not continuing, but watching you come undone was just as good."

Feeling confident, I braced my hands on his shoulders, straddling his waist. Licking up his throat, I ran my fingers up in his hair as I nipped his ear again. He groaned, thrusting his still-hard dick up, brushing against me. I bit back the moan, needing to get my words out.

"I decided you needed an incentive. Win, and you can have me, and," I turned, taking in Monroe. He hadn't been able to hear me, but must've known where I was going and nodded, licking his lips. Leaning back down to Wells, who still had his eyes shuttered, his grip tight on my hip, I finished the sentence. "Win, and you can have me... and Monroe. Tonight."

Wells groaned but nodded, opening his eyes to look at me on his lap. "I know this is more of your therapy mumbo jumbo, but I don't even care if it means I get to feel you around me later." He moved forward, sitting up, tugging the hair I'd forgotten he held in his other hand. "But don't for one second think I won't repay you for leaving me hard, and so fucking turned on before my fight. Payback is fair game, Kitten, and I *will* collect."

My body shuddered at the heat in those words, and I knew this back and forth between us had just shifted to something more. The gloves were off, and we were no longer tiptoeing around our mutual desire. Wells would wreck me, but I had a feeling I would enjoy it.

"Looking forward to it, Surly. Now, go and win, or I'll make you watch me fuck Monroe, and you won't get to join."

Wells groaned, kissing me hard before he lifted me off his lap and stalked to the bathroom. I turned to Monroe when the door shut and smiled.

"Time to jump into the deep end."

He smiled, cupping my cheek. "I've never been more ready for anything in my life."

We kissed for a minute before giggling like kids, getting up to fix our clothes. When Wells returned out of the bathroom, he was calm and collected, a smirk on his handsome face. He'd changed into tighter shorts like I'd seen fighters on TV wear. If I wasn't already wet for the man, that look alone would've done it.

"Are you guys going to watch from the VIP area or…"

"Where would you like us to sit?" Monroe asked.

Wells hesitated for a second before he answered.

"Would it be too much to ask to sit up front for my fight?"

"Not at all. When do you go on?"

"I'm the third one, so whenever that is."

"Do you want us to stick around here?"

He shook his head, a soft smile on his face. "Nah. I need to finish getting ready, and you're both distracting, honestly. So, go and watch the other two, and then I'll look for you when I come out."

"Okay." Nodding, I walked over, kissing his cheek, and Monroe did the same. The cute and small gestures between them were what melted me the most. Monroe took my hand as Wells started to tape his, and we made our way out of the room. Wells spoke up, stopping us before we exited.

"Save your voice, Kitten. Don't scream too loud watching me win. I want to hear you scream my name out later."

My cheeks heated at the declaration, my body tingling at the promise. Wells had once told me he was damaged goods, but as I looked at him over my shoulder, I couldn't help but fall a little more for the man he was showing me. He might be damaged goods, but so was I, and together we would mend our pieces into something indestructible.

FIVE

ATTICUS

My hand trembled, but I shoved it in my suit pocket, hiding my nerves. I needed a drink but was worried if I started now, I wouldn't stop. I couldn't afford to be anything less than perfect this evening. It wasn't meant to feel this strained with everything on the line. I'd wrestled all day with what the right call was, and when Sax barged into my office screaming that Darren had tried to take Loren, I knew he was right. He had me stretched too thin.

At least I understood what the third door was now.

He'd been implying Loren, so at least that was one less person to worry about. While I didn't care about Crash like family, I would protect him. I'd given him my word on that, but also, he was important to people who were important to me, intertwining his fate with my own. I couldn't sacrifice his well being for the greater good.

Which meant I either had to give into Darren or risk Camila.

I didn't see any other option, and I couldn't see a way out of this. I loathed the idea of helping him, especially if the container he received was what I believed it to be. I wanted no part in it. We'd been too distracted, though, either by our own merits or his misdirection, and I hadn't seen this coming.

I should've, but I hadn't.

At the risk of losing everything, the solution had become clear after speaking with Loren this afternoon. And now, I just had to pray it panned out.

"You okay?" Immy asked, leaning against the railing with me.

"Peachy. Why do you ask, Immykins?" I saw her smile out of the corner of my eye, and it loosened some of the tension that had grown in my chest.

"You seem, I dunno, more on edge than usual. Is it... is it because of me?"

Turning my head, I looked at her, confusion covering my face. "You? Why on earth would you think that?"

"I dunno. I guess because I know you didn't want me here. I overheard you and Loren earlier in the house. Sorry, I was loitering on the stairs and stopped when I heard my name." She shrugged, sheepishly.

"Oh, Imogen. It's not that I didn't want you here. I always want you with me when it's appropriate. I didn't think you'd enjoy this type of thing. But Loren was also right that I've become too overprotective, trying to minimize all the bad things that could harm you, and that's not fair to you. I never meant to isolate you or make you feel like you were incapable of being part of this world. You're so strong, and I'm proud of you daily for the battles you've overcome."

"Thank you, that um, that means the world to me." She politely wiped the tear from her eye, and I reached out, grabbing her, pulling her into my side. We weren't big on physical touch, but perhaps that needed to change as well.

"I've been doing a lot of thinking, and I want you to be more involved in things. That's if you want to, of course. I don't want to push you into this life, but I also know I can't hide you from it. I do need to make you aware and prepare you for whatever future you choose."

"I think I'd like to at least see what my options are. So, maybe I could learn more about this world outside of owning a business and also go to a regular school? I think I'd like to go where Jude is."

I paused, thinking about it. It wasn't an outlandish request. I'd attended a prep school, along with Sax. With Immy, we'd just always been more guarded, afraid someone would use her as a pawn to get to us.

What was worse, the fact it had happened anyway, or that it was by her own father?

Maybe Loren was right, and it was time to let her make her own choices. Jude was bright, and I liked him. It wouldn't be unwise to put a guard in at the school for him to begin with. Especially after the update Sax gave me after talking with Nicco.

"I'm open to discussing this plan with you if you'll

hear my suggestions to make sure your safety is covered."

Immy squealed, jumping a little in my arm. "Yes, absolutely! Oh, thank you, Attie! This is just the best. I can do all the things I've seen on TV, like join an after-school club and go to a dance!"

When she said it out loud like that, it made me realize how sheltered we'd gotten. "We'll talk about it, remember? There will be rules."

"Yes, yes, I know. Just let me bask in the knowledge I get to pretend to be a regular teen for a few hours."

"Okay. I'm glad that makes you happy. That's all I want for you, Immy, to be happy."

"I'm starting to be again, Attie."

It almost broke my heart, but the sounds around me reminded me I had to remember who I was here. Perhaps, this was the real reason I didn't want Immy here. She was my weakness, made me softer, and it was harder to wear the mask in her presence.

Kissing her forehead, I let her go and focused back out on the floor below. People were beginning to file into Upswing now. The first match was in half an hour, and the seats were filling up below. Sax wasn't here yet, and I felt empty without his dominating presence by my side. He'd stayed to help Nicco with the Jude matter and then to ensure our piece was in play before he would arrive here.

My phone buzzed in my pocket, and I relaxed some

more. Pulling it free, I sighed in relief when I read his message.

Saxon: On our way. Package delivered.
ME: See you in VIP.

Putting it back, I leaned against the railing, my heart slowing as things began to fall into place. I spotted Loren a few seconds later, her long legs a beacon for my dick in those shoes, as the red dress swished against her thighs. She looked more impressive than she had at the last fight, and she was covered more this time. It was something I appreciated about her, though. The clothes didn't wear her; she wore them. The outfit was only the vessel from which her seduction seeped, and I was starting to believe Loren could look sexy in a burlap sack if she wanted.

The golden retriever's hand sat at the base of her back, and she leaned into his touch. I hadn't been dramatic earlier when I said I didn't want to watch her with the others just yet. The way my hand tightened on the railing confirmed my assumption. A small part of me wanted to steal her away and command no one else touch her.

But she wouldn't respect that. And it would only make me lose her in the end.

I had to overcome this jealousy myself and not let it sour the careful re-do we had going for us.

When they made it to the top of the stairs, the guard

let them in, knowing who she was by now. Sax had most of them on her detail over the last months, her presence being more evident at our home as well. I liked the way they deferred to her, though, already understanding her significance, even if nothing had been said or made formal yet.

Before, I hated how well she fit into this. Now, it made me want to fuck her against the wall with the need of how aroused it made me.

I couldn't decipher if that was because I wanted to claim her so everyone else would back the fuck off, or if her demeanor and ability to bring me to my knees was the reason.

Either way, I had to shift the rock-hard cock in my pants before they neared, reminding myself we weren't there yet.

My dick only seemed to agree because of the yet.

I had to agree with him on that. I loved the fact 'yet' was now part of the equation for us and we had a second chance.

"Bellezza, I assume you left my fighter ready to win?"

"Oh, I think he'll definitely win." She smirked, and I had a feeling she'd done something to incentivize Mr. Young.

"Well, I'm glad you're here. Mr. Miller." I nodded, acknowledging his presence. "Would you care to join us for a drink? Anything to eat?"

"Oh, yes, that would be great. Thank you."

They followed me over to the teens' table, and Loren

sat next to Jude, easily pulling them into a conversation. I motioned for a waiter who quickly arrived, ready to take our order.

"We'll take one of each appetizer, and a round of drinks, whatever they're wanting."

"Yes, sir, of course." He looked around the table, taking their drink orders as they listed them off, and I watched Loren, wholly entranced. Since I'd allowed myself to admit my attraction, and she knew who we were, I didn't care to hide it any longer.

I listened to her talk with the kids and watched her, my arm perched on the back of the booth we found ourselves in. When my phone buzzed again, I didn't know if I was relieved or pissed this time, since it stopped my game of imagining Loren naked with no one else around.

Seeing it was a call, I excused myself from the table and walked over to a quiet corner.

"Darren."

"Just wanted to say hello, little Mascro, and make sure you got my message."

"Hard to miss a finger, Darren. You do realize if you hurt any more of her, I will come after you and return the favor."

"Ah, see, that's where we differ. I don't care about anyone but myself, Atticus. It's why I had to get Jaz out of the way because she was the only one I did care for. Killing her, though, it freed me."

The information was a punch to the gut, and I knew

he wanted it to be. Grinding my jaw, I breathed slowly to keep my emotions in check. I wouldn't fall prey to him.

"Did you have anything else to discuss, Darren? I'm busy. Your shipment will be delivered on time. I expect my cousin returned when it is."

"Or what?"

"Or I come and take her myself."

Hanging up, I didn't want to give him time to respond for fear I'd give myself away, or he'd say something else that would crack me. There was too much at stake to break now. I stood back in the corner, going over the plan I'd made earlier, looking for all the weak spots. It was the only reason I could guess she was able to sneak up on me.

"Atticus, is everything alright?"

Blinking, I looked up into chocolate eyes, so rich with depth and emotion, I sucked in a breath that her concern was directed back at me.

"Atticus?"

"Yeah, sorry. Just in my head, I guess."

"Anything I can do?" Loren reached out, brushing her hand against my arm, and the gesture was both soothing and intimate.

"I," I started but stopped. "Actually, there is something you can do. You can distract me." Grabbing her waist, I pulled her close, and this time her breath hitched, and I felt it throughout my body.

"Dis-tract y-ou?" she stuttered. "From what?"

"The things I have to tell you, but for tonight, can we

go back to being those strangers in a club? You enjoyed that, didn't you? Just being free without the strings of the world holding you down?"

Loren assessed me, her hands planted on my chest from my move. My arm wrapped around her waist, and it was my hand now that rested on her lower back. As she searched my eyes for something, I lowered my hand over her backside, watching her for any sign she wanted me to stop. When she stepped closer to me, I took it for an invitation and cupped her ass.

Bending down, I pressed her into me, feeling every inch of her body on mine. "I haven't been able to stop thinking about this ass since that night, you know? The way you rubbed it into me. You held nothing back in those moments. It was sexy seeing you so free, so uninhibited. Do you remember watching that other couple?"

"Mmhmm," she breathed. Her hands ran up my neck, and I felt her fingernails bite into the back of my scalp as she ran her fingers into my hair.

"I remember how you felt, too. And as much as I want to give in to you right now, wouldn't we be repeating the same mistakes as before?" She stepped back to look at my face, and I saw the decision she'd come to.

"Maybe, or maybe we wouldn't this time knowing what we do," I argued.

But Loren was smarter than me and apparently had a stronger will. "No, Atticus. As much as my body wants to say screw it and let you have your way with me, I'm not going to. If we're getting a do-over, we only get one, and I don't want to start it off repeating the same steps we took last time, even if the beginning ones were amazing."

Dropping my head down to her forehead, I breathed in her intoxicating smell of roses, my hands still firmly gripping her hip and ass. "I know you're making sense, but I don't want to listen. I want to lose myself in you."

"As romantic as that sounds, I think if we try hard, we might have something amazing between us. I just found myself; I don't want you to lose you just to be with me."

"I didn't mean it that way. I just don't want to think or worry for ten seconds of the day."

"Ten seconds? Wow, and here I thought it would last longer."

Stunned, I blinked, not expecting her to joke with me. When the realization hit me, I chortled, the sound escaping me in a loud guffaw. "Fair, Bellezza, fair. How do I already feel better just being near you and not even being sexual? I've been such a fucking idiot."

"I won't argue with you there because you have, but I also need to thank you."

"Thank me?"

"Yes," she nodded. "You, even in your dickishness, looked out for me. The bigger thing, though, you showed me a strength I didn't realize I possessed. Being angry at you helped me rise to the surface, and I like the woman I'm becoming."

"I like her too, more than I'm prepared to admit."

"By default, I think you just did."

Chuckling, I nodded, moving my hand to cup her cheek. "You know, I won't always be sweet. There's a dark side to me as well."

"Why are you always trying to scare me off, Attie? I see you, and I see me staring right back. Sax was right, we have a lot of similar aspects of ourselves, and it might feel like flint rubbing against one another from time to time, but all that means is we're preparing to spark. I'm kind of excited to see what ignites. Aren't you?"

"Yeah, Bellezza, I think I am."

Leaning down, I broke my number one rule with women, and I kissed her. Lips touching softly, I cherished the simple gesture for what it was, an acceptance of who we were, and a willingness to explore it together, dynamite and all.

"I have a feeling, Mrs. Carter," I purred when I pulled back, letting her know I was using it as a term of endearment. "That you're going to teach me a great many things, and I'm suddenly very excited to find out what they will be."

"You know, when you're not being a dominating asshole, you're actually quite sweet."

"Don't get used to it. I'm mostly an asshole, and I'll always dominate you."

"Oh?" Loren raised her eyebrows, a challenge forming there if I'd ever seen one. "Well, I guess that's something we'll have to see about then, hmm?" She straightened my tie, trailing her fingers over my neck, and then dragged her fingernails down my shirt. Pulling me closer with my belt loops, she placed her lips at my jaw as she spoke, brushing against my stubble as she did. "Try not to stare too long at my ass while I walk away." She kissed my jaw, and I watched, stunned, as she pivoted and walked away.

Almost as if pulled there like a magnet, I found my eyes seared to her ass as it swayed, and I gulped. Loren was showing me she wasn't scared to tangle with the likes of me. I needed to show her who I really was. Then, we'd know.

Stepping forward out of the dark, I peeked around the corner and watched her walk all the way back to the booth. Before she sat down, her head glanced over her shoulder, right into my eyes. The smile she had on her face was smug and all too sexy. Loren winked and sat down, falling back into the conversations at the table.

"She's something else, isn't she?" Sax asked, surprising me from behind. Looking over my shoulder, I eyed him. "How long were you listening?"

"Long enough to hear her remind you that you could be more than just 'The Suit' and that she's not what you're used to. Loren's going to turn your world upside down in the best way, and part of me just wants to pull up a chair, grab some popcorn and watch. But I also can't wait to jump into the deep end with you, my friend, and ride this crazy train all the way to forever station." Sax smiled a toothy grin, the look so uncommon on his face, I didn't recognize him for a second.

"Forever? Don't get ahead of yourself there, Sax. She surprises me, but there's still tonight and the benefit to get through first."

"Nah, you'll see. The package is in play. There will be a status update soon on Little Red."

He patted me on the shoulder, walking over to the booth. Sax reached down when he made it, pulling Loren up into his arms in a smooth move and sitting down with her in his lap like it was so natural, he didn't even have to stop to think about it. It was something I envied about him.

Forever felt like a long shot with our current enemies, and the update our plan had moved forward only made me slightly less anxious it would blow up in my face. What was the point in forever, when forever could end tomorrow? Sax could dream of a forever for both of us. I'd make sure we lived to get one.

SIX

LOREN

Sax led Monroe and me down to the lower level, the last fight had ended a moment ago. Everything felt more extreme this time, and I didn't know if it was because I was more aware of my surroundings, was here with five gorgeous and slightly dangerous men, or because Wells was fighting this go around.

Perhaps it was all three.

My whole body buzzed, my skin sensitive to every touch and brush of fabric that caressed it, making me a panting mess. My nerves were so heightened, I felt everything tenfold, my pussy throbbing from each heated look and touch—to think I'd even orgasmed earlier.

Sax pushed open a door, and we walked out onto the first level. The sound exploded around us, and I stepped back into Monroe in surprise. Sax glanced back at me in concern.

"You okay, Spitfire?"

"Yeah, I just wasn't expecting it to be so loud."

"Ah." He nodded, understanding on his face. "There's a sound barrier upstairs to help block some of it. There are speakers in the walls to amplify the announcers, but the crowd is muted. Do you want earplugs?"

"No, I should be fine. I just wasn't expecting it. I'm good."

Sax linked our fingers, and I turned, holding out my hand for Monroe, offering him my other hand. He smiled, taking it, and we walked down the aisle toward some seats together.

"How's Levi?" I asked Monroe. He'd stepped out a few minutes before we moved down here to say goodnight to him. One of the neighbors who was on the approved list was watching him tonight. She had a young boy his age, and they got along well. Levi had been excited about seeing his friend, helping relieve some of the guilt Monroe felt for leaving him so soon.

"He's good. Barely even wanted to talk to me." He chuckled, not upset about it. "They were watching some YouTube videos and playing Roblox. So, basically, he's having the time of his life, and I just need to quit worrying."

"I like this plan." I smiled over at him, squeezing his hand. Sax directed me to our seats, and we found ourselves in the front row a few seconds later. I'd been expecting some steel folding chairs, but the ones down here were luxurious. Sitting down, I was pleased with how comfortable they were, and I knew Atticus had gone through all these details himself. Sax leaned over as we waited, his arm going to the back of my seat.

"What were you and Atticus talking about earlier?"

"Oh, um, nothing really. He needed a distraction, so I helped. It was actually a good conversation."

Sax's lips lifted up, but before he could retort, music started playing, and the emcee stepped into the octagon ring, pumping up the crowd.

"Alright, ladies and gents! Are we ready for our next fight? We have Crash versus Berserker."

"Fuck," Sax cursed, peering down at me and then to Monroe. "Don't go anywhere unless there's an emergency before I get back. Stay with the golden boy, or grab a guard. Trust no one else unless it's someone you know. Do you understand, Spitfire?"

Nodding, I swallowed, his fear palpable as he spoke. "Is Wells going to be okay?"

He didn't answer, gritting his jaw, and I knew it was his way of not lying to me. "I'll be back. Stay put."

"Okay."

Monroe pulled me closer, and I curled into him, the excitement changing to fear at the way Sax had acted. Peering up at him, I watched as he looked around, trying to assess danger.

"Do you know this other fighter, Berserker?"

"No, but I'm guessing that wasn't who he was supposed to fight."

"Oh, shit. Jude and Immy!" I turned, forgetting Sax's

command in the chaos and wanting to make sure they were fine.

"Ssh, they're fine, Lo. Atticus, Nicco, and a whole slew of men with dangerous looks are up there."

"Ah, yeah." I blushed. "Thank you."

"You know, you're really good at that mom thing despite not having done it before."

The comment was innocent, but it hit my sore spot, and I stiffened, letting go of his waist.

"Yeah, thanks." I folded my arms over themselves, the earlier desire falling away to fear as goosebumps rose. Looking around, I tried to keep the panic growing at bay, but it opened the door for the memories I tried so hard to suppress to enter.

"You'll never be a mom."

"You can't possibly know anything about children if you've never had kids."

"If you're unable to even give me a child, what are you good for? Nothing. You're worthless."

The lies kept trying to slither their way into my mind, and I kept kicking them away. But each kick felt heavier and slower than the one before. The abduction and the realization about the men I was dating began to weigh me down, too. The fear from today, the grief I'd experienced, and now panic had me running around in a circle of chaos.

A hand turned my chin, the reassuring touch

soothing me amongst the awful things swirling in my head.

"If I said something wrong, I'm sorry. I didn't mean that how it sounded. I just wanted you to know how amazing of a job you're doing with Jude. You're changing his life, and you make it look easy."

Shaking my head, I said the truth that had been buried. "He makes it easy, and we're changing each other. We're misfit penguins, after all."

"What does one have to do in order to join this club?"

Looking up, I found only acceptance, reassurance, and support in his eyes. "Well, I guess the first thing is to be a misfit. I'm not sure you fit that, Mr. Perfect."

"Oh, Lo, I think you're the only one who sees me that way, and I love you for it. But I'm far from perfect. I know I stepped in something here, and I guess this isn't the right place to have a serious conversation, but I'm sorry for whatever I said that made you feel like you had to protect yourself around me."

"It's just, I guess there's still a lot we don't know about each other. It's exciting but also scary. It's hard to remember that when it feels like I've known you my whole life."

"I feel the same. And each day I get to learn something new, I fall for you even more. So, can you tell me what it was so I don't repeat it? I never want to hurt you or feel that wall between us again if I can avoid it."

Biting my lip, I debated. He deserved to know, but was this the best way to share it? "I uh, well, you see, um." My awkward rambling was cut off when the announcer came on and introduced the fighters.

"In the right corner, we have Crash, weighing in at 188 lbs with a 6-0 win record. This is his first fight in this weight class."

Wells walked out, a stern look on his face. When he caught sight of us at the end, he relaxed a little but kept his gaze forward until he got to the line. He stopped, waiting for the announcer to introduce his opponent. I watched, cataloging everything I could, looking for any detail that he wasn't ready for this. He stared ahead, focused and determined. His posture was relaxed, only a slight bounce in his step, which I could only assume was to keep his muscles warm, something from our training peeking through.

"In the left corner, we have Berserker, weighing in at 195 lbs with a 10-2 win record."

"He looks confident," I whispered to Monroe, drowning out the announcer. He nodded, not wanting to pull Wells' focus either, and we waited to see what would happen next. Once both contestants were in position, the emcee motioned for them to enter the ring. This wasn't like the one from the last place. It was an actual octagon ring, mat, and all. I tried to convince myself that meant it would give better protection to Wells, protecting him from injuries, but it fell flat, even my subconscious not believing the lie.

I glanced around, hoping Sax would be back, but he was nowhere to be found. When the bell rang for the fight to start, I jumped, the noise, once again, surprising me. Berserker surged forward, and I gripped Monroe's arm tighter. I knew Wells was a formidable opponent, but caring for him now meant I was scared for him.

The first punch missed, but the second one landed, and I cringed as the sound of skin slapping skin sounded out around us. This close, I could hear each excruciating blow and watch as the blood and spit flew from the force. The crowd around me hollered and screamed for more, encouraging each fighter to hit harder.

"I'd thought I'd enjoy this more than I do," I admitted to Monroe. Looking up, I watched as he tracked each move, grimacing when a brutal blow landed.

"Yeah, it's always difficult watching him fight. Don't get me wrong, it's hot when I'm not worried, but something about this guy doesn't leave me with positive vibes."

"I know what you mean."

When the guy had taken off his outlandish robe, I blinked, convinced they'd called the wrong opponent. I didn't know much about weight classes, but the weight they'd read off earlier didn't seem to match the man in front of me. Wells kept ducking and weaving his hits, sneaking them in when he could. The bell rang for the first round, and I sagged in relief. Wells walked over to a corner, a staff person handing him some water to rinse his mouth. I watched as he swished it, spitting it into a bucket before he put his mouthpiece back in.

"Um, should there have been blood?"

"Yeah, it's not uncommon, but that doesn't mean I'm not worried. The cut on his brow looks bad, too." The med guy wiped it, dabbing something on it. The whole time, Wells kept his gaze focused, not looking over at us. I watched as he controlled his breathing, slowing it down, and I wanted to kiss the man for keeping his head straight.

When the bell sounded, I wasn't ready for it to start. They traded blows evenly for the next two rounds, both sides getting in a few good hits. Wells was beginning to tire, his arms slowing as he swung them. By the end of the 3rd round, I couldn't take it anymore.

"How many rounds do they go?"

"They go 5 unless there's a KO."

"And we're on which round?"

"Four." Monroe looked down at me. The same worry reflected back. Taking a deep breath, I pulled him with me. The guards didn't stop me as I marched myself up to Wells' corner. He blinked when he saw us, confused.

"What are you guys doing up here?"

"I'm coming to remind you what's at stake. I thought you were a man to come after what he wanted. But I guess you'll be using your hand tonight while I ride Monroe." I glared at him, my arms crossed, but inside I was a mess. I wanted to pull his stupid face down and kiss him, making sure he was okay. But that wouldn't help in this situation. Instead, I decided to see if some reverse psychology would help. That and banter really was our strong suit.

"Kitten, are you doubting me?" he growled, some of his fire returning as he stood up from the stool he'd been sitting on.

"What's to doubt? I thought you KO'd people in the first round. And yet, we're on the 4th, and here you are still sitting. So, Surly, I guess you've met your match? Or are you too old to swing it with the young guys?"

He gritted his teeth, his fists clenched as he pierced me with his glare. He flicked his eyes over to Monroe, who shook his head, waving his hands out in front as if he wanted no part. Spinning, I pulled Monroe's head down and kissed him. Some hoots and hollers rang out from the crowd, but when I pulled back, I glanced over my shoulder and spotted the fire back in Wells' eyes.

"Well played, Kitten. Don't. Go. Anywhere. I expect a winner's kiss."

"You gotta be a winner first."

He smirked, shaking his head, but when the bell rang that time, he walked out with a jaunt in his step and determination on his face, and I knew he'd finish this. Monroe and I stayed where we were, and he pulled me back into him, wrapping his arms around my waist. Bending down, he spoke into my ear, leaning his head on my shoulder.

"I can't decide if that's really brave what you just did or really dumb."

"Probably a little bit of both, but I think he needed it. Look."

Sure enough, Wells' punches were quicker, and he was lighter on his feet as he kicked high, landing a solid kick to the chest. His opponent went down, and this time he didn't get up. Nerves began to flutter in my lungs as the referee started to count, slapping the mat with each number. When he got to two, the guy tried to get up but fell back, not moving again. The ref jumped up when he hit one, grabbing Wells' hand and raising it high as he announced Crash the winner.

The whole time, Wells stared at me, nothing but heat in his eyes.

Perhaps it was because of this we didn't notice the guy move or his manager hand him something, but when he sat up, he lunged for Wells, catching my attention.

"Noooo! Move!"

Wells had been watching me so closely, he noticed the instant I said it, jumping out of the way. The blade crossed his ribs as the assailant fell forward from the momentum. It felt like slow motion as the next few seconds played out. Guards rushed the ring, pulling Wells to one side for safety and pinning the other to the ground, along with his managers. I stood, frozen in fear, my hand to my mouth as I waited to see if he'd been injured. It had been too close to tell if the knife had only grazed him or had made purchase.

When he struggled against the guards to be let go,

knocking the medic's hands out of the way, something in me snapped, unfreezing me, and I flew toward the ring, Monroe hot on my heels. When Wells spotted us, he stopped fighting, waiting for us to approach.

"I'm fine. Just let me go," he growled, glaring at the guard. When they saw me, they finally let him free, and he staggered from the change but quickly righted himself. Grabbing my hand, he pulled me in the direction of the locker room. Reaching back, I linked fingers with Monroe, and we created a weird follow the leader as Wells weaved through the crowd. When we made it to the dark hallway, he didn't stop, tugging us along and entered the room he'd been in earlier. Wells kept going until he made it to the bathroom, only dropping my hand as he went inside.

Following him, I took the washrag he was using to wet and wrung it out. As I gently began to clean the area, I focused on his cut, which I was glad to find was superficial, barely breaking the skin.

"Are you okay?" He grunted, and I felt his body move like he'd shrugged his shoulder.

I heard Monroe scoff from the doorway, and I found him leaning against it when I looked over. "You're pissed; just admit it. That was a shit move they pulled, and it could've been so much worse. You're lucky you can't seem to take your eyes off Lo, or you'd be bleeding out on that mat upstairs."

I didn't acknowledge Monroe's words, too scared of their accuracy, and I just focused on cleaning Wells up.

There were several other scrapes from the fight, but nothing seemed deep as I trailed the washcloth over his body, tuning them out for my inspection. When I finished, I looked up into Wells' eyes and found him watching me.

"Thank you, Kitten."

Nodding, I smiled. Placing the wet rag down, I pulled him into a hug, shocking us both for a second. His arms wrapped around me a moment later, and I sighed into his chest, finding it easier to speak to him this way.

"I was so scared."

"I know. Me too, Kitten. I'm just glad it's over. I should've said no when they told me the fighter I was supposed to face bailed out ten minutes before, so I had to fight outside my weight division. I was just too amped up, wanting this moment to fix things... to fix me."

Looking up, I stared into his dark espresso eyes, so full of regret it was a wonder I'd never noticed before. "I don't know the full story of everything, but I've gotten to know you. You don't need to be fixed, Wells. There's nothing broken about you. I know my words don't magically fix the hurts you've felt, but I hope you can start to hear my voice over the others, urging you to believe it. That's all it takes, you know. Believing something different. Let me be the different voice until you can hear yours."

"You know, I should thank that brainless blonde at Windy City gym."

"Why's that?" I scrunched my nose up, wondering if I'd misread everything between us.

"Because, Kitten, she sent you to my gym to piss us both off, but it turns out, you were exactly who I needed to walk through those doors. I'm sorry you were scared. It was dumb of me to do that. I promise to use my head more."

"You better," Monroe demanded from the door, and we both turned to look at him. "It's not just you anymore, asshole, so remember that."

"I'm trying to, Roe. I'm trying. Speaking of..." he peered down at me, his eyes lighting up with mischief. "I do believe I won, so that means I get my prize now." He bent down to capture my lips when a loud throat-clearing had us all freezing and peering out into the main area.

Sax leaned against the back of the couch, his legs stretched out in front of him, a cocky smile on his face. Atticus stood straight next to him, and I had a feeling he was the one who cleared his throat.

"If I may interrupt, I wanted to check you were okay, Mr. Young?"

"Yes. It was just a graze. Thankfully, I saw Kitten's reaction and moved out of the way."

"Very good. He's been taken down to the station by Agent Clark and won't be fighting in our arena, and hopefully others, for a while. They'd like a statement from you, but I pushed it off until tomorrow."

"Thank you. I appreciate it. I just want to go home after that fight."

"Yes, I imagine you do." Atticus' eyes flicked over to me, and his comment about squinting when I was with the others came to mind, and I smiled. It would be good for him to get used to it, so I didn't move or try to make this easier on him.

"Lore, if I may offer a suggestion?"

I nodded, hoping he wasn't about to erase the progress we'd made. "Perhaps, Jude could stay over at our house this evening. We have plenty of rooms for him to use, and then he can finish his work with Mrs. Hildebrand in the morning. I know they're working hard to get everything ready."

Shame wanted to rise up, coating me for forgetting about Jude for a second. But it had been a tense situation, a crisis, and I'd gone into survival mode for my immediate surroundings, knowing he was safe. If anything, it proved I trusted Atticus to protect him.

"Yes, that would be great if he's okay with it. If not, then he can come home with us."

The corners of his lips tilted up, and my heart sputtered. "I believe he will be fine with it. He and Immy were discussing some epic battle they wanted to have, so I think he'll be more than pleased with the prospect. I will ensure that they have separate sleeping dwellings." He looked at me sternly, expecting me to be relieved.

Smiling, I waved him off. "It's all good. I already had the sex and condom talk with Jude. He's good to go."

I'd never seen someone's face turn red so quickly. "You, what?" he sputtered, and I couldn't hold it back anymore. Laughing, I found myself bending over at the waist, everything hitting me from the day. When I finally caught my breath, I pulled myself together, wiping the tears.

"Sorry, yes, I've had the talk with him. I'm responsible like that. But no, I'm not worried about them having sex tonight. Immy's nowhere near ready for it, and Jude isn't the type of young man to take advantage, nor do I think he's ready, either. But you know, one day, they might take that step, and I'd appreciate it if you didn't murder my foster son."

His face had returned back to its normal color, but his jaw was tight as he looked at me. "We'll see, won't we." He turned to go but stopped, stomping over to me, pulling me from Wells arms. The force had me falling into him.

Atticus's hand gripped my chin as he peered down at me. "I'm squinting, not blind." His lips pressed hard into me before he stepped back and stomped out of the room. Sax watched me, an impressed look on his face.

"You learn fast, Spitfire. I'm seriously craving some popcorn now, though." Tilting my head, I gave him an odd look as he sauntered over, cupping my jaw in a completely different manner than his predecessor. He grinned, taking his time, not caring that the other two behind him were watching.

When he pulled away, I was panting, my body

following him as he left. "Be good, Spitfire. Try not to say my name when you cum." The sexy asshole winked, sauntering off without a care in the world.

The two behind me stepped closer, one on each side. "I don't know what you see in the first one, but I get the second one," Monroe admitted, fanning himself.

"I don't know what she sees in me either, but I'll take it," Wells said, turning to us. "But am I missing something? When did you start kissing Atticus?"

Rolling my eyes, I tugged them out of the room. Their comments had broken the tension and replaced it with a giddy energy that filled us as we left Upswing. The fight had reminded us what was important, and a sense of urgency and desire filled the three of us as we hopped into the waiting car.

SEVEN

WELLS

My heart felt like it might beat out of my chest with how fast it pounded. I'd run the gamut of emotions in a matter of minutes—determination to prove to Kitten I could win, brief elation when Berserker stayed down, fear when that asshat tried to stab me, and now overcome with lust so powerful, I worried my cock would snap off, it was so hard.

When the car door shut, it acted as a gun for my libido, sending me racing toward the finish line. The two people I'd wanted for months were finally mine, and it was time to claim them.

"*Kitten*, time to pay your debt. You should start by sitting on my lap," I growled.

"But, that doesn't sound very safe. We can't both wear a seatbelt, and, like, won't they hear us? I'm not so—"

"Kitten, you have two seconds before I demonstrate to you why you should listen to me." Softening my voice, I bit back some of my need coursing through me, wanting me to fuck her into next week, consequences be damned. "*Please*, Kitten. I promise to keep you safe."

Loren finally moved, sliding over onto my lap, facing me. Her red dress stretched tight across her legs, hindering her from sinking all the way down. Placing my hands on her hips, I squeezed, kneading the flesh beneath me, a slight growl escaping as I pictured her riding me. Leaning up, I captured her mouth, needing to release some of the lust pushing me. My tongue swirled needily with hers, and I could've drowned in her purrs for an entirely different reason this time.

Pulling away, I lifted her by the hips and turned her, so she was sitting on my lap but facing the other direction, her legs falling down between my spread ones. With one hand, I gripped her throat, tilting her head back to look at me. Locking eyes, I stayed frozen for a moment, enjoying the way I possessed her.

Trailing it down her front, I grazed over her breast until both of my hands were at the hem of her dress, and I pushed it up to her hips. Just as I hoped, her legs were now free and fell open, revealing her drenched silk panties. I could feel the wet patch from her arousal on them, and it gave me a satisfied feeling, knowing she was as turned on as me. Returning one hand to her throat, I made her look at me as I plunged my fingers into her soaking cunt, the sensation causing me to buck up, my erect dick rubbing her backside.

Kitten moaned at the sudden sensation, her eyes closing, and my fingers tightened, reminding her I was there.

She opened them, and I smiled. "Good girl, keep your eyes on me for now." Looking down at her, I focused on her eyes as I finger fucked her relentlessly and felt her begin to tighten around me. Before she could fall over, I pulled out my fingers and licked them clean while she watched.

"Roe, on your knees before Kitten. She needs assistance." I didn't look at him, but I knew he'd follow my command. Loren writhed in my arms, her eyes still focused on me, a little frown on her face at the fact she didn't get to cum yet.

"Payback, Kitten, remember?"

I watched as she put it together, her frown turning deeper, and I wanted to chuckle at the cuteness. Leaning down, I nipped her lips, pulling back to whisper in her ear. "Be a good girl and keep your eyes on me, and I'll let Roe lick you clean."

Loren sucked in a breath, but a look of determination came over her, and she smirked, wiggling in my hold. Now that my hand was only on her throat, she had more range to move. Each little grind rubbed up against my dick, and I didn't know if she was doing it on purpose or if it was a lucky occurrence.

When I felt her hand cup me through my shorts, I knew she was up to something. I realized too late that she should've been squirming in pleasure if Monroe was licking her like I'd ordered. Looking over to his spot, I found him staring at me smugly. He moved close, our noses almost touching.

"Things have changed, Wells. I'm not the gullible and willing young stud you remember. You have to earn the right to dominate in this threesome now."

Kitten gasped, and then a small chuckle left her. "I think he liked that idea. His dick twitched beneath me," she purred.

Looking back to her, I watched as she licked her lips, her pupils dilated, and I knew I was in trouble with them. I thought I could come in and tell them what to do and somehow keep my feelings out of it, but Roe was right; this wasn't some purely sexual exchange. It meant something now.

Kittens' hand slid up my cheek, cupping it, and I looked down again, finding kind eyes staring back at me. She pulled my face down, delivering me a sweet kiss. When she let go, she gave me a cheeky wink. "I have an idea."

She lifted herself up some, and the next second, I felt my shorts lowered and my cock hitting the air. When Loren sank down on my cock, I didn't even have time to think about it as I felt her wrap around me.

"Shit, fuck. You guys together are dangerous. I know that was you, Roe. So, you'll listen to Kitten with your Jedi mind talk or whatever, but not my orders? Rude."

Loren seated herself all the way on my dick, and her hands lowered to the seat next to my thighs. I could feel each slight movement she made, and I dropped my hands down to her hips, planting them there.

"And here I thought you were concerned about

safety, but then you go and sit yourself on my cock in a moving vehicle, Kitten. You're gonna keep me on my toes, aren't you?"

"Wouldn't be any fun if I didn't."

Sliding my hands down her thighs, I took them and slid them over my legs, locking them to the seat with mine. If she was gonna play, then I'd play too. Holding her still, I cocked a smile and looked down at her right before I thrust up. Her eyes closed, a moan filling the car. I went to do it again when I felt him. Stopping mid-thrust, I panted as I looked down at the man kneeling on the floor of the SUV.

"Roe?"

He licked up my cock and Loren in one swipe before going again; this time, he cupped a ball in his hand before sucking it into his mouth as I watched, transfixed by him. When he was pleased with himself, he looked up, winking.

"Fuck," Kitten and I said at the same time before giggling. We needed the tension breaker, and I started to move with abandon as Monroe kept up his efforts. It had somehow become a race to see who would cum first, me or Kitten. And well, I liked to win, so I was giving it everything I had. The car started to slow, and I knew it meant we had to be close to their place, so I hooked her knees under my arms and lifted her effortlessly up and down, my cock sliding in and out in tandem with the movements.

Monroe must've given up on me cumming and

helped me with Kitten, sucking her clit into his mouth as I pinched her nipple through her dress. With her high heels still on, dress hitched up around her hips, she'd never looked more provocative. And despite my efforts to hold back, I found myself tumbling over the edge a second later as the car came to a stop.

"Shit. Sorry, I didn't think."

"Ssh, help me readjust my dress before the magic doors open, and my doorman sees my goods. George has already caught me kissing. I don't really want him to see my lady bits. I'd never be able to look him in the eyes again."

While she babbled, Monroe and I helped adjust her clothing, and I pulled my shorts up. We were all finishing the adjustments when the door opened, and I laughed, getting her meaning. One of the guards snickered, but when he caught me watching, he cleared his face and stepped out of view. I didn't have the intimidation the other guys did, but after being around the complex the past few months and fighting in the rings, it had given me some street cred, it seemed.

"Excuse me, Miss," the guard said, stopping us before we made it to the door. "I, um, Sax had a message he'd like for me to give you." He cleared his throat, looking uncomfortable.

"Okay, Elijah, what is it?" Loren asked, watching him, and I wasn't surprised at all that she knew his name.

"He said, and I quote, 'Spitfire, last chance to lose these goons and ride my cock all night, but if you decide to stay, just know that I'll be, um, stroking my dick and thinking of you. Don't forget your promise.' And I'm to send him your response post haste." The man cleared his throat again, shuffling on his feet as he rubbed the back of his head, his cheeks reddening in embarrassment.

I couldn't take it, and a deep laugh escaped me. Pulling Monroe to cover Kitten, I leaned in close and whispered in her ear. "Take off your panties, and then go ask George for an envelope and marker."

Loren looked at me funny but did as I asked, carefully sliding them off and putting them in my hand. Monroe shook his head at me as she walked inside to talk to George. "You're starting shit."

"Me? The big oaf had the balls to make a guard proposition our girl on my fight night. He better be glad this is all I'm doing. Next time, I'll send him a picture of us both fucking her."

"You'll do no such thing!" Loren gasped. "You will not use pictures of my body as some pissing contest. Nothing is ever deleted from the internet, and I will not risk my job over some petty rivalry. Now, here, what are you up to?"

She handed me the envelope and marker, raising her brow in question when I didn't answer right away. I was still stunned by her statement. "Why is it so hot when you go all bossy, Loren?"

"Hmm, I'd say you have some deep-seated teacher fantasy or something which probably stems from—" I pinched her lips together to get her to stop talking.

"Kitten, the next words out of your mouth will only be, 'yes, Wells, that feels so fucking good.' Got it?" I let her lips go, and she huffed, crossing her arms, but didn't say anything. Smugly, I stuffed her panties in the envelope, not wanting the stodgy guard to touch them. Uncapping the marker, I left the top in my mouth as I motioned for Monroe to turn around so I could use his back to write.

Once I was finished, I sealed it, capped the maker, and handed the package to Kitten to deliver. She glanced at the item, chuckling, and then walked over and gave it to Elijah. The guy looked down, a smile wanting to creep up, but kept it off his face as he placed it in his jacket and returned to the SUV.

Loren giggled as she walked back and took my hand when she reached us, making my heart soar. Monroe glanced between us, trying to figure out what I'd written. Holding out my other hand, I'd let him decide how he wanted to proceed since we were at his place of residence. When he smiled, linking his fingers with mine, I was sure my feet were no longer on the ground as we walked inside.

"So, are you not going to tell me?" Monroe asked a few minutes later when the elevator doors closed.

It was Kitten who answered him. "It said," she giggled, "in case your hand gets tired, I warmed them up for you."

Roe sputtered, slapping me on the shoulder in laughter, and I smiled smugly as the elevator climbed.

"You didn't get mad at that, Loren?"

"Nah, Sax was kind of asking for it, and at least this way, it kept it contained and isn't splashing my naked body on the internet." She shrugged one shoulder, looking over at us.

"Speaking of naked, I can't wait to get you both under me," I purred, pulling them both closer. "In fact, I think you guys should get started."

They glanced at me, not sure what I meant, so when the elevator dinged, I improvised. "New plan." I lifted Kitten over my shoulder, smacking her ass for good measure. She let out an adorable little yelp as we moved out of the elevator. I kept one arm banded around her legs, making sure to keep her dress covering her naked ass.

"Whoever's place we're going to, Monroe, get the door open pronto."

He didn't hesitate, taking off ahead of me to unlock his door and let us in. I stalked to the first surface I found and dropped Kitten down onto it. She had a pout on her face and her arms crossed. I think she meant for it to be intimidating, but it was too cute.

Brushing my thumb over her lip, I caressed her cheek before tilting her head back as I gripped it. "Kitten, I know that pout isn't for me. Now, where do you want to be ravaged, and are there any limits?"

She blinked at me, looking over my shoulder for a second to Monroe before she peered back at me again, worry fixed on her brow as she began to fidget. "I'm suddenly feeling very out of my depth, if I'm honest. I, uh, didn't have much experience before, and um, this is beginning to feel very overwhelming. Can you perhaps be more specific and assume I'm only a notch or two above virginal teenager?"

Now, it was my turn to be stunned. I hadn't expected Kitten to utter those words or to ever feel so out of her depths. There were moments she oozed sexuality that I never would've imagined she felt unsure about anything.

"Okay, new plan. Grab on tight, Kitten. It's time to relocate. Roe?"

"I got it."

Scooping up Loren, I was pleased when she didn't hesitate and wrapped her arms and legs around me. She might feel unprepared, but the realization she trusted me filled me, and I'd never felt more worthy in my life.

Following Monroe, I took us to his bedroom, deciding it was the most comfortable place to explore. When I made it to the bed, I smirked down at Kitten before I launched her onto the surface, her little scream of surprise fueled me, and I pounced on her before she had time to yell.

Kissing her deeply, I sank into her body, feeling every inch of her under me. When the side of the bed dipped, I pulled back, turning my head to Monroe. He watched me with a hungry gaze, his eyes hooded.

"Your turn, Roe. What are your limits?"

He licked his lips, looking down at the beautiful creature beneath me before looking back up. "I want to say nothing, but that's not true. I haven't been with another man since our time in college, so I don't think I'm ready to jump all the way in yet."

Pulling him by his neck, I kissed him deeply, his words meaning something to me. He hadn't needed to be faithful, but he had, and it only made me love him more. Blinking my eyes open, I held his gaze for a moment, softly caressing his cheek with my thumb.

"I don't deserve half the concessions you've made for me in your life, but fuck, if I don't love you more for them. I love you, Roe. I just wanted you to hear me say that."

Looking back at Loren, I found her licking her lips, a soft breath catching in her throat as she watched us. "Have something to say, Kitten?" I purred, wanting to fan the flames a little.

She swallowed, clearing her throat before she tried. "It's just, it's really hot watching you two show your love for one another. Like, don't get me wrong, seeing two hot guys kiss while I'm underneath one of them, mega hot. But hearing you profess your feelings unhindered, it's the kind of stuff romances are made of. I don't know how I got to be lucky enough to be part of it, but I'm glad I am. I get to see a whole new side of you both, and it's the hottest fucking thing."

She gasped a little at the end, her voice going husky with need, and I felt her rock up into me. My grip on Monroe tightened as I closed my eyes, trying to stop from creaming in my shorts. A small part of me felt strengthened by the realization I'd earned the right already to dominate our threesome, and I grabbed hold of it, wanting to remind myself what it felt to be strong.

Looking back at Monroe, I grinned devilishly. "What do you say, Roe? Do we want to show Kitten just how awesome it can be with the three of us?"

"You read my mind."

Almost in sync, we turned our hungry gazes to Loren, both looking at her with unshielded lust. "We're the lucky ones, Loren, and now, we're going to prove it." Lowering myself, I pushed up her dress, and Monroe managed to work it free above and unzipped it. Finding the place I sought, I dove into her still dripping cunt and fed like a starved man. I'd never wanted a woman so fiercely before. Need for her consumed me, and I couldn't seem to quench the hunger raging through me.

Plunging my fingers into her, I sucked on her clit, twirling my tongue as I drank up everything I could. I somehow managed to tune everything else out as I worked, just enjoying her, so when I returned back to the room and looked up, I found Loren trembling as she came, her moans filling the room with their sound.

Smirking, I licked my lips, making sure to clean every last drop of her up, wanting to savor it all. She lay panting, her body jerking in aftershocks. Monroe was naked now as well, and I watched as he stroked his cock slowly, just watching Kitten come undone.

I'd wanted tonight to be the start of us, and it had

exceeded my dreams a thousand times over.

Moving over, I took Monroe's dick into my mouth, and I found myself smiling. I'd never known what I'd wanted in life. I hadn't had a family to base my dreams on, and stupidly thought living life on my own was the way to go. But as I sucked him down, barely giving him time to blink before I took him deep, I knew this was it. It didn't even matter that there were other people in Loren's life or that Delgado hadn't forgiven me for siding with the Mascros, intent to make me pay, his knifing a real reminder of the dangers I faced.

None of that mattered, because the only things that did were the two people currently writhing on the bed beneath me. I might not control a company or make millions. I might barely only own my home, and drive a beat-up car with nothing in savings. But none of those things mattered anymore to me. I'd chased that life once, and it had left me broken.

But these two, they were piecing me back together and showing me how to truly live. They were the true end goal, and I saw that now.

So, as Monroe came down my throat, his body going taut as he exploded, I couldn't help but smile again as I licked up every drop of him.

Flopping down between them, I curled my arms around them both, knowing I'd do anything to keep this.

I was a man who'd been faced with his mortality tonight, and I found my two angels willing to show me heaven on earth.

EIGHT

LOREN

The next week passed in a blur, and despite the new knowledge I had, nothing seemed to have changed, which was a relief. Jude and I spent our week going about our routine, and when Friday night rolled around, I found myself spending it between Wells and Monroe again. Waking up with them both was becoming one of my favorite ways to greet the morning.

"Good morning," I yawned, wiping the sleep from my eyes. Monroe smiled, kissing me before he climbed out of bed, putting on some plaid pajama pants.

"I'll be right back. I need to grab Levi from his sleep-over. On second thought," he said, giving me and Wells a look. "I'll make some breakfast and you two can have some time together."

I blew him a kiss, snuggling up to Wells, not minding the plan at all. I enjoyed discovering a sweeter side to Surly I hadn't witnessed yet. I laid on his chest, listening to his heart for a while before he spoke, moving me up toward him, sharing a pillow.

"Do you know how incredibly beautiful you are? Sometimes I look at you, and my breath gets caught in my throat," Wells whispered, smoothing my hair back as he peered at me. Our faces were so close, our noses practically touched as we laid side by side.

"I think you got hit in the head more than you realized sparing with Nicco." Wells had been training all week, determined to be in the best shape so he could fight again next month.

"Stop, don't dismiss your beauty, Kitten. I don't say things only to make you feel better. I mean what I say. You should know that."

I watched his dark eyes as the pupils flicked back and forth between mine, and eventually, I nodded. "I'm not trying to say I'm not pretty. It's just, no one's ever looked at me like you are. I don't like to admit my ex-husband and mother got into my head, making me feel worthless. I'm supposed to be above it all. I'm a therapist, for fuck's sake." I sighed in defeat, ducking my head a little, not comfortable with his intense glare. Wells didn't let me hide, though, pushing my chin up, holding it in his grasp.

"Do you think doctors never get sick? Or that athletes never miss their shot? Or that bankers never miscount? Hmm?" His eyes drilled into me, waiting for me to respond, and I knew he wouldn't let go until I did. Huffing, I sighed, accepting what he was getting at. "No, I don't."

"Your job is something you do, not who you are. I had to learn that the hard way."

"Will you tell me about it one day?"

"Yeah, one day. I'm still trying to come to terms with it myself."

"Thank you for reminding me I'm more than just a therapist."

"Oh, Kitten, you're so much more. Maybe I should give you a visual to help you remember." He lowered his head, kissing along my collarbone, and I was lost to his touches.

As much as I enjoyed discovering this new sweet side, I loved our banter. It wasn't pointed or mean anymore, but fun, and I liked that. It helped me use my assertiveness and find my voice, something I found all the men were doing in different ways.

Wells brought out the sassy woman I never knew I could be. Sax made me feel like fire and stirred an insatiable need to uncover hidden desires. Nicco had a unique way of making me feel beautiful in my own skin and showed me how to ask for what I wanted. Monroe was my comfort and someone I could relax my walls with in a way I'd never been able to before. And well, Atticus, I was finding he was my backbone. He showed me how to stand up and demand things, his bossy nature a front for how he protected those he loved.

I didn't know how I ended up in this position with five guys wanting me and willing to share, but I wasn't going to question it. For once in my life, I was entirely in control and I liked the direction it was headed, which led to tonight. Anxiety crawled up my throat when I let myself think about this evening, and all it could entail. Not only would I be on a date with Atticus, but I would finally discover all the hidden secrets I'd been ignoring, or to be honest, unwilling to see.

Tonight, I would no longer be able to hide behind my ignorance. No mask could conceal the truth when it was laid out in front of you. Everything had limits, and I was at mine.

Now I just hoped I could handle whatever it was they shared.

I knew I was ready. I'd accepted that when I'd pulled the string, and I knew nothing in life was black or white. I could see that more clearly now than ever before. In this moment in Wells' arms, I realized my anxiety wasn't about what I would learn, but whether or not I would care.

I was in so deep with these men, I didn't think anything would make me walk away, and for some reason, that was more terrifying than any truth they could tell me. I was falling in love with them, and that meant I could get hurt.

But the reality was, I'd risk it all to be with them, betting I was strong enough to withstand it.

"Lor, are you ready to go?" Jude asked, stepping into my room.

"Hm, yeah." I nodded, looking over my shoulder at him. He'd spent most of the morning finalizing things at the center. Atticus had allowed Imogen to help, so they'd been able to spend all morning working together. I was pleased Atticus was taking my advice to heart and letting her be more of a teenager.

Stuffing the last of my clothes into a bag, I heaved it up onto my shoulder, walking out of the room with him. We were getting ready at the Masters' place, and I'd packed us both a bag for later, assuming we'd end up there after the party and it was better to be prepared.

Grabbing his arm, I walked with him out of our apartment, locking everything.

"You excited about tonight?" I asked, as we headed to the elevator. He nodded, thinking it over.

"Yeah. It was interesting getting to plan something to this scale. I don't think I want to ever do it again, mind you." He chuckled, pressing the down arrow. "But, it was a good learning experience. My favorite part was picking out the artists to feature. It was a nice feeling being that person to make their day, you know?" Jude turned to me, a slight smile on his face.

Nodding, I squeezed his arm. "Yeah, it is. I'm glad you got to do that. I didn't ask how you felt about staying at the Masters' place again. Are you okay with that? We didn't really talk about how it was last weekend for you."

He blushed, dropping his head a little, his hair falling across his forehead. "It was fun. Immy and I stayed up watching movies. Nothing, um, happened, though. If that's what you're after. There was a guard stationed in the theater room." He peered up, eyes wide. "Not that anything would've if he wasn't, I just meant, so you know I was telling the truth."

Knocking his shoulder, I smiled as I kept my face forward. "I trust you, Juju. You've never given me a reason not to, for one, but I know you're a good kid. And we had the talk, so if things were to happen, that's okay with me. Just maybe don't let Atticus know. He doesn't seem as understanding with that kind of stuff. Just remember what we talked about. Wrap it up."

The elevator dinged, and he bolted, wanting away from the conversation. Chuckling, I followed him, having way too much fun with the whole thing. When he handed his stuff to the suited guy waiting outside, I found myself wanting to poke him a little more. "I'm too young to be a grandma!" I shouted, a giggle escaping at the end.

Jude had one foot into the car, the door open, the inhabitants blocked by his body. He turned slowly, his eyes wide as he gaped at me.

"What? It's true!" Giggling, I handed my bag to Topher, who laughed with me. Though when I climbed in, I wondered if he was laughing at me or with me.

"*Spitfire.*"

The name rolled off his tongue, and I instantly

heated. "Oh, hey, Sax. How's it going?" I asked, playing it nonchalantly. Jude leaned against the other window, looking like he wanted to be anywhere but in this vehicle, his cheeks tomato red.

"Nice try," Sax said, grinning like the Cheshire cat.

Ignoring him, I buckled myself in, fidgeting with my hands in my lap. "I have no idea what you mean."

He hummed but thankfully let it go, grabbing my hand and wrapping his big one around mine. I looked over at Jude, nudging him. He finally turned to me, giving me a classic teenager look of non-amusement.

"Sorry," I mouthed, cringing. Thankfully, he relaxed and smiled back, his shoulders dropping. The rest of the car was quiet, all of us too afraid to say anything to disrupt it. When we arrived at the mansion, we climbed out of the vehicle and I found Atticus waiting for me inside.

"Loren, it's good to see you. A hair and make-up team is waiting for you and Immy."

"Now?" I asked, looking at my watch. The benefit wasn't for five hours. I'd hoped to have some hang time with Sax or Nicco.

"I was told this was even pushing it." Atticus raised an eyebrow, and some panic set in. Shit, maybe this had been more work than I'd given him credit for. Nodding, I followed along as he directed me to a room. Looking over my shoulder, I saw Sax and Jude hurrying off in the other direction. *Chickens!* Narrowing my eyes, I turned back to ask Atticus a question, but found he was also scurrying away like his ass was on fire. It didn't exactly fill me with confidence. Just what had I'd gotten myself into?

Pushing open the door, I entered what could only be described as Hell. Taffeta, silk, and a gazillion ruffles filled the room. It seemed I would die from overexposure to hairspray, sequins, and bronzer. Oh, joy.

When Immy saw me frozen in the doorway, she squealed, running over to me. "Isn't this amazing? Attie wanted me to have the full experience, especially since I probably won't have the opportunity to attend a real prom or dance." She practically jumped with joy, and I melted. I could do this for Immy. Who knew? Maybe it wouldn't be as terrible with her around.

"It's great, Immy." She took my arm, whispering conspiratorially.

"Though, I'm trying to work on him to let me attend school with Jude. He seems to be thinking it over. Any advice to push him into the yes category?"

That was news to me, but I didn't say I disagreed with her idea. I guess it would depend on how everything played out tonight, but Immy could use some normal teenage experiences. It was right then, I decided I'd help her get it.

Walking with her over to the make-up artist who kept checking her watch already as she eyed me, I pulled her close. "Actually, I just might."

The next few hours were something I hoped to never experience again, and the mantra "for Immy" was starting to lose some of its effect. Still, when the torture artists deemed us ready, I'd never sighed in relief so hard. Grabbing Immy's hand, we walked out together, willing to take on the world in high heels, silk, and enough hairspray to last a lifetime.

If anything had solidified my opinion of who the Masters were, it was evident that while there might be some skeletons in their closet, they had deep and wide hearts with the capacity to do great things when they tried. I made a vow to trust in that knowledge and myself.

Because there was no turning back. I was all in whether I wanted to believe it or not. And the way three men's eyes raked over me when I descended the stairs only confirmed it.

It was time to embrace my darkness and learn to balance in the light. That was a promise I could make to myself; no, a vow, because promises could be broken.

"Loren, you look..." Atticus paused, clearing his throat. "You look ravishing. Thank you for agreeing to be my date. Shall we?"

Atticus extended his arm, his sharp tux cut to perfection, and I had to remind myself I couldn't lose my cool yet. But three men in tuxes looking at me with hungry eyes were apparently my weakness, and I was faltering fast into a puddle of goo.

Wrapping my arm through his, I let him lead me out of the house. Sax gave me a wink, and Nicco smiled wide as I walked by, hunger in both of their eyes. My heart raced with excitement, and as I scooted into the limo waiting at the curb, I smiled with glee that finally, everything would make sense, and I wanted to enjoy this fairy tale moment.

Jude and Immy were already seated inside, and I smiled at the two teens, both looking more adult than I wanted them to. There was no denying they made a cute pair, though, even if they weren't willing to admit it. Immy wore a simple black dress that hit a few inches above her knee and had some flutter sleeves. The wow factor, though, was the back of the dress, which was open. Jude was wearing a nice navy suit that Monroe had helped him get, and he looked handsome with his hair brushed back, though he still needed a haircut.

When I felt a body scoot in on my left, I turned in surprise, until I realized who it was. *Sax.* Smiling, I linked my hand with his and sat back as we headed toward the center. This would be a night to remember.

NINE

ATTICUS

Clearing my throat, I wrestled with the right words to say. This would be everything. I'd debated with myself on having Jude present, but as much as I wanted to avoid imagining my baby sister dating, he would be in our lives regardless due to Loren, and because of that, he deserved to know, too.

If she told the golden retriever one, that was up to her, but right now, the people I wanted to tell were here. When everyone looked at me, I cleared my throat again, finding myself fidgeting. Straightening my hands, I looked back and forth between the pair.

"Lore, I promised to give you answers. While I think it would be wise to let Jude in as well, I will let you make that decision."

She glanced at him, and he nodded. "Thank you, I appreciate you acknowledging his importance in my life. He accepts the responsibility of the information you're about to share, and I believe he's mature enough to handle it."

I waited ten seconds, giving them both one last chance to back out. When they didn't, I took a breath, filling my lungs full and letting it out slowly. I'd never had to tell anyone this before, and I found it difficult to know where to begin.

"You asked Sax last week if he was in the mafia, and the short answer was yes. That would be the mainstream definition or classification. However, the word has become bastardized, and I find it doesn't encompass everything we are. It's why I wanted to show you, using your reasoning, that actions mean more than words. I get it, because it's hard to sum up everything we are into one word. The world will call us bad guys, corrupt, and villains. I do not deny there are times those might be true, but as I think you can understand, we are more than one thing, more than a classification used to help people sort the do's and don'ts."

I paused, needing a moment to say the next part. Her eyes never left mine, and I found I didn't want to look away either. If I did, I might miss a reaction, a clue to how she felt about it. She gave me a slow nod, and I took it to mean to continue.

"I'm not going to lie and say I haven't broken the law or protected my family, however I saw fit, because I have, and I don't regret it. At its core, the mafia is about family. It encompasses more than just bloodlines, though, that's the important piece. As a family, we rise above others and stand stronger together. We prosper, suffer, and celebrate together. My father," I sneered, "sought to ruin the family in a way that dishonored our legacy and our name. He used the family to prosper only for himself, aligning with those who no longer upheld family values and were only concerned with lining their pockets with riches. That is not who we are. We don't hurt or use our family to gain leverage. It goes against everything we believe in."

Her eyes flicked briefly to Imogen, and I knew she understood then. I wasn't positive how much my sister had shared, but Loren was brilliant, and I knew she'd at least be able to connect things.

"In the past, our type of families have been connected to the criminal underground, our businesses prospering in the illegal markets. Our family, in particular, is one of the big three families in Chicago with a stronghold. Our specialties include money laundering, gambling, and, until a few weeks ago, antiquities. The one we don't advertise, though, is secrets."

"Secrets?"

"You've been to one of our clubs, and well, we use a lot of the rooms and staff to gather information. But we also offer the opposite for a price—complete confidentiality. Several public figures use our club as a safety measure to ensure their hidden desires and secrets never get into the wrong hands. In the past nine months, I've also been redirecting most of our cash flow from illegal businesses to legitimate ones. The arena last night, the club, and a few others are the new direction I'm moving the family in as we rebrand our name and what it means to be a 'made man.'"

I watched to see if she'd have any questions, but she only stared back, waiting for me. I briefly shifted my gaze to the other occupants, finding everyone fixed on me. It was time to reveal the dirty part, and I prayed I'd done enough so far to show we weren't the real villain.

"There was a great fallout around fifteen years ago, and the city was covered in bloodshed. Sax and I were earning our stripes, and it's still a time that haunts us. It started when the daughter of the second most powerful family died. She happened… she happened to be someone close to Sax and me, and her death rocked us both. Her family claimed we'd killed her, knowingly giving her laced drugs. Her death created a divide and the next five years were full of turmoil as the top three families fought it out for dominance. It was at a great cost to everyone that a truce was finally made. Maybe if I hadn't been struggling with my own grief, I would've noticed it sooner, but I didn't. I'd turned to destructive ways of revenge and violence to soothe my soul, but it almost destroyed it."

I dropped my eyes that time, not wanting to admit my failure. If I'd been more involved, if I'd insisted he included me more, if… if… if… There were so many what if's I'd grown dizzy stuck in the loop.

"This past year has been difficult for our family. My father, known as the Grim Reaper, had been hiding his misdeeds from me. It's only after his death that I've discovered how far back he'd been planning this. When he…" I paused, the bile rising in my throat each time I thought of what he sacrificed for his own fortune.

"Used me as collateral and killed my mother in the process," Immy supplied. I turned to her, surprise on my face. Her voice was strong, and she held my gaze, unwavering.

Once again, Loren had been right. I'd been babying her, underestimating the woman she was becoming—the one she'd been groomed to be her entire life. I didn't miss the way she clutched Jude's hand, though, reminding me it was okay to lean on others. Grinding my teeth, I breathed out through them, needing my heart to slow. I wasn't ready for my baby sister to step into this life.

Loren placed her hand on my forearm, shocking me. When she squeezed, I whipped my head back to her, holding her gaze. Her calming presence and reassuring smile helped me focus on her and not fall down the path of self-hatred for failing Imogen.

"His crimes were too many to let stand, so I did the one thing I never thought I'd have to do. I killed my father and took his place as head of our family."

I was expecting her to recoil in terror or even disgust, but Loren stared back, her gaze unflinching as she processed it.

"I can imagine how difficult that was for you. While I've never been in the position where I've had to consider taking a life, I know you must've felt it was the only solution. You're brash at times, closed off, and like to be in control. But you're not a vicious man, Attie. I'm still getting to know you, the real you, but I do know that. If you thought that would scare me or send me running, I'm sorry to disappoint you. Perhaps, a year ago, it would have. But I've witnessed things myself this past year that have changed me, reshaped who I am. The dark parts of the world have edged into my life. So, while I can't understand what killing a person is like, I know you don't take enjoyment from it. I can see how much it still haunts you and how you doubt yourself over it. From what I know," she shifted her gaze to Immy, her expression softening before she turned back to me, "it would've been difficult to not make that choice."

Shifting forward, I slid my hand up her neck, my thumb on the pulse point there, feeling the movement. Mindful we were in a car with my sister and her foster son, I leaned my forehead against hers, and watched as she sucked in a breath.

"Bellezza, you see me as better than I am, giving me more credit than I deserve. I'm not the hero here. The hero would've made sure it didn't happen in the first place. While I'm working to make our family better, bringing us into a new era, I'll never have clean hands. There are too many sins already staining my soul to ever be good enough for you," I whispered. "I tried to push you away, keep you out of our lives and away from the danger, but you kept showing up, and danger found you anyway."

"You only see one side of yourself, Attie, the part you're ashamed of, the one you've had to become to survive in a world where death and deceit are traded as commodities. I've found that evil can hide in plain sight just as easily as good can conceal itself in the dark. You don't have to work to be good enough for me because you already are."

I stared, not believing this moment was real. I closed my eyes, hers fluttering closed as well, her lashes almost touching my cheek. I could've stayed in that moment with her forever, content to be that close. A throat cleared, reminding me we weren't alone, and pulling me from the perfect bubble.

"Um, while I find this all very sentimental, could you maybe wait until the teens are out of the limo to start making out? I don't really want to watch my therapist and friend swapping spit with my brother. Love you both, but eww."

Sputtering, I pulled back, and the sound of Loren's giggle went straight to my cock. "Fine, brat," I teased. "Don't think I didn't notice you holding hands. Payback is fair play; remember that." Her cheeks heated, but she rolled her eyes, playing it off.

"Um, I have a question," Jude asked, raising his hand, and I nodded. "What do you mean by Loren being in danger?"

"Oh," Loren said, looking between Sax and me. "Well, there was the bombing, and then there's been a man following me."

"And why am I just now hearing about this?" Jude demanded, leaning forward and giving Loren a look. I wanted to smile at his protectiveness, but I smothered it with my hand. Sax, however, did no such thing, snorting out a laugh and reaching across and offering Jude a fist.

"You're alright, little watchdog."

Jude blinked before raising his own and bumping it with Sax's. He smiled and then turned back to Loren with his brow raised, waiting for her to answer.

"Well, um, there's just been so much going on, I didn't want to worry you."

He sat back, crossing his arms. "Consider me worried."

Loren laughed, smiling at him. "Noted."

"In regards to your stalker, he's the son of our rival and the one who," I gritted my teeth, blowing out a breath, my eyes shifting to Immy, the words unable to leave my mouth. Loren gasped this time, and something about her being more upset about Darren made me smug. "He's also the brother of the girl who died, Jaz," I sneered, the info he'd revealed last night at the forefront of my mind. "He's responsible for your Mr. Young's injuries a few months back and the downfall of his career, and the attack last night. Darren Delgado is not a good man. I could list more of his misdeeds, but we'd miss the benefit if that was the case."

"So, what will you be doing to ensure he doesn't approach Lor again?" Jude asked, giving me a pointed look.

Chuckling, I nodded, respecting his protectiveness. "I think you'll find your guardian is very capable of protecting herself, but she does have a guard detail."

"I have a what?"

"Oops," I snickered, knowing full well I just outed Sax.

He glared at me before looking at Loren. She didn't miss it, and turned to glare at him, slapping his chest. Sax grabbed her hand, clutching it, the tension shifting. Thankfully, the limo rolled up to the center in time to stop whatever was about to happen. I cleared my throat, needing to say one more thing.

"The people in this car are the only ones you should trust. My father left our family in disrepair, and I'm not convinced there isn't another mole in our ranks. Sax is my second and Nicco, my underboss. There are a few guards I trust, but to keep it simple, just keep it to us three."

"Okay." She nodded, looking around at everyone. "I understand."

"Me too," Jude replied.

"Good. Now, I want to show you some of the good that the Mascros can do." I motioned for the door to be opened, turning back to take Loren's hand. When I did, I found her face ashen, and I didn't understand what had happened in the small time frame.

"Lore? What's wrong?"

She looked up, fear on her face. "Mascros? Your last name is *Mascro*?"

"Yeah, sorry, we don't use our real name in public much unless we need to for power moves."

Her face didn't change, though, with the news. She swallowed a few times, and I watched as she worked to blank her face, all the emotion leaving her, and a cold dread filled me.

"Okay, sure, yeah, that makes sense. Well, I guess we better get to the party then." Loren nudged me, but I wanted to stay and figure out what had just happened. Opening my mouth, I was about to tell the teens to leave when Mitzi intercepted, pulling us all from the space.

"Mr. Mascro, you're here. And Loren and Jude, oh, lovely! We're all ready for your entrance." She smiled wide, and I nodded, donning the mask of the Suit and sliding out of the limo. I offered my hand to Loren, and she placed hers in mine, but the moment she was clear of the car, she dropped it, smoothing down her dress.

I didn't miss it, the subtle shift in her demeanor, and as we entered the benefit, I never felt regret so heavy in each step. I'd known this was how it would end, but I'd let hope sway me, the allure of her in our lives too tempting to ignore.

It didn't matter. Mascros were good for one thing, and one thing only—the destruction of dreams.

TEN

LOREN

Mascro. The name swirled in my head, and I felt sick. It couldn't be the same family. Right?

It seemed too coincidental, though. Some of the information Dayton had revealed started to click, aligning with what Attie had shared, but I still didn't want to believe it.

Because if it was true, then it meant…

I couldn't fathom that thought.

Goosebumps spread over my skin, and I shivered, covering myself with my arms. I walked along in a daze, unsure how to proceed. What did I do here? If it wasn't the same man, would I only cause pain by making them believe something that wasn't real?

Ethically, he was a client, and confidentiality dictated I didn't share without his consent.

But… and I'd never felt a *but* so hard in my life before.

But what if he was their father?

But what if he was the monster who sold Immy?

But what if he was the man Atticus believed he killed, but he was, in fact, very much alive?

'What if' had never felt so scary.

A hand brushed my shoulder, and I jumped, knocking into the body behind me. Hands landed on my hips, and I steadied, their weight helping to ground me. Jude looked at me in concern, and I realized his mouth was moving, but I couldn't hear any sound.

Nicco stepped in, cupping my face, and the body behind me moved closer, encompassing me in a bubble of tuxedoed men. Nicco's eyes gazed at me, his thumbs brushing over my cheek. It probably messed up the torture artists' hard work, but I didn't care; his touch felt nice. Leaning into it, I closed my eyes and sighed as the world around me returned.

"Beautiful, are you back with me?"

I nodded but kept my eyes closed, enjoying the feel of his hands on my face and the ones on my hips that had to be Sax. I felt terrible that I'd ditched Attie, but right now, he made things too confusing.

"Do you want to tell me what happened?"

"I…" I swallowed, my throat dry. "I can't. I'm sorry." My eyes opened, and I found him frowning. Nicco didn't push, nodding that he accepted my answer.

"Okay." His hands dropped, and I instantly missed their presence. Thankfully, he took my hand, not leaving me altogether. I sighed in relief, worried I was going to screw this up. Sax's hand went to the small of my back as he moved to my side, letting Nicco guide us. The scenery and people blurred together as we walked.

We stopped at a table near the front of a stage where Atticus waited, holding out a chair for me. I spotted his jaw tick, and I knew he was upset with me, assuming this was about what he'd told me.

But it wasn't. Not really.

Attempting to repair things, I stepped forward and kissed his cheek, lingering there for a moment before I stepped back and took the seat he offered. He stood stunned for a millisecond before snapping into action, pushing me in as I lowered.

It was one of those perfect chair pushes you saw well-mannered men achieve, but anyone who hadn't had etiquette training failed miserably at.

Immy and Jude sat across from me, with Sax on my right side and Nicco next to him. It was the first time I noticed the hierarchical position between the three of them, and I realized being out in public meant they had to take on their roles. Nicco was more subdued than usual, and it made me wonder how much I'd been neglecting him lately. I'd barely spoken to him at the fight, and we hadn't spent any alone time outside our tattoos. Shit.

I needed to figure this out because I wanted our unconventional relationship to work. It meant something to me, and I was determined to keep things equal as much as possible.

Atticus leaned close, whispering in my ear, his breath

tickling me. "I do hope nothing I've said scared you. You mean something to my family, and I'd hate to see that stop."

I turned, intrigued by the change in his words. He'd said family. Our faces were brought close together as I looked him over. "Just your family? Not you?"

"It's clear my past changed how you feel. I was prepared to accept it. I was expecting it, honestly."

His eyes fell, and my heart broke for him. The tension between us had been back and forth for so long, I could understand his reluctance to trust this calm. Running my hand up to his chest, I grabbed hold of his suit lapels, pulling him the last few inches between us. In the background, I faintly heard Sax tell Immy and Jude to turn their heads or go get dessert. Knowing my overgrown protector had my back, even with his friend, gave me the confidence to seal my lips to Atticus'.

It wasn't a passionate kiss, our surroundings inhibiting us from more, and keeping it brief. But it was significant, and I knew Atticus understood that. I'd just claimed him in front of the upper echelon, my peers, and perhaps his to a degree. It meant everything.

Drawing back, my hand threaded his hair at the back of his nape. His vulnerability had been my undoing. His brashness was his shield, his protection; he sacrificed everything for his family.

And if I let myself acknowledge the elephant in the room, the secret knowledge I had now, his father hadn't instilled confidence in him. The fact Attie was compassionate with a morality of his own making after having Dayton as a father was a testament to his strength.

"Oh, Attie, this has nothing to do with what you told me. If anything, you sharing it with me endeared you to me. You make sense to me in a whole new way."

"Then what was it? Because I'm just as adept at reading people as you are, Lore, and I know what I saw. You put your barriers up. If it wasn't because of what I told you, then why?"

Blowing out a breath, I searched his eyes, glancing around the table to find Sax and Nicco watching me just as intently. I briefly searched for Jude, knowing it was pointless since Imogen was with him, and while Atticus had been loosening the restraints, he would never let her be anywhere unguarded. Just as I thought that, I spotted Beau's familiar head. He caught me staring and winked before going back to his two charges. They were talking to some other teens, and it was heartwarming to see them finding peers.

Turning back, I knew I couldn't avoid him any longer. His face was already stern when I met it, not liking how long I'd left him waiting. The fact he was a literal mafia boss put a whole new perspective on his control issues. Opening my mouth, I searched for the right answer, willing the words to come to me.

"I... hmm. This is difficult for me to say, but... I can't tell you," I cringed, dropping my eyes. I didn't want to see his disappointment. I thought I'd feel better putting that out there, but I didn't. Atticus was staring at me when I looked back up, but it wasn't in anger like I expected.

"I'm guessing it has something to do with your job?"

I nodded.

"Very well. As much as I want to demand you share whatever made you close yourself, I won't. I respect your profession Loren, and I appreciate the fact you take it so seriously. It validates my decision to bring Immy to you in the first place."

Sighing, I nodded, relief flooding me, and only a little bit of disappointment he wasn't demanding I tell him. It would be easier if he had, removing the guilt from myself.

"Something tells me that a part of you wanted me to demand you spill, Bellezza." He moved forward, whispering the last part in my ear as he casually freed my lip from between my teeth. "Don't forget what I said about this lip."

Atticus moved back a centimeter, our faces still extremely close. "I won't demand it, but I ask if it involves my family, that you tell me before it's too late. I believe highly in the concept of being two steps ahead of my enemies."

I nodded, the words climbing my throat to share it right then, but they wouldn't come, stopping at my tongue each time. The ingrained ethical dilemma of crossing that line kept halting me.

Mitzi crossed the stage we were sitting next to, taking the microphone offered to her, and Atticus and I broke apart, falling back into our seats. My hand shook under the table, and Sax reached over, linking our fingers together, and I instantly calmed.

Now that my decision was over, I felt worse than I had.

I think I was making a mistake.

Mitzi spoke about the generosity of Atticus to the center and the help Jude had been organizing it. She called him up on stage, and I sat up straighter to listen. I watched him smooth down his navy suit, taking the podium from her. He'd grown so much from the shy teen I'd met back in January. Jude went on to share his experience interning, his enjoyment in selecting the artists, and what it meant to share art that spoke to him.

A tear fell down my cheek, and I quickly wiped it away. Leaning forward, I grasped Atticus' arm. "This… seeing Jude up there, this is everything. Thank you."

He smiled at me, adoration in his eyes. "Of course. I'm glad I was able to find something meaningful. I took your words to heart, you know. I want to show you how I feel and that I'm truly sorry for my boorish behavior."

"Only you could say boorish and get away with it."

"Is that a compliment?" He smirked, some of the light returning to his eyes.

"If you have to ask, you're missing the point," I smirked, sitting back. I heard a sniffle next to me, and I turned, finding Sax rubbing his nose. He caught me looking at him and glared.

"Allergies."

"Uh-huh."

Chuckling, I let it go as Jude returned to the table, and we all congratulated him on his speech and how well he did.

"Why didn't I know you were doing that?" I asked, giving him a pointed look this time.

"Oh, I guess it slipped my mind." He ducked his head, his cheeks heating.

"Uh, huh." I clicked my teeth, liking being the one to give him shit this time.

Mitzi came back on a few minutes later, announcing the silent auction would begin soon, and that dinner would be served in an hour.

"Lor, there's a picture I wanted to show you in the auction. Will you come with me?"

"Of course." I began to stand when Atticus placed a hand on the back of my chair, stopping me.

"How about we all go?"

Nodding, he stood at my acquiesce, pulling my chair out, and I inwardly swooned at the gesture. As a group, we made our way to the room the art had been set up in. Atticus eyed Imogen's dress now that he could see the back, making a face, but I was happy he didn't make a scene.

He leaned over to whisper. "Why do I feel you were the one to encourage that dress?"

"What's wrong with it?" I asked, blinking my eyes innocently at him. He growled, the sound going straight to my clit, and I gasped at the sensation.

"Careful, *Bellezza*, don't forget what I told you about lies."

He nodded his head forward, and I turned slowly, finding Nat and Stacy waving at us. Walking over, I embraced them both, happy to see them.

"You both look gorgeous! How are you? Cami with you?"

"No, she didn't answer at her apartment either," Stacy answered.

Nat bit her lip, glancing at Atticus before excusing herself. I watched as she approached him, and they walked off out of sight.

"What's that about?" Stacy asked.

"I don't know." I shrugged. I didn't think for one second that Atticus was interested in Nat or vice versa, but it did worry me that she'd taken him away to talk. Secrets were starting to pile up, and I couldn't find my way out of them. When I spotted Jude motioning for me, I excused myself from Stacy to join him.

"Is this the one?" I asked as I approached. He nodded, fidgeting as he waited for me to see. Gasping, I clasped my hand over my mouth as I stared at the photo. Tears rushed to the surface, and I did nothing to stop them this time. "Did you do this?"

He nodded, and I finally wiped my tears before I pulled him into a hug, clinging to him. When I felt like I could speak without crying, I drew back and peered at it more. I noticed Jude wiped his eyes too, but I let it slide, the emotion too real to diminish today. He'd used photos

I'd taken when I was younger, photos he'd taken of me, his own images, including ones of him, and had morphed them into a collage. As I stared, tilting my head, a shape began to emerge.

"Is that…"

"A penguin," he answered, a bright smile on his face. He pointed to the piece's title, and my tears wanted to explode out of me again. *Misfit Penguins.*

"Oh kid, you're gonna make me a sobbing mess."

He laughed. "Sorry, I just thought we needed a family picture."

Any chance I had of keeping them at bay broke, and I started crying again. I felt a large body pull me into their arms, and from the scent of fresh cotton and slight sandalwood, I knew it was Sax. He held me for a while, rubbing my back before he gave in and asked the question.

"Spitfire, what's wrong? Who do I need to beat up? What did you do, little watchdog?"

"Me? Nothing, I just told her it was a family portrait. I didn't think she'd cry this much. Lor, I'm sorry if it was presumptuous."

His doubt had me pulling away, wiping my eyes. "Jude, no! I'm not upset at all. I'm overcome with emotion because it means everything to me. *Everything.*" I reached out, grabbing his hand as best I could with Sax's arms wrapped around me still, holding me to his chest. At the rate I'd been crying tonight, I was scared to look at my face. Jude looked at Sax, a satisfied look on his face as he took in the big man, causing me to laugh.

"Loren, it seems you've decided to humiliate your father and me further," a voice from behind said. My blood went cold, and I turned, my eyes spitting daggers at my mother. Today was not the day to mess with me, and Jacqueline Hanover was about to discover why.

"I'm sorry, I didn't realize I'd asked your opinion. In fact, I never have, and yet you think you can give it whenever you feel like it. Well, not anymore. I'm done, Mother. I know you and Brian are up to something, and I *will* find out. So, you might as well come clean now and save yourself some humiliation."

I saw fear flash for a second before she swallowed, lifting her nose up in the air. "I don't know what you mean. Clearly, this was not the black-tie event I expected if they let riff-raff like your companion in. I think it's time for me and my money to leave. I'll be sure to tell my friends on my way out. Your event is going to fail, just like everything else in your life has without me."

Scoffing, I prepared to let her have it again, but someone else stepped in.

"Mrs. Hanover, Jacqueline, is it? I don't think we've had the displeasure to meet yet. That's been on purpose on my end, at least. It's good you're leaving, since you couldn't afford anything here, anyway. Isn't *that* right?" Atticus asked politely, an air of regalness she'd never be able to replicate dripping from each word. He continued on, not giving her a chance to respond, and I could kiss the stubborn man for how brilliant it was. It was entertaining when his ire wasn't directed at me.

"As for your friends, *who* are they exactly? If what I've heard in the circles are true, you've hit up all your rich friends for a loan, and they've all declined you. Seems your poor behavior has finally caught up to you, Jacqueline. So, please do enjoy your trip out of the benefit. We don't need anyone of *your* kind here."

"My kind! Listen here—"

"*Mr. Mascro*," he offered, and she blanched even more. "And as for 'your kind,' I mean rude, obnoxious, and too blind to see the beautiful gem of a daughter you had. And I do mean *had*. You'll do well to remember that it's past tense and stay the fuck out of your daughter's life. That *is* a threat."

Atticus turned his back on her, dismissing Jacqueline even more in front of everyone in the room. I didn't even have to think about my next move. Pulling him to me, I kissed him thoroughly this time. Sax's arms stayed wrapped around me the whole time, and his words about me between the two of them had me rubbing my legs together. Thankfully, Atticus seemed to remember we were in public still and pulled back before I practically humped his leg.

"If it only took putting your mother in her place to be kissed like that, I would've done it a long time ago."

"Nice try," I teased.

"Um, can I look yet?" Jude asked, and I laughed, peeking around Sax to see he'd turned Jude in the other direction. I looked up at him, and he shrugged. Chuckling, I turned Jude around, not even embarrassed.

"I think we're gonna need a code word or something, so I'm not scarred or continuously shoved into corners."

"Sure, JuJu." I smiled, feeling the happiest I'd ever been. Looking for the rest of our crew, a pair of dark eyes stood out from the crowd, staring at me. When they caught mine, I noticed their lips lifted in what most people would perceive as a smile, but it was a sardonic mask of the real thing on him. He faded into the crowd, but his message was clear.

He knew I knew who he was now, and it was only a matter of time before he played that card.

My heart raced, and goosebumps broke out at the implications of what he could do to the happiness I'd just found. My vow to trust myself surged up, and without any hesitation this time, I turned to Atticus, searing him with my gaze, the words tumbling free, uninhibited.

"I can't do this to you."

ELEVEN

LOREN

His face fell, and I realized how what I said sounded. "No, sorry. What I meant was, I can't keep this from you. I can't choose it over all of you. There's something significant I need to tell you. I believe it's life or death."

Once he'd recovered from my dismissal, he nodded, squaring up and moving, expecting the rest of us to follow. He spotted Nicco a few spaces ahead, grabbing him to whisper something in his ear. He took off in the other direction as Sax, Jude, and I followed Attie. He led us to a boardroom, and I watched as Sax and Topher, who I hadn't noticed, walked over to a panel in the wall and typed in something before a buzz filled the air.

I looked at Jude, and he raised his eyebrows with me. A few seconds later, Immy and Nicco arrived, and I realized what Atticus had done. It made me realize that Nat and Stacy were out there alone. Opening my mouth, I started to ask the question when Nicco answered for me.

"Beau is watching Nat and Stacy. They're safe."

Relaxing, I nodded, and he took the opportunity to kiss my cheek. My eyes fluttered closed for a second, and I soaked in the comfort of him. I'd missed him so much. Wrapping my arm around his waist, I pulled him to my side, not wanting him to leave. When I opened my eyes, I found his beaming at me, and my heart took off at the sight. I needed to make it a priority to focus more on each of them.

"Lore, you had something you wanted to share?" Atticus asked, pulling me from the gray-blue depths of Nicco. Licking my lips, I focused on the room and found Imogen snickering at me. Sticking my tongue out at her made me laugh, and it helped me loosen up.

"Sorry, it's just… Phew, this is hard for me." I blew out a breath, and Nicco wrapped his arm tight around me, and it helped. "When you revealed your last name in the car, the reason it took me by surprise was… was because it wasn't the first time I'd heard it."

I looked up at Atticus, finding him watching me. He nodded. "What have you heard?"

I shook my head, my mouth going dry. "Um, it's not what I've heard, but more of *who* I've met."

His eyes widened, not expecting that answer. I watched as he shifted his position against the table, attempting to find some sort of control. Atticus really didn't like being out of the loop.

"So, um," I started, falling over all of my words. Shaking my head again, I straightened my spine. They deserved to know the truth, and I needed to be brave and share it.

"When you said your last name, it took me by surprise. On my first day back to work after the bombing, I had a new client. What was odd about it was when a man walked in. It confused me because I typically only see women and teens. This man, he insisted on seeing *me* specifically, stating he'd been referred to me." At the mention of a man, everyone stiffened, watching me closely with intrigue.

"This client, he was very odd. He never felt genuine, and everything he did felt like an act. He would try to act scattered or shy, but I'd catch a glimpse of a dominant personality shining through. Everything was at odds with him. His speech. His words. Nothing made sense. Quite frankly, he freaked me out." Gasping, I turned into Nicco, clutching his chest. "Do you remember that day I crashed Ignite Ink with tacos after a weird client session?"

"Yeah, of course. You were really shaken up that day. Is this the same person?"

"Yes!" I turned back to Atticus, almost pleading with him. "For the past month, I've been trying to terminate sessions with him or refer him to someone else. I didn't feel like we were connecting, and he was playing this game with me. On the day I went to see Nicco, he'd been really off, and it seemed like he was going to hurt someone. He played it off as a fantasy when I questioned him, but it never felt right."

My body shuddered at the memory, needing to clear him from my mind. I looked around the room and found everyone peering at me. Even Jude and Immy were focused on the tale I was sharing. I knew the next part was going to be the hardest, but I had to get it out. *I had to.*

"I've been struggling because, ethically, I'm not supposed to share client details. But this... this seems important. And well, you're all important to me. Jude has shown me what it means to be a family, and so have all of you. I see that now. I get what you meant about the mafia being a poor word for what you are because you're right. It's so much more. When you stood up to my mother like that, you reminded me what was at stake. If I lost any of you, I don't think I'd survive it." I took in a deep breath, fighting back the tears. I'd cried so much this evening from happiness it was overwhelming to think about.

"I think I found a loophole. A way for me to technically not break confidentiality and help you stay two steps ahead, but I need you to let me say what I need to say and only ask questions when I pause. Okay?"

"Anything, Lore." Atticus watched me intently, and I could tell he knew this was important and would either destroy or strengthen the family.

Nodding, I glanced up at the ceiling for a second, gathering my thoughts. Righting myself, I held his umber eyes as I started.

"Is Mascro a common name in Chicago? Or are you related to all Mascros through some line?"

"It's a rare name, and every Mascro I've ever met here is family through bloodline to some degree."

"Okay, so by me saying, you're not the first Mascro I've met…"

"I can assume your client is part of my family."

One side of my smile lifted, but dropped as I continued. "Who is your biggest enemy?"

"Delgado," he said without question. I grimaced, trying to figure out how to ask it differently.

"Okay, who would you never want to see again?"

Atticus watched me, understanding he hadn't answered the previous with what I'd intended. "That's a lot of people, unfortunately."

Taping my lip, I focused on how to say this. "Let's say there's a person, and their existence, if accurate, could irrevocably change the course of things, as well as your own standing and belief." I started sweating, feeling like I was talking in circles. "Ugh, why do I have to care about morals!" I shouted, closing my eyes. Taking in some breaths, I rubbed my temple.

Nicco turned me inward, so all I could see was him. Taking my face between his hands, he soothed my temples with his thumbs, and I relaxed into him. "Beautiful, I get how hard this is for you. Having morals doesn't make you weak. It makes you strong because you stand for something. Your job, it's been the one consistent thing in your life this past year when everyone and everything abandoned you after your world fell apart. I know that it's hard to trust this new reality, and I applaud you for trying to find a way to share this without hurting anyone. But…" he took a deep breath, "if you're struggling this much, maybe you shouldn't tell us."

I heard Atticus disagree from behind, but I ignored him, focusing on the calming waves of Nicco's eyes.

"But?" I asked, smiling.

"But," he grinned, glad I'd asked. "Knowing what you do now about who we are and how this client acted, how do you know they weren't a plant to gain information from you? Or an imposter, even? It's hard to imagine anyone in our family acting so erratic as some ploy."

"What if I'm wrong, though, and the information only causes more harm? What if I'm some Trojan horse they're using? I'm hesitant because the thought of hurting any of you makes me want to tell you, but if it's a trap, then am I playing into that? Do they expect me to tell you or to keep it hidden? I feel like I'm holding a loaded gun and anyway I shoot, I'm hitting someone."

"Fair," he nodded, "but—"

"Loren," Immy cut in, pulling Nicco and my focus to her. "You once told me that the 'what if' game is a trap of your own making, one that has you going in circles, and you never get anywhere except dizzy."

"You're right." I nodded, smiling at her, realizing it had been what I was doing.

"And," she beamed, liking that she got to play therapist, "laying out all the information is the best way to get off the loop."

"Again, you're right."

"Well, I had an awesome therapist."

Sighing, I took her words to heart. I was trying to manage their emotions for them in this situation. Closing my eyes, I nodded, accepting what she was saying, knowing I had to trust I'd prepared her to deal with this, but most importantly, she wouldn't be alone. Opening my eyes, I looked at Atticus again. Thankfully, he wasn't angry with me, just patiently waiting for me to come to a decision myself. It made me respect him, thawing that block between us even more. It was practically non-existent at this point.

"Okay, remember that I don't have all the facts, only what I was told. It could be a trap to send you all into a state of recklessness, hurt you to gain leverage, or even distract you. But I agree that I need to present all the information to you, and then you can make an informed decision instead of being bombarded with surprises."

My hands shook as I looked between the two I felt would be most impacted by this news. "My client, his name… his name was Dayton Mascro, and I saw him. He's here."

It was silent for all of two seconds before utter chaos exploded around me.

TWELVE

IMOGEN

The words left her mouth, and I knew they were true. I'd thought I was going crazy the other day when I smelled his cologne, wondering if I'd regressed and only imagined things. I hadn't had a nightmare in a month, and the overcoming sense of fear that coated me each time I left the house had dissipated. So while I wasn't thrilled one of the men of my nightmares was back, it was actually comforting to know I hadn't imagined something.

My father was known for his mind games, and that was what this all was, after all. A game to him. He didn't care about anything other than power and control. This was the ultimate way to control us, through the woman who had entered our lives and started to put our pieces back together. Attie could deny it all he wanted, but she had. Loren was healing all of us, and somehow Dayton had known that and went for our heart, where it would hurt the worst. He wasn't an evil genius for nothing.

Ringing in my ears became noticeable, as did the pain

from my fingers that were gripping my chair. Slowly, I released a breath and tried to recall what Loren had taught me.

Breathe in. Think of something comforting—reading.
Breathe out. Exhale the negative weight—weakness.

I felt my body start to unwind some, and I kept going, focusing only on it and not the chaos around me.

Breathe in. Piano.
Breathe out. Fear.
Breathe in. Cozy sweaters.
Breathe out. Shame.
Breathe in. Jude.
Breathe out. Dad.
Now, close it off with a self-affirming power thought. My past doesn't define me. I'm stronger than the things done to me.

My whole body sagged, and I slowly lifted my fingers away from the chair one by one. Carefully, I opened my eyes, blinking as I came back to my surroundings. The first things I noticed were the arms wrapped around me, and this time when I caught a whiff of a familiar smell, it soothed me, my body melting completely into his for a brief minute.

Pulling away, I smoothed my hair back from my face and focused on the person closest to me, the shouts and noise too much for me still. Jude watched me, and any doubt I had that he'd look at me differently was cleared away. His brown eyes peered back, understanding in their depths. We hadn't talked about our pasts, often skirting around the edges of the bad things that had occurred in our lives. In our friendship, we'd found a safe place to be without any of the past defining us. It was one of the things I was most grateful for.

"Hey," he said, smiling. He dropped his arms, and instantly I missed their comfort. But it was probably for the best, not that anyone else seemed to be paying attention to us at the moment outside of Topher. When he saw me look over and cataloged I was okay, he nodded and went toward the others.

"Thanks for that. How long..." I couldn't bring myself to say the rest, but he understood.

"Not long. Your brother watched you for a minute, so did Loren, but when I told them I had you, they then started that." His eyes shifted over to the group of adults arguing. I couldn't hear everything, but mostly I could hear Atticus saying Loren was wrong or confused. Sax kept firing questions, and Nicco tried to get them all to stop shouting and sit down and discuss it.

"I know this isn't the right question to ask, but are you okay?"

"Yeah, I am." I smiled at how cute he was asking. "It was a bit shocking at first, but then it actually helped validate me." Jude scrunched his nose, not understanding, and it made me giggle a little. "It's a game, and I know he purposefully sought her out and had been planning for me to run into him or something at a place I felt safe. It almost worked when I smelled his cologne last week."

"What do you think it means, then? I thought Atticus… you know…" he shuffled in his chair, his cheeks heating a little.

I giggled again, not because the thought of my brother killing my father was funny, but the fact he was so nervous about saying it made me appreciate him so much more. Jude was the reminder that there was more to life than mob bosses and child brides.

"Yeah, he did." I nodded, nothing else to really add. I looked over at the grownups again, their arguing going in circles, and I knew I needed to step in. This wasn't how I wanted to spend my time at this benefit. Auctions were going on, and I hoped to be able to dance with Jude at some point. I wouldn't get to do any of that if they didn't resolve their shit soon. Taking Jude's hand, I kept my eyes forward, not wanting to see his face, and pulled him over with me. I nodded to Topher, and he stepped back, letting me through.

"I believe Loren."

It was all I said, but it worked as they stopped and turned to peer at me. Loren smiled, and it gave me the strength to say more.

"The other day, I had a slip, I guess, a moment where I fell back into that time. I snapped out of it quickly, but it bugged me because it had happened so quickly. I shook it off, and we went on to our dress fittings. It was later when I realized what had triggered me, my brain working to solve the puzzle even when I wasn't focusing on it."

I took a deep breath and felt Jude squeeze my hand as Attie looked at me expectantly. His arms were crossed, and I could tell he was about to deny anything I stated. Holding his eyes, I gave him the evidence I hoped he'd believe.

"It was his cologne, Attie." Looking over at Loren, I asked her for the clarification I needed. "You saw him that day, didn't you? Right before we met?"

She nodded. "I did. It was our last session, actually. The one where he was very manic and spouting off a lot of different information like how he..." she stopped looking over at Atticus. I knew I didn't need to hear anymore; the information I did know haunted me enough.

"There's your proof, Attie. You can argue with her, you can get mad and call her a liar, but I believe her. You know as well as I do that Dad had his cologne specifically made for him because he was too important to wear something everyone else did." I rolled my eyes, some of the things my dad had lamented on seemed so self-serving now. But at one time, he'd been my world.

"It doesn't mean—" Atticus started, and I did something I never thought I'd be able to do; I held up my hand, halting him.

"Save it. This is exactly what he does. Mind games.

Whether or not it is him, it has to be taken seriously. If it is, then you need to prepare for that. If it's someone impersonating him, then you need to prepare for that. Neither option is something you can sit on, and arguing whether or not Loren is right is wasting time. The fact that someone took time to target Loren, tell her things, and time their appointments to intersect with me are the things you should be concentrating on. Now, I'm going back out there to bid on some art, eat some cake, and then dance with Jude. Do you have a problem with that?"

Attie's jaw ticked, and I watched him mentally fight with himself as his body relaxed. I waited, knowing it was important for him to accept me as a viable part of this family, not someone to brush aside.

He blew out a breath, and I glanced over at the others, finding Sax watching me with pride, Nicco beaming at me, and Loren going all misty-eyed again. When I landed back on Atticus, his eyes had also softened, and he pulled me into a hug. It was so uncharacteristic that I tensed at first. When I realized what he was doing, I let go of Jude's hand and wrapped my arms around him. My brother, not the mafia boss, held me for a few minutes, his head in my hair as we stood there. I could feel his heart against my cheek and the way his body trembled slightly. He was struggling with this, perhaps more than I had.

"You carry so much, Attie; you don't have to carry this for me. Thank you for doing it up until now, for showing me how to be strong and compassionate. But I can take it. I'm not a wilting flower," I whispered.

"You're not, and while I hate this for you, thank you for reminding me how strong you are. I love you, Imogen, and I want the world for you beyond this."

"I love you too, and because of you, I have the world. I know you don't want the mafia life for me. I don't even know if I want it. But right now, I have my world, and I'm happy. Let that be enough for now. Let's fight our demons together."

He pulled back a little, grasping my arms as he looked down at me. "You're the best thing to ever come out of this family. Your mother would be so proud of the woman you're becoming. Thank you for reminding me how strong you are and how strength is different for each of us. Go, enjoy the party, and we'll be out in a few." He kissed my temple, squeezing my forearms, and I stored it away as a win. This was something I wanted to remember and replay over and over.

He let me go, and before I could take a step, Loren wrapped her arms around me too. Smiling, I hugged her back, enjoying this newfound affection in our lives.

"I'm so proud of you. I watched you, and you fought back against your memories, gaining control, and it was beautiful. I'm so honored to have witnessed it, even if I was the one to have caused it." I shook my head, not wanting her to carry that guilt.

"No, Loren, don't think that way. I'm glad you told us. Maybe I'm naive and just read too many books, but the bad guys succeed by creating doubt and fear in the heroes. Transparency and authentic communication are utter kryptonite to villains. You taught me that, too."

"You know, you're so right." She laughed, and I squeezed her tight before pulling back.

"He chose you because he knew it would hurt the most, you know." I shrugged, knowing it was true. "Either because he hoped he'd break you down by keeping the secret or causing this infighting. He underestimated you, though. But he got one thing right."

"What's that?" she asked, peering at my face.

"You're our heart, and he hoped to stab us in it. The thing he doesn't understand, the thing he'll never understand. You're not our weakness, but our strength. You've helped us all to become better versions of ourselves, even if some are slower to it than others." I shifted my eyes to Attie quickly, but she got the message, and we both smiled.

"Thank you for that, for reminding me the smallest things make a big change over time." She pulled Jude closer, holding both our hands. "Now, go and enjoy. We'll be along shortly. Jude, put down the biggest bid on yours. I don't want anyone else to have it."

"It's not for sale, Lor." I watched as Jude blushed, my heart growing warm. He really was the sweetest boy.

We stepped away from the adult huddle and headed toward the door, with Topher following. When we got out into the hallway, it felt calmer, and any last dredges of tension fell away as we walked.

"That was pretty amazing back there," Jude said, bumping my shoulder. My cheeks flamed, but I smiled, enjoying his praise. He cleared his throat as we entered the central area. "So, um, were you serious about wanting to dance with me?"

"I mean, yeah, if you want to. I don't want to force you." I kept my eyes focused, not sure I could take it if he made a face of revulsion or something. Jude was undoubtedly my best friend, and my feelings for him were complicated. Well, I guess they weren't, really. I liked him. And at times, I felt like he liked me too. I didn't have many normal interactions, though. We held hands at times, but was it only him being a supportive friend? We talked all the time, and I shared almost everything with him. I could be myself around him and never got bored of talking to him.

But what if that was normal for a friend? How did I know if it was more? He made my heart race and my palms sweat, and I often got butterflies when I first saw him. I cared what I looked like around him, and I couldn't wait until the next time I got to spend time with him.

But did he feel that way? I didn't know.

I knew Loren said I should say something. But each time I started to, anxiety overwhelmed me, and I swallowed my words, unsure of myself.

Perhaps I should read some different books to get a better perspective. The YA fantasy ones I tended to gravitate toward did nothing to prepare me for being a teenager with a crush.

"I don't think you could ever force me to do anything. I mean," he stuttered, talking fast, "not that you aren't strong, just that I always want to do things with you. Wow, hope that doesn't sound lame."

Giggling, I turned my head, taking in his expression finally. "No, it doesn't. So, cake first, then we brave it?"

"Yeah, though I have to warn you, I've never danced before, so I'm bound to step on your toes."

"That's okay. It will be my first time too. We can brave it together. So, what kind of cake did you pick out for this event?"

As Jude went into an explanation of the three types he'd chosen and why, I found myself smiling so hard my face hurt. My father might be back, but I wasn't the same girl he'd once known. I'd climbed through the fire, fortifying myself with armor so tough, it would take a hell of a lot more to break me this time. I knew what it felt like to have people care about me, and now I had something to fight for.

My father had tossed me aside once, thinking my only use was my vagina. He made a vital mistake assuming women were weak and non-threatening. I'd be sure to show him just how wrong he was.

Dayton Mascro thought he had broken me once. He hadn't. If anything, he'd shown me what I was capable of.

My tutor was a dumbass, but something he'd made

me read the other day resonated with me, and I knew it was time to claim that part of myself.

"*What the caterpillar calls the end of the world, the master calls a butterfly.*" — Richard Bach.

I was the master of my life now. It was time I showed my father just how deadly *this* butterfly could be.

THIRTEEN

NICCO

Once Immy and her entourage had cleared the door, the silence in the room became deafening. Mas didn't want to admit he'd been bested by his little sister or that he'd played right into his father's hands, but as Immy had stated so clearly, he had. This was a mind fuck, and Dayton wanted us unfocused.

Though I wasn't convinced yet that it was the Reaper.

I'd seen Mas that night, and he'd been shaken, certain he'd killed his father. So, I'd be the one to ask the hard part, Loren had already done enough tonight.

"Mas, I know you don't like to talk about it, but…" he glared at me, daring me to ask the next part. I raised my brows in a challenge, not scared of his glower. "How *sure* are you that you killed him?"

"Very," he growled. Loren sighed, raising a hand to her head.

"Listen, whoever he is, he knows a lot about you. Let me just ask you if anything he told me is accurate, and then we go from there. Okay?" I heard her mutter, "It's not like I haven't already broken confidentiality. I might as well go all in." She shifted on her feet, bringing a smile to my face. Atticus rolled his eyes, but Loren smiled, patting his arm.

"First, I need to sit; these shoes are not meant to stand in for hours."

Before she could take a step, Sax swept her up into his arms, smirking down at her as he walked over to an armchair and sat in it with her. She giggled, not bothered one bit by his behavior. It confirmed what I knew to be true; we were all meant for each other. This felt natural.

Atticus and I sat in the other chairs, facing them, and waited for Sax to quit nibbling on her neck. When he gave no sign of stopping, whispering something in her ear instead, Atticus grew impatient, snapping at his oldest friend.

"Cut it out, Sax. This is important. Keep your dick in your pants for once."

"Challenge accepted," he purred, lifting his eyes to Mas.

Laughing, I covered my mouth with my hand when my cousin turned his glare on me. "You're not helping." Lifting my hands, I pleaded innocence. It was Beautiful who finally got the big man to stop when she whispered something back to him, biting her lip when she pulled away.

Looking at me, she then glanced at Atticus, debating where to start. Blowing out a breath, I watched as she came to a decision, a resolve coming over her.

"He had dark hair with some salt and pepper and was probably around sixty. He was tall, always dressed in a suit, and I suppose he was handsome in a conventional way." Sax growled, tightening his grip on her, but Loren didn't react, lost in her memories as she tried to pull relevant information.

"Dayton gave off a weird energy. He always felt like danger, in a way that makes you want to run away from him, but he would purposefully make himself appear less intimidating. He slouched, fidgeted, and would be soft spoken or with a stutter. He spoke of a fallout with his son; how he had disappointed him, siding with his sister."

Mas stiffened, sitting forward more as she spoke, and I wondered if he was starting to take Loren's claim more seriously. I believed Loren. She wasn't one to lie or create false hope.

"He was strict on responsibility and family..." she trailed off, almost like it clicked for her. Shaking her head a little, she blinked, refocusing on us. "I don't know how much is accurate, but he mentioned killing someone once and wanting to kill, well, um, you." She swallowed, but when Atticus didn't say anything, she continued. "Our last session, he shed a lot of information. He spoke of a brother, um, Benny, I think."

Bolting upright, I startled her with my sudden movement. "What did he say about Benny?"

Her eyes took on a sense of sadness, and I knew it wasn't going to be good. "You can say it. I never believed the lie he told me about my father. There were too many questions surrounding his death, but I hit a brick wall any time I tried. Eventually, I stopped."

"Well, um, apparently," she stopped, looking between Mas and me. "Benny was having an affair with your mom, Atticus, or at least she was, according to Dayton." Loren shifted in Sax's lap, clearing her throat.

"Is that all? I feel like you've purposefully left something out to protect my feelings, Bellezza. You don't need to. I have very few."

She looked up, sucking in a breath as she looked between us again. I had a feeling whatever she'd held back included me too. I watched as she started to pick at her nails, rubbing her forefinger over her thumbnail.

"I… don't know how to take that. But you're right, I can't manage this for you. Dayton told me that he sent Benny and Shayna on a forever trip, but before he left, he made sure to let Benny know he'd known about his affair and had taken retribution by stealing his heir. He, um, raped your mother, Nicco…"

"Wait, but that would mean…" I turned slowly to Mas, looking at him. His face was full of shock as well, his brows high as he stared at me. He blinked, his features returning, and he looked at Loren. I didn't know how to feel. I hadn't known Benny, only the stories I'd been told, so it wasn't devastating news to be told he wasn't actually my father.

But…

If Dayton was my father, then it changed things. I

didn't know how yet, but I could tell it was something significant.

"What do you mean by 'forever' trip? Are you implying he had them killed?"

"That's the phrase he used, but knowing what I do know, and the atrocities he's committed against you and Immy, I'd put money on that. He killed your mother and his brother because they loved one another."

"It tracks with what Ethan told us, connecting the dots a little more," Atticus said, looking at Sax.

He grunted, deep in thought.

"Ethan?" Loren asked.

"Head of another family. There are three main ones in Chicago; Mascros, the Delgados, and the Rawles. Ethan is the head of the Rawle family. He recently aligned with us in exchange for giving him our shipping portion. When he was at the compound, he mentioned that Benny and Dayton were in love with my mother, Shayna, but that Dayton won out in the end. I believe that there were actually four of them that were in love with Shayna."

Loren nodded, processing the information. "You know, he made a vague statement about his friends and winning her. I can't recall it exactly, but that could fit. So, does that mean you believe me?"

Atticus stared for an extended period before he spoke. "I don't know. I believe someone with information on my family was in your office. That whoever they are intended for us to doubt if you did ever tell us, but that mostly they enjoyed being close to you and getting one over on us. You said you're no longer seeing this client?"

She shook her head. "No, the day that he dumped the info, he also told me he'd no longer be needing counseling. After weeks of being creeped out by him and attempting to get rid of him, I was just glad he was gone, honestly. But when I saw him tonight, it smacked me in the face how he made me feel. Dayton is up to something."

"Did he ever ask you for information?" Sax asked.

"Um, what do you mean?"

"Did he ever cross lines by asking about your life or others?"

"Yeah, he did, but I never told him anything."

"Very good, Spitfire. What about items? Did he ever leave anything behind and then magically find it next week?"

Her face paled, and she nodded. "Yeah, he did. Why?"

"He probably bugged the office to see if he could gain information, I'd assume. So he either didn't know Immy wasn't coming there anymore and hoped to gain something, or his purpose was something different."

Loren shivered, doing a full-body shudder at that. She started to fidget more, and I could tell she was feeling creeped out now, her resolve falling away with each revelation. "Do you, um, have a photo of your dad or anything?"

"Not digitally. Dayton was paranoid and had his presence routinely scrubbed from the internet. The only photos of him are hard copies, though he was known to destroy those at times too. I know there's the one at the compound at least, the one with Benny and Shayna in it as well. I'll send someone there to grab it. If Dayton is here, or someone is masquerading as him, which is more likely, then they've gone through great lengths to stay hidden this whole time. I have a feeling any paper photos have also been destroyed. It would be what I'd do if I was trying to fake an identity."

"So, you believe me?" she asked, fear in her voice.

"Yes, Bellezza, I believe you met someone who is targeting us through you. I won't jump to the conclusion that my father has returned from the grave until I see it for myself. There are some things you can't put the lid back on once it's out, and dealing with Dayton again after all this time, well, it would change me, and I'm not ready to be that man yet. Not when I just got you in my life. My father… doesn't make it easy for me to be the best version of myself. And if he's come to hurt you or Immy again, I won't hesitate to exorcize that demon."

"How are you so sure it's not him?" I asked. Mas never talked about what went down. He turned to me, a stoic expression on his face.

"Because I shot him and then set the building on fire. So unless he's a fucking Phoenix, I don't see how he could've survived. Plus, I have his bones to prove it."

Nodding, I let it go, trusting Mas to have covered his

bases. I zoned out as they talked more about potential doppelgängers who'd have access to information. When I felt Loren's hand on my cheek, I realized I'd been lost in my thoughts more than I'd realized.

"You okay?" she asked, curling up in my lap. Wrapping my arms around her, I pulled her closer, breathing her in as I placed my nose in the crook of her neck.

"Yeah. I will be. It's just a lot to process. I don't really care about Benny, I barely knew him, but it means that…"

"I'm your brother, and Immy's your sister. In fact, it seals your position even more since we're full siblings. You have Costa and Mascro blood in your veins."

Nodding, I tried to process all of this. "Does that mean I can call you big bro?" I teased.

Atticus relaxed, shaking his head at me. "Try it. We'll see how well that works, squirt." He smiled, some emotion leaking through. If I didn't know better, I'd think Atticus hoped it was true. He cleared his throat, looking at everyone. "Before we get too ahead of ourselves, let's test our DNA just to verify. Especially before we tell Immy, I don't want her to get her hopes up."

"Yeah, you're right. You'll need more time to try to win her over for favorite brother. I see your play there, big bro."

Mas rolled his eyes at me, but I caught the slight smile on his lips. "Keep it up, smartass."

Loren giggled, and the sound helped ease any weird tension. "Come on, Beautiful, dance with me."

"Okay." She smiled, kissing my lips briefly before climbing out of my lap. The other two headed out of the room, and I lingered back with Loren, walking at a leisurely pace, swinging our hands. When we got to the dance floor, I gathered her up in my arms, the music soft and perfect for swaying.

"I like dancing with you, Beautiful."

"I like dancing with you, Stud." Chuckling, I shook my head at the name.

"Can I ask something of you?"

"Of course," she answered.

"Stay with me tonight? I'm going back to the house, so you'll be where everyone is. We don't even have to do anything. I just want to hold you in my arms and wake up with you next to me."

"I'd love to."

"Yeah?" I smiled, my body relaxing, knowing I'd get to hold her tonight. After a few songs, we walked around, bidding on auctions before they closed. When it was time for the meal, we made our way back to the table to eat some food. When things started to wind down, I turned to Atticus, getting his attention.

"How long do we have to make an appearance here? Can we leave yet?"

He assessed me, looking up at the stage and then back. He gave a slight nod in answer and then turned his head to get one of the guard's attention. Whispering something to one, he tossed his napkin on the table, holding out a hand for Loren. She quickly shoved the bit of chocolate cake on her fork into her mouth, a small moan leaving as she inhaled it.

All three of us were glued to the utensil as she pulled it out, her lips pursed around the tines. "Shit," I mumbled, attempting to discreetly shift my cock.

Loren's eyes opened, staring at the hungry looks I had to assume we wore. "What?"

Chuckling, I stood and walked over, slapping Atticus' stunned hand out of the way, and took Loren myself, pulling her toward the exit.

I suddenly felt like the young stud she called me, ready to report for duty.

FOURTEEN

LOREN

The moment I was alone with Nicco in the elevator, I shoved him up against the wall and kissed him. He resisted for all of two seconds before his tongue was tangling with mine as well. The rest of the benefit had been a slow torture of dancing and eating, then the excruciatingly long limo ride where he ran his fingers up and down my arm casually as he held me. If Jude and Imogen hadn't been in that limo, I would've had two nights of car sex.

Something told me limo sex would need to be added to the must-have sex list I'd just made in my mind.

Temptation to have elevator sex was high, but I wanted it to last longer with Nicco. It was like our first time all over again, and something about that concept excited me. We were getting a second chance, and it meant everything to me. And this time, I wasn't as hesitant or shy as I'd been the first night.

Nicco's hands cupped the globes of my ass, squeezing firmly through my dress, and I moaned into his mouth. He broke away for a second, kissing along my jaw to whisper. "Are you sure, Loren? I don't want you to feel like you have to."

"Nicco, if you don't fuck me in the next minute, I will go and pound on Sax's door and have him fuck me up against yours. Is that what you want? Because what I want is to feel you inside me. I appreciate the concern, but I'm good. And I'll be even better with your cock inside me. Is that okay with you?"

"Fuck, Beautiful." He kissed me hard then, his cock thrusting toward me to show me how turned on he was. When the elevator stopped, he lifted me up before I could protest and marched out of it, a man on a mission. Looking down at me, he smirked.

"I don't know what's sexier. The fact you ask for what you want now in the dirtiest and most delicious way, or that you were willing to dole out some punishment there. I never thought I had a kink before, but I'm kind of liking Domme Loren with her masochistic tendencies."

"Well, you can only blame yourself, as you were the one who taught me how to ask for what I needed."

"You're so right, Beautiful. I guess it's time I remind you of that as well."

His eyes heated more, and Nicco bent down to ensnare my bottom lip with his teeth. I was so transfixed by him, I didn't notice we'd entered a room, and the next second I was tossed onto a surface. Nicco wasted no time and pounced on me the second I landed as a small yelp left me.

He captured it with his mouth, and his hands went to work, finding all the zippers and buttons on the dress. When he drew back, he had a smug look on his face, and when I glanced down, I understood why. Sitting up, the fabric slipped from my body into a pool of silk, leaving me in nothing but my underthings.

"Fuck, Loren. I made myself forget just how magnificent you looked." My breath caught, the huskiness of his voice going straight to my pussy, the ache almost unbearable now as it throbbed with need. Lifting up a little, I pulled the dress out from under me and gently laid it to the side. I desperately wanted to get busy with Nicco, but the dress had cost a small fortune and deserved respect.

Nicco undid his bowtie, the strands hanging down, and I licked my lips. What was it about that look that just did it for me? He was still completely dressed as he kneeled over me, only his bowtie undone, and I wanted to melt into a puddle on the bed at how erotic it looked. He stepped off the bed, kicking his shoes, his eyes never leaving me. I took the chance to climb off the bed and moved the dress to a chair, carefully laying it out. When I turned back around, Nicco had his shirt off, now standing only in his tuxedo pants.

His eyes were hooded, and I watched as he licked his lips. Enjoying the seduction, I slowly brushed a strap off my shoulder and then the other before reaching back to unclasp my bra. Nicco swallowed as I slowly lowered the cups, dropping it to the floor. He stared for a long while, just taking them in as he breathed heavily.

"Fuck, I think your breasts have gotten even better since I last saw them."

Tilting the corner of my lip up, I sat on the edge of the bed, practicing my best interpretation of a seductress. Spreading my legs, I ran my hands up my thighs, teasing my pussy as I hooked my thumbs into the fabric and slid them down. His eyes moved down to my wet center, and I worried his heart stopped for a second when he stood utterly still, not even making a sound. Once I dropped them on the floor, I scooted back on the bed and rested against the pillows. Feeling incredibly horny and confident, I spread my legs again, teasing myself through my tight curls as I touched my clit.

A moan escaped me, and he jerked forward, wrenching his own pants off and crawling toward me on the bed. My eyes fluttered closed as he neared, and I plunged a finger into my dripping wet cunt.

"Fuck, Beautiful, I think you're going to kill me," he breathed into my neck. Opening my eyes, I found him caging me in as he peered down at me, his arms to both sides of me. Remembering his new tattoo, I reached up, tracing my hands over the feather bent into the shape of a heart.

"It's beautiful."

"Not as beautiful as the woman I got it for."

Something about that sentiment had my breath catching, and I looked up, finding the heat replaced with a different emotion in his eyes. I didn't want to jinx myself, but it almost looked like love. Cupping his face, I pressed my lips to his, sharing this moment with him, reconnecting on all levels.

It didn't take long for the kiss to turn heated as he greedily devoured my lips and tongue. He pulled me down to the bed, pressing his naked skin into mine, but continued to kiss me for a while. It was nice, the kisses expressing all the pain, regret, and hope we both had for us. It was a cleansing by a fire of our own creation, and I couldn't think of a more perfect way for us to have it. I completely dropped all of my shields, forgiving him wholly, and surrendered to the first man who showed me the woman I could be.

Breaking the kiss, Nicco smoothed my hair back off my face, cupping my cheek as he stared down at me with love. It was so clear to see, and I was a fool if I denied it. "Beautiful, do you feel up for a little fun?"

"With you? Always. I trust you to know my limits. I've always felt safe in your arms, Nicco."

He groaned, touching his temple to mine. I felt his dick rub against me as he rocked a little, hitting me just right. "Loren, you're the most amazing woman. You make me feel like I could conquer the world. Hearing you say that makes me feel good because all I've ever wanted was to have someone feel that way with me, and you do it so effortlessly. I might be stupid for saying this, and it might be way too soon, but I don't care. I know how short life can be, and not taking your chance when it's staring at you right in the face is a colossal mistake. So, I'm going to do it and hope I don't ruin anything."

He paused for a second, searching my eyes, and opened his mouth again. But an urge rose up in me, and I found myself saying it first, needing to show him.

"I love you, Nicco." He froze, blinking down at me with his mouth open. "Shit, was that not what you were going to say? You were probably going to suggest anal or something, weren't you? Well, whatever, I don't care if I embarrassed myself, because I do, I love you."

He slammed his lips down to mine, his tongue waging war on my mouth. I felt the tip of his cock at my entrance, and I was done waiting. Wrapping my legs around his waist, I tightened them and pulled him to me. He slid in a little, halting himself with wide eyes as he stared at me.

"Shit, woman, I think you're gonna kill me. There's something I need to tell you."

"Tell me later. I need you, Nicco."

He groaned as if it pained him, but he obliged and thrust the rest of the way in. My eyes widened when he did, and my breath caught as I felt all of him in me. He felt wider, and something was very different. I could feel it rubbing against me in a way that a penis never had before. My back arched, my head falling back as I grasped his arms, and I moaned.

"What... is... that?" I gasped out. Nicco smirked down at me, a mischievous glint in his eyes.

"Since you were so impatient," he said, thrusting in and pulling out again, "I didn't get to tell you, that not only do I love you, Loren Carter, but I got something during our time apart." He narrowed his eyes down at me, clearly not impressed I'd beat him to the punch. "So, as a punishment to you, you'll have to wait to find out."

He thrust in deeper this time, and my eyes rolled back, and I was lost to the sensation, words not able to come. Nicco plunged in and out of me a few times, and I detonated quicker than I ever had before. As my body shook, I knew whatever he'd done, I needed more of it.

When I came to, I blinked, a slow smile spreading across my face. He watched me with a satisfied grin, his eyes twinkling in delight.

"You gonna tell me now?" I asked, my voice raspy.

"No, I think it will be more fun if I don't. Plus, now that you've cum, it's time for that fun I was talking about."

"It wasn't that?"

"Oh, Beautiful, that was just the appetizer. Now, it's time for the main course."

He leaned back and flipped me over. I went willingly, my body pliable to his demands. I watched as he grabbed his phone, and a confused look spread across my face. If he was going to record us; he had another thing coming. Lifting myself up on my elbows, I turned back to give him the same speech I'd given the other night when he placed a finger over my lips. He pressed a call button, flashed it to me, and then sat it back down on the end table. In the next second, he was kissing me, and I forgot all about the phone.

Nicco raised me up, banding his arm over my breasts as he plunged up into me. A moan rang out, and I wrapped my arm around his neck. His fingers plucked at my clit, and he thrust in small bouts, while whatever he'd done, rubbed deliciously along my walls.

Gasping, I couldn't stop the sounds leaving me as each thrust had me close again. Nicco dropped me back to the bed, grabbing hold of my hips and lifting them up higher to him as he found an unrelenting pace, pistoning in and out. It was so rough, the bed moved with each thrust, and I found myself coming again as our skin slapped against one another. A loud bang had me jumping, but Nicco didn't stop. I glanced over my shoulder and found him smirking, but he kept his eyes on me, not concerned about the noise.

"Think you have one more in you, Beautiful?"

"Y-e-s," I panted.

"Good." He pulled out, and I whimpered, missing the fullness. Nicco lifted me up and turned us in the other direction, and that was when I realized what the loud bang had been. Suddenly, the phone call made sense. Nicco had taken my bluff and turned up the stakes. Sax stood, leaning against the wall, his thick cock in his hand as he watched us, no shame at all for interrupting.

I gasped when I saw him, licking my lips at the sight.

He smirked at me, lifting his eyes to Nicco. "I figured since you called, it was an invitation."

"I called?" Nicco asked as he sat on the edge of the bed, slowly lowering me onto him. Ever since I'd pulled him into me, he'd been meticulous in making sure I didn't get a peep at his dick. At this point, it felt too good; I didn't care and would wait to find out. I tuned out their conversation as he slowly bounced me up and down on him. Placing my hands to the side, they touched the bed, and I soon found my own rhythm, rubbing my new favorite thing inside me.

Moaning, I was surprised when I felt fingers lifting my chin a second later. Opening my eyes, I found Sax in front of me, his glistening cock at eye level. Licking my lips, I grasped the base of him, stroking his monster as best I could and watched as he moaned, his head falling back.

The three of us found a pace, and I began to lick around Sax's dick, taking him into my mouth slowly, as my lips stretched around in order to contain him. When Nicco was close, he sped up, and I tried to take Sax deeper, but there was only so much dick I could reasonably take before my gag reflex was triggered.

"Good girl, Spitfire. Relax your jaw some more."

Doing as he said, he weaved his fingers through my hair softly, massaging my scalp. My jaw was hurting, but I persevered, using my hand to stroke the base where I would never be able to reach as I sucked the tip. My own moans echoed around him, until Nicco pulled me back toward him, taking my jaw into his hand to kiss me hard as he finally found his release. I quaked around him as well, entirely spent after three orgasms.

When I opened my eyes, I found Sax watching us with a lusty gaze as he threw his head back with a moan. Hot cum splashed out of his cock onto his stomach and hand, and I found myself wanting to lick it up, but not sure if that would be weird. So I did nothing, just catching my breath, with Nicco still impaled in me.

The oddness of the whole thing got to me then, and I giggled and then couldn't stop. The men, thankfully, joined in, and when we stopped, I realized we'd fallen back onto the bed. Sax went into the adjoining bathroom and cleaned himself up, and I pouted a little at not being the one to do it. When he returned, he carefully cleaned me, bending down to kiss me thoroughly. When he pulled back, he whispered in my ear. "Next time, just lick it up, Spitfire."

My cheeks heated, but I nodded, and he winked, kissing me quickly before walking out of the room. Nicco chuckled but didn't say anything else, pulling me back to his chest to cover us up. His arms wrapped around me, and I didn't miss how his thumb stroked over the tattoo he'd given me on my wrist. It brought a smile to my lips, and I sighed in happiness. As we laid there in bliss, I remembered my question.

"Are you going to tell me now?

"Of course, I'll tell you a million times if you need me to. I love you, Loren."

It was so sweet, I didn't correct him. Reaching up, I kissed his nose. "I love you, Nicolai."

Grinning, we fell asleep, and I felt protected and safe. I'd learned a lot tonight, but it hadn't changed how I felt about them; if anything, it only made me want to love them all more. I'd also shown myself I could be brave.

Now, if I could just figure out how Nicco's dick became magic.

FIFTEEN

ATTICUS

My patience had left me ten minutes ago, making my irritation grow the more I stared at the phone, waiting for it to ring. When we returned from the benefit, I'd received another envelope from Darren telling me to be available Sunday morning. At least this time, there weren't any body parts with it, but I didn't like having to bow to his schedule. My spy had been successful infiltrating so far, so I had to believe Darren had no clue. If he was onto my subterfuge, though, I was afraid Loren would never forgive me.

The phone lit up finally, and now it was my turn to make him wait. After a few rings, I picked it up, not greeting him. His low chuckle sounded out, and I gritted my teeth. His arrogance would be his downfall if I had anything to do about it.

And I would, or die trying.

I was determined to eliminate him for all the pain and horrors he'd caused in my life and to the people I loved. I just hoped I'd be here afterward.

"Little Mascro, so good of you to take my call."

"What do you want, Darren? I have better things to do."

"Oh, I bet you do. That pretty little therapist, perhaps?"

Gritting my teeth more, I kept my mouth shut. He could believe what he wanted, but I wouldn't be foolish enough to give him any information freely.

He chuckled again, finding my silence amusing, and I wanted to smash his face in. My hand gripped the arm of the chair, the wood creaking under the pressure.

"Very well, very well." He sighed heavily before continuing, mimicking that he was disappointed. "My delivery arrived intact and on time. Thank you for that. It seems you can follow directions when properly motivated."

I could hear the smile in his words, wanting to bait me again, but I held firm.

"Tsk, tsk, little Mascro, you're no fun. Fine, I'll get to business. Seeing how well that went, I have another job for you."

"No." I knew it was coming, but the audacity of his request had me rejecting it instantly.

"Ah, but we've been having such fun, little Mascro! Don't break up the team already."

"We're not a team, Darren, and you know this. I paid the debt you claimed my father owed. Therefore, our partnership is over. You will release my cousin, or I'll have to retaliate. And Darren, you don't want me to retaliate."

"Oh, aren't you so cute making threats like you matter." He laughed, the sound maniacal, and it made my blood run cold.

"You know the code, Darren. Tit for tat. It's been reciprocated even from the grave as it was my father who struck this bargain with you. I owe you nothing else. Adhere to the code and release her, or I'll be forced to enact the brotherhood clause that our fathers agreed upon after the great fallout. Are you prepared for the repercussions if you break the code, Darren? I'd hate to see your new venue fail before it even opens. You have twenty-four hours."

I hung up, not letting him have time to respond. He knew as well as I did what the code stated, and for all of his bravado, I didn't think Darren had it in him. The next twenty-four hours would be imperative on whether or not a war would start again on the streets of Chicago.

At least this time, I was prepared. I wouldn't let him take anything else from me.

Picking up the burner phone, I sent a message to my spy.

ME: Status?
Spy: No visual yet
ME: Approximation?
Spy: Soon
ME: I gave him 24hrs. He should start scrambling.

This is our chance for him to make a mistake.
Spy: Understood
Spy: How is she?
ME: Safe
Spy: Thank you
ME: You have my word. Be careful.

Taking a deep breath, I shut the phone off and stuck it back in the hidden panel on my desk. Rubbing my temples, I already had a headache, and it was only 7am. No doubt, Darren had wanted to find me off-kilter after the benefit by making it so early. I'd only gotten a few hours sleep, too anxious to sleep any more after the information Loren had shared.

Part of me believed her, knowing my father was creative and always had a contingency plan. But the part of me that had shot him, and saw him fall to the ground as I escaped the burning building, didn't know how. I'd never told anyone the full story of that night. Not even Sax. My shame and guilt had kept me from wanting to relive it. But now, I was worried I'd missed something. In my panic, had I slipped up, allowing my father to escape and survive all these months?

If I had, I'd never forgive myself for allowing him to hurt Imogen again. That was a burden I couldn't place on her.

My hands shook as I lifted the gun at the man I'd once admired. He'd been missing, not wanting to show his face once he realized I disapproved of his plan. Sax had taken on the hunt for Imogen while I tracked the Reaper down, knowing I had to be the one to do this.

"I expected more from you, Atticus. I taught you better than this."

"That's where you're wrong. I taught myself the important things. I used to admire you, you know? I used to look up to you and thought you were the greatest man to ever live. But these past few years, I've seen your cracks, the destruction, and vileness you so desperately tried to hide with good deeds. I know what you did, father," I spat, the bile wanting to emerge at the thought.

He smiled, his lips curving up in a vicious smile. "Oh? Do tell me, Atticus, how you manage to think you're so much better than me? Your hands are just as dirty!"

"I've never raped anyone! Or molested children. You're a disgrace to the Mascro name. This is not what Grandfather wanted our family to become. You've tainted all the goodwill he built all because of your greed and incessant need for power."

"Bravo!" He clapped, shooting me an indecipherable look. "Let me tell you something about my father, the man you look up to so much. Who do you think taught me? Hmm? His whole family motto was a lie, a pretty facade for the other families to believe, while he secretly bought up all the property and businesses he could get out from under them. We own a fucking empire, and you want to what? Make it legitimate, so we lose half our profit? You're the

delusional one, Atticus. I see now that I chose wrong. I should've made your—"

I didn't let him finish, no longer caring to hear him. Firing the gun, I jerked back from the recoil, my hands sweaty as I attempted to realign my grip. Dayton chuckled, and I searched for where he'd ducked. I spotted some blood on the ground and followed it. Taking a step, a shot rang out, hitting the wood next to me. Jumping back, I peek around the large container.

It had taken all day, but I'd finally tracked him down to an old warehouse on the docks. He'd been staying in one of the shipping containers. Based on the number of items in it, he'd been planning this for a while. It was a mini office and room with clippings all over the wall.

When I'd entered, I hoped I could have a reasonable chat with him, but that quickly dissolved when he showed no remorse for his part in Imogen's capture and rape. I'd raised my gun when he laughed about it being good for her. We were out in the warehouse now, too many containers to get a good line of sight. He wasn't stupid, so I'd need to catch him off guard. Trying to visualize the area in my head, I guessed the pattern of containers, hoping they followed a similar route as another warehouse we owned.

Heading in the other direction, I took a few turns and then doubled back in the other direction, praying it would lead me behind him. Dayton had thankfully stopped spewing hate-filled insults, but it also meant I had no idea where he was. A sound up ahead had me freezing, and I counted to ten before I slowly took a step and peeked around the corner.

I found my father muttering under his breath as he spread gasoline over a pile of papers. He was probably trying to cover his tracks and erase all information on his future plans. Too bad he wouldn't need them where he was going. Raising my gun, my hand no longer shook, and I aimed it at him with a steady arm.

"Your reign is over, Dayton. It's time I took over the family and made us what we're meant to be, not this perverted sense of family you've made us. You sicken me."

"That's rich coming from you, son, now isn't it?"

He looked right at me, and I fell into his trap. When I realized he was distracting me, I looked over to see him tossing the lighter onto the pile of papers. I watched it fall in slow motion, his fingers waving as he turned to retreat. I rushed forward, for some reason trying to catch the lighter despite being too far to do so.

When I realized the lunacy of my actions, I raised my gun and fired off a few shots. I heard one hit him in the back and the other in the leg. He cackled like it was great fun, turning to fire one himself. I dove, the fire igniting in the same instant, and a whoosh sprang up behind me. I could feel the heat of the flames on my skin as I crawled forward. Standing, I turned back once more, finding Dayton lying on the other side of the fire, not moving. Shooting once more in his direction, I raced back out the way I came, the fire licking my heels as I ran. The smoke was thick by the time I made it back around the front, the circle I had to make not doing me any favors.

Coughing, I pushed open the door, the hot handle

scalding my fingers at the touch. Gasping in the clean air, I fell to my knees, the gravel biting into them through my suit. Another loud boom had me standing again and moving forward to get out of the blast range. I stumbled again, but this time, an arm reached out and grabbed me. I tensed, raising my gun, but found Sax there.

"Immy?"

"I got her. She's..." he cleared his throat, emotion thick, and shook his head, not able to finish it. I didn't know how to face my sister after this, knowing the pain I'd allowed to happen. Dayton had fooled me, and it had cost my baby sister her innocence. It wasn't something I could ever return to her, but I vowed to never let her down again, doing whatever it took to make sure she survived this.

"Reaper?"

"Shot. Dead."

He nodded, helping me over to the black car I'd driven. We sat on the hood of the car, watching the flames rise until there was nothing left of the place. It took a few hours, but there was nothing left to save by the time the fire department arrived. Sax and I walked through the ruins and made our way to the spot where I'd last seen my father. Nothing remained there but a pile of ash and bones. Crouching down, I reached back for a bag and placed the bones and ash into it. This would be a reminder of what power cost. It was the dawn of a new era for the Mascros, one where we could be proud of our heritage and what it meant to be family.

That was the promise, no, the vow, I made on that day.

The day I killed my father, I rose up, and took the mantle of boss.

"Mas." I jerked, my knee colliding with my desk as I sat up. Blinking, I found a grinning Sax in front of me.

"What?" I asked, craning my neck. Shit, I'd fallen asleep, the few hours catching up to me.

"Are you listening?"

"Hmm?" I looked up, finding him watching me in concern now. "Sorry, I didn't get much sleep. Darren insisted we talk this morning, and the little I got was restless."

He sat down, no longer joking, as he observed me. "What did he say?"

"Nothing of importance. I told him he had 24hrs to release Cami, or I'd enact the code."

He sucked in a breath, but a pleased expression came over him. "Well done. I bet he didn't take that well."

"No, not at all."

Sax chuckled, leaning back. "Any other updates?"

"If you mean if I've discovered if my dead father is still dead, the answer is no."

"What are you thinking?"

I shook my head. "I don't know. The things he told Loren… not many people would be privy to that detailed or secretive information. But… we both saw him. I just can't fathom it. Not until I have the proof back."

"So, are you sending the bones out?"

"Yes. I already had them sent over to the lab. It could take a few weeks to get anything back, though."

"Why do they make it look so fast on TV?"

I raised my eyebrows at him. "It's TV, Sax. Seeley Booth doesn't exist in real life, nor does Temperance."

A loud chuckle left him as he bent over, slapping his knee. "I knew it!" He pointed at me, and my face reddened. The lack of sleep had caused me to slip.

"I may have caught a few episodes on reruns. Don't read into it. Now, I spoke with our friend, and so far, no visual, but they're confident there will be soon."

"Good. I think I found something on the little watchdog's brother. I'm going to check it out today, and I'll let you know what I find. Are you still going to ask Loren?"

"Yeah. I need to speak with Jude too. Can you send him this way?"

"Are you going to tell Loren about Cami?"

"I'm hoping I won't have to, but if it goes bad tomorrow, I will."

He nodded, getting up from his seat. I read through some emails, finding a few about the fight expo this summer, and I forwarded them to Luca. Clicking on the cameras, I checked in on my cousin in the holding cells, but he was asleep and not entertaining. I would need to deal with him soon, but everything kept piling up, and I put off the things that weren't as important. And Joel wasn't at the moment.

A knock at the door had me looking up to find a nervous Jude standing there. "Come in." I motioned for him to sit in the chair across from me. He did, a little nervous, but kept his head up, and I respected that about him.

"You wanted to see me, Mr. Mast—I mean Mr. Mascro?"

"You can call me Atticus, Jude." He nodded, and I sat back, steepling my fingers together on the armrests. "I wanted to talk to you about Imogen."

"Okay, what about her?"

"It hasn't slipped my notice that the two of you spend a lot of time together."

"Yeah, um, we're friends."

"Only friends?" I lifted a brow in question, waiting him out.

"Yes." He nodded again, swallowing.

"Perhaps I didn't ask that question correctly. Do you only want to be friends?"

Jude held my gaze, not wavering. "I think that's a conversation that Imogen and I should have first with all due respect, sir."

I stared, trying hard not to smile. The little shit had balls. Maybe I was being unreasonable. I couldn't keep Imogen locked up forever, and if she was going to be with someone, I would want them to be a good person. There was no doubt that Jude was. He'd lived a hard life but had risen above his circumstances and hadn't fallen into the traps of the streets. Sitting up, I leaned on the desk.

"Fair. I have a proposition for you then, Jude."

"You're not going to pay me to stay away or something? Because there's not an amount that I would take. Immy is my friend, and that's invaluable."

I couldn't keep the smile hidden any longer, and the corner lifted as I watched him. "No, you're right, and I think you're the type of person that she needs in her life. I was going to ask for a favor, and in return, I'd owe you something."

"I'm listening." He crossed his arms, sitting back in his chair now like he had the power. It only made me smile more, and as both sides lifted, a short chuckle escaped.

"Imogen has asked to attend a real school, and I'm considering it. However, there are a few concerns I have, and this is where I think I could use your assistance."

He sat up, a smile on his face as he nodded. "Okay, of course, yes, that would be great. I think she would love it. I've never liked school before, but Timber Creek Prep is different." His words tumbled over each other in excitement. Holding my hands up, I halted him.

"Slow down. There are some steps first before you get your hopes up. If I was to look into it, though, would I be able to count on you to watch her while she's there? You know who we are now, and it's not safe for Immy to be out in public alone. While I'll send a guard, they're not always able to blend in as well or allowed access to everything. This would be where you come in."

"Respectably, sir, I think Imogen is much stronger than you realize. As her friend and someone who cares about her, though, you don't have to owe me a favor to keep her safe. I'll do that because that's what friends do. Maybe she can join me in training to learn some self-defense as well?"

"You're learning self-defense?" I asked in surprise.

"Yep." He grinned smugly. "Or, well, I still need to ask, but Nicco suggested it after my brother, you know." Jude's face fell a little, and I nodded, understanding what he meant.

"Well, I guess that's not a horrible idea. I'll make it happen. You have honor, Jude. That's a hard trait to learn. I'll still grant you a favor one day if you ever need it."

"I feel like I might have to sell my soul to accept that, but I'll keep it in mind in case I ever find myself in a situation with no solution."

Jude got up, and I stared, stunned. He was more perceptive and wise than I'd given him credit for. Imogen had done well making him her friend, and I'd have to learn how to be okay with it if things developed more.

Picking up my phone, I noticed the time and decided to ask in person. Loren wanted action, so I needed to show her I was committed to this. Locking my door, I headed down the hall, excitement bubbling up, helping to erase the fear I would lose all this.

SIXTEEN

LOREN

I was being attacked.

Walking into the room that had become my second home since I'd been here, I was surprised when two forces of nature attacked me, taking me down to the ground. Their happy licks and snorts were delightful, and I tried to grab them in my hands to hold them still as their little butts wiggled in excitement.

"Aw, I missed you guys too," I cooed at Barkley and Fort.

Looking up, I found a smirking Wells leaning against the wall. I'd hoped he was here and had ventured down to see if we could get in a workout. With all the events of the past week, it had been a while since I'd run or done anything physical, and nervous energy had built within me. I didn't want to examine it too closely yet, but I found it often dissolved when I could exert myself in something.

Sex, however, didn't seem to work the same as punching a bag.

Because if that was the case, I'd definitely banked enough sexual activity for at least a week of no exercise. I felt a little smug about that fact, but I found myself liking that I could be. Cami would be proud. The thought of her made me miss her more, and I realized I was starting to get worried. Perhaps I should stop by her place and check on her later and make sure she wasn't sick and one of those people who refused to ask for help? Yeah, that sounded like her and was probably the case.

Filing that away, I got the dogs to calm down, and I sauntered over to the sexy man holding up the wall. He didn't move or say anything, but his eyes heated, and his smirk grew as I approached.

"Hey, you."

"Kitten."

I pressed my body into his, kissing him. His hands went to my waist, and he captured my offering with his lips, his tongue making a greedy sweep of mine. I'd only meant to greet him, but Wells was on a mission, it seemed, and I gave in to the desire coursing through him. When his hands started to roam, I moaned, rubbing myself against his hard length. The dogs began to make a noise behind us, barking in a warning, and we broke apart, panting.

A second later, Jude and Imogen walked through the door laughing and then converged on the dogs when they noticed them. Thankfully, it gave us more time to right ourselves and walk over to them. I eyed their clothes, both in loose-fit ones that neither wore regularly.

"What's up?" I asked, bringing their attention to me.

Imogen looked up first, a small smile on her face. "Um, well, I wanted to ask Mr. Young if he would be interested in giving me and Jude self-defense lessons. Sax mentioned it would be a good idea for Jude, so I decided I wanted to do it too when he told me about it. That is, if you're willing, Mr. Young. If not, I can bug one of the guards. It's just," she paused, glancing over her shoulder to see if any were near. I didn't spot the usual three I'd come to know as Beau, Topher, or Elijah, and Immy relaxed a little when she didn't either. "It's just, they won't really teach me anything because it goes against their creed to harm a woman." She stopped, her eyes going wide, and her head started to shake back and forth quickly. "Not that I think you harm women," she sputtered.

Jude laughed next to her, and she calmed some, turning to stick her tongue out at him before addressing Wells again. "What I meant is, that it makes them feel like their job is obsolete if I can defend myself, and they would never go all out in the training because they'd be scared of hurting me. But I don't think you have the same hang-ups; at least, I'm hoping you won't. I just... I think I need this, especially if *he's* back."

Wells flicked his eyes to me in question, and I mouthed "later" to him, and he nodded, looking back at the two on the ground with the dogs. He stood with his arms crossed, a frown on his face that I knew was all for show.

"Hmm," he muttered, moving his hand to rub his chin. "I'll do it on two conditions."

They both looked up, excitement peeking through as they eagerly waited.

"One, call me Wells, none of this Mister shit. Two, assuming you can find a way out to my place, help me look after the dogs. I'm finding myself away from them more and more, and it's not fair for them to be cooped up so much in the house. They need to run and play. So, if you can stop by and do that a couple of times a week, that would help me a lot."

"Absolutely, that'd be no trouble at all, Mr., er, I mean, Wells," Imogen said with hope shining through.

"Hm, I seem to remember you like it when I call you Mr. Surly," I purred into his ear before I walked over to the bench to wrap my hands. I heard him growl softly, making the smile I wore grow with each step. Pushing his buttons was so fun that I now understood the attraction to that whole trope of enemies to lovers.

I zoned out as I started on my punches, Wells not needing to monitor me as much anymore now that I had a good understanding of how to stand and punch. During my breaks, I watched him with them both, seeing that softer and patient side I often noticed when he was with the dogs. I guess Wells had a soft spot for kids as well. It made my heart feel squishy, and a blush rose to my cheeks. I quickly drank my water and then went back to my kicking, not at all imagining Wells holding a baby —nope.

The reality of that image slammed into me, and I staggered, the pain hitting me square in the chest with force at the realization I couldn't give him that. I'd been doing so well, so it wasn't surprising that my dark thoughts wanted to surge up and poison the small amounts of happiness I'd found. As I breathed rapidly, clutching my chest where I could feel physical pain, I wrestled with myself.

"Give in. It would be so easy to fall into the despair and let it swallow you. It feels good. Let it consume you. You don't have to care anymore when we're around," the darkness promised.

No, that wasn't true, because I cared. I had people who cared about me, too.

"Do they really care, though?" the thought whispered.

Forcing myself to open my eyes felt like lifting a 50 lb bag of sand. But I did it, and I found both Barkley and Fort at my feet, leaning into me, their whimpers drawing my attention as I slowly moved my arm down to scratch Barkley's head and then Fort's. My arm felt like it moved through quicksand, the weight of the world on it as I pushed through it for the action.

Lifting my head, I saw the other three were still practicing, thankfully not having noticed I'd stopped. Wells glanced up, though, his eyes capturing mine, and he held them while he spoke to the teens. It was the reminder I needed as I held them—Wells' eyes always held so much emotion.

Pain would always be present. Things in life didn't

magically get better over time or feel any less hurtful. Pain hurt. No argument there.

But life was about balance.

Yes, sometimes things would hurt me, and I couldn't control those moments when I would be reminded of my grief out of nowhere, but I didn't have to give into them like the thoughts wanted me to. Because life wasn't just pain, just like it wasn't always winter.

There was love, joy, and hope. There were dog kisses and friends who made me laugh. There were teens who showed me strength as they figured out the world. There were mafia men, damaged and broken men who showed me they were capable of more than one thing and that they could cherish me.

There were so many things in my life that I didn't have to give in to the pain, letting it swallow me whole.

Losing my child would never not hurt.

Losing my ability to bear children at all would never not bring me pain.

But they weren't the only things in my life, they didn't define me. I could hold both the pain of those losses and the joy of all the others together without having to ignore one. It was the lightbulb moment I needed for myself to understand their relationship and how they affected one another. I felt the fissure in my heart fill in, no longer dividing the two sections but sealing them together as one.

And the thing that bridged that divide—love.

Love for myself, love for others, and love for whatever my future would bring.

Vowing to myself to always remember this moment, I closed my eyes, securing it away. To the observer, it might seem like a woman stood silently petting two dogs, but internally, a battle had been waged and won. No one else would know the significance of this, but I would, and I would protect it at all costs.

As my body relaxed, accepting this new state of being, I felt the dogs lessen the pressure against me as they laid down, looking up. Dogs really were magical beings, and I knew my idea of training them both hadn't been a foolish one, and I grew even more excited at the possibilities ahead of me with the both of them.

Sitting down, I loved on the two of them, losing myself in their soft kisses and pets.

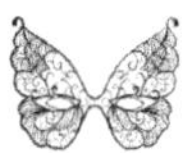

JUDE and I gathered our belongings, ready to head back to our place. We'd had lunch and showered, and I knew we needed to get back and prepare for the week despite not wanting to leave. Pushing the last item into my bag, I zipped it up and pulled it off the bed, making my way out the door. I came up short when I found Atticus standing on the threshold, his fist raised to knock.

"Atticus!" I smiled, leaning up to kiss his cheek. It still surprised me at times how much our dynamic had changed once he let his walls down. His hands fell to rest on my hips, and when I pulled back, I found him smiling at me.

"Loren, I was wondering if I could ask you on a date?"

"You were wondering, or you wanted to?" I teased.

He chuckled, bowing his head. "Apologies, yes, I want to. You take my breath away, that sometimes, I find myself fumbling for words."

It was said so innocently, but it had my heart racing. Atticus was so much more than the man he presented to others, and I wondered if he knew the one he shared with the people he trusted was worth more than the cold, distant one. Knowing his history now, I doubted he did.

"I would love to go on a date with you. When?"

"How about Wednesday?"

"Perfect. Anything I should know?"

"Hmm, I like the idea of surprising you, but I will tell you that you can dress casually. I'll even, um, wear jeans."

His face scrunched up at the thought, but something about seeing the always-suited man in a pair of blue jeans had me squirming. Atticus didn't miss it and was suddenly smiling, pushing me up against the wall.

"Something tells me you like that idea, and now I suddenly find myself wanting to wear them all the time. The things you do to me, Bellezza," he whispered, rubbing his nose up the column of my neck.

I dropped the bag, my arms wrapping around his

neck as I threaded my fingers in the back of his hair. It was such a luxurious thing to do, the strands thick and silky; I moaned at the sensation. The sound caused him to growl, the vibration sending shivers down my body, and I desperately wanted to lift my leg and rub up against him. It hadn't even been 24 hrs yet since I'd last been fucked, but I wanted it again, badly. Between kissing Wells and now Atticus, I was bound to rub myself all over the next person like a cat if I didn't curb this.

"The need to take you into this room, slam the door, and not let you leave for days is so high right now." He thrust a little into me, showing me how turned on he was as well. The move caused me to whimper, and Atticus nipped my neck in response. "But," he purred, managing to pull himself back with Herculean strength, "I'm respecting what you said the other night at Upswing. I want to earn your trust with your heart before I fall prey to your body."

"I'm starting to regret saying that. Are you sure that was me?" I joked, straightening myself. I found it a little easier now that his body wasn't pressed into me.

"I'll see you Wednesday, Lore. Let me know when you're done with work, and I'll pick you up."

"Okay." The sound came out breathless, but thankfully, Atticus pulled himself away, walking quickly in the other direction. It took a few moments, but I eventually gathered myself and made my way to the foyer. Jude was waiting and gave me an odd look when I stepped off the last step, but thankfully didn't say anything.

I was kind of sad when only Beau went with us, not getting to say bye to Sax or Nicco, but it was probably for the best, so I didn't make a fool of myself in front of my foster son.

Jude and I decided it would be a good night for laundry and takeout when we got back. Queuing up Netflix, I sat back as a load whirled in the machine, and I knew this was the life I wanted to have. Snuggling with Jude on the couch as we watched some show, eating greasy food, and knowing that there were men out there who cared about us was everything.

My life wasn't perfect by any means, and I still had shit to work out with my ex-husband and mother, but it was one I'd made on my own, and something about that made it mean more.

SEVENTEEN

LOREN

I had one more client before my date with Atticus, and I tried not to let it distract me too much. It was difficult, though, when the random thought of Atticus in jeans and what that could mean would pop in my head. Heading to the front, I ignored the suited man that now sat in our waiting room. I'd officially been given a guard, despite my protests, though Sax admitted there had always been one, just not in the lobby. And with Dayton potentially out there, the guys weren't leaving me alone.

Doris and the other girls gave me questioning looks, but I ignored them, hoping they would just let it go. I knew there was only so long before they would ask and I didn't know how to respond to it yet. Today, Beau was here, and he smiled when he saw me. I think he was my favorite, and I didn't seem to be as grumpy about them being here when it was him. I wondered if Atticus knew that and had sent him today to make sure I was in a good mood for our date.

What was I thinking? Of course, Atticus knew! That

man was perceptive when he wanted to be.

"Jill." The petite teenager looked up, a soft smile on her face as she gathered her things and walked toward me. Today, her head was down more, and she shuffled her feet. All thoughts of mafia bosses and bodyguards fled me, and I focused on the girl in front of me.

I thought it strange that she was always alone. While that wasn't uncommon for teenagers, one with her history of trauma, you'd assume her parents would be shadowing her every move. It was something I filed away, adding to the puzzle and information I had on Jill.

When she made it to the couch, I shut the door and wished I had one of the dogs with me today. Jill looked like she could use one of them. I needed to seriously look into what it would take and quit just hoping I could do it. For this client alone, I would follow through with it.

"How's your week been, Jill?"

"Oh, it's been fine." Her voice was small, and she stared down, fidgeting with her sleeves.

"Can you tell me a high and low?"

"Not really." She kept staring, not meeting my eyes.

"Would it be okay if I sat closer today, Jill?"

She shrugged, so I stayed put, not taking that as the answer. Leaning forward, I tried to cut some of the space between us, hoping it would help ease some of her tension.

"I can't help but notice, Jill, that you seem more withdrawn today. In my experience, that typically means something has happened. Do you want to talk about it?"

She looked up a little, meeting my eyes for a second before dropping them. "My nightmares have been bad this week, and my parents don't like it when I wake up screaming. It's just… it's been tough being at home. It makes me miss school, but then I think about *him*, and then I'm right back in it. I can't seem to get myself out of this loop."

I nodded, processing her words. "That does make it difficult to feel like you have a safe place to process everything with support. Has there been anything in particular that your dreams have focused on, or anything you can think of that might've been the triggering event for these thoughts?"

"Um, I guess lately I've been seeing all my friends post about training and gearing up for competitions, and it made me miss it. I feel useless here not getting to skate or even train. I sit in my house all day, do my school online, and just think about how different my life is now. It makes me angry to think of the things I'm missing, of the things he took from me!"

"That would be upsetting, Jill. I'd be angry too. Your anger is valid and needs to be heard. What do you do when you're feeling this way?"

"Nothing. I shove it down because my parents want me to be okay, so I do it. But I'm suffocating inside, Loren." Tears came to her eyes now, and I knew the struggles she felt. An idea began to form in my head, and I wondered if I was crazy for thinking it.

"You're wrestling with a lot of big emotions, Jill. I'd

like to help you learn to process them so that you don't feel that suffocation. I think there might be some ways as well to increase your support in your life. Is there a reason you're doing online school versus attending?"

"At first, it was what I wanted. I didn't want to go back to a school I'd been at where everyone knew me and would talk. But now, I dunno, it's just been what I've done."

"Okay, what if I talked with your parents about maybe enrolling you into a school? Would that be something you'd want? In my experience, if you can fill your day with new things, it helps not focus on the things you've lost. Plus, having new friends that aren't reminding you constantly of your trauma could also be good. Getting you involved in some activities will help you process those emotions you're struggling with, too. There's a Youth Center not far from here that I think you might enjoy. I know ice skating has always been your goal, but it doesn't hurt to find some new friends or interests until you can do it again. What do you think?"

She smiled, nodding, her eyes forward, and I knew that while this was a small win, it wouldn't be an easy fix, but maybe, Jill could find some support and not feel so alone in her healing. We spent the rest of the time talking about things she would like in a school and some activities she'd always wanted to try but hadn't had the time with her skating commitments. She had a list to take with her, and I made an appointment to call her mom and talk with her next week. Jill was apprehensive, but I encouraged her to let me be the bad guy if needed. She left with more pep in her step, and it felt nice to know I'd helped her find that.

Not every session was a win, but when you had those moments where the client seemed to click with something, it buoyed you up until the next one. Once the door shut, the realization that it was time for my date hit me, and I hurried back to my office, grabbing my bag, taking it with me to the bathroom. I could've changed in my office, but ever since the guys said Dayton could've, and probably did bug it, the thought of undressing in there unnerved me.

Changing into jeans, I left my blazer and chemise on and quickly brushed my hair. Spraying on some spritz, I gargled some mouthwash and then stepped back into my boots. Turning in the mirror, I felt confident, and several butterflies fluttered to life inside me. Taking out my lipstick, I spread it on, liking the red and how it had started to become my look. It was bold and sexy, and it made me feel those things as well.

Placing everything in my bag, I grabbed the rest of my stuff from my office and made my way to the lobby. Doris gave me a once over, a knowing look on her face. Waving, I didn't stop to talk, my face already heating at what she could be thinking. When I stepped into the lobby, Beau was gone, and in his place stood Atticus.

Holy shit. I was not ready for the man who stood before me.

The top half was a causal interpretation of his normal

everyday wear. He had on a sweater and blazer. It was the jeans, though, that stood out. When he said jeans, I hadn't really believed him or expected they'd look like *that*. Tight material wrapped around thick thighs, and I suddenly found myself wanting him to turn so I could see how his ass looked in them.

Fucking. Hell. Atticus might kill me tonight.

"Lore?" I heard a slight chuckle in his voice.

"Oh, sorry. I'm just…" I waved my hand in front of him. "I wasn't really expecting that. It's a good thing you don't wear those very often, or I think you'd kill all the women in the vicinity."

He snorted a cough, stepping forward and grabbing my elbow in his hand to pull me closer. "The only woman I want to see me in them is you. Now, are you ready?"

Nodding, I followed along in a daze, not sure how to take this side of Atticus. When we started toward the back entrance, I looked down, realizing he'd linked our hands together. Jean wearing Atticus was smooth. I would need to gird my loins tonight, or I'd be in trouble.

When we stepped outside, I was shocked when I didn't see the blacked-out SUVs I'd become so accustomed to. Instead, a black, sleek car was parked there. Looking around, I had to assume it was for us, but the lack of guards had me turning my head, seeing where they were hiding.

"What are you doing?"

"Looking for the guards. Where's the SUV?"

He chuckled, stepping in front of me and placing his hands on my waist. "Tonight, it's just us. No boss, no guards, no ghost fathers. Just you and me." He kissed my neck, and I wrapped my arms around his; the feel of his body pressing into mine felt divine.

"For some reason," I gasped, "I don't trust that statement is completely honest." Atticus chuckled into my neck, and the sound was becoming my new favorite addiction. I also was beginning to realize he had an obsession with kissing me there.

"Fair, Bellezza," he cooed into my ear before nipping it between his teeth. "You won't *see* the guards. Everything else, true." Atticus continued caressing his lips and teeth along my neck, dipping down into the collarbone where my skin was exposed. A throaty moan left me as I ran my fingers through his hair, not caring we were in the middle of an alley.

With a pained groan, Atticus pulled back until our noses touched. "I want you so bad. I just wanted you to know that." He kissed me but drew back after one swipe of his tongue, leaving me panting as he pulled me toward the car. I didn't know much about luxury vehicles, but I could tell this one was expensive. He opened the door for me, and I slid into the seat, the leather so soft under me, I practically melted into it. I was still groping the seat a few seconds later when he closed his door.

Atticus smirked but didn't say anything, starting the car. The engine purred to life, and I could feel the power of it as it rumbled underneath us. As he pulled out, I sank back into the seat, watching him as we drove. It was a unique experience to see him so carefree as he maneuvered around streets and cars.

"See something you like there, Bellezza?"

"It definitely has potential," I teased. The corner of his mouth lifted, and I wanted to lick it. It seemed all Atticus needed to do was take off his suit and the stick up his ass fell away. When he pulled up to an old theater a few minutes later, my brow creased, not expecting this as a date spot.

"This is where we're going?"

"Mmhmm." I saw the corners of his mouth tilt up, but he kept his face neutral, not giving anything away. He climbed out of the car, and I unhooked my seat belt, reaching for the door. I blinked when it opened, and a hand reached down for me.

"Do you have super speed or something?" I laughed, eyeing him as I climbed out.

"Just properly motivated."

My face heated, and I knew the fight to not give into Atticus was useless. He linked our fingers again and pulled me toward the entrance. Someone opened the door for us, bowing their head at him, and we made our way into the theater. It was an old-fashioned one with maroon and gold designs on the carpet and thick drapes spread throughout. It reminded me of the classic theaters where black and white films were shown. There was a counter to the side and the smell of popcorn hung in the air, but we didn't stop. Atticus took me around a corner, pulling me up a flight of carpeted stairs with a grand railing. Up top, he turned to the left, leading the way to wherever he was taking me.

Other than the person who'd let us in, there wasn't a single other person in view. He pulled up to a door, taking out an old-fashioned key; he unlocked it and opened the door for me to enter. Dipping my head in thanks, I stepped through and stopped at what I encountered.

The space was a balcony that overlooked the theater below. And while that was impressive all on its own, it was the elaborate setup that had me frozen in my tracks. It looked like something out of a bohemian photoshoot. Poufs, low couches, and lounges close to the ground were in a circle with an ottoman in the center filled with a spread of plates. A bottle of champagne cooled in an ice bucket to the side, and a cart of desserts waited along-side it. It was casual, and opulence all rolled into one unique setting.

Atticus' hands landed on my waist, and he moved the hair off my shoulder, placing his lips on the pulse point of my neck. He briefly kissed it, trailing his nose up to my ear.

"Do you approve?"

I had no words, so I nodded, completely speechless.

"I thought we could watch the movie you shamed me for not seeing." His words surprised me, and I turned with an accusation on my tongue.

"I've never shamed you!" My words started off strong, catching themselves toward the end. The heat in his eyes, the closeness of our bodies, and the whole scene had my brain fritzing when I faced him.

He gave me a pointed look, and I bit my lip to hold in the moan that wanted to escape. The growl that left him hit me straight between the legs as he leaned forward, rubbing his thumb over my lip to release it.

"One," he said, pulling back. I blinked, not knowing what that meant.

Atticus used my stunned nature to pull me over to the low couch and sit us down. He started to fill plates full of food and poured us drinks. I watched in awe as he grabbed a little of everything with such ease it surprised me.

"What kind of food is this?" I finally asked, my words returning.

"It's Indian. Have you ever had it before?"

Shaking my head, he looked surprised, before a huge grin spread across his face. "Well, then you're in for a treat." He rolled something up in a flatbread shape and then brought it up to my lips. "Here, try this."

I held his eyes as I took a bite, the flavor exploding across my tongue, and I moaned. "Mm, that's so good." He smiled, giving me another bite. We spent the next ten minutes with Atticus feeding me bites of his favorite things and telling me the first time he'd tried Indian food.

"When I was in school, one of my classmates invited

me back to their restaurant. I didn't often do things with my peers as you can imagine, but I happened to think his sister was cute, so I hoped to get an in with him," he said, chuckling. "Well, to my surprise, I discovered I loved Indian food, the girl, not so much." He smiled, taking a bite of Chana Chaat, my new favorite, and I found I liked the carefree Atticus a lot with his bent knee and jean-clad legs.

"I've never really tried too many things. It wasn't considered appropriate, so thank you for introducing me to something new."

Atticus leaned forward, capturing my chin in his hand, holding my focus to him. "You have no idea the things you've brought into my life, Bellezza. It was the least I could do." He leaned forward, the taste of the curry on his lips adding to the kiss. Just as before, he stopped before it could go deeper, letting my chin go.

"Are you ready for the movie?" I nodded, my body still buzzing from the kiss he'd given me, words not forming in my head. Some of his mysterious magic happened, and the lights dimmed, the movie starting on the screen below. The railing in front of us lowered, giving us an unhindered view.

"Whoa, that's fancy." Atticus chuckled, pulling me back into his arms. Leaning against his chest, I sighed, enjoying the feel of him. When the opening credits began to roll, I turned, a shocked look on my face, slapping his chest playfully.

"I'm not even mad you think I shamed you on this

one. You needed to be. So, if it brought us to watching it, then I'm okay with that."

He rolled his eyes but didn't deny the fact he'd missed out on a classic movie. It was quickly becoming one of the best dates of my life, watching *The Princess Bride* on a private balcony, surrounded by a luxurious picnic. I even quoted the movie as it played, and Atticus didn't get annoyed, only laughing at my enthusiasm.

Looking over as Wesley rolled down the hill as he said, "As you wish," I found him watching me.

"Are you even watching it?" I teased. He smoothed my hair, his fingers lingering there as he ran them through the strands. "I'll be honest, I watched it after you told me about it, hoping it would give me some clue into you. And I knew if I ever did watch it with you, I'd be more focused on you and not the movie."

"That's," I shook my head, not even knowing how to take it. Blinking up at him, my breath caught, and I leaned up, kissing him this time. Atticus didn't pull away, and I found myself straddling the very thighs I'd been drooling over in jeans all night.

He shoved off my blazer, my silk chemise exposing my shoulders to the air, and I gasped. Following his lead, I pushed his blazer off and even went as far as to lift his sweater over his head as well, leaving him in only a tight undershirt. Smoothing my hands up his chest, I rocked into him, all thoughts leaving me.

Atticus brushed his thumbs over my nipples, and they pebbled under his touch. His warm palms met my stomach as he pushed the silk off. Breathing heavily, I lifted my arms, discarding the garment to the floor. He stared, swallowing as he took in my breasts in the white lace bra I'd worn. Atticus bent his head, taking the peak between his lips, and I moaned, rocking forward more. I needed to feel his skin, so I pulled the shirt from the back as I tried to find a way to get it over his head and not have him leave my breast.

In the end, he pulled back, smirking at me as he pulled his shirt off the rest of the way. When it was clear, he full-on smiled at me, and I forgot my name for a few seconds as I ran my hands over the muscles on display. He wasn't as built as Sax or Wells, nor was he as tattooed as Nicco, but Atticus was yummy on a whole other level.

I unhooked my bra, dropping it to the floor, and I watched as the powerful mafia boss gaped, losing himself for a second as he swallowed. He reverently reached his hand up, rubbing his thumb over my nipple, causing my head to fall back, and I rocked. It was all it took to break any restraint he'd had. Atticus surged up, surprising me as I wrapped my legs and arms around him.

"Sorry, but I've had a fantasy playing out in my head for weeks, and I need it to happen now."

The thought of Atticus imagining fucking me a certain way had me moaning as wetness flooded me below. The throbbing was intense, and I needed some relief soon. Atticus dropped me to my feet, spinning me around to face out into the theater. We were at the edge of the platform, and for a second, my breath caught. Thankfully, Atticus hit something on the wall, and the railing raised again, making my fear dissolve.

Atticus came up behind me, his hands traveling over my body as he groped my breasts, his thumbs unable to resist touching the hardened buds. "Now, place your hands on the railing, and try not to move."

Doing as he said, I sucked in a breath when I felt his hand come around to the front, lowering my zipper. Slowly, he dragged it down, brushing his fingers over my pubic area in the process. Sucking in a breath, I was about to cry out when his fingers returned, pushing into me, the fabric of my panties not hindering him. Curling my hands around the rail, I pushed my butt back, wanting more. His dark chuckle made my legs shake, but thankfully he obliged, and his fingers retreated, pulling my jeans and panties down in one jerk.

Atticus knelt down, lifting my feet to step out of them before his tongue met my clit from behind. He licked from front to back, the evidence of my arousal apparent as I soaked his tongue. I was about out of my mind with need, a pained groan leaving me at all the teasing with no real relief.

He pulled me up, and my hands left the rail as my body became parallel with his. I could feel his naked skin against my backside now, the hard cock I'd been rocking up against rubbing between my butt cheeks. His hand came to my throat as he tilted my head back to him.

"I want you so bad, Lore. I don't think I'll be able to

do anything else until I feel you around me, but I won't take it. Tell me, have I shown you enough to earn this?" I knew he meant what he said to be sweet, but something about it felt off to me. Turning, I took his face between my hands, staring into his eyes.

"I'm sorry if I've made you feel like you weren't enough. That wasn't my intention. I've been hurt by people who made me feel that way, and I wouldn't want to make someone else feel that. But to answer your question, you've shown me that you respect me, that you care for me, and that you aren't going to take our relationship for granted, and that's what I needed without knowing how to say it or ask for it. I want you, Atticus. So, please, make me yours."

"Oh, Bellezza, we're both fools. I've been yours since that night at Illusion." His lips slammed into mine, and he lifted me up. I thought he would sit me down on the railing, and some panic entered me, but when he went around to the chaise lounge, laying me down on it, I relaxed.

"I thought your fantasy—"

He shook his head, placing a finger over my lips. "This is better than any fantasy."

I didn't get a chance to respond as he pushed in, filling me. My head rolled back at the sensation, and I wrapped my legs around his waist, wanting to keep him there. He chuckled, pulling my chin to look at him.

"This isn't going to be gentle, Bellezza. I *desperately* need you." He groaned, almost in pain at having to restrain himself, and I noticed the fear that I wouldn't be okay with whatever he needed on his face.

"I trust you."

Something about those words had his eyes shuttering closed as he breathed. His hand dropped away, and he leaned back on his haunches, angling my hips up more, holding me there with his hands. Atticus gave me one look before he pulled back and then slammed into me again. The force was intense, and I soon lost myself to the impact as he impaled me. A few seconds later, I felt him tense, pulling me to him tight as he held me there. I blinked my eyes open, finding Atticus staring at me, a look of horror on his face.

"What? Are you okay?" I asked, trying to sit up to comfort him.

"I, um, I... fuck, I can't believe I came that fast and you didn't even, you know."

The concept of the stone-cold mafia boss being shocked about losing his load so quickly and concerned I didn't orgasm had me laughing.

"This isn't funny, Lore. I'm sorry." He stared down at me, a stern look on his face, his arms crossed. He seemed to forget the fact he was still balls deep in me, too. It only made me laugh more, and to remind him, I squeezed my walls, feeling him suck in a breath at the pressure.

"Oh, is that how it's going to be?" he breathed, some of the tension leaving him. He bent down, lifting me up and walking back over to the railing. The movie still played, though it was at the end, and I laughed at how much we'd miss due to our preoccupation.

He placed me on my feet, and before I could ask him what was going on, he plunged his fingers in me, tweaking my nipple as he unmercifully finger fucked me against the rail. As I came down from an orgasm a minute later, he plunged his dick in and thoroughly fucked me up against the rail this time, my screams echoing around the theater as an epic sword battle waged on screen.

At one point, I worried the railing wouldn't hold, but as we both came again a few minutes later, I was pleased to note it had stayed. This time, Atticus pulled me down to the ground, and we laid on the blanket, watching the last of the movie while we ate dessert.

As the credits rolled, the screen going dark, his thumb trailed up my arm in a caress, neither of us wanting to move, content to stay where we were for the moment.

"Lore, there's something I need to tell you."

Rolling over, I perched my arms on his chest, tracing the raven tattoo before I looked up into his eyes. "What's up?" I smiled, loving this dynamic between us.

He brushed his thumb over my face, cupping my jaw. "It's about Cami," he said, regret heavy in his voice.

As I lay there after one of the best dates of my life, I was reminded why these moments were so important to have. Because life was always there waiting to throw a curveball.

EIGHTEEN

LOREN

Thoughts swirled in my head, and I couldn't find one to land on. It had been two days since my date with Atticus, and I was still on edge from what he'd revealed from Cami being taken, the brotherhood code, and the spy he sent in to save her. I'd wanted to rage at him, but in the end, I hadn't. I didn't like his choice, but I knew my real anger was directed at someone else.

The door dinged, and I looked up from the little table I'd been sitting at for the past thirty minutes. Restless energy had me getting here early, hoping some coffee would help me relax. It had not. The battered sugar packets and torn napkins gave away my nerves as I stood.

"Hey."

She smiled at me, but it wasn't the usual one I'd come to know from her. The realization she might be struggling with this too had me softening, some of my anger receding.

"I'm sorry," she blurted, tears brimming at the

corners of her eyes. "I wanted to tell you, but I knew you'd tell me not to do it, and I couldn't just sit here and not try. Please understand, Lor."

Sighing, I pulled her to me, wrapping her in a hug. Smoothing my hand up her back, I stuffed my anger down, realizing it wasn't about me at this moment. My anger was coming from a place of fear and hurt, and she didn't need to hear that. I could tell she'd already beaten herself up enough as it was. I'd be the friend she needed, the one she'd always been to me.

"Oh, Nat, I'm not mad. I mean, I was, but I'm not now. I don't understand, but Atticus said it was your choice if you wanted to tell me. I *know*... you know." I pulled back, raising my eyebrows, and she smiled, laughing as she wiped her tears.

"Okay, so it seems you have some stuff to spill, too."

We sat down, and I pushed the coffee I'd gotten her across the table before I grabbed her hand, feeling like she needed the support. Over the next half hour, I filled her in on the fight, the benefit, and Atticus coming clean to me. I didn't share anything about Dayton, not wanting to pull anyone else into my ethical dilemma.

Nat shared how she'd gone to Cami's apartment, and neither Lark nor Seb had heard from Cami in a few days, saying she'd gone to stay with her sugar daddy. Nat could tell something wasn't right, and had been officially worried. She'd called Atticus, hoping to set up a meeting to discuss looking for her. To Nat's surprise, he'd invited her over immediately and wasn't shocked when she admitted to fearing something had happened to Cami.

"When I mentioned I was worried, he just stared, assessing me." I nodded, knowing exactly the look she was referring to. "When he leaned forward, I about shit my pants, thinking I'd overstepped. I know who *they* are," she whispered, "but outside of Mason and Nicco, I avoided contact for the most part. Atticus had asked me to keep an eye on Climax, paying me double to ferry people, especially women, so they didn't get themselves in bad situations. But other than that phone call, I hadn't ever talked with the man before."

Nat took a breath, sipping her coffee, and cleared her throat. Peering up, she watched me, gauging my expression. I didn't know what she was looking for, but I held her eyes, attempting to convey acceptance and understanding. She sighed, taking one more sip before starting again.

"I haven't told you much about my life. You know I live with my mom, have a little girl, drive on the side, and I'm in school to be a beautician. But you don't know much about my life before Lily."

Reaching over, I squeezed her hand, shaking my head. "Nothing you say will change how I feel about you, Nat. You're my best friend, and I'm here for whatever you have going on. I'm not going anywhere."

She sniffled, squeezing back. "You remember when you asked me where I'd been all your life because you could've used a friend like me?" I nodded, focused on her. "Well, truth be told, I could've used a friend like you more." My heart warmed at the thought that she considered me such a good friend, but my intuition warned it wasn't for a good reason, much like mine hadn't. It was one of those times an innocent comment had more weight than intentionally intended.

"My life," she chuckled, the sound watery, "it hasn't been easy, but it was what I'd known for so long. I hadn't thought life was different, you know? My family hails from a long line of petty criminals and con artists, and I was groomed to follow in their footsteps. I was taught how to pick a lock, lie with ease, and pickpocket like a pro from an early age. It was second nature to me, and I never questioned it. My father would have races, and we'd see who could lift something from strangers the fastest without getting caught. I'm not proud of it, but I was really good and often won, gaining praise and attention from my father. Things changed when I was twenty-one and I met Mason. I was visiting Chicago for my first solo heist. God, saying that out loud makes me want to shake myself."

She shook her head, a self-deprecating laugh leaving her. Nat leaned back, her eyes going to the ceiling as she seemed to gather herself. When she returned forward, she gave me another watery look before taking a sip of her coffee. Wiping her eyes, she steeled herself, focusing on my mug.

"My father had hoped it would be the one to set us apart from the rest of the family, the haul that would put our name on the map. Instead, I met a boy, screwed up my job, and my whole world turned upside down. I'd hadn't realized how sheltered I'd been, and while Mason wasn't a law-abiding citizen, he gave me a home when I needed it. He taught me basic things and showed me stealing wasn't the norm. Outside of Lily, the only good thing he ever did for me was that. He opened my eyes, and I knew I couldn't go back. I changed my name, got a real job, and started a life I wanted to lead."

"That's a lot to deal with at that age, Nat. Why would you think I wouldn't understand?"

She shrugged, her eyes going to the table. "Most people hear con-artist, or petty criminal and don't really see value in believing that person. It wasn't easy to change, and I struggled a lot. When I found out I was pregnant, it was the last push I needed to stop. I wanted to be better for her, to bring her up in a life different from my own. Mason was decent during that time, helping me to appointments and being attentive. But as things progressed, he withdrew more and more. I didn't notice it at first, but once she was born, he was hardly there. And when he was, he was high or stoned. I was desperate one night, sleep-deprived, and so broke, there was barely any food left in the house. So, I did the one thing I said I wouldn't… I called home."

She sucked in a breath, the story difficult for her, and I squeezed her hand, reminding her I was there. Nat took a wobbly sip, but I watched her straighten her spine and look me in the eyes.

"My mother, she was overjoyed to hear from me. It turned out that my father was in debt. So when I hadn't returned with the payout he'd expected, he'd been desperate, and tried to rob a store. He was shot and killed, and my sister had run away, not wanting to be connected to our family anymore. My mother begged me to let her come to Chicago, promising we could make an honest life together, and maybe one day, my sister would return. So, that's what she did. I moved out of Mason's, got my own place, and became committed to being the best mom I could be. My mother has been amazing, and we both work multiple jobs to provide for the life we want Lily to live outside of crime. But it's hard, I won't lie, I've been tempted at times to just take what I need to make it easier on me, but then I see her face, and I remember the vow I made to myself."

"You've done an incredible job, Nat. I'm sorry it's not been easy, but you're so strong, and I love the person you are. You helped me when you didn't have to, so I know you've done that for others as well. I'm so glad you made the choices you did to be here because I don't know what my life would be like without you in it. I know I'd be lonelier, and I wouldn't have you as a best friend."

She smiled, reaching across to hug me as we both cried a little. "Lor, you have no idea the amazing woman you are, either. I'm glad we found one another, too."

Pulling back, I grabbed her hand again, wanting to

know how this connected to Cami. "And now, how did you end up being a spy for Atticus?" I whispered.

"When I talked with him about Cami, he told me the truth, how Darren Delgado had taken her and was using her to threaten him to do something. I could see his desperation, and I saw an opportunity. I hate myself for saying this, Loren, but the weight of doing it all on my own was just too much to bear anymore, and I hope you don't think less of me. I'd gotten Lily's tuition bill for next term that day and it has to be paid in May, or she loses her spot. I know she doesn't have to go to a private school, but I wanted to give her the best chance with her bloodline being a crook and mobster. So, I made a proposal to Atticus."

I nodded, Atticus having told me the conversation he had. "But he countered?"

She nodded, smiling. "Yeah, he did. He really is a good man, Lor." She blew out a breath, her hair flying away a bit at the motion. "I knew I couldn't sit by and do nothing with Cami in danger, and he offered to make a fund for Lily for her schooling. Not just this year, but all the way through college. He also set up an account to make up for all the support that Mason has missed. I won't have to work two jobs anymore, and my mom can just work at the diner now as well. He promised to keep them safe while I was doing this so there wouldn't be any retaliation, and if anything did happen to me, he'd provide for them both. It was the salvation I needed, the risk worth it. I asked him not to tell you, hoping we'd get her back soon, but when Darren didn't hold up his end of the bargain, I knew he wouldn't keep my secret forever. I'm sorry I didn't tell you, but I was scared you'd hate me or look at me differently, and I couldn't fathom it."

"Oh, Nat. I could never. I think what you're doing is really brave. It scares me, and I'd never have been able to do something like that, but I love that you can. I want Cami back too, and if this also gives you a better life, you were right to take it. I don't begrudge you that, and I don't believe it was taking the easy way out, either. I think in your attempt to do it differently than your own upbringing, you went to the extreme, not realizing that it's okay to ask for help. It doesn't mean you're conning people. I hope you can see that there are true friendships and family."

"I'm learning that." She grinned, letting out another breath.

"So, have you had any luck yet? What has it been like having to step back into that role?"

"Such the therapist," she teased, and I shrugged. You could take the girl out of the office, but you couldn't take the therapist out of the girl. "It hasn't been as bad as I thought. At first, I was really nervous, but because I changed my name and played it safe since we've been here, no one really knows me. Mason's non-involvement helps, too, and not many people know he's Lily's father, so my connection to the Mascro family is practically non-existent. I slid into Delgado operations fairly easily, and I've been making some connections. It's just, now is where it gets dangerous because Darren isn't operating by the code, and he's gone off-book. I don't know what it means that he broke the brotherhood code, but I know it's not good. Be careful, Lor. I know you've encountered him a few times. I wouldn't put it past him to try again."

I nodded, accepting the fact it was a possibility. Out of instinct, I looked to the table where Beau sat, the mention of safety reminding me of my shadow. His eyes weren't on me though, they were on Nat, a look of concern on his face. *Interesting.* I turned back to my friend, taking a sip of my coffee to hide my smile. It seemed Nat had two admirers now, and it was my new mission to assist her in letting men into her life.

We talked for another hour, just catching up, and I felt the barrier I hadn't realized was between Nat and me fall away as she let me all the way in. She'd always been the fun girl, the cool one who didn't seem to have any troubles, and it made me realize that maybe everyone wore a type of mask, shielding who they really were from others. It made getting to see beneath it valuable, a commodity you couldn't buy or trade for; it made vulnerability priceless.

Hugging her goodbye, I walked with Beau back to my condo. He was one of the few who listened to my wishes and walked with me instead of behind me. It made me feel awkward when they were following, just a voiceless shadow trailing me. Even if we didn't talk, like

Beau and I often didn't, it was nice having him next to me, making it feel more friendly.

As we walked, I ran through the rest of my day. Since it was Friday, my day off from clients, and Jude in school, there wasn't anywhere I needed to be. It was the last day before his spring break, reminding me to check into some campuses we could look at and plan a photo date together. Organizing the lists in my head, I didn't see her until I felt Beau stop me with an arm out in front of me. Blinking at the contact, I looked over and spotted her waiting for us.

"Christine?"

When she saw me, she relaxed, and we met at the door. I found myself embracing her, something I wouldn't have even thought of doing months ago. "How are you?" I asked when I pulled back. She'd been radio silent for a few weeks, and I'd been nervous. Brian had gotten out on bail and so far had been quiet, but I knew the retaliation would come. There was no way he'd be able to let it go. I'd been worried he'd take it out on her instead.

"Sorry, I was trying to tie up some loose ends and gather the things I needed. And well, I found something, Loren."

Her words filled me with dread and relief. As we made our way up to the apartment, I knew whatever it was, this time, I could handle it. I was done with letting Jacqueline and Brian dictate my life, and that included how I felt. Pulling out my phone, I sent a message to the group chat I'd set up for the guys for instances such as this, so I wouldn't have to send out five different ones. So far, they'd all been quiet, ignoring the presence of one another. I guess it was squinting in text form.

ME: Christine is with me. She found something. Going up to my apartment now. If anyone is free, you're welcome to join me. No more secrets.

I put my phone away as we stepped through the door, knowing if anyone could, they would come, and Beau would let them in. Facing Christine, I took a deep breath as I watched her pull out a piece of paper.

"Okay, what is it? What's this trust about?"

She bit her lip, twisting her hands. "I think you might want to sit down for this."

NINETEEN

MONROE

I yanked off my tie, and tossed it onto the bed as I sat down. Sighing, I hung my head, rubbing my hands through my hair. I thought my battle with Brittni had been over when I'd gained custody of Levi. The reality was it had only begun. Today was her arraignment and charges were officially filed against her, but she'd been let out on bail, free to see Levi as long as it was supervised. It was ironic, in a way, but I didn't want her to have any contact. Especially with my current role as the prosecutor's star witness.

It wasn't how I'd intended to spend my time in court, but at the end of the day, the only silver lining was that I got to come home to Levi. And if it helped keep her locked away from him, then so be it. I'd sit through however many hearings I had to.

Sitting up, I unbuttoned my shirt and laid back on the bed, staring at the ceiling. Turning on my side, I pulled the pillow closer, sniffing it. It might be strange, but I could still smell a faint whiff of Wells' cologne and

Loren's perfume. It somehow mixed together on the pillow they'd laid on, creating my new favorite smell. Snuggling with it, I dozed off as memories of our time together replayed in my head.

When my phone vibrated, I jolted a little, the feeling waking me from the midday sex dream. Sleepily, I reached into my pocket, bringing it close to my face to see who was texting. It was the group message Loren had made with a message from her. Clicking on it, I sat up when I read it. Quickly, I brushed my shirt all the way off and grabbed a sweater out of the closet, putting it on as I made my way to the door.

Within two seconds, I was unlocking Loren's door with the key she'd given me, and I bounded into her living room, sliding to a stop. She was sitting on the couch, Christine next to her. They both looked up at my arrival, mixed expressions on their faces.

"What is it? What did you find?"

"I haven't told her yet," Christine admitted, and I exhaled in relief. Loren was used to dealing with the heavy stuff on her own, and I wanted to show her she didn't have to. Not ever again. I'd be the person for her to lean on when she needed it. It was something I could do for her, offering her that reprieve.

Walking over to the spot next to her, I sat, taking her hand in mine without even thinking about it. Our level of comfortableness had increased over the past few weeks, and I no longer had to think about my interactions with her. It had become that natural.

"Okay, let's hear it," I said, hoping to spur Christine on. Before she could respond, Loren's phone rang, causing her to jump. I picked it up for her, finding an incoming video call from Atticus. Hitting accept, I found Loren smiling into my neck as I answered with a smirk.

"Hello, suited one." Atticus stared at me, clearly not amused. His eyes shifted to Loren, who was barely visible at the bottom, and I watched him relax. It was the first time I'd witnessed some real emotion from him, even if it was slight.

"Lore, I'm here." He ignored me, which was the usual, so I tilted it down so he could see her. She nodded, her hair tickling my neck.

"Thank you, Attie."

"You're gonna be placed on the table. I have better things to do with my hands." He rolled his eyes, but I caught the slight tilt of his lips and the crease around his eyes easing.

Sitting it down on the table, I used some of Jude's books to leverage it up so he wasn't looking at the ceiling and then gave my attention back to Christine.

"Christine, apologies, I didn't ask how you were? Paisley?"

She smiled, a serene look crossing her face. "We're so much better thanks to your and Loren's help. I feel awful that it took me that long to leave, but I'm glad I did. Paisley is a different child."

"I'm glad we were able to help. Do you need anything else? I know Brian's been out. Has he tried to contact you since?" Loren asked, letting her worries go for a second.

"No, thank goodness. Whatever you said to him has kept him away, which made it easier to find what I needed."

Loren's hand tightened in mine as we waited for Christine to take a breath and a sip of the water she had. When she took a deep breath, her eyes lifted, and she held Loren's. It made me respect her for not taking the easy way out.

"Brian was real careful. He didn't leave much at my place. The last time he was there, though, he must've been distracted because I found something that connected some of the other information I'd overhead. Did you ever find anything else out about the trust?"

A throat clearing from the table had us remembering Atticus was listening in. "I've recently uncovered some information that I think connects to your mother and ex-husband, Loren."

Christine nodded, accepting she didn't need to know, and continued. "Well, good, it might help make sense of it all. The thing Brian left behind was an invoice to a storage facility. The name was strange, though, so I looked it up." She pulled out a torn piece of paper and handed it to Loren.

"Descendents Storage," she read, "I've never heard of it. He must've gotten it after our divorce."

Christine froze, a panicked look on her face. "Something tells me it's not a regular storage facility, and he's had it longer than they've been divorced?" I asked, my heart sinking when Christine nodded, fidgeting in her seat.

"I'm sorry to be the one to tell you this then, Loren. But it's a storage facility for um, ovum… mature oocyte cryopreservation."

"Ovum? Like women's reproductive eggs?" She asked, her nose scrunching in confusion. "Why would he be storing anything there?"

"I, uh, I don't know. But he's been paying a monthly fee for three years."

"Three years! But that was when we were still married…"

Loren froze, her face going white, and I worried she was about to pass out. When she didn't appear to be able to form any words. I moved the phone to her hands and walked Christine out.

"I knew it would be hard to hear, but I hadn't expected her to shut down like that," Christine admitted with remorse on her face.

"Hey, it's not your fault. She needed to know all the facts to make an informed decision. Loren has that now, no matter how difficult it might be to hear. So, thank you. You'll call me if you need anything?"

"Of course, Monroe. I'm glad you got Levi back. You really are a good dad."

"Thanks, Christine. Let me know when you get to wherever you're going, okay?"

"We will."

I gave her a hug once the elevator arrived and headed back to Loren's apartment. I let myself back in and immediately noticed the silence. I'd hoped she'd talk to Atticus while I was gone, but it seemed that hadn't lasted. When I stepped into the living room, I found her curled up on the couch in a ball, the phone laid on its side as she stared at it. I couldn't hear from here, but I guess she was listening to someone because I saw her nod before she laid it flat.

I paused, hesitating for a second before I remembered my assurance earlier that I didn't have to second guess anything with us. Walking over, I didn't ask her what she needed because I knew she wouldn't know, or at least she wouldn't know how to ask for it. Scooping her up into my arms, I carried her to the bedroom. She didn't fight me, but curled into me. I laid her on the bed, my body curling around hers, and I stroked her hair, giving her time to tell me when she was ready. I didn't know how long we laid there, but eventually, she rolled over, looking me in the eyes.

"Hey."

She smiled, her hand reaching out to trace my face. The slight touch had my eyes closing as I felt her run her fingertips over the bridge of my nose, my cheeks, and lips.

"You have such a handsome face." She leaned forward, kissing me softly. I smiled at the gesture, opening my eyes when she pulled back.

"Thank you."

"What's it like being a man and not questioning that compliment?" she laughed.

"Oh, you think just because I said thank you, I've never felt insecure about my looks? Huh?" I moved forward, grabbing her around the waist, tickling her.

"Sorry," she gasped between laughs. "It just seems easier sometimes to be a guy."

Pinning her to the bed, I loomed over her, pressing my body into hers. "Guys are just as insecure about things for your information. They're just different, I suppose. It's nice to hear it from you, and I trust you and value your opinion."

"You make it sound simple when you put it like that."

I stared down at her, noticing the way her eyes wouldn't meet mine. Cupping her face, I brought her attention to mine. "What's really going on, Lo? I doubt what you're really worried about is your ability to accept compliments, which, if we're giving them out, I think you're the most gorgeous woman in the world, and I hope you believe that."

She blushed but didn't shake her head, making me feel like maybe she believed it a little. Her mouth opened, and she started to tell me what she thought when someone pounded on the door. We both looked at one another, frozen for a second, before I rolled off, trotting to the door. Peeking through the peephole, I found Wells leaning against it, giving me a sinful look.

"Let me in, Roe."

Laughing, I opened the door. The rush of dogs surprised me as they bounded into the room, only stopping when the leash pulled. Wells had a smirk on his face at my shocked expression, knowing I wouldn't have expected them.

Rushing him, he dropped the leads as I pinned him against the door, my forearm against his throat. He could quickly get out of the hold if he wanted, but I think he liked it when I showed some dominance, that or I'd shocked him enough to stay still.

"You think you're funny, don't you?" I growled, my eyes heating as I felt him swallow, his pulse beating against my arm.

His hands landed on my hips, and he pulled me into his rock-hard erection. "I know I'm hard as fuck right now for you, so what are you going to do about it?"

"Barkley! Fort!" Loren's voice called as she walked down the hall, finding them. Their barks and paws gave away their happiness at seeing her. Stepping back, I let go of Wells, adjusting the steel rod in my pants. He groaned, stepping forward and pulling my chin to him.

"This isn't finished. I expect you to take what you want later."

The desire in his words had me whimpering as I nodded, licking my lips in anticipation. We both turned to find Loren watching us, her arms crossed as she held the two leads. "I swear, every time I think I find the hottest thing, you go and up it." She sighed, fanning herself. "So, how did you manage to get the dogs in here? I've been hounding the board for weeks with no results."

Wells stalked forward, grabbing her by the hips and kissing her deeply, and the erection I'd just managed to lose found a new reason to raise its head. When he pulled back, he kept hold of her waist, and I swear Loren swooned a little. I was right there with her. Not that I wished Wells' past on him, but the man he was becoming was dangerously charming, and I was kind of glad he hadn't been this way all along. I didn't know if I would've been ready for him back then.

"Atticus," he said, shrugging. "He called me and said to bring them and that he'd have everything approved. I saw the text after my workout, so I figured you could use them. Though, if I know Roe, I bet he had some spectacular make-you-feel-better activity up his sleeve."

Leaning against the wall, I shrugged, liking that he thought that about me. "It may have included a joint bubble bath followed by cuddling naked in front of a fire on a bearskin rug."

Loren laughed, reaching her hand out to me. "Well, I don't have a fireplace or a bearskin rug, and Jude will be home at some point. But the bubble bath, that actually sounds nice."

"Done." I kissed her on the cheek, walking back to her bedroom to start the water. Once I had a suitable temperature, I looked through her supplies and picked out a few I liked, dumping them in. Once the water was going, I walked back into the bedroom, finding

Loren and Wells getting the dogs settled for the moment.

Lifting my sweater over my head, I dropped it to the floor, toeing off my shoes and socks. When they heard the clink of my belt, they both turned, stopping to watch me as I pushed my pants and boxers down in one go, stepping out of them. Winking, I turned, my still erect cock pointing in the direction I was headed.

The water was at a reasonable level, so I shut it off and stepped in, settling back against the corner. Loren had one of those jacuzzi tubs. It would've been perfect for two people, but three would be tricky, but I had faith in us to figure it out. My cock peeked out of the bubbles, and I grabbed it, giving it a tug, my head falling back against the wall. I hadn't wanted this to be sexual, only to provide Loren with some comfort.

Using all the things that would make me soft, I kept repeating them over and over in my head. When I felt the water rise, I opened my eyes to find Loren smiling at me. Holding out my hand, I pulled her down into my lap, laying her against my chest.

"This is perfect, thank you." She brushed my chin with her nose, leaving me a kiss. Wrapping my arms around her, I pulled her tight to me, loving the feel of her against my skin.

Wells stepped in a moment later, settling between my feet, taking Loren's legs into his hands as he reached up to me.

"I vote for a bigger tub when we all get a place

together," Wells grunted, causing Loren and me to look up at him.

"A place together? Did you just say you wanted to move in with us?" I asked.

"I'm pretty sure that's exactly what he said," Loren said, agreeing.

Wells lifted a corner of his mouth, not answering as he laid his head back, his hands wrapped around my foot and hers. We looked at one another, shrugging. It was quiet for a while as we all soaked in the tub together.

"You ready to tell us, Kitten?" Wells finally asked. Loren sighed, nodding.

"Yeah, I am."

I sat up some, taking the washcloth and running it over her skin in soothing motions as I pretended to wash her. Slowly, I massaged her neck, arms, and back as I dropped water over her skin.

When Loren started to speak, it was low, her voice barely above a whisper. "I was pregnant once," she said, the words freezing my movements. "When I was about 33 weeks, I had a fall, and it started premature labor. Everything is a blur and disjointed. I don't even remember how I fell, honestly, just the pain and fear are clear. I know that they put me on medication to slow down the labor, and there were a lot of tests performed. No matter what they tried, though, the labor couldn't be stopped, and I was rushed into emergency surgery."

She sucked in a breath, and I pulled her back into my

chest, wrapping my whole body around her. I felt her tears hitting my arms, and I knew this was hard for her. Wells leaned forward, linking his hand with hers.

"What happened next, Kitten?"

"No, Wells, she doesn't have to tell us."

He glared at me, shaking his head, not listening. "*Kitten.*"

A grunt left my mouth as I moved to kick him in the balls for being an asshole right then. Loren stopped me, placing her hand on my shin. "No, it's okay, Monroe. I need to do this. I need to say it. I know it's important."

Rubbing her arm, I kissed her temple, trying to give her all of my strength.

"They rushed me into the room, and I remember the look on the nurse's faces. It's so vivid when I look back, their stares of pity are locked into my memory, and I knew my odds weren't good. I prayed to whoever would listen to just grant me this one thing. I'd been good my whole life. Surely I deserved this? I was owed that much, I thought. When they finally pulled my baby out, I was exhausted, the delivery taking so much out of me on top of all the drugs and trauma my body had been through in the past twenty-four hours. I followed the nurses' movements as they took her over and started to clean her up. The doctors were working down below, but I wasn't even focusing on that. I watched the nurse use that sucking thing, cleaning her eyes and throat. I kept waiting for her to cry, to hear her voice. Their movements became more frenzied as they shouted things, turning her over. I cried out at that point, and they moved to block my view. It felt like hours as I waited. When the nurse turned, my baby was wrapped in a blanket, and I thought I must've zoned out and missed her cry because they were bringing her to me."

She looked up, glancing between Wells and me, tears streaming down her face. I looked over at Wells, and I saw his pain at hearing her story, and I let go of the anger I had for him. He knew she needed to do this and had been willing to push her when I hadn't. Loren sucked in a breath, wiping her eyes. She grabbed both of our hands as she told the last of her story.

"They placed her down on my chest, and I stared at the most precious face. She was so beautiful. I didn't hear their words at first, too happy to stare at my baby, thankful she'd been given to me finally. But when she didn't move or make a sound, I looked up to meet the nurse's eyes, and the sadness I saw there told me everything I needed to know. She told me that they'd done everything they could but that she was just too small, her lungs underdeveloped to handle the birth. That's when I knew it didn't matter that I'd been good my whole life. The world didn't care. It took what it wanted, and it had taken my baby. When they took her away, a piece of me left with her."

"Where was your husband during this?" Wells asked, a growl slipping out through his teeth.

"I don't know. I never asked. He was there when I woke up later. My mother had met me at the hospital when it first happened. That was back when I thought they both had my best interests in mind."

"How does what Christine told us connect?" I asked. She turned to me, some of her fierceness returning.

"When I woke, Brian told me I was responsible for losing our child and that my incompetence had caused me to not only lose the baby I carried, but any future ones. The labor had been difficult, and I guess while I was watching them with Violet, they were trying to save my life. Apparently, there'd been extensive scarring on my fallopian tubes, making it impossible for me to ever conceive. It doesn't matter though, because they also told me I was infertile."

"I'm not a doctor or anything, nor a woman, but that doesn't sound right. Did *you* ever talk to the doctor?"

"No." Loren shook her head, a puzzled look coming over her face. "But that's the part that doesn't make sense. If I'm infertile, why was Brian paying to have ovum stored? And just whose are they?"

"I think I might have the answer to that," a deep voice said from the doorway, causing us all to jump. The dogs were sitting next to his legs perfectly still, and not for the first time, I realized just how much power Atticus weaved.

"Fuck, dude," Wells hissed, sitting forward to cover his junk. "And you two," he glared at the dogs, "some watchdogs you are." They both whimpered, laying down with their heads on their paws. Atticus rolled his eyes, but never once looked at us.

"I'll give you a minute to, um, get decent." He turned, and a sound I hadn't expected to hear from Loren erupted out of her as she lost herself in a fit of giggles. I looked at Wells, and we soon found ourselves joining her. Clothes were tossed into the bathroom, only causing us to laugh more.

"Don't run into any walls while you're squinting," Loren shouted, giggling even more as she started to climb out of the tub. The only response she got back was a one-worded reply.

"Two."

The door shut, and I looked at her, and she shrugged, but I noticed her face heating as she dried off. The three of us dressed quickly and made our way out to the suited man, who seemed to have all the answers.

TWENTY

SAX

Shifting my leg, I sighed when the asshat across the street still hadn't moved. I'd been trailing him for the past hour, and all he'd done so far was sit on this stoop like a pigeon. I was already bored and about to call it quits when Spitfire's message came through.

Deciding to leave and see what the douche she'd been married to was up to, I stepped out of the shadows and turned in the opposite direction. Of course, that was when Mason, Cami's brother, pulled up in his souped-up piece of shit. He was one of those dumbasses who had hydraulics that cost more than the actual car. He revved it up, and I stepped back, watching.

Cameron walked forward, leaning down into the window, and exchanged something with Mason. He stepped back, righting himself, and put whatever Mason had given him in his pocket. The obnoxious car jolted forward as the tires went up and down before he gunned it, smoke billowing behind him as the loud muffler rattled from the acceleration.

I watched Cameron glance both ways before he took off again. My phone buzzed again, and I was officially out of patience. Spitfire needed me, so it was time I enacted my asshole gene. Crossing the street, I let the shithead get a few blocks over before I increased my speed. When he was about to pass an alley, I sped up and yanked him into it before anyone saw me.

He squirmed under my hold, but I glared, promises of death in my eyes as I stared down at him. "I'd calm the fuck down, Cameron, if I were you. You don't want my arm to slip and accidentally crush your esophagus. Sometimes, I just don't know how strong I am, and well, mistakes occur. I'd hate that to happen to you."

The kid froze, all pretenses of bravado fading away, and I could've sworn the faint scent of ammonia filled my nostrils, but it was hard to tell in the alley full of piss to begin with.

"Now, I need to go take care of something, so you're gonna go with my good friend Topher. And when I'm ready to see you, I'll come and visit, and then you can tell me all about how Mason is connected to you. If you play along, then I won't have to break any fingers or other appendages you might be a little more attached to and have less of to spare. Though," I spat, looking him up and down, "that might be small too. Jude is ten times the man you are. Some big brother you turned out to be."

I let him go, shoving him toward Topher, who grabbed him, ushering him to the waiting SUV. He paused before climbing in, looking over his shoulder at me. "If you know Jude, then he's in trouble. I was only doing what I thought was best. I didn't know what I'd gotten myself into until it was too late. Please, I'll tell you anything, just keep him safe because you're right. Jude is better than all of us."

He stared at me with panic, and Topher waited to see what I would do. Eventually, I nodded, acknowledging his words, but not giving anything away. If he cared about Jude, it would be a lot easier to get him to talk, even if that meant I needed to lie to do it. Topher dipped his head once the boy was secure, walking over to me.

"The warehouse?"

"Yeah. Don't be too nice to him, but don't rough him up too much, either. He's Jude's brother, and I don't want the kid to hate me if it turns out his brother was trying to protect him. But feel free to scare him a little and let him know we're the bigger threat."

Topher nodded, walking back to the SUV, pausing at the door, and glancing over his shoulder. "I like Jude. He's a good kid. Though, I hear you're only in second place because you scare him. Do with that what you will. I don't pretend to know anything about how your relationship works."

My eyes narrowed, and he swallowed, averting his eyes. "Second place for what?" I finally asked, making him remember I wasn't someone who needed his opinion about my relationship status, and he'd do well to remember it. Topher swallowed, a slight smile breaking free as he opened the door. Before he got in, he looked at me and said, "His favorite daddy."

A laugh broke free as I sputtered. His comment had caught me off guard. The door shut before I could respond, so I flipped them off, knowing he'd see it. Shit, I didn't know if I liked I was second, merely because I scared him or hated it. When it came to Immy, I definitely wanted to scare the kid to keep his sausage to himself. But… when it came to Loren, I wanted him to see the value I brought and not just be scared of me. It would be a tricky balance to navigate.

Pulling out my phone, I hit redial on the call I missed, not even looking as I made my way over to my bike. It felt nice to have made progress on Cameron, and hopefully, I'd be able to solve one problem on our list.

"Where are you?"

"I'm on 10th. Topher is taking the weasel to the trap. Mason was here."

"Fuck. Okay, send someone to follow him and bring him in."

"Already done," I said as I straddled my bike and unhooked my helmet from the bars. "Update?"

"It's not good. I'm headed to her place. I called Mr. Young to take the dogs over."

"Shit. If you're calling in the dogs, then I know it's not good."

"Her ex…" he started, his teeth grinding through the phone as he tried to keep his temper in check. I could picture him sitting at his desk, his hands wrapped around the desk chair as he tried to reign in the anger. Atticus didn't like being out of control, and the fact he was struggling told me whatever it was, was bad and how much he'd finally let himself care about Loren.

"Fuck," I hissed when he didn't say anything else; his silence spoke volumes. "Alright, I'm heading there. What about the golden boy and the kid?"

"The first is already there, and I haven't been able to reach Nicco. I'm having Beau pick up Jude from school and bring him to the house. I'm not sure what will go down tonight, but I didn't want Lore to have to worry."

"Ah, guys, look, the coldhearted asshole cares. I think I just shed a tear," I teased, hoping to calm us both down some. My own heart pounded in my chest, and I knew it wouldn't do me any good to ride that way; no matter how much I wanted to storm the castle and sweep my princess up, I couldn't. Not right this second, at least.

"Very funny. Stop by Ignite on your way over. I'll see you in a bit."

He hung up, knowing I'd follow his order despite wanting to ignore it. It wasn't a request, though, and as much as the kid irritated me at times, he was part of our bro club now, and I needed to respect that. As I drove over, my mind tossed around words to describe our group, helping me to avoid thinking about the things weighing heavy on my mind.

Bang brothers? No, it sounded like we all sexed one another up, and I only wanted to fuck Loren. I'd have to look something up because nothing else was coming to mind or get the kid on it. He was more of the creative one anyway.

I pulled around to the side, parking my bike next to Nicco's, some relief that he was here coursed through me. When I stepped in, Cassandra smiled wide, giving me her best flirtatious grin.

"Well, well, look what the cat dragged in. I do believe it's my lucky day."

"Oh, Cassandra, you know a love like ours would never last. But oh, would it be beautiful."

"You're right," she beamed, chuckling.

"The kid here? He hasn't been answering his phone."

She nodded, leaning over the counter. "Been in with a full back tat most of the day. He should be finishing up if you want to wait."

"Nah, I'll interrupt." I smiled wider, winking, and she shook her head, knowing there was no stopping me.

I walked to the back, ignoring the other employees as I made my way to his studio. The door was shut, and I could hear music coming from underneath. I didn't bother knocking but turned the knob, stepping into the room. Nicco was crouched over, the full tattoo of a fallen angel on display. He glanced up at me briefly, but went back to what he was doing. I leaned against the wall and watched him work. Nicco really was talented, and it was no wonder his business was such a success.

Five minutes later, he finished, turning off the gun and setting it to the side. I didn't give him time to do anything else before I delivered the message I'd be sent to do.

"It's Loren. She needs us."

Turning, I strode out of the room, nodding briefly to Cassandra, and made my way to my bike. The back door opened as I was snapping on my helmet, and Nicco stood there, breathing deeply.

"Fucker, you can't just say that shit and then walk away."

"Sure I can. Check your phone, dumbass. She's not in immediate danger, but some shit is going down, apparently. Clean up and then head there; cancel the rest of your day if you care about her. That's all I'm going to say. It's your choice from here, Nicco. I did this as a courtesy to Spitfire."

He was still breathing hard, but his anger had left, and he nodded before stepping back through the door. A second later, my engine purred beneath me, and I tore out of the space, making my way to her place. Finally, I could hold her and figure out what all this shit was about instead of trying to figure it out in my head. I wasn't doing well with the unknown, and a panic was rising in me.

I pulled into the garage, parking in one of the guest spots, and strode into the building, barely even stopping to acknowledge the old man at the door. He'd gotten used to us over the past few months at least and knew we were there to protect Loren, some of us more closely than others.

I was tempted to take the stairs as I pushed the button for the elevator, the need to be up there with Loren riding me hard. Fuck! I'd never felt this much for someone before, and while that should scare me, it only made me want to be with her more. It felt like once I quit being a dick and opened my eyes to the beautiful creature in front of me, nothing else sufficed. Loren had become my whole world, and when I wasn't orbiting around her, my entire existence felt off kilter.

It probably wasn't healthy, but I never claimed to be mentally stable to begin with. Doubt there was any way to be stable when you had to kill as part of your job. There was something you either had to shift or ignore to keep it from haunting you. In my case, my morality lay with Mas and now with Loren. Whatever I had to do to keep the people I cared about safe had no limits.

When the elevator finally dinged, I exhaled in relief as I stepped onto it. I heard footsteps running toward me, the cadence familiar, and the asshole part of me wanted to hit the close door button. As the doors began to shut, I sighed, rolling my eyes, and hit the button to hold them open. Nicco slid to a stop a second later, looking at me in relief as he sagged against the wall to catch his breath.

Grumbling, I stabbed the door close until they shut, finally moving upward. We didn't speak to one another; there wasn't anything to say. Nothing outside of Loren would help either of us at this moment.

When the doors opened, I used my size to take longer

steps, eating up the space quicker than stumpy legs. I didn't knock, doors holding no value to me at this moment, and entered her place. Atticus was pacing in the living room, his head snapping up to meet mine when he heard me.

"She's, um, dressing." He grimaced, and I laughed, feeling better knowing she wasn't destroyed. Nicco walked in a few seconds later, nodding to Mas before taking a seat. He spread his legs, leaning back as he rested his head on the cushion. I looked at him, realizing how beat he looked.

"Kid, how long had you been working on that tat?"

He rubbed his temple, but kept his head back and his eyes closed as he answered. "Six hours and something. I'm beat. You going to tell me what's going on now, old man?"

I walked around the island, opened the fridge, and ignored his comment. At this point, it was how we showed we cared for one another, anyway. Grabbing a glass out of the cabinet, I filled it with juice Loren had. Taking an apple out of the fruit bowl, I walked over and sat it down next to him before I sprawled myself out on the couch. Kicking him with my foot, I waited until he opened his eyes, peeking at me. I nodded toward the food, and he sat up, a smile on his face.

Ignoring his glee, I sat back myself, stretching my arms out. Atticus sighed, coming to sit next to me. "While we wait," he started, addressing Nicco, who was sipping the juice. "I got the results back from the lab."

Nicco sat up, his entire focus on Mas as he waited. "I'm still not convinced it's Dayton, but whoever Loren met with, he wasn't wrong about the fact Benny isn't your father. We're brothers, Nicco."

A wide grin spread across the kid's face, and he launched himself out of the chair, surprising Mas in a hug. Atticus glanced over at me, a wide-eyed look on his face as he awkwardly patted Nicco. "Ah, big bro, I'm going to have so much fun with this." Nicco pulled back, and I could tell that he really was excited about the news despite his jokes.

"You're brothers?" Loren's voice asked as she stepped into the room, taking in the scene. I sat up, noticing their wet hair and the two dogs trailing after the three amigos. Barkley spotted me and rushed over, nuzzling into my side. Fort might've been a grumpy fucker, but Barkley, she was pure sunshine. I'd grown fond of the dog and had started carrying treats around in my pocket to give to her when I'd see her. Patting her head, I scratched behind her ears, giving her some love while Atticus conveyed what he'd just told Nicco.

"How do you feel about it? Both of you?" she asked.

"I'm cool. They've always been family to me, so it's not a big stretch for me," Nicco exclaimed before taking a bite out of the apple I'd given him.

"It's different," Atticus started, and I turned to him, curious as to how he felt about it. "I'm not against it; I'm just not sure how to feel about it yet. It makes me wonder what Dayton had planned and why he never revealed it before. There had to be a purpose."

"Outside of that, though, it must be nice to have a brother?"

"Oh, yes, like Nicco said, he already was family, and he's acted like a brother, especially to Immy, since he moved in with us. It doesn't change any of that."

Nicco smiled, eating his apple, and I wondered if this was a bigger deal for him than he was admitting. He wasn't alone anymore, and as an orphan myself, I knew what that felt like.

"But we're not here to talk about me," Mas started, waiting for the others to take a seat. Realizing there weren't enough places, I reached over and pulled Loren until she was in my lap. Snuggling with her, I wrapped my arms around her, cocooning her in my embrace.

"Mm, better," I breathed, her giggle soothing me in all the best ways. I didn't realize how much I needed her touch to soothe the broken edges in me.

Grumpy grumbled something but took a spot on the floor, Fort sitting near him for pets. Barkley laid at my feet, and I wanted to brag about it, but I felt having both the dog and Loren's attention might sting a little, so I let it go for now. Happy pulled a chair over from the table, taking a seat. Once we were all positioned, we all looked at Mas, and that was when I realized we were like the fucking dwarfs.

Mas was clearly Doc, and Nicco was a toss-up

between Bashful and Sneezy or Clumsy, as I liked to think of him.

So which one did that make me?

Ah, hell. I was the mute one, wasn't I?

Well, if I was going to be Dopey for anyone, it would be Spitfire.

TWENTY ONE

LOREN

My heart thumped loudly in my ears as I sat on Sax's lap. The past few hours felt like a car wreck as I swiveled from one emotion to the next. My body even felt like it had been hit by a truck, the pressing weight of the information slamming into me. When I would surface, and see the guys around me, my heart was full. I'd laugh, and feel giddy, to only be reminded that things weren't okay.

When Christine revealed what she'd found, it felt like I was right back to that day when it felt like I'd lost everything. Atticus had soothed me through the phone, whispering to me to stay with him. I wasn't certain, but it sounded like he sang me a song at one point. The language was all different, none of the words making sense, but the cadence and deepness of his voice made me wonder. I wish I'd been present enough to hear it, or even have recorded it. That would've been something I'd like to have witnessed, or have forever.

Sax's hand rubbed my arm, the motion reminding me

that they were all here, in my living room together. It was odd having all five of them here like this, but at the same time, it also felt right. These were the men who made me feel like a woman and that I could do anything. I was glad they hadn't made me give any of them up. I wasn't sure I could at this point, even if they tried to make me. They were welded to me now, in it for the long haul.

I listened to them talk, finding it interesting to hear what they chatted about amongst themselves. Their banter was cute, and I found myself smiling. Atticus noticed, his hand smoothing across my ankle to get my attention.

"Bellezza, are you ready to hear the truth?"

"The truth?" I asked, still feeling like I was floating.

He nodded; his dark eyes that always revealed nothing bore into me with intensity. Atticus was worried about me, and he was letting me see it. I sat up, moving off Sax's lap, and sat wedged between the two men. Something about this moment told me I needed to hear it clearly, and as much as I enjoyed Sax's touch, it was too easy to fall into. I didn't want to dull the pain now, to only be smacked with it later when I was alone. No, this, I needed to hear with no barriers.

Peering up, I stared back for a few seconds before nodding, assenting to Atticus' news.

"I called the place that Christine found and confirmed that there is a storage locker for Brian Carter that was purchased three years ago on November 14th."

I let the information sink in, the realization it was the day after Violet's birth settling in. Nothing made sense, but I had a feeling it was about to.

"That was the day after Violet died," I whispered, the memory of holding her as I cried alone in my hospital room rising up. Now that Wells mentioned it, where had Brian been? My mother was there, and it was one of the few times I'd ever witnessed real emotion on her face. She'd been devastated as much as I had. It was the one moment in the past three years that I held on to, reminding myself she cared.

But was it real? Had she cared about me or something else?

"From what I overheard," he paused, taking my hand. The movement was so out of character that I savored it, linking my fingers with his. This was Atticus, the man who cared too much and was scared to show it. "You were told that due to the emergency delivery, there was scarring on your fallopian tubes causing you to be infertile. Is that correct?"

I nodded. I couldn't look at anyone else, but I felt Sax's hand on my back and Barkley at my feet, giving me the strength to hold his gaze.

"I'm assuming your mother or Brian told you this?" Dipping my head in acknowledgement, I sucked in a breath, waiting for the sucker punch that was indeed to come.

"They lied to you, Lore. The tests showed that when

you were admitted, you tested positive for chlamydia, which was what led to the scarring and infertility."

I reared back, shaking my head from side to side. "No, that's not possible. Before Nicco, I'd only slept with Brian. How could I be pregnant and have an STI?"

He looked at me, not with pity, but with a ferocity that made me close my eyes at the intensity. Taking a few deep breaths, I calmed my heart and thought about what he was telling me. Atticus wasn't lying to me; there was nothing to gain from it. But Brian...

I thought I'd dealt with the divorce and had moved on, but this... *fuck.*

He'd been cheating on me long before I lost the baby.

I didn't know why that mattered, but shame I'd been carrying around for not being enough of a woman to give him a child, for being depressed when I lost my baby, and not fulfilling his needs as a wife, that shame dispersed into nothing. It felt almost magical as the pain and burden of those things, of never being enough for someone, lifted at the realization it hadn't been me.

Brian was the one at fault there. Brian had been the one who hadn't taken our vows seriously, breaking them and everything in our marriage. It wasn't me who wasn't enough. It was Brian.

Lifting my head, a force of determination rose up in place of the shame, and I squared my shoulders back, ready for the rest.

"Brian cheated on me. He gave me chlamydia." I said it as a statement, not needing to question it.

A noise behind me had me wanting to turn, but I tuned it out, knowing I needed to stay with Atticus or I'd fall into the hole and never rise. Atticus was the raft I needed to cling to at this moment. His sturdy assurance, combined with his no-nonsense nature, was the stability I needed. I didn't need someone to protect my feelings; for once, I just wanted the fucking truth, no matter how much it might hurt. And Atticus had never bowed away from saying something.

"Yes, Bellezza, it appears so. But… that's not all." He took a deep breath, his chest rising at the inhale as he slowly let it out. Something about that small action endeared me to the man he was. He would tell me how it was, but it wasn't easy, it did cost him something, and I liked knowing that.

"I finally have all the pieces, and I'll share with you how and why I believe your mother and ex-husband have been colluding together. Do with my exposition what you will, but I feel I'm close to the mark."

"Okay."

"Your mother, while she comes from a well-bred family line, it seems when she married your father, it was an arrangement. He needed the clout of a high-class marriage, and she needed the financial backing. Her family had gotten into trouble and were hemorrhaging their assets. A deal was brokered between the Wood-fields and Hanovers."

"Things like that still go on?" one of the guys asked.

My mind was too busy rolling the information around to verify who.

"Yes, more than you think," Atticus said, acknowledging whoever asked. "The only one with any inheritance remaining was a great, great grandmother. When she died, she left it in her will to set up a trust for her future descendants. It listed you and any children you had as the trustees. It is my belief that your mother hoped to gain access to this through you or even the birth of your child. That is the detail I'm not positive about when it all started with her and Brian, but somewhere along the way, he became aware of it and part of the plan. In my opinion, maybe he wanted a divorce sooner, or to not marry you at all, but your mother promised him something if he did and produced an heir. The past few years, your mother has been reckless with her finances and has gotten herself in trouble. She put a lot of her stock into the um," he paused, his eyes flicking over to Wells. "Into a stock that crashed."

"Fuck," Wells hissed, and I turned to him, curious how it connected, but also not caring. Whatever his part was, I didn't blame him. That much I knew to be true.

"Whatever it is, it doesn't matter, Wells. It sounds like she made a choice on her own. That's on her, not you." He nodded, but I could see some guilt there. Atticus squeezed my hand, pulling me back.

"She lost a lot of the wealth she'd gained since marrying your father, and panicked. She started using other avenues to gain it back. These have all failed as well, and she's gotten herself into a hole now that she can't get out of without something significant happening. I believe she hid it from your father, but he's now aware. There's a lien against their home, most of the clubs they belonged to have banned them after declined payments, and some of their possessions have been repossessed. This trust you have the right to is her last hope of getting out of debt. That's why she's been so desperate. I believe that the thing other than Barkley they had to bribe you with is your ovum."

"But how? And that's what you meant the other night at the benefit? Why she left so quickly?"

He nodded. "This is where I'm not sure of the sequence of events, whether it had been planned or a happy circumstance she took advantage of. When the doctor told your mother about the risks of the delivery and the test results, she was given a choice. Apparently, she had power of attorney over you for all medical procedures."

"What?" I gasped, jerking back at the information. It shocked me so hard, I reared back, bumping into the body behind me. Sax's hands landed on my hips, and his nose and mouth made their appearance on my neck. It was the grounding I needed to not lose my shit. When I opened my eyes, Atticus continued.

"It was in the paperwork I found today. I'm guessing Brian had you sign something when you weren't aware. Still, she had the authority to make decisions for you and requested they perform a transvaginal aspiration to retrieve the healthy eggs directly following labor. You wouldn't have known as you were focused on the nurses and the doctors already working on closing you up. It wouldn't produce a scar either, leaving you clueless. When you woke up the next day, your grief was so heavy, you would've believed anything they told you." His voice was soft, trying to, for once, soften his tone in consideration for my feelings. It didn't matter; everything he said was accurate. My grief had consumed me, and I hadn't thought I needed to guard myself from them. I never would've believed my husband or mother would lie to me.

"Which brings it back to whether it had always been planned as a means of blackmail, or if it was bribery in a last-ditch effort to gain control of the trust."

"Anyone else feel like they've just stepped into an episode of the Rich and Famous?" Nicco joked. "Shit like this actually happens? Though what I can say, I'm apparently a surprise heir to a potentially not-dead father, so I guess shit like this does happen. Huh. Perspective is a weird thing."

I turned to look at him, my face breaking into a smile at his nonsensical babble. He was sitting back in the chair, his ankle crossed over his leg in much the same way Atticus did often. Nicco had a contemplative look on his face, and for some reason, it pulled me from the cliff I was about to dive off. I slowly looked around at the men gathered here, realizing we all had things we'd carried, and the knowledge of that made me feel not as alone.

Nicco had just discovered he wasn't an only child, and his father might've killed his mother.

Monroe had gotten his son, but still had to deal with his ex-wife and if co-parenting would be possible.

Wells carried so much shame for his choices; it blanketed him and made him push others away.

Atticus carried the weight of protecting everyone on his shoulder, never allowing himself any happiness.

And Sax, he had something buried so deep, I worried if he didn't talk about it soon, it would swallow him.

None of us were perfect, and we all had our own crazy shit, as Nicco put it, but we weren't alone, and that made me feel like nothing was impossible.

"What I want to know then," I started, everyone's attention on me, "how do I gain access to the trust and my eggs, and how are *we*," I emphasized, "going to handle Jacqueline and Brian?"

"We?" Wells asked, a smile on his face as he absently patted Fort.

"Yes, we. I know you all don't necessarily know one another or hang out watching sports or whatever guys do. And I know that some of you," I teased, looking at Atticus, "have to squint to ignore the other guys I've found myself attached to. But we *are* a we, and it means everything to me that you're all here for me. I honestly have never felt this way about people before, which only confirms what I said the other night. So, yes, what are *we* going to do?"

They all smiled at me, and I felt it through my entire body. This unconventional relationship would work because we would make it. I didn't care what others thought. I'd already lived that life, and it had been lonely and miserable. If people wanted to talk about me, point fingers, and call me names, so be it. I'd be too busy having mind-blowing orgasms to give a shit.

"The best way to get back at your mother and ex-husband is to hit them where it will hurt. It won't be enough to take what is yours. You need to make a point, an example of them in a way that will matter to them," Monroe said, meeting my eyes.

"That's an excellent point."

"I might have a suggestion that not only solves your problem but also could set the stage to get Cami back."

"I'm listening." I waited for Atticus to speak, but he looked at Monroe first.

"Mr. Miller, I believe it's only fair that you understand the possible consequences of your choice. But I can guarantee that I would never let anything happen to your son, and in fact, by joining with us, I could help you more if you allowed it. You can verify with Mr. Young how authentic my word is."

I held my breath, having not considered this. Of course, it would be bad for Monroe to be connected to the mafia. I hadn't told him anything yet, and a small part of me was probably scared he'd leave, and I would have to let him go, knowing it was the best choice for him and Levi. He held Atticus' gaze for a while before looking over at me and then Wells before returning to Atticus.

"I appreciate the honesty, Mr. Masters, and I do believe you are true to your word. I'm not naive, nor am I a stranger to the darker parts of this city, despite my outer appearance. I pride myself on making the best choices for my son and myself. And well, being with Loren and Wells is the best choice I can make. That will never not be the right decision. You have changed Wells' life, and for that, I'm grateful. You've also helped Loren and me more than most people. So, while I can assume you're not just a restaurateur, I can accept it as an accept-able risk because the rewards are worth it. *They are*," he finished, looking between Wells and me, officially making my heart swell with love for him.

"Then I'd like to first tell you my last name isn't Masters, but Mascro, and I'm the current boss of the Mascro crime family." As Atticus conveyed his story to Monroe, I leaned back into Sax, rubbing my hands up his arms. Sax had given me so much in our time that now I wanted to make sure he knew I was there for him too.

Pulling his head down, I rubbed my hand over his beard, holding him there so I could whisper. "I want to know everything about you, the good and the bad. You don't have to protect me from the truth. You've shown me parts of myself I didn't know existed, and this is what I can do for you. Please, let me." He pulled his head back a smidge, staring at me for an extended time before he nodded, kissing my forehead.

"Okay, Spitfire." He didn't need to say anything else.

When I looked back, I found the others watching me. Smiling, I sat up, but I didn't hide or feel embarrassed. "So, how are we going to use the mafia to take down my mother?" I grinned at the thought, a laugh wanting to bubble up.

"Easy, by throwing the most exclusive party at our estate in the suburbs and inviting her. We lead the rat to the cheese and then drop the trap. Never underestimate the value of good cheese, Lore." Atticus smiled at me, and it was at such odds with our conversation, I couldn't help but snort.

"And how will that help with Cami?"

"Exactly the same reason. We invite Darren to join us. And while the cat's away, we steal the mouse."

"Bro, I'm kind of worried about your obsession with rodents as your metaphors," Nicco jibed good-naturedly.

Atticus gave him a look, but I could see the tiniest tilt at the corner of his lips, and I knew it pleased him to hear Nicco call him brother. Seemed my cold-hearted Attie was melting, and I couldn't wait to see the complete transformation.

"So, when is this event?" Wells asked, surprising me.

"Sunday."

"As in *this* Sunday?" I squeaked in question, gesturing with my hands. "Two days from now?"

"Precisely."

"You're fucking insane!"

"On the contrary, I'm practically a genius," Atticus countered, only making me laugh more.

"Why does that not surprise me?" I rolled my eyes, smiling at him. "So, what now?"

"What do you mean, Spitfire?"

"Well, we dealt with my emotional wringer, made a plan for two days from now to sort out our enemies, so, what's next on the mafia agenda? World domination? Knocking some heads together? Capping some people in the knees?"

It was quiet for all of two seconds before all five men busted out into laughter. I sat back, a blush on my face, accepting the fact they thought I was funny.

In reality, I'd been mostly serious. Guess I needed to brush up on my mafia knowledge. Good thing I had three hot mafia men to teach me.

TWENTY TWO

LOREN

Kicking my foot to the floor, I closed the book I'd been trying to read for the past hour. Considering I was still on the same page, I was calling it a lost cause. I'd curled up on a chair in the library, hoping to pass the time, but I think it was time I gave up. Blowing out a breath, I looked over at the two teenagers who were sitting at a long table looking through colleges on Imogen's computer.

"Find any that interest you?" I asked, my voice disrupting the quiet that had settled around us. Fort picked his head up, instantly wanting my attention. Barkley was over by Jude as he casually scratched her as he scrolled. She'd become his shadow over the past few days, making my heart happy.

"Hmm, yeah, a few," he responded, looking up.

"Cool, just let me know what day you want to go. I'm off all week to do things with you." He smiled at me, and I knew I'd made the right call.

"Looking forward to it."

"Lor, did you know there was a music program at Jude's school?" Imogen asked excitedly.

"Yeah, I did. Timber Creek's a good school, and their music program has won a lot of prestigious awards. How's it going with convincing Attie?"

"Pretty good, I think. He told me to get the info and present it to him. That's the first time he hasn't said no, so I'm feeling hopeful." Jude hid a smile, having told me about Atticus' plan to enroll her there, and him keeping an eye on Imogen at school unbeknownst to her.

"That's great. I think I need to go for a walk or something. For once, sitting is driving me crazy. You guys okay in here?"

"Yep," they both answered, not even glancing over.

"Alright. Don't forget, Levi will be here later. Thanks for volunteering to watch him."

"It's gonna be a blast," Immy beamed, looking up this time. She was more excited than any teenager I'd ever met before about the prospect of babysitting.

"He's the cutest and a huge Potterhead. I'm sure you'll get along great."

"I can't wait."

"Be good. I'm going to explore some."

"Bye," they mumbled, already back to talking about whatever they were looking at. It made me happy to see them so excited about their futures. I couldn't fault them for not wanting to engage with an adult.

Getting up, I nodded to Elijah, who was standing outside the library. I didn't know if it was for them or me, but I had to assume the kids when he didn't follow. Sometimes, Atticus' paranoia about Jude and Immy made me chuckle, and the need to push his buttons arose just so I could watch him react.

Walking through the halls, I realized how much the past two days had been a test of my patience. At first, I'd needed the time to decompress and process everything Atticus had discovered about my medical history. Once the numbness wore off, I quickly switched to anger and had to rein in my impulsive streak to run Brian over with my car. I spent a lot of time kicking the shit out of the punching bag in the gym, at least it was cathartic.

And when Wells finished the session with an orgasm, even better.

Atticus hadn't wasted any time sending out the invitations to my parents, ex-husband, and Darren on Friday night, which might've been what made me anxious. It was difficult to sit around for two days, knowing what was to come, but it gave me more time to prepare what I would say when I saw them. The lure to give in to that dark part of myself was tempting me, just like when I'd kicked Brian in the balls. I knew I was close to the edge of falling over, and the darkness had never looked more enticing than it did right now.

I wanted revenge and justice for the things they'd done to me. I craved it like nothing I'd ever craved before.

And it wasn't just the fact they'd manipulated and lied

to me, but the years of emotional abuse and gaslighting had trapped me in my own mind, limiting me from being who I was meant to be. It was the worst kind of prison because it was so hard to escape your own self-defeating thoughts.

Nervous energy vibrated under my skin as I walked the hallway, and I didn't think punching anything would help today. We still had hours before we needed to get ready for the event, so perhaps some mischief would help. I just had to find someone in this place willing to help me out.

I'd always thought Atticus' mansion home in the city was impressive, an entire building used for his own personal needs. The estate, though, was on a whole different level. When we arrived here last night, Wells made a face stating he liked the mansion better. I kind of understood what he meant, though. Everything was grand and luxurious, but it didn't have Atticus or Immy's feel to it. If I let myself think about it, I could feel Dayton in some of the decor.

Perhaps that was why this place gave me the creeps.

It was beautiful and impressive, but there was a layer of darkness coating everything. The longer I was here, the more I could feel the menacing things that had likely occurred in these rooms. There was darkness and shadows in every corner, and it was saturated with danger—and not the good kind.

"Good morning, Mrs. Carter. Anything I can help you find?" the head of staff asked.

"Loren," I corrected with a smile, "and, no. Thank you, I'm just looking around."

She nodded, continuing on her path, but I didn't miss the disapproval in her gaze at me being able to wander wherever I wanted. Atticus had made it clear, though. While the teens were to be watched, I had free rein of the place. He'd warned me that some of the older staff might have an issue with it, but I hadn't thought anything of it. Now, I was beginning to see what he meant.

Atticus had convinced us to head to the estate Saturday night, so we would be on the premises for Sunday and not have to stress over it. Monroe was arriving at lunchtime with Levi after the supervised visit with Brittni, and then we'd all be here. It felt strange, but also like we were becoming this modge-podge family that I loved. With all the kids looked after while the grownups attended the party, it helped reduce my worry about them. Knowing they were safe made it easier to follow through with our plan to ensnare the three mice.

I just didn't think these mice were blind, not all of them, at least.

It also benefited us that the kids were on spring break since the party was taking place on a Sunday evening. It gave us time to make sure everything was safe before we returned to town with Atticus striking back against Darren. He'd broken the code, whatever that meant, but I feared what he might do in retaliation. However, I knew it needed to be done. Cami had to be rescued, or I worried I'd never see my friend again. If I let myself think about what she was going through, I'd fall into the pit of despair, and it would take a lot to pull me out this time. Too many things were occurring, and it all seemed to hinge on this party. So instead, I locked it away, compartmentalizing it until I could fall apart safely.

When I came to a long hallway with portraits on the wall, I slowed to see if I could spot one with Dayton in it. Atticus hadn't been able to locate any yet, and the one he'd been banking on using at some secret place had been mysteriously stolen. It was hard to know what to believe with all the evidence disappearing. The results of the bones were our best bet now until Dayton decided to reveal himself.

"Find anything interesting, Beautiful?"

I felt Nicco come up behind me, his arms wrapping around my waist, and I leaned back into his hold. When we got in last night, it had been late, and we'd all been shown to rooms. It had felt weird to sleep in this house alone, so I hoped that wouldn't be the case tonight.

Though, I hadn't really been alone last night, only alone in my bed.

Sax had snuck in at some point, taking guard from the chair in the corner. While I was surprised to find him there and not in my bed, I wasn't surprised to see him in my room. He'd been my shadow since Friday, and I had a feeling whatever I was dealing with had triggered something in him, causing him to grasp on tight to me. I didn't mind though, it was nice to have his reassuring presence wherever I turned, even if only in the shadows.

"Not really. I thought you were going over security with Sax?"

Nicco and Sax had worked on the security details this morning and meeting with the guards while Wells trained. It left me to my own devices since I hadn't been able to find Atticus earlier. I figured he was doing something for this evening, so I left him to it.

"We're done, and I decided I needed some time with my girlfriend."

"Oh?" I was glad my face was hidden because it definitely heated at his words. I liked that he called me his girlfriend more than I wanted to admit. It was silly, but it felt nice. He snuggled down into me, his lips brushing against my neck as he spoke.

"Will you come with me to see something?"

"Of course." I tilted my head back just enough to brush my lips against his jaw. His hands flexed on my hips at the motion, and I wanted to moan out, but I held it back, curious to see what he had to show me.

He spun me, grabbed my hand, and pulled me down the hall. When we were halfway down, another familiar face stepped out of a door. I'd need to remember how I got to this hallway because it seemed to be where all my guys were, and I'd want that knowledge for the future.

"Kitten, coming to surprise me?" Wells asked, ignoring Nicco.

"Um, no. I didn't know you were here. Nicco wants to show me something."

"Hm." He flicked his eyes over, holding Nicco's stare,

and I could've sworn I saw a flicker, but then he returned back to me with a smile. "Mind if I tag along, then?"

I looked up to Nicco, expecting him to be upset, but instead, he shrugged, his face only showing curiosity. Nicco continued to surprise me in his maturity, and I needed to remember to quit underestimating him in moments like this.

"Of course, Three. Why not." He chuckled, pulling me along. Wells rolled his eyes but cozied up to my other side.

"Number three?" I asked, confused at what it meant.

"Nothing," Wells said, but I didn't miss the smile that Nicco had on his face.

We came to a door a little of the way down, and I would've missed it if Nicco hadn't pointed it out. It practically blended into the wall, the random knob sticking out slightly, the only clue to its presence. Nicco pulled it open, gesturing for Wells to go first. I had a vision of Nicco tricking us and pushing Wells in there, only to lock the door and run. A laugh bubbled out of me, and they both looked over with curious expressions.

"Sorry, just, sorry." I shook my head, trying to stop the laughter from rising up. Wells stepped into the room, brushing up against us both as he did. Nicco hadn't moved out of the way, making the space tight for Wells' frame to make it. I bit my lip as a moan now wanted to leave me at the touch.

"Naughty minx," Nicco whispered, and I relaxed, letting my poor lip go. Winking, I followed Wells, making sure to brush my hand and maybe grab Nicco's special package as I walked in, smiling when it was him holding in a moan this time.

Once I had devious ideas out of my mind, I looked around the room and gasped at what I'd walked into. The furthest wall was all glass. Another was full of plants; flowers of all colors in bloom. The opposite wall had benches, couches, and loungers with a waterfall feature in the middle that trailed down the wall. It was calming and exotic in the same breath.

"Wow, this place is magical." My voice came out breathy, my hand hovering over my mouth as I took it in. Wells was looking out of the window, so I walked over to see what he was looking at. It looked out onto the lawn, and a green maze, like something out of *The Secret Garden*, loomed in front of me.

"This is one of my favorite rooms, and not everyone knows it's here," Nicco said, coming up and standing next to us.

"Thank you for sharing it with us," I whispered.

"Yes, thank you, Nic. I'm so glad to have intruded on this," Wells teased with a dour expression. I bumped his shoulder with mine, narrowing my eyes at him. Nicco only laughed, not caring, wrapping his arm around me.

"Well, Three, I'd planned to eat out Beautiful with the waterfall in the background, so dismiss this room all you want, but I'm betting when she screams around me, the acoustics in here will be outstanding."

I sucked in a breath, looking over at Nicco, his

flirty smile on full display. Cupping my cheek, he placed his lips on mine gently, belying his earlier statement. When a body pressed into me from behind, I moaned. Wells moved my hair out of the way, leaning closer to whisper in my ear as he nibbled.

"Oh, I think I can play this game and see whose name she screams the loudest. That's if you're up for the challenge, *Nic*?"

Nicco snorted. "I'm always *up* when Loren's around. Try to keep up."

Before I could open my eyes, Nicco had me in his arms and carried me over to the couch bed by the water. He laid me down gently, his lips sealing back to mine as my back landed on the cushions. Hands began to roam, but I couldn't keep track of whose they were as Nicco's tongue swirled with mine, and I lost myself in the sensations of his kiss. When I felt cool air, I gasped, opening my eyes to see Wells smirking down at me as he pulled my pants off.

Nicco looked over, rolled his eyes, but began to trail kisses down my abdomen in earnest. Wells moved up to my top, pushing it over my head and unclasping my bra. Once I was completely naked, they both descended on me, somehow finding a way to work in tandem.

Wells swirled his tongue around my nipple, his hot mouth making them pebble as he ravaged me. Nicco didn't hold back, apparently taking the competition seriously as he thrust his fingers in and licked up my core like a man starved. My back arched as my legs spread wider, an indecent sound leaving me.

"Yes, Beautiful, tell me how it feels."

"So good."

"If I was between her legs, she wouldn't even be able to speak," Wells teased, moving his mouth closer to mine. I cupped his cheek, opening my eyes to find him hovering over me. His eyes fluttered closed at my touch, and I melted at the vulnerability he kept showing me. Running my fingers through his hair, I brought his mouth to mine as Nicco began to suck on my clit.

Reaching my hand down, I cupped the hard length through Wells' pants, squeezing it as best I could. He pulled back from the kiss, allowing a moan to escape as Nicco continued to plunge into me. I watched as Wells shoved his pants down, freeing his erection. Licking my lips, his eyes heated as he grabbed his cock and stroked it once, rubbing the bead of cum over the tip with his thumb.

Extending my hand, I beckoned him forward, wanting to touch him. One of my hands traveled down to thread through Nicco's hair, and the other squeezed around Wells as I tried to stroke his thick cock. I was a writhing mess as they both touched me. When Nicco took it upon himself to plunge three fingers into my dripping wet pussy, I almost combusted.

"Fuck," I breathed. "Ah, yes, right there."

Just as Nicco expected, the sounds of my moans echoed around the room.

"Here, Kitten, something better for your mouth." Wells inched forward, leaning so I could take him in. Sucking the tip, I swirled my tongue, trying to focus as Nicco worked me over. Before I could take Wells further, an orgasm rocked through me, and I tried to remember not to bite down as my whole body locked up.

"Fucking hell, Nic. You did that on purpose," he hissed.

"Since you decided to make sure she couldn't scream my name, I thought I'd give you a taste of what I'm capable of." I could hear the teasing in Nicco's voice, and I smiled at their easy banter. If I got to be the one who benefited from their contest, they could battle out orgasms all they wanted to.

"Fine, my turn now." I barely registered the words before being lifted and hauled over a shoulder.

"Where are we going?" I breathed, my voice barely above a whisper.

"You'll see."

I could hear the smirk in Wells' tone as he walked a few steps and set me down on my feet. He looked at me for a second, kissing my nose before he spun me around and pressed my body up against the glass. I hissed as the cold surface met my skin. Wells' hands skated down my body, groping my ass cheeks and smoothing his hands over them. He pressed into me, leaning to whisper into my ear.

"I really want to take your ass, Kitten, but I have a feeling you're not ready for it yet. So, I'll have to get you ready for that, but right now, I want to hear you scream so loud, you fog up that window. Think you can handle that?"

"Mmhmm," I moaned, the neediness practically vibrating through me at his words.

Wells tilted my hips, my hands falling to the glass as he pulled me to an angle where he needed me. My breasts were smushed up against the surface, and the pressure felt oddly pleasant against my nipples. Leaning my head back, I peered over Wells' shoulder to find Nicco sitting close by, stroking his newly pierced cock. I still couldn't get a good view of what he'd done, but the silver was evident over the entire length, making me even more curious. He winked when he caught my eyes, and I knew he wouldn't be sitting back for long, even if Wells had tried to keep him out by positioning me where he'd have limited access.

In my eye fucking with Nicco, I'd lost track of Wells, so when he surged up in me, I audibly gasped. "Fuck."

His deep chuckle vibrated through my back, but he didn't rest long before he was pulling out and then ramming back in. His pace picked up, and I found myself pressing against the glass as he thrust into me.

"Fuck, Kitten. You're so wet. I love how nice I slide in you. I'll have to thank Nic for getting you ready for me."

"Nice try, Crash. You're the opener. *I'm* the headliner."

Wells snorted, but pulled me harder, determined to make me shout his name the loudest. "Tell me how it feels, Kitten. Let him know who's making you feel good." His hands tightened on my hips, sure to leave fingerprints there I'd feel for days. I liked the idea of that more than I wanted to admit.

"It feels… so good, Wells," I gasped. "So, good. I'm gonna…"

"Say my name louder, Kitten."

"Wells," I moaned, my eyes rolling back the instant his name left my lips. How I managed to stay standing had to be all him because my body went limp as it spasmed around his dick. Wells joined me, his cum squirting up inside me, and I felt him sag against my back, kissing my neck softly as he soothed my skin in small circles. My face was pressed against the glass, and sure enough, there was a fog print there.

"Not bad, but I think I'll do better," Nicco purred. He stood against the window next to me, not caring his dick was practically touching us or that Wells and my faces were smooshed together. He leaned in, kissing me like he had all the time in the world.

"What the fuck," Wells hissed.

I jerked back, worried he realized he couldn't do this, and I'd have to figure out how to be with them both. But when I turned, I found him staring down at Nicco's cock instead. A laugh bubbled out of me when I took in his face.

"Like what you see, *Three*?" Nicco purred.

"I…" He shook his head, looking up to meet my eyes. "*Damn*, Kitten, you get to have all the fun. I'll concede to that. I don't want my ego to be too bruised, but I'm man enough to know when I'm beat... and a little jealous."

"Never say never, Three." Nicco winked but yanked me to him, no longer wanting to go slow as he smashed his lips to mine. He backed me up until my legs touched the sofa, but he didn't lower us down.

"Feel like putting on another show?"

Nodding, I couldn't find words as Nicco spun me and sat down on the edge. He spread his legs, his cock bobbing with the move, and skated his hands up my thighs, grazing his fingers over my soaked core.

"Turn around, Beautiful."

I did as he asked, and he pulled me down, and I realized what he was doing. Bracing my hands on his thighs as I started to feel him enter me, the metal rubbing up against me. This time, since I knew the piercings were there, I could feel them even more with each brush against me. Once I was seated, he lifted my legs and moved them to drape over his, opening me up to Wells. Leaning back on his chest, I watched Wells walk forward, his thumb propped precariously on his lip as he stalked toward us.

When Nicco started to move, I fought to keep my eyes open, so I could watch the sexy man in front of me. My pussy was so wet at this point, Nicco moved in and out of me with ease. One of his hands reached up to tweak my nipple, and I wrapped my arm around his neck. When Wells was closer, I was surprised when he didn't stop, but dropped to his knees, bringing his face directly in line with my cunt.

His eyes flicked up to me, and I tried to read the emotion there as he brushed his thumb over my nub. I moaned at the touch, my eyes no longer able to stay open. Every part of me was so sensitive, it felt like a live wire with each touch.

"Yes, God, that feels so good. It all feels so amazing."

Wells took my moan as permission, and he sealed his mouth over my clit, thrusting his finger into me alongside Nicco's dick, making it even tighter.

"Fuck," I moaned. "You two are gonna kill me."

"I think he's going to kill me too," Nicco moaned into my ear, his voice husky.

Wells only hummed against me, but it was the last bit of pressure I needed, and my toes curled, my muscles tensed, and I felt the orgasm rock through my whole body as I locked up, every nerve ending exploding into a tiny million pieces.

"Ah, yes, Nicco… Wells," I screamed, along with a bunch of other nonsensical things, but I was too far gone to know, barely remembering, they wanted me to say their names.

"Shit," Nicco shouted, holding me to him as he thrust up one more time before he stuttered inside. When I finally stopped trembling, I opened my eyes, my breaths coming out in hard pants, and found Wells sitting back on his knees licking his lips with a satisfied smile on his face—a shiny face, drenched in my cum.

"I win," he said.

Sputtering, I peered up at Nicco, who looked as wrung out as me.

"Yeah, you do," Nicco agreed, laughing at the end. "Fucking hell, Three." He shook his head, laughing at the last five minutes.

"I think this is my favorite room too," I said.

"As long as we all know you screamed my name the loudest, it's my favorite too," Wells chimed in.

Laughing as I laid on Nicco's chest, I never thought I'd be lying naked with two guys who were barely friends, drenched in cum, and feel this happy.

"Fine, round 1 goes to Crash. Just means we have four more."

Sighing happy, I realized I couldn't wait for more.

Twenty Three

WELLS

The tie around my neck reminded me way too much of my past, the feeling even more suffocating now. Suits used to be as familiar to me as breathing, wearing them day in and out to a job I believed was the answer—the answer to feeling like I was enough.

In the end, the suit, nor the job, were the solution. Turns out, it took losing everything to realize I had to find that for myself.

This tie, though, was going to have to go. Yanking it off, I bent at the knees, sucking in deep breaths as I clasped it in my hand. The stupid thing had almost sent me into a panic attack. I didn't care what Atticus said; I wasn't wearing it. I couldn't risk going back to that guy who only cared about money and fortune. Not when I had Monroe and Loren.

"You okay, Wells?"

Nodding, I sucked in a few more breaths with my head between my legs before I stood, tossing the tie onto the bed. Monroe walked over, taking my hand in his and rubbing his thumb over the palm.

"You sure?"

"Yeah, I am now. I just… can't wear that. It's too…" I couldn't say the words, but Monroe understood.

"As nice as your ass looks in those pants, it is odd seeing you in a suit after all this time. I'd be lying if I didn't admit it made me think about that time too and wondering when you'd leave again."

Stepping forward, I grabbed his jaw, forcing him to look at me. "I'm sorry I put you through that Roe, truly I am. But I'm never leaving you again. Don't you get it? I love you. I've always loved you, and I'm not risking that for anything else."

I wrenched him closer, pressing my lips to his, and held the kiss there for a minute until I felt him relax. Pulling back, I searched Monroe's eyes to make sure he understood. A radiant light shone back, and I felt my whole body let the tension go as I realized he wasn't leaving either. I didn't want him to doubt me, but it didn't mean I didn't doubt myself a little still. I'd borrow his faith in me until I could trust myself.

"I love you too, Wells." I smiled, liking how it sounded coming from him.

"Good. How did Levi take coming here?"

"He was excited. Of course, I didn't tell him the mafia part, just that they were important people like the president, so there would be people here to guard them. He was able to understand it without asking too many questions. It's when he goes back to school I'll have to figure out how to keep it a secret." He rubbed my back, his hand moving naturally up and down. "How's your day been? Did your training go well this morning?"

"Yeah, it did, actually. There's another fight in a couple of weeks, and I'm feeling ready for it. Granted, that's if it's actually my weight class this time, and none of that shit is pulled."

"Sounds like if we take this guy out, then we can all relax. Shit, I still can't wrap my head around this mafia stuff. Even growing up and knowing street gangs were real, this feels so made up. But then I looked around, and all the evidence was slapping me in the face. It's just hard to accept it."

I nodded, sitting on the bed to slip on my shoes. "Believe me, if you'd been around some of the warehouses, it would be easier to believe. But I'm glad you weren't around those places. You're too good for them."

"Ah, is that your version of like, sweet talk, babe?"

Grunting, I felt a smile tug at my lips as I tied my shoe. "Sure, though I think I'm much better at dirty talk. I reminded Kitten of that today, in fact."

"Oh? Sounds like a story I need to hear."

"Nicco decided he wanted to have a contest to see who could make her scream their name the loudest. So, of course, I had to show up." I looked up, finding Roe straightening his tie in the mirror before moving his hair around to where he wanted it.

"Now, I'm really jealous I missed that. Nicco strikes

me as the type to be hiding a lot of interesting kinks. How was it, though? Being naked around another guy? Have you thought about that? That there might be orgies in our future?"

Sputtering, I stared in shock at my oldest friend, not sure where this side had come from. Standing, I walked to him, trapping him against the sink. "You surprise me every day, Roe. I'm such a fool for not realizing it sooner. If we had time, I'd show you just how happy I am to have you in my life." I kissed his neck, thrusting my hard on into him a little.

"To answer your question, it wasn't weird, actually. Maybe because it was Nicco and not the other two. Those guys have big dick energy like none other, and I don't know if I can handle being around that just yet."

Monroe chuckled, returning to finish getting ready. "You're not wrong, but I think it might be fun to watch." He lifted his eyes, meeting mine in the mirror. "You're leaving something out."

Smiling, I shook my head, forgetting how observant he was. "Nicco was definitely a surprise. He wasn't jealous, though we did have a little competition. I think he might be a little into exhibitionism based on the show he put on, but watching Loren come undone around him was actually really hot. The most surprising thing was his pierced cock. So many thoughts and feelings went through me." I rushed out the last part, hoping he wouldn't notice.

"Really? I've always wondered what possessed someone to get one, but also cringed at the thought."

"Yes, that," I agreed. "It looked painful, but at the same time, I was curious about what it felt like. The sounds Loren made make me believe it feels pretty amazing."

"Is that all?" he asked, a perspective look on his face.

I shrugged my shoulder, feeling uncertain, hating he'd heard it in my voice. Monroe spun around, facing me. "Hey, what is it? Talk to me."

"I just, I'm worried I screwed up."

"You like him, don't you?"

I looked up, searching his green eyes, the paleness constantly reminding me of mint green. "I don't know what it is, and that's what confuses me. I love you, and I know I'm headed there with Loren. I don't feel anything like that with the kid, but he intrigues me. There's this weird tension at times, like he sees something in me, a hidden compartment. But, I just, I don't want to mess this up, and I worry if in my need to win, I went too far."

Monroe moved closer, taking my face between his hands. "I can't say I'm an expert on this type of relationship we've found ourselves in. I know that I love you and Loren. But I also know love can grow, and it's not limited. I would never hold you back. I just want to be there too. Does it seem like Nicco's into you?"

Blowing out a breath, I licked my lips. "I don't know. There have been some moments where things felt tense, and I don't know if that's just natural tension or if something more is there. He's not shy or scared about sharing, and his openness confuses me, so I don't really know if it's just that or more. I uh, kind of touched his dick when it was in Loren, but it was more of an in the moment type of thing, rather than a conscious thought. Fuck, I'm already messing this up. I'm jumping to conclusions and assuming things. I'm getting ahead of myself."

"Babe, stop, don't start down this spiral of self-hatred. It's better to talk about it. That way, if the moment happens, we both know where we stand."

"So, where do we stand?"

"Honestly, the thought of you kissing him... I don't know. Maybe it would be hot, or maybe I would want to punch him, but I'd also be lying if I didn't say Loren hasn't collected herself some yummy men. I've just never thought outside of you and a woman because even that felt too far-fetched. Now, I have the pairing I've always wanted; it feels risky to want more or even consider it. But I see how happy Loren is and how nice it felt on Friday to be included in this little makeshift unit, and I can't deny how much I like being part of it. It's scary, but doesn't that mean it's worth it too? I don't think the other two are into guys, but I hope to get to know them better. I want to, at least. But I know for certain, without a shadow of a doubt, that you, Loren, Jude, and Levi, that's my family. If I can add four more people too, I'd be happy to have that. It's kind of the foster kid dream, isn't it?"

"You make it sound so much better and easy. I get all

up in my head and start to beat myself up. You're truly a good person, Roe. You make my life better just by being in it."

"Oh, Wellsy," he smiled, "you have no idea the magnetism you have or the strength you encourage in others. Let's just agree that we're both lucky, and then we can show each other later how grateful we are, preferably with Loren, if we get the chance."

"You have the best ideas." I smiled, kissing his lips and feeling better. I hadn't realized how much guilt and shame I'd been carrying around. I still didn't know how I felt about Nicco. Most of the time, he annoyed me, and then other times, I thought he understood something about me, but I didn't know what that translated to in a relationship. I'd never done one outside of the sneaking around with Roe we'd done as teens. As much as I didn't want to admit it, I was out of my league when it came to matters of the heart. I was glad I had him and Loren to show me the way, at least.

"Come on, let's go see our hot girlfriend and take down some evil villains." He grabbed my hand, pulling me out of the room.

"I like when you get commanding," I said, checking out his ass as he charged forward.

"Oh, yeah?" Monroe blushed, ducking his head a little as we stepped into the hallway. The house was full of people now, from staff and waiters working the event to the family members who were now in attendance. They eyed us with caution as we passed, not sure what our presence here meant. Atticus warned us that they might be cold toward us as outsiders, but we were protected. I saw one of the guards I'd come to like, nodding when he met my eyes. At least with Topher around, I knew no one would start anything.

We stepped into the backyard, and I caught sight of the maze off in the distance to the left, a slight smile tilting the corner of my mouth at the memory. The area we were in had been decked out with tents of food, tables, and lights all around. Flowers were spread out, speakers set up, and men and women mingled in their finest.

"You remember the plan?" Monroe whispered.

Scoffing, I nodded. "Don't let Loren out of our sight. Watch the scumbag and monster mom, and under no circumstances do we engage with dildo."

Monroe sputtered, a loud laugh escaping him and causing some guests to look over and eye us. "Shit, Wellsy, warn a man when you're gonna go and get all funny."

Laughing, I laced my fingers with his, not caring if these stuck-up people watched, and walked over to the burly giant standing stoically off to the side. Sax eyed us as we joined him, but didn't say anything. He'd been unusually quieter these past two days, and I felt something brewing within him, my own experience with self-loathing and fear recognizable in his eyes.

"You need to talk to her before it explodes on you, or worse, her. I won't pretend to know anything about you, but I know the look in your eyes. I have it at times, too. Don't let it destroy everything."

He looked over at me, his jaw tensed as his nostrils flared a little as he bit back his words. Eventually, he swallowed whatever retort he had and nodded, returning to his scanning of the crowd. We stood there with him, waiting, not wanting to interact with the others since we didn't really know them or who was friend or foe. When Nicco stepped out of the doors a moment later, I ignored the way my pulse picked up, attributing it to the Goddess who stepped through a moment later with the boss man himself.

"Fuck," Monroe whispered in awe, swallowing audibly next to me. Sax only grunted, but we were all in agreement. Loren was fucking stunning. She had on a tight white dress with a black top that was see-through to an extent. It cupped her breasts, providing a show of cleavage, and all I could think about was dripping champagne there and licking it up.

Every eye was on her as Atticus led her through the crowd, stopping for no one, only giving them a polite head nod if he saw fit. They made their way to us, and I didn't miss the way Nicco smirked at me as he went to stand next to Sax. Loren smiled when she neared, but as Atticus told her, she didn't let go of his arm, staying by his side. While it seemed Atticus had accepted us all in her life, he didn't want to announce it to the family yet when we were dealing with our enemies. Instead, he cautioned us all to keep our hands to ourselves until they were dealt with.

It was harder than I thought not to reach out to her. But at least I had Monroe, grounding me to him as his fingers squeezed mine.

Atticus waited for everyone to settle down before he started to speak, his arrival the official start to the party.

"Welcome, family. It's so good to see you all here tonight and celebrate the Mascros and the new adventures we're taking. Before I get started, though, I'd like to raise a toast to us." A staff member handed us all champagne flutes as she walked by, and Atticus waited until most of the crowd had them. He raised his glass, indicating for everyone to follow.

"To the Mascro family, may we continue to grow, sharpen our skills, and above all, rise to the top. We are family foremost, bonded by blood second, and one house above all. *We are Mascros…*"

As he finished it off, everyone joined in, and we all took a sip in celebration.

A slow clap started as everyone lowered their glass, and the crowd parted for him as he moved forward, carrying on his clapping like he was a fucking cheerleader, here to celebrate.

"Well done, little Mascro. You know, I almost believed that speech myself. But then again, I know all your secrets, so it's hard to bullshit me." Darren Delgado, the man who'd left me for dead in an alley, the man who'd set me up to take the fall for his failed scheme, the man who'd apparently been stalking Kitten, and had a fighter stab me weeks ago stood in the middle of the crowd with a Cheshire grin on his face.

The glass in my hand began to creak as I gripped it hard, the urge to walk forward and punch his fucking lights out overcoming me. It was Sax, though, who put his hand on my shoulder, giving me an imperceptible nod to cool it. Monroe squeezed my hand, and I breathed, remembering what was at stake here.

Looking at Loren and how strong she stood, I sucked in a breath, hearing her voice in my head to calm.

"Not yet, Surly."

Darren Delgado would get his due. I just had to be patient. And for once, I had the right people beside me to do it. I guess Monroe was on to something, we had become our own little unit, and I had to trust in that.

The three assholes had no idea who they were messing with.

TWENTY FOUR

LOREN

My skin pebbled in goosebumps as he walked through the crowd. Men and women parted for him, many sneering as Darren walked by, not pleased with his presence. Several others regarded him cautiously, understanding the dangerous man in their midst, and probably the most interesting were the few that seemed pleased by his arrival. I filed their faces away to share with Atticus later. It was nice having a job too, helping me stress less about what was at stake.

It also helped me not focus on Darren and the immense urge I had to kick him in the balls for thinking it was okay to use Cami as a bargaining chip.

When I'd met him on the train, I'd thought he was an attractive man. He was tall, probably around forty, and well built. He had eyes that pierced you and cheekbones most would kill for. His dark hair was slicked back now, and the effect only added to the whole evil persona he had going for him. His suit was tailored to his body, providing a menacing ensemble. Assessing him under this new light, I realized how much Darren had held back in our encounters. He'd used charisma to attempt to win me over, shielding the sinister man that was beneath. There were no attempts at hiding who he was now.

Darren was evil incarnate, and genuine fear bubbled up as I looked at him.

He continued to slow clap his way up to the front, and I scanned the crowd to see if the other two had made it yet. The staff had been given their pictures and were told to bring them straight to us, but Brian wasn't great at following directions and would attempt to find a way around an escort. It appeared, for now, we only had one threat to worry about.

Atticus' hand brushed my lower back, steadying me, and I took a deep breath to calm my nerves. My whole body had been shaking, and I needed to keep it together, or I'd faint in front of all these people. Slowly, I tilted the flute up to my mouth, pretending to take a sip. Sax had warned me not to eat or drink anything unless someone I knew had handed it to me, but the motion gave me time to collect myself.

I swear I heard a growl behind me at my action, and it made me smile, bolstering me. I wasn't alone.

Lowering the glass, I leaned in closer to Atticus, feeling his warmth along my side, and slowly turned my gaze to meet Darren's. As I expected, he was staring right at me with that stupid grin on his face. Gripping the glass, I stilled my hand from tossing it in his face. The urge was strong, but the goal was to keep him here as long as possible to give Nat and Beau ample time to get Cami out. For her sake, I'd rein in my grievances.

Atticus didn't utter a word as Darren stopped in front of us, leaving this to me. His warm pressure on my back, the slight flex of his fingers, gave me the go-ahead. We hadn't practiced this, assuming Darren would be by later, but I could roll with it.

"Darren, how nice to see you in the light of day and not surrounded by your goons attempting to kidnap me. What is it, three failed attempts? Pity." I pouted dramatically as the words left my tongue, and a sense of derealization took over me. Who was this woman? It felt odd to play this part, like an out-of-body experience, but I didn't appear to be mucking it up too bad yet.

Darren smiled wider, shaking his finger at me. "You," he started, "you were more difficult than I bargained for, gorgeous. I bet your screams are so beautiful; it's a pity I won't get to hear them. *Yet.*"

The growls behind me rose, and it sounded like we were in a bad werewolf movie with the amount of noise they made. It made me smile, though, as did Atticus' continued silence and the way his hand flexed on my back at Darren's implications. He trusted me in front of his whole family, showing me I had what it took, that I was strong enough to stand next to him.

Snorting, I shook my head, sighing. It was kind of fun acting dramatic to get a rise out of him. "That's where you're wrong, Darren. You'll never get to hear them. I only consort with worthy men. And well, from what I hear, you don't fit into that category. Now, I believe some festivities need to begin, and you're rudely interrupting. Enjoy the food, though." I waved him off, hoping I wasn't screwing up.

Atticus pulled me a little closer, and I caught a smile out of the corner of my eye. "Yes, Darren, please, enjoy some food." Then he turned his back on him, addressing the men behind us. Nicco stepped closer to me as Darren began to throw a tantrum at Atticus' dismissal.

"Fuck you, Atticus! I already have one pretty little Mascro pet. What's to say I don't add another? Where's that sister of yours? I was so looking forward to tasting her."

If he was hoping to get a reaction out of Atticus, he chose wrong, but the family around him, on the other hand, began to stiffen and circled him. Darren was arrogant if he thought walking into the lion's den by invitation meant he was immune to retaliation.

"Be careful, Darren. You're not protected here," Atticus admonished, barely glancing over his shoulder at him.

"Aren't I, though?" He crossed his arms, a smug look on his face, and I worried he was up to something. A commotion over his head caught my eye, and it seemed the last two guests had arrived.

"Always so fashionably late," I muttered as Brian and my mother were escorted toward us. It was pretty hilarious watching the two of them be brought forth like naughty children. I didn't miss the way Topher, one of the guards I'd gotten to know, held Brian's arm tighter, either. Smiling, I brought the glass up to my lips to hide behind, almost absently forgetting not to take a sip. The next second, the flute I held was pulled from me, and replaced with another.

Sax gave me a pointed look, and I smiled, his caring nature on display as he placed the other one on a tray. At least this way, I could drink without worry. That was one thing we didn't need with all the balls we juggled.

"Loren! What on earth are you wearing? You look like a common prostitute dressed that way. What's going on here? We need to talk immediately!"

Rolling my eyes, I pushed my shoulders back at the slurs my mother made. "I can't work out which bugs you more, that I look like a prostitute or a common one?"

Jacqueline seethed but didn't respond to my question. My ex-husband stood quietly, but I could see the anger rolling under his skin and the hatred he glared at me with. He was still mad about the garage debacle, no doubt, and the night he had to spend in jail.

Atticus addressed the crowd again, calling the party to begin as the food was brought out and the music started to play louder. It didn't mean eyes weren't on us still, but at least they couldn't hear our every word as they pretended to eat and socialize with the family gathered.

"Darren, I have some business to do first, so please, do eat, and I'll call for you when I'm ready."

The two guards who'd brought up Tweedledee and Tweedledum surrounded Darren, forcing him to follow, his big entrance derailed. It was kind of funny when you thought about it.

Once he was out of hearing range, Atticus gestured to the thorns in my side and directed them to a table we'd set up at the front. Walking over, Sax pulled out my chair but stayed standing behind me. Atticus had shared with me that while Sax was his trusted counsel, not everyone knew yet, and for events such as these, Sax liked to keep his role as enforcer and personal guard. It allowed him to watch and hear things better.

Nicco sat on my left, with Atticus on my right, encompassing me in a mafia-brother sandwich. Monroe and Wells sat to Nicco's left, leaving Brian and Jacqueline to sit closer to Atticus. I watched as Brian made a face before taking his seat, and I smiled, holding in a laugh at his discomfort. Hands landed on my thighs from both directions, and I smiled wider.

"Mother, it seems you and Brian have been busy. I never knew you two to be such pals. I've learned so, so much."

"I don't know what you're referring to, Loren. I don't have friends."

I held in a snort because she wasn't wrong. Jacqueline didn't see people as companions. Everyone was viewed in terms of their bank accounts and what they could provide for her life. They weren't friends, but mere commodities and doors to leverage to get her where she wanted to go. I wish I'd realized it sooner. It might've saved me a lot of grief over the fact my mother didn't seem to care about me. But she didn't care about anyone other than herself, and she didn't even try to hide it. At least not with me.

"You're right, Mother, my apologies. It seems your *business* partner and you have been busy. There, is that more accurate?"

She stiffened, but didn't say anything. I hardened my eyes as I stared her down.

"The question I'd like to know is, what were you planning to do with the contents of storage locker 8374?"

She sucked in a gasp, looking over at Brian, who gritted his teeth, but didn't speak. I didn't know if he was smart, or just that angry. When neither answered, I had to assume they wanted to know how much information I had.

My hand tightened on the table around the fork I'd picked up, and I felt Nicco pull it down, lacing his fingers with mine, rubbing his thumb over the top of my hand in a soothing gesture. I took a few seconds to count in my head, needing to keep my breathing even. It would be so easy to unleash my anger, but that was what they wanted. I could see that now. I needed to be cold and unattached to get through to them.

"Last chance to come clean." Jacqueline began to fidget but still didn't open her mouth. I didn't know if I was relieved or disappointed. They weren't trying to lie to me for once, but they also didn't deem me important enough to be honest with. There was a fine line between truth and lies, after all.

"Fine, have it your way. I'll just have to keep it to myself rather than share what I've been up to in the past two days. If you have nothing to offer, your presence is no longer needed. You might've been able to manipulate me in the past, twist things around to get what you wanted, but I'm not that person anymore. I will prosecute you to the letter of the law for the things you've stolen from me, and I will make damn sure that every one of your peers knows it, too. In fact, starting tomorrow morning, there won't be a single person in Kenilworth who doesn't know the scum you both are. But I'm not stopping with the suburbs, your names will be worthless throughout Chicago by the time I'm through." I sat back, taking in some joy at seeing my mother and ex-husband's faces turn red. "Though, now that I think about it, you've already ruined your reputation all on your own. Isn't that right, *Mother*?"

She stuck her nose up, scooting back to get up. "I came here, hoping you were willing to listen, but I see that you've let yourself become some whore for these men. No one will take you seriously, Loren. Wait until I tell your father this."

She stood, turning on her heels, but was stopped by Topher. She huffed, and he only smiled, taking her arm. Brian stood slowly too, buttoning his jacket, an evil smile on his face. I knew he was about to launch an attack. I just prayed we'd planned for it.

"Your mother owes me a significant amount of money, Loren. I have no quarrels with you. I just want what was promised. You can pay her debt for her, or more like, you should." Brian turned, waiting for me to ask. He was an expert in that particular manipulation tactic, and I hated it with everything in my body. He'd make a statement, but wouldn't finish it, leaving it hanging, so you were forced to ask him in order to find out. Rolling my eyes, I sighed, tired from this game.

"And why should I?"

"You're not the only one with new friends."

Atticus had enough, not liking the threat, and narrowed his eyes on the asshole I used to think loved me. It was clear now he only loved himself.

"I'd be careful with threatening Loren, Mr. Carter. You might not have understood the precious gem you had, but I do. More importantly, *we* do. If you come after Loren, you'll be facing all the men in her life who care for her. And we're not corporate scum that you can bully into getting what you want. I invited you here as a courtesy to give you the chance to do the right thing. If you choose to ignore that, well, that's all on you. I plan to fight you in a different way."

"You don't scare me, Mr. Mascro," Brain spat, stiffening his spine in indignation that Atticus was calling him out.

"That's too bad. I should. And well, *he* certainly should." Atticus gestured behind Brian. Sax had walked around the table, and was now glaring down at Brian, and I watched as my ex winced when he spotted Sax. But his ego was too big, and he pulled his shoulders back, acting as if he didn't care.

"Am I free to go, or will I be treated like a criminal?"

"Your purpose has already been served, so you may go, but I wouldn't go far. There will be some people visiting you in the morning. Do yourself a favor, and don't make it hard on them."

Brian sneered, but Sax clapped his hand on his shoulder, directing him out of the party.

"Are you sure this was the best play?" I asked, anxiety filling me now that they'd gone. I'd never stood up to my mother or Brian in such a public way. It was terrifying and exhilarating all at the same time.

"Definitely. They've been photographed, and they will be in the paper tomorrow. We'll hit them on multiple fronts. Socially, financially, and publicly. Their names will be mud by lunch tomorrow."

"And my father?"

He turned, looking me over. Atticus hadn't wanted to give my father a pass, but I insisted he deserved a chance. "If he went along with my associate, then he has nothing to worry about."

Nodding, I sighed, some of the anxiety leaving me that Brian and my mother were gone. I knew it wasn't over with them, but we'd shown our hand, or the part we wanted them to see, sending them running for once. Now, we just had to sit back and wait, and hopefully, they would hang themselves. If not, Atticus had an ace up his sleeve. But it was the waiting I found so difficult.

Nicco's thumb rubbed in a circle on my leg, and I turned to look at him. His smile settled me, and I leaned into his side, needing his constant reassurance.

"Two mice down, now it's time to see if our trap worked for the big cheese," Nicco whispered, kissing my temple. I giggled, his use of Atticus' metaphors making me relax. After we nibbled on some food, I looked around the table, seeing the unease, and I knew it was time to face the last obstacle.

Standing, I held hands with Atticus as we walked over to confront Darren. Except, as we headed toward him; he was no longer where we'd last seen him.

Shit, this couldn't be good. I looked over at Atticus, but instead of shock, he had a satisfied gleam in his eyes. Well, then.

TWENTY FIVE

ATTICUS

Loren tensed next to me when she didn't spot Darren, but I knew he wouldn't remain sedentary. He was too used to being the biggest dick that he believed he could get away with anything. But not this time. I didn't want to admit my father had taught me some good lessons, but my favorite was using one's own hubris against them.

And Darren was an arrogant asshole, and I'd wanted him to stray.

Everything was falling into place, and Loren had performed beautifully. I'd hoped for her to gain some power, not only among my family who were present and watching every little interaction, but also with the two people who'd made her doubt herself. I knew what it would mean for her to stand up to them, and I wanted to give her that. No amount of me telling her, pushing her, or even baiting her, would do as much for that belief than her feeling it herself.

And fuck, if it hadn't been sexy as hell to watch.

Loren continued to prove my first impressions wrong, showing me more and more she belonged with us—to us. Watching her shine made me question what I'd been scared of in the first place. I'd been the one too scared to admit it, knowing my life would forever be changed. Seemed I still had things to learn myself.

"Don't forget whose place he's at, Bellezza. Darren will do nothing here without my knowledge. I've had eyes on him the whole time. I wanted him to think he was smarter than us, only to remind him he wasn't. The children are safe."

She relaxed, squeezing my hand, and I knew that was where her first worry had gone. Loren was compassionate and protective of those she cared about, and I was glad to be included in that now.

"Let's go see what trouble Darren's gotten himself into, shall we?" I smiled, the corners of my lips tilting up. I'd almost suggested moving this setup to Climax for what I had in store for him, but then I realized I could bring the parts of the club I needed to the house and control the situation even more. I'd been working on it all morning, and I planned to make use of it later with Loren.

Nodding to Sax, I watched as he and Nicco walked ahead and turned down a hallway. Briefly, I glanced over my shoulder at the other two. "This is one of those moments where you can choose how much you want to be involved and know. Fair warning, the more you step into this life, the more dangerous it becomes. I vowed to protect you at all costs, and I meant it. But this is your choice."

I waited to see what they'd do. They looked at one another, and I watched as my fighter deferred to the golden one. I got it, Monroe had more to lose, and I respected Wells for that simple act. I hadn't been sure about him at first, but he continued to surprise me with his determination and loyalty.

"If this involves Loren, then we're all in," Goldie stated firmly.

Nodding in respect, I turned and put them out of my mind, knowing they were adults and had made their own choice. Nicco and Sax were standing guard outside a door, and I stopped again, needing to check with Loren. This would be the ultimate test in some ways if she could accept me fully. Turning, I pulled her face close to mine, cupping her cheek. Leaning in, I rested my forehead against hers.

"Are you sure you're ready for this, Bellezza? You might not like the man I become in there."

"Attie, no matter how many masks you don, you're still *you* at your core, and that's the man I've fallen for. Your darkness doesn't scare me. I've had to stare my own in the face. I'm well acquainted with the horrors of life more than you know. Whatever you have to do in that room, don't hold yourself back on my account. I'm here with you for all the good and bad. I'm not picking only parts of you, I see you, and I know your heart."

"Oh, Bellezza, I can't wait to test that theory later

when I can get you out of this dress." My heart sped up at her words, my breathing uneven as I tried to rein in the need to fuck her against this wall. My hard as steel cock pressed against the zipper, and I cursed under my breath at denying myself. Kissing her quickly, I turned and went to the place in my mind where all the dark parts of me lived.

I opened the box, letting the shadows out, and embraced them for what they were. I'd always been ashamed of these feelings for liking some of the things that Dayton had taught me. I didn't want to be like him, and to admit that anything he'd done was good or helpful felt wrong. But Loren had pulled it all out from under me, showing me I didn't need to hide.

The urge to hurl wasn't present either, and I wondered if after all these years, my aversion to lying and doing the things I couldn't stomach had been something else this whole time. With that thought, I stepped through the door, the mask of the cutthroat mafia boss firmly in place.

Dark reds and blacks filled the space we'd turned into a mock club room. I knew Darren would find it difficult to ignore the chance to snoop and leer at the attractive females I'd hired to work as the catering staff and placed in his vicinity. Except these women weren't *just* caterers.

A smile fought to creep up my face at the sight in front of me, but I managed to keep it off—barely.

The two stooges behind me, though, didn't, and I

caught the soft snort of laughter followed by a cough as they tried to curb their reactions. Peeking out of the corner of my eye, I even found Loren fighting a smile, but her profession lent her a particular ability to mask her expressions better.

I stopped in front of Darren with Loren at my side, and for the first time, I felt thrilled at not doing this alone.

Darren's glare did nothing to take away from the scene. Sax walked around to the left and Nicco to the right, flanking our sides. Emma walked over, handing me the key to the restraints, her leather getup squeaking as she moved in the nine-inch heels she wore. The two women who worked with her moved away from Darren, grabbing their clothes as they dressed.

"He's all yours, Mr. Mascro. I have video, photos, and an extra special audio recording of him crying like a little baby I'm thinking of using as my ringtone." Emma grinned wide, a maniacal smile on her face, and I knew I never wanted to piss her off. After all, she was the city's best dominatrix, and she ran a tight ship.

Loren snorted at her comment, and a rare smile threatened to spread across my face, but I kept it hidden.

"Thank you, Madam. I'll be in touch. Your fee and a generous tip have already been transferred to your accounts. You're free to stay and enjoy the party if you like."

"Always a pleasure, Mr. Mascro." She winked, eyeing Loren as she started to walk around our group. "If you ever want to get into the biz, hun, give me a call. You have the hot librarian thing going, and I bet you'd make a mean dominatrix." She stopped, looking her over and at the men around her. "But I also teach classes."

Sax growled, and I thought Loren would shrink away in embarrassment. Instead, she surprised me by looking at the woman and smiling coyly.

"Thank you, that's very kind. It's not something I'm interested in at the moment, but if that ever changes, I'll give you a call. I can tell you do great work, and it would be a privilege to learn from you. You're all beautiful, by the way, and I'm a little in awe of you, honestly." Her cheeks blushed slightly, not from embarrassment, but from arousal, and I found myself wishing for the second time in ten minutes I didn't have to deal with this scumbag.

"Ah, honey, you're a wet dream yourself. Please, do give me a call. I teach *all* kinds of classes." The two other girls nodded, smiling, before following their Madam out the door now that they were dressed. Emma had stayed in her leather pants, boots, and bustier, putting the whip back around her waist like a belt.

Bringing my eyes back to Darren, I let myself smile at the predicament he found himself in. "Oh, Darren, it sucks when you're not the smartest person in the room, doesn't it? What was it you told me? You knew my weaknesses? Thank you for reminding me that I knew yours too. And just a friendly heads up, whatever you think my weaknesses are, you're wrong. Now, it's time to have a little chat."

I clicked the remote in my pocket, a screen falling down on the side wall. It revealed a square with Ethan Rawles and his second, along with the next powerful family in the Chicago area. Brianna O'Sullivan and her second flicked onto the screen, a coy smile on her face. She'd been eager to join forces when she heard there was an opening. With Darren breaking the code, he'd inherently given up his place on our informal coalition.

He groaned against the ball gag, pulling against his restraints, but the girls had done an excellent job as they hooked him to the bed, and there wasn't any give for him to gain. I pulled the ball gag loose and backed up, not putting it past him to spit on me. As soon as it was clear, he sneered. "You're going to regret this, little Mascro. You have no idea who you're messing with."

"Oh, that's where you're wrong, Darren. You'll do nothing to me because I have everything recorded like Madame Emma said. While that won't do much to hurt you, it will damage your reputation and let your family members know just how much you like... this." I motioned my fingers, looking him up and down, trying not to laugh before I brought my eyes back up. "Now, I'm all for people exploring their kinks and the freedom to like whatever they want, but I don't think your family, the one you've built on being the biggest male asshole, will understand your need to wear a diaper and be called 'little boy blue' now will they?"

"My family doesn't care."

"Well, that's good for you then. I'm glad to hear the Delgados have embraced inclusivity in their ranks. But here's the problem I have. You took something from me and didn't hold up your end of the agreement, breaking the brotherhood code. That doesn't even get into the way you disrespected my family with the heinous actions you committed against my sister, your attempts to take Mrs. Carter, and the audacity you had to rig *my* fight against *my* headliner. So, how I see it, you owe me a pound of flesh now. That's not even getting into you working with my father or killing Jaz. You've been walking around like you had no impunity for too long. It stops here."

He laughed, but I could see fear creeping into his eyes for once as he flicked them over to the screen. When he caught sight of both guests, he tensed but didn't drop his sneer. The fear in his eyes couldn't be ignored, and it fed the monster in me that wanted to make him pay for everything right here, right now.

But I had to play the long game, which meant being smart about this. I still needed him to lead me to whoever was impersonating my father.

"You can't touch me, Atticus. You don't think my family knows I'm here? You were the stupid one if you thought inviting me to your own family party meant you could take me out. Your guests there won't do anything either if they want to remain where they are."

"Oh, I'm not going to take you out here, Darren. What would be the fun in that? This wasn't even a challenge. You fell for every trap I placed, and it really makes me wonder just who's in charge. I know you've had to have killed your father by now, or perhaps have him locked up somewhere. And since I've killed my father, who you were colluding with, it makes me question who you're hiding behind now?"

I watched his face closely for any sign. There was a slight widening of his eyes, a tightness in his smile, but otherwise, he held his composure. But there *was* someone, I just didn't know who, yet.

"You sure about that, Atticus?" He attempted to roll his eyes, but I caught the quiver. Whoever it was, Darren was scared of them.

"Keep your secrets, for now, Darren. I will uncover them, though. But we do have matters to discuss. You broke the code and the penalty for that is to lose your standing in our circle. I've asked the Rawles and the next powerful family to be here as witnesses and to vote on your fate."

He glared, but had nothing else to say, knowing he couldn't get out of this. "Do you deny you kidnapped my cousin, sent me her finger, and then broke your agreement to return her to me?"

Darren continued to stay silent, so I moved forward. "Answer me!" I shouted, my anger rising as I thought about all the heinous things he'd done to Imogen.

"*No.*"

It was all I needed, so I stepped back, straightening my tie. Loren grabbed my hand, and I instantly felt grounded. "Then with the Rawles and O'Sullivans as my witnesses, I hereby dethrone you as the second most powerful family and all the benefits that garnered you. As head of the Chicago crime family coalition, I move to make the Rawles seat number two, and promote the O'Sullivans to seat three. You will be able to petition for your place in five years as per the guidelines on the brotherhood code."

"You'll regret this, little Mascro," he sneered, pure hatred in his eyes.

"No, I don't think I will. We might be mobsters, Darren, but it doesn't mean we live in chaos. You willingly broke one of our most basic codes. You dug your grave. I just hope your family understands."

I felt the vibration in my pocket, and I glanced over at Sax. He read his phone, his shoulders relaxing, and looked up, giving me one nod. Turning back to the grown-ass man in his nappy with a rattle, I exhaled even more.

"I've taken back what is mine, and if you attempt to retaliate for any reason, then I'll release this footage, and you'll find out how forgiving your family is on top of losing their clout. I'm not stupid, Darren. I know a war is coming, and this is only the opening shot, but I think it's time you understood you weren't the biggest threat. You'll do well to remember that."

I dropped the key onto the bed out of his reach, nodding to the screen, and headed out of the room. I bowed my head to the two guards at the door, indicating for them to enter. I'd given them strict instructions earlier to not help him out of the cuffs, but once he was free, to escort him off the property and make sure he didn't talk to anyone or touch anything.

Once we were free of the room, I sighed and stepped into a secondary office, the others following. "We can take a few minutes to gather ourselves, and then we need to go and mingle. Loren, I want to introduce you to some of the more important family members."

"Attie," she whispered, stepping toward me. Her arms trailed up my chest, pulling me toward her by the lapels of my jacket. "Take a minute and just relax. You were amazing back there, but I know stepping into that role takes a toll. So take a minute, and just be here with me."

I looked down at her, and I let myself do what she asked. Her eyes were full of acceptance, and I realized what I'd been worried the most about—her leaving. But she wasn't; she understood that part of me and wasn't running away.

"God, you're perfect for me, Bellezza. I'm so sorry I didn't see it sooner and all the pain I caused us. I was an idiot. You belong with me."

"It's okay. I think we both needed it, to fight for something to show us we're still alive and not just a frozen statue of ourselves."

Kissing her softly, I ignored the others and the noises of protests they made at my words. I didn't care. Loren was mine, and they'd have to get over it. They could be in her life, but it didn't mean I had to acknowledge it when it was her and me. The possessive asshole in me wouldn't allow it. This was how I was handling it, and I needed it for now.

Taking a few breaths, I felt myself relax more, the tension leaking from my body. Blowing out a breath, I nodded. "Thank you. Ready?"

"Yeah. Just one thing?"

"Anything, Bellezza."

"Cami and Nat, are they safe?"

I smiled, rubbing my thumb across her cheek. "Yes, they're on their way to the safe house now. Give them a few days and then I'll set up a video call."

"Oh, thank goodness they're safe. Yes, I'd love to see her. I guess we shall go mingle, now."

Loren smiled wide, happiness radiating off her as she linked our hands together and pulled us from the room. Sax nodded that the guards were with Darren and the children were safe, the last of my tension leaving me.

I'd been confident in my plan, but there had been a small voice whispering it wouldn't work, and I was a fool for doing it this way, not killing Darren right here. Shoving the hand that was shaking as the adrenaline left my body into my pants, I straightened my spine and walked with Loren back into the crowd. I'd needed this win, and it felt nice to come out ahead for once.

This was the feeling I wanted to capture and keep in a bottle—family, acceptance, and peace.

ON CAMERA, I watched Brian and Jacqueline be served with court papers. Brian thought he could buy his way out of his part in everything, but he still had sins of his own to pay for. He slammed the door in the courier's face, and a vindictive smile spread over mine. Jacqueline hadn't been as dramatic, but her reaction to the news reporters at her door was more entertaining.

From the newspaper to every little magazine she subscribed to, I had her face plastered with the words, *"Scandal shakes North Shore."* There was nowhere for her to run, nowhere to hide, and no one to bail her out of the mess she'd found herself in. She was penniless, a social pariah, and disgraced beyond measure. It was more fitting than death for the woman who'd abused Loren for years.

It didn't mean I wouldn't take the chance if it presented itself. The urge to run her over with my car was there, but I didn't hate any of my vehicles that much.

Picking up my phone, I found myself smiling for once at all the messages. It felt good to be on top.

Ethan: We've secured his territory and I've
divided it up with O'Sullivan. Delgado's name is
trash. Good job, Mascro.

Beau: Doc has looked over Camila and has her on some IV's. Some abrasions and scrapes, but nothing else major. He suggested PT for her finger. Camila has some info she'd like to discuss with you.

555-3958: Papers delivered. Father willing to meet. He was surprisingly agreeable.

Bellezza: Good morning, handsome one.

Staring at her picture, I let myself hope for a future. It was within my grasp as our enemies fell one by one.

TWENTY SIX

LOREN

The breeze cooled my face, and I closed my eyes for a second as I breathed it in, enjoying being outside at this time of day on a Thursday. I was beginning to think spring was a booster shot for the soul. It came in, shook out the cobwebs, and made you want to get up and move, to be out in it and explore. There really was something significant about seasonal depression.

Though, to be fair, the past two years, I'd been all-season-depressed and was only now able to appreciate the beauty that was spring.

The feet approaching behind me broke my reverie, and I blinked open my eyes and turned to find Sax. I'd known he was there for a while, but I'd waited until he was ready to show himself.

"Hey," I greeted, smiling at him.

He didn't say anything, but moved closer to me, and I took his hand. Sax had been different the past few days, but I knew it wasn't about me, or at least not in the way I'd assumed at first. He'd closed himself off a little, but not in our connection. Sax still touched me, kissed me, and watched me. I didn't doubt his feelings for me. This was something to do with him and his past, and I'd tried to wait it out.

The therapist in me was struggling to not manage his feelings for him, to make this better however I could. But that was a trap I was trying not to fall into anymore. I couldn't be his emotional life preserver, but I could be there with him as he tried to figure it out. It was just hard to remind myself of that. But if ten years of marriage had taught me anything, it was that I had a tendency to want to save people, or fix them, when they only needed me to hold their hand.

So, here I was, holding his hand and reminding him I was here.

Leaning into him, he wrapped his arm around me, and I laid my head on his chest. We stood like that for a while, just looking out at the park as Jude played with the dogs. It was carefree and peaceful.

We'd been back in the city for four days, and I missed the feeling we had at the estate. I didn't necessarily miss the estate, that place had too many dark secrets, but I missed us all being together. It had been nice to feel like a unit, a real family, and I missed being able to walk into any room and find one of my guys or the kids. There had been so much laughter and companionship that now everything felt emptier.

"Spitfire, I was wondering if we could go on a date?"

Smiling, I nodded, tilting my head to look up, his tall

frame making me crane my neck. "I'd like that a lot, Sax. When were you thinking?"

"Tonight?"

"It just so happens, I'm free."

I felt him relax, and a rare smile graced his lips before he pulled me closer. Leaning down, he kissed my forehead, lingering there for a moment. I didn't miss how unsure he'd sounded or how much I missed his confidence and dirty talk. Whatever he was dealing with was bigger than those things, and I knew Sax needed to do this in his own way to find his way back to who he was.

"When are you heading to the campus?" he asked.

Looking at my watch, I knew it was soon. "Probably in about ten minutes. We're gonna grab lunch at a place near the campus, and he has an interview with someone at 1 pm. I should be home no later than 4 pm, though."

Sax brushed my hair back, his thumb staying on my cheek. "I have some things to do today, so Beau will accompany you. I'll pick you up at 6 pm."

"Okay, I'll be ready."

"Wear something casual. Pants will be better for the bike."

"Oh? I get to ride again?" He smiled and then dipped down to kiss my lips. It was brief, but I felt his emotions all the way down to my toes.

Sax pulled back, staring at me for a second before letting go, and turned to head around the building. I missed the warmth he'd brought me with his presence immediately. That man was dangerous, but in all the best ways.

Taking a deep breath, I slowed my racing heart and squelched my hormones as I walked closer to Jude. Fort saw me and barreled toward me. Wells had gone over a few commands for me to work with the dogs on, so I snapped my fingers and pointed where he was to stop. "*Hup.*" Fort's legs scrambled under him as he tried to slow his momentum and right himself to follow. It wasn't perfect, but it was an improvement, so I bent down, scratching his head.

"That's a good boy." His dog pants in my face told me he was pleased, and I gave a treat as I clipped his leash on.

"You ready?" I asked Jude as I stood. He already had Barkley leashed and was walking toward us.

"Yep." He smiled wide at me, and we both headed back to the apartment to grab our things and drop the dogs off with Monroe. They weren't great at being alone yet in a condo for an extended period of time, so thankfully, Monroe and Levi were going to spend some time with them. He also had a few days off to spend with Levi and deal with Brittni's case. The beginning of the week had been heavy dealing with our families, so I was glad to have this time with Jude.

We walked back out of the condo within fifteen minutes, waving bye to George as we started our journey, cameras in tow.

"So, we have a little over an hour before we need to

eat. Do you want to head to campus and shoot some film there, or just take shots as we go along?" I asked.

"Let's keep it relaxed and just shoot things we see as we head there. You never know what might inspire you."

"Spoken like a true artist." I bumped my shoulder into him, smiling. Jude's face blushed, and he ducked his head. "We haven't gotten a chance to talk much since we got back to the condo about things, but how are you doing with… you know, everything?"

Jude snorted, laughing at how I'd phrased it. "You've never asked me about my past much, but I didn't grow up in the best of circumstances even before my parents died. I'm honestly not even sure if the story Cameron told me is true, and I wouldn't put it past him to lie to try to save me. He was a good brother to me back then, always trying to protect me. But we lived on the streets, and I saw things that I'd hoped to be able to forget one day, but I don't know. It's something that stays with you no matter how much you try."

We kept walking as he talked, moving around pedestrians, and I looped my arm with his, needing to comfort him in some way. As we stopped for the train we needed, he turned to look at me.

"Foster care wasn't necessarily safe either. It's why the center was so important to me. It gave me a place to be that wasn't the streets or home. I don't fault Cameron for falling into whatever mess he did. I'm sure he saw it as an opportunity to get himself out of the dark hole our life had become. I don't want to follow him, though, and that's where I'm glad I met you. My life has opened up to all these possibilities, and it feels like I have a real chance at changing the course I was on."

I squeezed his arm, trying to hold the tears back. "I'm glad to hear that, Jude. It's all I wanted for you."

"But," he started, smiling at me.

"Sorry, sorry, I interrupted your big speech."

"Yes, yes you did."

Laughing, I mimed, zipping my mouth.

"But that's not the only, or the most important thing, Lor. You gave me a chance to be part of something I only read about in books. Being a misfit penguin with you is the dream I was too scared to have. In addition to that, I now get to meet and know all these genuine and fierce people. They might be a little scary to some, but I've looked darkness in the face, I've seen true evil, and no matter how many muscles Sax has, it doesn't change who he is. Besides, if the Mascros were the actual villains, then I wouldn't let you anywhere near them, and it would be no contest who my new daddy would be."

Sputtering, I felt my face redden as I tried to make sense of what he had just said. The smirk on his face conveyed everything I needed to know. "Why, you little punk!" Laughing, he ducked out of my reach as he stepped onto the train and avoided my slap. Beau stepped on behind us, and I smiled, forgetting he was there. He dipped his head but stayed near the door as Jude, and I settled on the seats.

"Monroe, right?" I whispered conspiratorially. "Wait," I turned, a realization forming in my mind. "Did you say something to one of the guys? What do you think about me dating all of them, anyway?" I rushed out.

Jude snorted, shaking his head at my flustered state. "I like them. They make you happy and can keep you safe. And yeah, I joked with Nicco that he was in third place after Roe and Sax, and only because the big man scared me," he whispered.

"So that must be why Nicco referred to Wells as number three. Can they move up or down?"

"Oh definitely, it's kind of become this little game I play with them to push their buttons. Nicco seems to be the most invested. I told him Wells moved up because of the dogs."

"Do me a favor, don't tell them I know. I can have some fun with this." Laughing together, we colluded the rest of the train ride on how we could poke fun at the men. Beau leaned down and whispered something to Jude when we stepped off the train. He about choked on his laughter but nodded, doing a fist bump with him.

Oh man, I had a feeling this was going to land me in trouble, but I loved seeing Jude forming relationships with the people who had become important in my life as well.

As we made our way to campus, we stopped and took photos of things. Jude was a lot more advanced than me and talked about the composition, juxtaposition, and perspective. Me, on the other hand, I just took pictures of things I thought were pretty. I liked seeing him in his element, though, and I wanted to cultivate his passion, so he never lost it like I had been forced to.

"Oh wow, this is delicious. You gotta try this, Jude." I gestured to the fried macaroni and cheese ball I'd just taken a bite out of. We were trying out some new food truck goodies that we'd scoped out, and so far, it was living up to the hype.

"Oh man, those are incredible. Here, try this." Jude shoved over some street tacos, and I grabbed one, almost moaning as the flavor exploded on my tongue.

"I don't know what's my favorite. It's all been so good. Beau, what do you think?"

I'd finally been able to convince him to sit with us and eat despite his insistence to stay back. "I think I vote for the BBQ. You can't find chicken like that just anywhere."

"Mmm, yeah, that's true. I'm glad we just got a bunch of things. I'm finding I don't like to choose."

Jude snorted, but I ignored him. Well, I did for all of two seconds before I stuck my tongue out. Laughing, I looked down at the time and realized we needed to go.

"Shoot, Jude. Your appointment is soon. We need to head over there."

The three of us quickly gathered our food and drinks, tossing the trash into the can as we waddled our way toward the stone building. Once inside, I nodded to Beau that I would head to the bathroom and for him to stay with Jude. He didn't like it but finally agreed and waited outside the door to the room he was in.

Reliving myself, I sighed, zipping my pants and hurrying to the sink to wash my hands. The sight of my flushed cheeks, windblown hair, and bright eyes stopped me. Each time I looked into the mirror, it felt like I'd found a new version of myself. Squaring my shoulders, I tossed the paper towel into the trash and headed out the door, feeling strong and confident.

I nodded to Beau when I spotted him, headed in his direction. My phone began to ring, and I stopped to pull it free from my bag. When I saw the caller, I motioned I'd be outside. He scowled at me, but I'd seen scarier glances from Sax and Atticus, so he did nothing to thwart me from my mission.

Once I was free of the doors, I answered. "Cami, oh my God, girl. Are you okay?"

"Hey, Lor. It's good to hear your voice," she wheezed, and my heart broke for her.

"Where are you?"

"I'm safe. Atticus has us at a secure location. I'm here with Nat, Lily, and Nat's mom. I just wanted to thank you." Her voice was so soft, and unlike Cami, it had me shaking my head. Sitting down on the bench near the door, I tried to press the phone to my ear more so I could hear her better.

"Thank me? I didn't do anything. I'm just glad Beau and Nat got to you in time."

"Hmph, well, I disagree. You deserve all the thanks

girl. I know you played a part in distracting Darren, and it just, well it means a lot to me."

"You're my friend; of course, I'd do whatever it took to help you."

"I'm glad I met you and have a friend like you."

"Oh, Cams, I know this must've been an ordeal, and you're probably not in the space to talk about it yet, but I'm here for you when you're ready. I won't even charge you my fee," I teased.

Cami chuckled, the sound coming out with half her usual exuberance, but it was still nice to hear some of her cheer back. "That's so kind of you. But seriously, I'd love that. I know I can't hide from it, but yeah, right now, I just want to heal and head back to Lark and Seb as soon as it's safe."

"Tell me more about them."

Cami sighed dreamily, and she told me how they'd met and became a triad. I wanted to ask how Darren had fit into that, but I knew it wasn't the time. Yet.

"Well, as soon as you're ready for visitors, let me know, and I'll stop by. I'm off this week to spend time with Jude, but he's playing hockey with Monroe one day and doing something with Immy another, so I have some free time."

"I'll hold you to it. It'd be nice to see your face. I love Nat, but she's momma birding me so much, I might try to make a break for it. Not to mention, I need to hear the scoop on all things 'Loren has a harem' because don't think I didn't hear all about that."

Laughing, I shook my head, despite her not being able to see it. "Is that what we're calling it? I think it needs a better name, but I'll gladly share all the deets. Rest up and let me know when you're ready for a visitor. I'm glad you're back, Cams."

"Me too, Lor. Me too."

We hung up, and I sat back on the bench, settling on to it. It had been good to hear from her, but it didn't make my worry go away. There were so many balls in the air. I honestly had no clue how Atticus kept them all straight. When his name showed up, I answered it, surprised to find it was a video call.

His face filled the screen, and he gave me one of his disapproving eyebrows. "Three," was the only thing he said before the phone clicked off. I sat there stunned, confused at what his numbers kept meaning. Though, I was a little worried, a smidge angry, and a whole heap of turned on from it.

Well, fuck. That could only mean one thing. I was in trouble.

TWENTY SEVEN

SAX

I stared across the table at the twerp, but it did nothing to quell the anger surging in me. No, that wasn't quite right—the fear and anxiety. It had been a crippling realization last Friday that I was too happy.

When Atticus called to tell me what he'd discovered, it hit me that I'd only been kidding myself. Even with the other guys in the relationship, I was beginning to wonder if I could make her happy; if I would be enough. She'd get tired of me eventually, and the allure of dating a giant, bearded, and perverted mute wouldn't be fun anymore.

Grinding my teeth, I slapped the table, the kid sputtering in surprise, but it still wasn't enough. I needed to punch something, and he just wasn't cutting it. Violently, I shoved away from the table, the screech of the chair across the floor ringing out as thoughts swirled in my head.

I wasn't enough.

In fact, I knew I wasn't, not on my own. But was I

holding on to false hope that I could be with the others? Or was that a deluded fantasy as well?

I was too damaged. That was the reality.

Hearing Brian had hurt Loren and violated her in such a horrific way, had made me want to run out and kill him. I didn't even question it. It popped into my head, and I was halfway to the door before I realized it and stopped all thoughts of murder.

Picturing what Loren would think of me when she heard, how my spitfire might look at me differently, had frozen me in indecision. This need inside me, this thirst to make the people who hurt her pay, couldn't be extinguished, and nothing short of vengeance would satisfy it.

It was the inevitable look of disgust on her face that halted my actions.

So, I'd rushed over, held her close, and watched over her as much as I could. But the pain didn't go away. The fear and the panic only intensified, and the monster inside me grew. I'd lose her.

Glaring at Cameron as I leaned against the table, towering over him, I tried to pry the location out of him through sheer will. Unfortunately, it didn't seem to work and only made him hiccup louder, his snotty nose and tear-streaked face a disgusting sight. He clearly wasn't as important as he thought, the mere fact he had no interrogation training a dead giveaway.

Pushing off from the table, I stomped out of the room, slamming the door behind me as he cried louder. The sound of my stomps echoed around the warehouse with each step, giving a fair warning to my mood. A few guys nodded, but I ignored them; nothing but the assholes who deemed it okay to hurt Loren, and my quest to not become the monster living in me occupied my mind.

Images of how upset she'd been swirled through my head, reinforcing my need to take care of them. If they were gone, they couldn't hurt her anymore, and I began to think I would rather that be the possibility than lose her due to my own choices.

This way, I could be prepared for it. If I was going to lose her, I'd rather it be by me than someone deciding to take her away. At least through my own actions, I could mitigate the damage if I took out all the things that could harm her.

Pulling that string, though, felt like defeat, and I was slowly losing control. I could feel the edges of reality slipping, and soon I would either succumb to the desire to rain down my own form of justice, or I'd crack under pressure.

I couldn't afford to do either. Something had to change.

Right now, finding information was something I could handle. Ignoring everything, I headed to the next cell. Time to see if Mason was willing to play.

Wrenching open the door, I watched his smug face spread wide as he took in my pissed-off demeanor. He really should've learned by now not to play with fire. Walking up, I pulled back my fist and punched him, finally finding something to mete out my rage. Unfortunately, while it felt good, my punch might've been a little overkill, considering I punched him unconscious.

"Well, fuck," I muttered, turning to leave.

Locking the door behind me, I leaned back against it and sighed.

Topher looked at me, giving me a long look but keeping his thoughts to himself. When I couldn't take it anymore, I snapped.

"What?"

"Nothing, man." He held his hands up in a placating gesture, only pissing me off more.

"Don't say nothing! You've been looking at me so close; it's like you're trying to see what size boxers I wear!" I glared at him, lifting my eyebrow. I caught the small corner of his lip twitch, and some of my anger quelled. "What's on your mind, Topher? Spit it out, already."

"It's just," he started, swallowing as he met my eyes. "I think you're running from the wrong thing and looking for something to make sense when it's not going to."

Fire burned inside of me, and I glared at him. "And, just what do you know?"

"I know I've been in this family for a long time and that Loren is the first person to come into it and make all of you hardened mafia men smile. I know that unspeakable things happened to our princess, but I see her laughing and blooming into the beautiful woman she is now. I see our family prospering for the first time in years. I see a family who had started to hate what it meant to be a Mascro stepping up and taking pride in the name. I see all these things. And I see you on the brink of losing it all because you can't handle your feelings."

I deflated at his answer, my whole body sagging against the door like a wilted flower. Slowly, I looked up, finding him watching me.

"But what if I lose it all?"

The fear inside me escaped, and I asked the first honest question. It wasn't that I was damaged or not good enough; those were just easy excuses to take away the responsibility of having to own up to my choices. And those scared me. I didn't know how to live in this ambiguity. I didn't know how to handle not having control and caring about someone so good.

Topher watched me as I debated with myself, before finally lifting one shoulder. "What if you do? Nothing in life is guaranteed, man. You know that more than anyone. Every day could be our last. Our lives are dangerous, and that's the truth. Every second is a hair fracture away from being in our favor or not. It doesn't mean that you shouldn't live it to the fullest. If you live in fear of what you're going to lose, you never appreciate what you have. Life's about a culmination of moments. Don't miss out on them because they're not perfect, or you're worried it could all go away tomorrow. That's what makes them perfect to me. The futility of life is a gift that should be cherished, not feared."

"When did you become so wise?"

He shrugged that one shoulder again, a small smile on his face. "Standing against walls gives someone a lot of time to think."

Snorting, I nodded in acknowledgment of what he said and made my way out of the warehouse. Topher was right about the family. They had changed in so many small ways. Even the reality that we had prisoners was a change. The Reaper would've just killed them. But thankfully, Atticus had a better mind and knew they could be useful. So he kept them.

Though, the same couldn't be said for his uncle. He was too polished, too seasoned, and it would've taken a long time to break him—time we didn't have.

It was also a risk we couldn't afford. His silver tongue and promises of fortunes could sway anyone, and he would've escaped. That wasn't a risk worth it. So, Joel, Mason, and Cameron occupied cells, and Uncle Seth had met a different fate.

Stepping out into the sun, I blinked as my eyes adjusted to the brightness. Tilting my head up, I stood still, feeling the warmth on my face. I tried to remember that good things could happen without something bad happening around the corner. Loren had taught me that, and I needed to honor her knowledge and expertise, even if it was out of my comfort zone.

Slinging my leg over my bike, I revved the engine as

I tossed on my helmet and skidded out of the warehouse lot. Without even thinking about it, I found my way to Pops, inwardly knowing he was the one I needed to see. Pops understood me, this life, and had a way of saying things that resonated. He'd be able to straighten my head or at least point me in the right direction.

The bell over the door jingled as I walked in, a few of the guys nodded when they saw me. I kept walking, not in the mood for chitchat. Though, to be fair, I never was unless it was Loren. I'd listen to her read the fucking obituaries and still want to hear more.

And therein lay my problem. Loren was my whole world, and I didn't know how to function anymore. I would get someone killed if I didn't find a way out of this mind trap I'd found myself a prisoner of.

"Saxon Wessex, you look like someone stole your favorite bike, but since I heard that beast a mile away, that can't be it. Sit, tell me what's troubling you, son."

With a large exhale, I folded my large frame down into his tiny chair and felt the weight of everything lift slightly. Pops had been the right call. Rubbing my hands on my thighs, I clenched my fingers back into fists, lifting my head.

"For the first time since I was a little boy, I'm scared, Pops. I'm so fucking scared, and I don't know what to do about it."

The words fell effortlessly from my tongue, and when I lifted my head to meet his eyes, I expected to find a grim look; instead, I found a smile on Pop's weathered face.

"It's about time you opened yourself up to someone."

"That's all you have to say? I came here for help!"

Pops snorted, shaking his head. The pen he had in his left hand flipped over as he tapped it against the desk. "You have the answer, son. You don't need me to tell you."

"Wow, and here I thought you'd be some form of emotional comfort." Huffing, I slouched back, the chair creaking beneath me. Pops laughed louder, and I regretted coming here. I leveled him with a deadly stare, and he finally held his hands up, calming himself.

"Sorry, it's just so reminiscent of me. I can't help but find humor in it now."

Sitting up, I leaned forward on my thighs. "What did you do, then? Tell me."

He sighed, looking at me with a look of nostalgia. "What's your heart telling you, boy?"

"To run away with her and lock her in a tower," I growled. He gave me a look, not accepting my answer, but I held onto it, not budging.

"And how do things feel when they're trapped?"

"Safe."

Pops rolled his eyes. "Dangerous chaos. If you lock away the beautiful creature who has captured your heart, you'll ruin everything beautiful about her and create something neither of you will be happy with. Fear is unavoidable."

Slamming my fist on the desk, I didn't miss the fact he didn't even flinch. "So everyone keeps telling me, but I find that unacceptable. I can't do nothing. I can't."

"You're smarter than this, Saxon. You're so used to protecting everyone else that you've forgotten how to enjoy life. Your beautiful flower might be safely locked away, but she'll wilt right before your eyes. You'd do more damage than anything in this life ever could. Do not fear the bee; fear the honey drying up. Without the bee, we can't appreciate the sweetness the honey has to offer. Don't limit yourself, Saxon. The bee is more scared of you than you should ever be of him."

It was on my tongue to protest, but somehow the way he said it washed over me, soothing away the anxiety and settling into every fiber of my being. Topher's words mixed in as well, and I knew I was making this bigger than it needed to be.

Taking a breath, I exhaled slowly, meeting his eyes. A look of pride shone in his, a soft smile on his face. I'd never known my father, and Dayton hadn't been the man I thought he was, but Pops, he looked at me like I'd done something right, and that felt nice.

"Okay, old man. I'll take what you said to heart. Thank you."

"I'm always an open ear for you, Saxon, you know this. Now, tell me more about this woman who's tamed you."

Laughing, I shook my head, a huge smile coming over my face. Over the next thirty minutes, I told Pops all about Loren, Jude, and the men who'd somehow managed to become part of our family in the past month.

"You know, that's what the mafia was meant to be before it became the criminal underground. *Family*. It's not as crazy as you think that you've found yourself in this type of relationship. If she's as magnificent as you say, and I have no doubt about that, then it bears to reason Atticus and others would take notice too. It's smart. A woman in the mafia has a harder path ahead of her, but with all of you… she'll blossom into the mafia queen our family needs. I thought at one time that Shayna would be that, but that was before Dayton got his paws on her."

He sighed, shaking his head, but I didn't miss what he said. Sitting up straighter, I placed my forearms on the desk, staring straight at him.

"Tell me everything you know about Shayna Costa."

Pops smiled like he was happy I'd finally asked the right question. When I left his shop an hour later, my heart felt better, but my mind swirled with everything I'd just learned, and I wondered if some secrets were better staying buried.

But Atticus and I didn't work that way; no matter how hard it might be to hear, he deserved to know. I just wished I wasn't the one having to tell him.

TWENTY EIGHT

LOREN

Knocking on the door, I swallowed before entering, taking a moment. A mix of apprehension and excitement warred in my stomach at what could lay beyond the threshold. Turning the knob, my heart rate picked up, and I pushed my shoulders back as I stepped through.

Atticus' eyes burned through me, lighting a fire within. I didn't miss how he trailed them over every inch of my body. I didn't miss how his nostrils flared or how his pupils seemed to grow in size. But I especially didn't miss how he gripped the arms of his desk chair, the wood creaking under the pressure.

Unsurprisingly, when Jude had finished his interview, Beau informed us that Atticus had invited us over to the house for dinner. I heard the invitation for what it was, though—an order. It didn't matter that I had plans with Sax, Atticus called and we ran.

The darker part of me that had been activated meeting these men wanted to rebel and decline the carefully worded invitation and ride off into the sunset on Sax's bike. Jude's excitement about seeing Immy and my own need to see the others won out in the end.

Which meant I had to push buttons another way. I was starting to wonder if I had a bratty side or if years of suppressed rage had bubbled up, needing an escape. Whatever the cause, it had me standing at Atticus' office door wearing his dress shirt, tie, and nothing else.

It had been an impulsive decision I made on my way here, sneaking into his room to grab the items and then ducking into the bathroom to change. I'd purposefully avoided looking at the guards, hoping if I didn't know who they were, I wouldn't feel embarrassed later when I met their eyes.

Denial? Perhaps, but it was the best I had at the moment.

Stepping in, I shut the door, turning the lock. My eyes never left him, and I watched as he swallowed, scooting his chair back.

"Bellezza," he growled, lighting every nerve ending in my body.

As casually as I could, I walked forward, bypassing the chair I usually sat in, and walked around to his desk. My heart was dangerously close to leaving my chest at how hard it pumped, but I stayed the course.

"Yes, Attie?" I cooed, batting my eyelashes. I ran my fingers over the silk tie I wore, drawing his eyes down at the movement. I made it around the edge of his desk, pushing myself to not stop. Moving his chair, I caught the smirk filling his face as he watched me hungrily. He didn't block me, giving me the courage to continue.

Once the chair was pushed far enough from the desk, I perched myself on the edge in front of him.

"The baser part of me wants to ravage you right now on this desk."

"But?" I asked, hearing it in his voice.

"The logical part of me knows I have a business call in twenty minutes, and in no way would I be finished by then. You're a fine course, Bellezza, and should always be given the proper respect."

His words filled me with fire while also making me swoon. Scooting back, I braced my feet on the edges of his chair.

"Hmm, well, maybe I could help you with your call?"

"The only thing you'll help with Loren is distracting me beyond measure."

I smiled, liking the idea of distracting this man. His hands landed on my feet, slowly rubbing them. Despite his words, his hands seemed to have other ideas creeping up my legs. Sliding my feet forward more, I pulled the chair closer.

The corner of his mouth lifted as he looked at me. "Why do I feel like that only made you more determined?"

Smiling wider, I didn't confirm as his hands found their way to my thighs. His face was close enough now that I could bend down and thread my fingers through his hair. Atticus' eyes closed at the touch, leaning into my fingers as I applied pressure, a soft moan leaving his lips. His dark hair was silky, the length just long enough to grab onto the strands. The shorn sides tickled my palms as I ran my hands up and over them.

Moving my legs out of his chair, I braced them over the armrests and pulled him in closer. Atticus' hands slid to my backside, and I pulled his head to me. We were in some weird hug, but it worked, and I felt his body relax as I massaged his head. This hadn't been what I intended, but it seemed to be what he needed. Running my fingers through his hair, I held him close to me, letting him be vulnerable in a safe place.

His hands started to move, and I soon felt the cold air hit my butt cheeks, the shirt moving up. Atticus hissed when he met my skin, warming the cold flesh with his warm palms. "Bellezza, it seems you came in here with a plan."

It wasn't a question but a statement, and I did nothing to confirm it outside of pressing my fingers deeper into his hair. A sound of pure pleasure met my ears, and I smiled. It was addictive, feeling in control and eliciting these sounds from him.

Atticus pulled back, his pupils blown as he looked at me with unfiltered lust. He surged up, towering over me, bracing his hands on the desk next to my legs. The growl that left him had me gasping, leaning back at his proximity.

"Are you going to take what you came in here for, or are you going to falter under pressure?"

My heart raced, my spine straightening as I grabbed hold of the tie that dangled in front of me. I knew he was baiting me, seeing if I'd rise to the challenge, but it was the push I'd needed, continuing to prove that Atticus understood a part of me I was only beginning to.

"Your mouth could be used for something else instead of pissing me off," I said, pushing him back into his chair and tugging him forward as I trapped him against the desk with my legs. We both knew he could break it, but he let me take control, submitting to me for once. Wrapping his tie around my hand, I pulled him closer, my breath hitching as power coursed through me.

It was a dangerous emotion, one I could easily become addicted to, but one I knew he wouldn't let me drown in. His umber eyes smoldered, lighting my skin on fire as I held him in my grasp. I unbuttoned the bottom of the dress shirt with my free hand, the tails falling over my legs. My wet pussy was on perfect display, my desire evident for Atticus to see. He growled, his eyes glued to my glistening folds, and the sound pushed me over the edge.

Using my leverage, I positioned his mouth where I wanted it. Atticus didn't waste any time, licking up my core, his tongue hot against me. A moan escaped me, my head falling back, but I didn't let go of the tie, anchoring him where I wanted. His arms wrapped around me again, pulling me closer, and my back fell onto the desk.

I was lost in sensations, Atticus devouring me like only he could. Each lick and flick of his tongue was done with such precision, I was a sopping and spasming mess within seconds. When he plunged two fingers into me, I arched up, screaming out my orgasm. My hand let go of the silk material, my fingers were cramped, and my body tried to come down from the high it had just felt.

Clamping his hands on my thighs, he held me to the desk, making his way up my body with kisses. When he came to a button, I looked down briefly, wondering what the hold-up was. His eyes met mine, a devilish smirk on his face. "I have half a mind to rip this off you, but I think I like you in my shirt too much to ruin it. Don't move, or your number increases."

I sucked in a breath, my body trembling with his promises, and I tried to hold as still as possible as he painstakingly unbuttoned them. By the time he reached the top one, my body vibrated, the brush of his knuckles against my sensitive flesh too much. I struggled not to fall over the edge again. A whimper left me as he pushed the shirt off, the black tie I'd taken falling perfectly between my breasts.

"Fuck, that's the sexiest thing I've ever seen." I saw the moment his eyes hooded fully, and his hand dropped to his belt buckle, unleashing it from his pants. Atticus started to untuck his shirt, his hunger causing me to breathe heavier in anticipation. The chime on his phone startled us both, and we turned to stare at the device as it lay on the desk.

He groaned, closing his eyes as he remembered his meeting. He picked up the phone, glancing at it, almost like he debated answering it. Atticus looked from me to the phone before sighing and sitting back in his chair as he answered.

"Let's make this quick," I heard him utter into the phone as a brilliant idea filled my mind. Sitting up on my elbows, I watched him. His eyes were on me as he listened, one hand tapping aggressively against the arm of his chair. "Uh-huh," he mumbled, focused on me.

Licking my lips, I sat up further. His eyes narrowed, but I didn't stop. Moving my foot, I brushed it against his leg, feeling up the length of him. His hand clamped down on me, stopping my movement. Smirking, I placed my other foot, stroking him, knowing he couldn't hold on to both of them. Satisfaction filled me as he closed his eyes, pressing his lips together to hold back a moan.

"Mm-hmm. What does he want in return?" Atticus' voice was pained, so I took mercy on him. I circled my breast with one hand, pinching my nipple with my thumb and forefinger, inching the other hand toward my apex. Spreading my legs on the desk, I touched my clit, dipping down to gather some of my essence, swirling it around. Biting my lip, I held back my own moan and looked at Atticus.

His eyes were locked on my hand, his tongue peeking out to wet his lips. As I plunged my fingers in, he covered his mouth to suppress a moan. His eyes flicked up to me, liquid heat licking every inch of my body.

"Is there anything else? I have something that needs attention in my office."

Smirking, I kept up my pace, my own eyes falling closed as I started to find my own release again. A strangled groan had me opening my eyes, finding Atticus still on the phone. His free hand rubbed the very prominent erection in his pants, and his eyes promised me retribution when he was free. Figuring I had a limited window of control, I slid off the desk, pushing his chair back. Squatting down, I finished unzipping his pants and pulled out his length. Atticus sucked in a breath, his eyes closing as I wrapped my hand around him.

That seductive power raced through me, and I licked his tip, spreading the drop of precum over my tongue. Stroking him, I sucked down, working my hand and mouth together. I'd hated giving my ex blowjobs and hadn't ever been good at them. But expanding my sexual horizons like I had recently, I'd discovered my passion for bringing my guys to their knees. I still felt amateurish in my blowjob abilities, but the sounds Atticus made encouraged me, and I sucked, hollowing my cheeks as I took him as far as I could.

Looking up, I found his eyes on fire as he stared at me, his mouth tense. There was so much emotion in his eyes, ranging from desire, respect, and devotion. When I licked the tip, taking him into my mouth again, I saw the moment his switch flipped.

"We'll finish this later," he barked, tossing the phone onto the desk, the case clattering against the surface as it slid. I didn't stop, knowing whatever those numbers had been for were about to be revealed. I'd finally pushed

Atticus to his breaking point, and I smiled smugly as I sucked him.

In one movement, he stood and pulled me up, his cock falling from my mouth as it slapped against him. He twirled me around, slamming me down onto the desk, and sheathed himself in me. I didn't have time to moan as he started pounding into me at an unrelenting pace. My hips slammed into the edge of the desk, and I knew there would be bruises there later. The knowledge that I'd tipped the put-together Atticus over the edge made me not care, though.

Grabbing the edge of the desk in front of me, I tilted my head back to take in his face. Atticus' head was thrown back as he thrust himself in and out of me. His fingers dug into my skin, the sound of slapping skin accompanying our moans and the creak of the desk. I watched his face, entranced with how blissed out he looked to be in me, and it pushed me to see what else I could glean from Atticus.

Pushing back against him, I lifted my body off the desk, twisting my head to look at him more fully. He stopped when he felt me move, looking down at me as I smirked at him.

"We'll see how long that smirk lasts, Lore, when I'm dolling out your punishments in a minute."

"You say that like it's a bad thing. I think you're the one who's all talk, Attie. Now, fuck me like you mean it."

Lifting off the desk completely, I wrapped my arm around his neck, bringing his face closer to mine. "Show me I'm yours," I whispered, kissing him. He growled but took my kiss, battling my tongue for dominance. His pace started again, and he moved one hand around in front to pinch my clit as he pounded into me. My legs shook, my walls clamping around him as my orgasm built. He dropped me down to the desk, fucking me with such vigor, I knew I wouldn't be walking right later.

A moment later, my orgasm detonated, and I broke into a million pieces. Atticus roared out his own release, and just as I started to come down, his hand struck against my butt cheek, somehow sending me into a third orgasm. When I came to, he had me cradled in his arms, nuzzling my neck with his nose, peppering me with kisses.

"Sorry if I distracted you from your call," I mumbled around a yawn.

"What did I tell you, Bellezza? Don't lie to me."

I opened my eyes, a smile pulling at my lips. "Fine, you're right. I enjoyed disrupting it very much. I think I should do it more often."

"Hmm, we'll see."

Giggling, I cupped his cheek, pulling his face to my lips. "Thank you for knowing what I needed."

"I see you, Bellezza. No thanks needed. I'll always push you and remind you when you go off course."

"I know."

He smiled, kissing my nose. "Go take a bubble bath. You're gonna want a soak."

"Good idea." I kissed his cheek, getting up to leave. I

pulled his shirt back on, buttoning it up as I made my way to the door.

"And Bellezza, that was only one. You still have three left, and they're never the same." His eyes heated, a smirk crossing his lips as he watched me.

I sucked in a breath, not missing he'd added a number, my cheeks heating at the thought. Stumbling out the door, I fell into Sax's arms as I did.

"Spitfire," he breathed. His face was solemn, not even noticing what I was wearing. "I'm ready to talk."

We headed off toward a hall I hadn't been in when Atticus stopped us. "She's been ordered to take a bath first. Perhaps you can get it set up and then come and see me, Sax. I have a feeling you have something to share with me as well?"

Sax stiffened, but didn't deny Atticus' words. He nodded, not looking back, and led me to a door. It was the most magnificent bathroom I'd ever laid eyes on. When we walked in, I wondered if this was where he'd intended all along or not.

I watched his motions as he filled the tub, adding things to the water as he did. When it was half full, he nodded for me to step in. I did as he directed, wincing when my pussy met the water as the heat licked up my body. Once I was settled, I looked up at him—my beautiful neanderthal—ready for whatever he had to share, praying it wouldn't rip my heart out.

"I have a lot of demons in my past, and I worry I'll darken you too much, but I'd like to give you the opportunity to decide for yourself because I know I can't live without you and I'm done running."

Sax proceeded to tell me about his past and how he came to live with the Mascros. Through his whole story, he had a resigned look on his face, like he already knew what I would say. When he finished, he kissed my head before standing. I opened my mouth to stop him, wanting him to know what I thought.

"Not now. I need to go over some things with Mas and I want you to really think over it all and not just make a decision in the moment. Can you do that for me, Spitfire?"

Nodding, I wiped a tear, wishing I could hug him. "Okay." Sax smiled weakly and left, and I sank down below the water, doing as he'd asked.

I thought.

TWENTY NINE

LOREN

Sax's words echoed in my head as I watched Wells train Jude and Immy on more self-defense moves. The dogs sat at my feet, content to chew on their bones. I'd been in here for a while, but I'd been so lost in my thoughts, it had felt like mere seconds. Taking in the sweat on the kids' brows, I knew it had to be almost time for them to finish. Damn, I'd been zoned out for forty-five minutes at least.

Arms wrapped around me, pulling me into a chest, and I leaned back, peering up at my captor. When I saw it was Monroe, I smiled at him. "Hey."

"You look like you have a lot on your mind, Lo." His brows creased, concern radiating from him.

"Yeah." I agreed, but I didn't expand, knowing it wasn't my story to tell, but it didn't stop the words Sax had said from repeating in my mind.

I killed a man when I was ten years old.

My mother bargained with my life and then took her own.

I'm not a good man, Spitfire. You should run far away from me, but I hope you won't because you make the darkness not feel so lonely. I need you, Loren.

I think what had taken me the most by surprise was the emotion I could hear in his voice, and feel in his body as he held my hand. Once he'd told me his story, and the fears he carried, he kissed me on the head and left me to process. I wanted to run after him even if I would've been dripping wet, but he asked me to stay, to relax, and give him time to talk to Atticus about something.

It was one of the hardest requests to follow in my entire life.

I could see his brokenness, but it was only the plea in his voice to give him space to manage his own emotions that had me staying put. Sax was a proud man, and he needed to feel strong at that moment. Being vulnerable had left him open, and I understood the need to create some space for a while.

And I could give him that, but it was all I would give him—a moment. I fully intended to seek him out later.

So right now, I was physically in the training room, but emotionally very far away. I needed to pull it together and be present with the ones I was with. When Immy landed a perfect jab to Well's instep, she beamed, her pride in accomplishing something evident for all to see. She was beautifully confident at that moment, and I hoped she got to have plenty more of those moments in her life.

"Good. Next session, we'll work on more resistant attackers. I've enlisted some of the guards to help."

"Sweet. Please tell me one of them is Beau?" Immy prodded, a giggle escaping at the thought. Wells smiled, a protective glint in his eye I'd never seen before. It seemed like Wells had fallen under Imogen's spell as well. It was hard not to when she turned those soulful eyes on you. You wanted to make the world magical for her.

"Dinner's in thirty. You guys might want to hit the showers beforehand. You kind of reek." I scrunched my nose up dramatically at the teens. Immy stuck her tongue out at me but headed off toward the hallway, Jude following behind her.

"Separately!" Wells shouted, causing both teens to blush. They didn't acknowledge his comment, but I saw it. His reaction was almost as protective as Atticus.

Heart, melt.

Monroe pulled me up, lacing his fingers with mine. Wells met us, giving us a salacious look. He bent down, patting both of the dogs, giving them some love before he stood, taking us in.

"Now, my shower can definitely fit more than one."

"I'll pass this time. I need to talk with Atticus about something. You staying for dinner?" I asked Monroe, looking up at him.

"Of course." He kissed my nose, letting me go. I

briefly kissed Wells' cheek, surprising him before I strolled off. In my haste earlier, okay, in my lust, I'd forgotten to broach the topic with Atticus I'd been meaning to. Giving myself a time limit seemed like the best course of action, so I wouldn't back out.

I didn't know why I was so hesitant to ask the question that had been plaguing me, but I was.

Nodding to a few of the staff and guards, I twisted my hands as I walked, my steps soft as I made my way to his office. The door was open, the light drifting into the hallway. I could hear the shuffling of papers, but not much else seemed to be coming from the space. Sucking in a breath for the second time that day, I knocked on the door frame, peering in.

Sax and Atticus both looked up, and I stopped, surprised to find them both here. Sax looked at me, apprehension on his face. For some reason, his presence was comforting, and I relaxed, walking into the room. I made my way to him, taking the papers out of his hands and sitting them on the side table. He didn't stop me, but he also didn't move. It felt like he was on a cliff, waiting to see if I'd save him or push him over.

Squeezing his hand, I turned and sat in his lap. It only took him a second before he seemed to break free from his frozen state, wrapping me up in his thick arms. He nuzzled down into my neck, his lips pressing a slight kiss there. Smiling, I looked up, meeting Atticus' eyes. He observed me as well, but there wasn't any fear or apprehension. Just pure appreciation for what I was doing for his best friend. He smirked, lifting his eyebrow.

"Did you need something, Lore?"

"I do, actually." I swallowed, the words becoming thick on my tongue. "I think I'm ready to move forward with obtaining what is mine. There's just one thing."

Atticus watched me, looking for any sign to indicate what I might say. Swallowing, I felt Sax's arm tighten around me, and Atticus nodded, telling me they stood with me. It was what I needed.

"I'd like to meet with my father. I want to give him the chance to choose a different path for himself."

"Are you sure? He stood by for years, compliant to her actions against you."

I nodded, understanding what he saw, but I couldn't get the shoulder squeeze out of my head. "I don't deny the actions he played in my life, but I also know a person isn't all black or white. They can change if they truly want to. My father, he could've stepped in several times, but I can see how hard it might've been to be married to a woman like her, especially if it was arranged. I don't think he's a bad man, just a cowardly one. I'd like to give him a chance that I never had to escape her clutches. If he's willing to make the effort, that is."

"You're too good, Spitfire," Sax whispered. "Your heart is so pure. I'm just happy you have room for me. None of us are deserving of the empathy you freely give."

My face warmed from the sentiment, even if I didn't

believe he wasn't deserving, because if any man was, it was Sax. "If only you could see yourself the way I do." I tilted my head up, kissing his cheek. Atticus had watched our exchange, his expression unreadable.

"He was agreeable with my associate, willing to provide information." He watched me, looking over every inch of my face. "Because of that, I'm willing to let him have a chance. Where would you like to set up the meeting? Do you want any of us present?"

I appreciated that Atticus accepted my ability to know if I could handle it or not, offering his assistance instead of trying to force it. I didn't miss his possessiveness threaded throughout, either. I thought about the potential locations, but in the end, I knew there was only one place that would do.

"Could we invite him over for brunch this Sunday?" I smiled, not ashamed a little pettiness had slipped through at the thought. What better way to poke my mom and test my dad's loyalties than to invite him over during the time I was forced to spend with her? My cheeks started to hurt at how wide I was smiling. I didn't know if Sax chose to ignore this darkness in me or if he accepted it as I did his.

"I think you answered your own question there, Bellezza."

Furrowing my brows, I tried to figure out what he meant. "Because I'm being evil to invade her precious brunch time?"

Sax chuckled, and even Atticus smiled at me, shaking

his head. "No, though it's nice to see you have an evil streak. You said *we*. This is just as much your place now. You're the lady of the manor. If you want to invite someone over for brunch, have someone's head chopped off at lunch, and an orgy at dinner; well, let's just use different rooms for them all."

I blinked, not sure which part I was more shocked over. *Lady of the manor. Head chopped off. Orgy.*

Yeah, it was definitely the orgy.

"So, does that mean you're not squinting anymore?" I teased, standing up and bracing my arms on the desk to stare across at him. I knew my shirt would be showing just a hint of cleavage, his eyes dropping for a nanosecond proving it. When he spotted the black silk, his eyes heated as he peered back up at me. I'd taken his tie and wrapped it around my breasts, feeling brazen earlier.

"I don't need to squint when you're in front of me, Bellezza; you're all I can see, smell, taste... you've consumed me, Loren. Things I never considered before are suddenly on the tip of my tongue."

We stared at one another, lost in the feelings coursing between us. Warm hands slid up my back, pulling me back to the present.

"As much as I'd prefer to have Spitfire for dinner, we do have guests waiting. I think it's time we scheduled that request you had."

I looked up at Sax, not knowing what he meant. He slowly drifted a finger over my skin, light as a feather, and it reminded me of the sensation room, and I knew what he meant.

"Yes, please," I purred.

"Saturday."

I turned back to Atticus, his eyes blazing, and I nodded. "It's a date."

AFTER DINNER, Jude had asked to see his brother. Atticus had debated, but when he looked Jude over, he nodded, seeing what I did—he was ready. Sax and Atticus were working on something, so they stayed back, sending Beau to take us. Monroe had to go home and get Levi to bed, leaving Wells and Nicco to decide what they wanted to do.

"I'd like to join you if that's okay?" Nicco asked, looking at Jude and not me. I got a little weepy at him being concerned about Jude and wanting to make sure he'd be okay facing his brother.

"Yeah, that would be great." Jude swallowed, nodding, and I watched as his shoulders relaxed some. Immy walked over and gave me a hug. Nicco gave her a look, and she rolled her eyes and hugged him, too. She hesitated for only a second when she pulled back before hugging Jude quickly, kissing him on the cheek, and saying a quiet "good luck" before bolting from the room. Jude's cheeks tinted red, but I didn't miss the smile that spread across his face, either.

I glanced at Wells, and he raised an eyebrow at me, motioning for me to walk. Rolling my eyes, I tried to hide how glad I was that he was coming too. The ride was quiet, the four of us in our own thoughts as we traveled to wherever his brother was being kept. When we pulled to a stop, I squeezed Jude's hand.

"No matter what happens, I'm here. That doesn't change anything. So, get your answers, but don't let it consume you."

Jude nodded, giving me a tight squeeze before stepping out the door Nicco held open. Before closing it, Nicco winked, and silence descended around Wells and me. He moved over into the vacant seat, pulling me into his arms. The dogs whined in the back, but Wells dropped his hand over the seat, scratching them until they settled. With our recent back and forth, they'd both gotten used to riding, and Atticus had even installed special crates for them to ride in the back.

As much as I dismissed his comment earlier about being the lady of the manor, I couldn't deny he meant it. He had made me a part of his life, and I could see it in everything. Atticus was all in, and well, I guess I was all in with the mafia.

Now, that was a statement I never thought I'd hear myself say.

"Penny, for your thoughts?" Wells mumbled into my hair.

I giggled. "I was just thinking how I never thought

I'd be involved with someone in the mafia. My life has turned out a lot different than I imagined it."

"Hmm, I kind of know what you mean, but I can't say I'm not happy about it, especially since it includes me, too."

"Your selflessness is huge." I laughed, enjoying the quiet moment with Wells.

"Hey Kitten, can I ask you something?"

"Of course."

"How do you see this all playing out?"

"What do you mean?" I asked, turning a little so I could see his face.

"Us? Are you just with the five of us now, or do you think it will be something permanent?"

"I want it to be permanent. Each relationship is different, but I know I need all of you in my life. Do you… do you not think you can be in this type of relationship long term?"

He smiled, calming my racing heart. "I'll be wherever you and Roe are, Kitten. I just wanted to make sure I fit into yours."

"I need you, Wells. I can't profess anything big yet, but I'm getting there. I know I feel for you deeply, and the thought of not having you makes me want to punch things. I thought my life was meant to be one way—the way my mother told me it should be. I'm learning it can be whatever I have the courage to dream it to be. Just as I never saw myself being in a relationship with someone in the criminal underground, I never thought I'd be with five guys at once, either. My life is full of adventure, love, and family now, and I'm honestly so happy with how it's turning out. Jude, Immy, and Levi are the kids I'll never bear myself, but who I love with my whole heart. Motorcycles, fighting matches, tattoos, and even kinky sex clubs are so far outside what I should do, but I couldn't imagine not doing them now. You're all a part of me, your lives have become my life, and I want to weather it with you until the end if we can."

Wells slammed his lips down to mine, heat, and passion fueling him. "You say you can't express big feelings, and then you go and say all of that. To a man like me, that means more than empty words any day. Never stop kicking me in the balls if I need it, Kitten."

"Deal." I giggled, loving all these new sides of Wells I was learning. He was more than he gave himself credit for.

"What I need to know, though, what is this kinky sex club you speak of?" He grinned, his hands smoothing over the back of my shirt as he waited for me to answer.

"Maybe I'll take you there one day. We'll consider it a field trip."

His eyes heated. "I'll hold you to that."

I leaned up for a kiss when the dogs barked, making us both jump. "Fucking hell, Fort!"

When he barked again, Wells sighed, dropping his head to mine. "I better see if they need to go. Fort's still training. Stay put."

I rolled my eyes but nodded. He jumped out, walking

around to the back, and I heard their excited huffs as they were leashed up. I turned, leaning against the head-rest, watching.

He had them both ready within seconds and walked them over to a small grassy area, leaving the trunk up. I couldn't see much, the darkness of the space keeping things hidden. Closing my eyes, I started to fall asleep as I waited for them to return. When I heard three pops a moment later, I bolted up. Had that been? Was I imagining things?

Silence met me, and I convinced myself I'd dreamed it. Except, when I heard a whine, it jerked me out of my denial, and I fumbled for the phone.

"Please, please, answer...."

I opened the door slowly, bracing myself for an attack, a canister of pepper spray in my hand as the phone rang.

I saw the prone body at the same instant it clicked over. But I heard nothing. I felt nothing. I was *nothing*.

The phone slid from my grasp, clattering to the ground, and I just stood there.

"Please let this not be real," I whispered, finally taking a step. Then another. Then another. Before long, I was running.

Dropping to my knees, a whimper left my lips as I frantically looked around, trying to figure a way out of this.

If only I could go back in time.

 THIRTY

NICCO

Jude was silent next to me as I walked into the warehouse. I wondered what he thought, heading into a place like this, or if he was even able to think about something like that. He seemed deep in thought, and I worried maybe we'd all jumped the gun too soon.

"Do you know what you're going to say?"

He shook his head, stuffing his hands in his pockets. "No, which is funny because there have been so many questions I've wanted to ask him for years." He stopped, turning toward me. "Yet, here I am, and nothing comes to mind. I guess… the only thing that matters is if he regrets his choice. If he doesn't, then I know he's not the brother I knew when we only had each other on the streets."

I watched him, the emotions playing over his face—fear, hope, and determination. Jude was as ready as anyone in his situation could be.

"What will his answer change in your life?"

Jude thought about it for a second, looking up to

meet my eyes. "A few months ago, everything. Now, I'm not sure it will have much impact on me other than whether or not he gets to be part of my life. I hadn't really thought about it that way."

"What do you mean?" I asked, kind of amazed at the emotional intelligence of this young man. I didn't know if it was Loren's influence, the life he'd lived already, or perhaps a combination of both, but I knew he was one of a kind.

"My whole life, I've looked up to my brother and wanted to be just like him. He was my hero when the world turned against us. I worked so hard to make him proud of me, always wanting his approval. But now… I don't need him to be that for me anymore. I don't need him to tell me if I'm a worthwhile person. Instead, I get to choose if he belongs in my life or not, and it has nothing to do with whether or not I'm worthy, but whether or not I allow it. It's kind of nice not needing his approval to feel good about myself."

"You're kind of amazing, you know?" I smiled, pushing his shoulder. "I don't know what the future holds for you, but I'm happy I get to be part of it. I think you're going to do amazing things, kid."

"Thanks." Jude blushed, ducking his head a little. This light moment in the middle of a warehouse used to house our family's enemies showed me what it was all about. I hadn't always been the biggest advocate for the criminal life, wanting to escape to a life of freedom and be my own person. The thing I'd gotten wrong, though, was that those things didn't have to be mutually exclusive. The things I wanted to feel I could have in the mafia. I just needed to open my eyes to the possibilities life granted me.

The mafia, the family… they weren't inherently bad. Just as the outside world wasn't exclusively good. Evil didn't exist in a vacuum, the same as love. It was time I changed my own definition and embraced who I could fully be. Jude showed me it was possible.

"Come on, let's go see if he is." Clamping my hand down on his shoulder, I walked with him to the door. The guard nodded at me.

"Sir."

"Good evening, we'd like an audience with Cameron."

"Of course, sir." He moved down the hall, leading us toward a door a few feet from where he'd been standing guard. The keyring jangled as he lifted it, unlocking the door. He pushed it open, nodding for us to enter.

"Do you want me to wait outside?"

Jude bit his lip but shook his head, clearing his throat. "I'd like you to enter if you're okay with that?"

"Absolutely."

He smiled, grateful to not have to face it alone. It was another reminder that we didn't need to be strong on our own, not when there were others to help us along.

Stepping in, we were greeted by Cameron sitting on a bed. He lifted his head at our entrance, his eyebrows raised in shock, followed by hope and regret as he registered his brother.

"Jude, I, uh," he swallowed. "I didn't expect to see you here. Seems you've gained some friends." He nodded toward me, his expression turning to granite as he cleared it of all emotion. Internally, I sighed, knowing he would lose his brother if he didn't drop that tough guy act.

"The difference, Cam, is I didn't have to sell my soul. So tell me, how much of yours is left?"

Jude leaned against the wall, crossing his arms over his chest. He had a look of determination, his jaw tight as he glared at his brother. He was holding his own and not letting Cameron run him over. Jude was stronger than he knew.

"I'm afraid you won't like the answer to that," Cameron mumbled, dropping his head. He took a few deep breaths, his shoulders moving from the action. When he lifted his head, the hard-boiled street kid was gone, and some of the aspects I caught in Jude were there.

"How about you let me decide that? I've been making my own decisions for the past three years as it is, so give me the respect that I deserve."

"You're right. I thought leaving you was the better choice. Seeing you now, I think I was right. You're too pure for this world, Jude. I sacrificed myself so you could have a future outside street gangs, drugs, and mobsters. So, tell me, what exactly are you doing here? How deep are you with the Mascros? Because I can tell you, it's not a place you belong. Especially—" He stopped abruptly, holding a hand to his mouth, halting his words. Cameron shook his head, groaning out in frustration.

"What do you mean, Cameron? Is my family in trouble?"

The protective ring I'd been feeling for the kid since I met him filled in completely, flaring to life in me. He called us *his* family. There wasn't anything I wouldn't do for the kid. He was right; we were family. Puffing up my shoulders, I held my head proud, waiting until he needed me.

While I'd been feeling sentimental, it appeared Cameron had a different reaction. He jumped back like Jude had struck him. His face screwed up, his eyebrows tight as he looked at his brother.

"Your what?"

"Family. Now, out with it." Jude stood tall, not backing down.

"Ouch, low blow, bro."

Jude sighed, rubbing his temple in such a way it reminded me so much of Atticus. Shit, he'd been hanging around the boss man too much. "You're my brother, yes, but you're not my family anymore, Cam. Family is there for one another. Family looks out for the well-being of its members. Family doesn't leave without a word, no matter the intention. Family apologizes when they mess up, but most importantly, family shows up when they're needed, *no matter what*. So tell me, how have you been there for me in the past three years? At most, I deserve an explanation, you fighting to make amends, and lots of groveling on your part. At worst, I deserve an apology and no judgment on the choices I've had to make in your absence. So, which is it going to be?"

His brother stared at him, shocked at what he was hearing. He opened his mouth and then closed it, giving the perfect description of a fish. "I, uh, I..." Cameron shook his head, rubbing at the temples. "Mom would be proud of the man you've become." He sat back down, rubbing his palms on his hands before he looked over at me.

"You're Nicco, right? You used to run the fight rings?" I nodded, not giving him my words yet. "I thought so. I've seen you there a few times when I was working." He blew out a breath, chuckling a little self-deprecatingly to himself. "Man, you never think you'll have this type of conversation with your kid brother." He looked up, and I saw the look Jude had been hoping for. Remorse. "You're right. I'm sorry for ghosting you, but I'm not sorry for leaving you, Jude. I only regret not keeping in contact; maybe then, you would've talked me out of some of the mistakes I made. But I do think you've been better off without me."

Cameron sighed but met Jude's eyes, determined. "I was so tired and thought I found an easy way to save us. But I found myself in the same trap Pa had. When we were on the streets, I avoided the bad people, holding onto the promise I made our parents. You probably don't remember them like I do, but they were good people once. Life hit them hard, and when Pa lost his job, he fought to find something. A few bad decisions, and he found himself in debt, deep. Mom worked so many jobs, but we still barely made it month to month. When they approached him, he was so beaten down that he didn't consider the risks or costs. With each job he did for Delgado, he became deeper into debt. He wasn't making any progress, and in the end, he got him and mom both addicted to the stuff he was selling. That last year, there were a lot of scary men around our house, but one in particular, I remember that he always creeped me out. When they were killed, I vowed to do different… but in the end, I failed."

Tears brimmed his eyes, and I knew his brother wasn't a bad person. He'd been faced with unimaginable choices and responsibilities at a young age. I could've been in his same position if I hadn't had Mas and Sax to guide me. Jude walked over, sitting next to his brother, grabbing his hand, seeing the same thing.

"It's not too late to make a different choice. Sometimes, you have to fall before you can see the right path to take. It's hidden beneath the weeds and brambles, but it's there; you just need to see it for what it could be."

Cameron nodded. "I avoided him the whole time we were on the streets, proud of myself for keeping us safe. I didn't realize how much we were suffering, though, not until we were forced apart. That was the first time I thought you might be better off without me. You were younger, easier to place. You've always been kinder, more intuitive, and families liked that. I was rowdy and constantly fighting, ready to make the world pay for the pain I felt. The homes I was in… it was a constant struggle. The day I graduated, they showed me the door, just a bag of my belongings, a metrocard, and the meager earnings I'd made washing dishes. I was so tired of fighting to survive. So tired of being seen as less than, of having to scrape by just to make it. He gave me a warm place to stay, new clothes, and a hot meal when he approached me. I was persuaded by the carb overload." Cam chuckled, making Jude grin.

"He manipulated me, waiting until I was vulnerable and then struck. He started asking for small favors until I was so indebted to him, I had no way out. I stayed away to protect you, hoping they'd leave you out of it. He said I had to pay off our family loan, which our Pa still had. I knew I'd never escape, but I hoped my sacrifice would protect you. And it seemed to work, for a while at least, that was until you were at that restaurant. I saw you there, and I… I refused. He knew you were important then. To me and… to *them*."

He looked up, meeting my eyes, and I knew what he meant. Darren had seen the opportunity in front of him. "He told you he would clear your debt if you brought him Jude." I didn't need to phrase it as a question; we all knew I was right.

Cameron nodded. "Yeah." He swallowed, looking

back at his brother. "I refused to give him any information and said you were just a kid from a foster family. I don't know how much he believed me, but he told me to approach you and pull you in. I kept putting it off until I couldn't any longer. I hoped you were brighter than me. I'd never been prouder when you proved me right." He smiled, and Jude stared at him in shock.

"You wanted to be brought here? Why?"

He chuckled, shaking his head. "I didn't know this existed. I just hoped you would be smarter than me and tell someone, not try to do it all on your own and save me. When that scary guy showed up, I'd never felt so much relief, hoping it meant it was over. I don't care what happens to me, I've made my choices, and I'll live with them. But maybe I can help you have the future you deserve."

"You're right, Cam. You are dumb." Jude punched him in the arm.

"Ow, that actually hurt."

"Good. I've been practicing." Jude beamed at him. "You're stupid to think I'd ever want a future without you. We're better together." He hugged his brother then, and I watched the moment Cameron accepted he was safe this time as he fell apart in his younger brother's arms.

I stepped out, wanting to give them some space. Jude exited a few minutes later, wiping his own eyes.

"You good?" I asked.

"Yeah, I think I am. What happens now? Does he have to stay here?"

I wrapped my arm around his neck, walking with him down the hall. "We'll talk with Atticus and see what he wants to do. If any information he gives us pans out, it will speak volumes for his intentions. I think he's legit, but Atticus protects his family tightly, so it will take more than an emotional reunion to sway him."

Jude nodded, probably already knowing the answer I'd give him. I nudged him, smiling. "This means I'm number 1 now, right?"

Jude chuckled as I nodded back to the guard as we passed, making our way out of the warehouse.

When we stepped outside, it took a few minutes for the scene in front of us to register. Shoving Jude back through the doors, I fell into my command, a hard mask falling over my face.

"Stay here. Do not leave."

I looked at the guard there, searing him with my eyes. "You're responsible for him at all costs, do you understand?"

"Yes, sir."

"Call The Suit. We have a red riding hood."

THIRTY ONE

LOREN

The tears streamed down my face, obscuring my view. My hands shook as I tried to put pressure on the wound, quickly becoming covered in blood, the warm liquid spilling over them too fast.

"No, no, no," I pleaded.

A wet kiss met my cheek, licking away my tears as Barkley whined next to me. Fort laid on top of Wells, attempting to cover him, his fur turning dark brown from the blood. It didn't matter though, it wasn't enough. A car backfired, and I jumped, looking up. Evil eyes gleamed in the darkness, staring back at me.

"Kitten," Wells wheezed, my eyes flicking to his. *"Run."*

"No." I shook my head, not willing to leave him. I didn't care. I wouldn't leave him to die alone. I wouldn't. At that moment, he was all I focused on.

"So… stubborn."

"Save your breath, don't you dare leave me."

"Never."

Movement around me pulled my focus, and I tensed, fearing the end. I fumbled for the pepper spray I'd dropped, hoping I'd get one spray off before I was shot, too. My hands slipped on it, the wet blood making it slick from my fingers as I tried to contain it. When I saw it was Nicco, I left it, sagging in relief he was here. Faint sirens could be heard, and I prayed they were headed to us. I had no clue where we were or if it was even possible for them to get to this place, but I hoped. I couldn't begin to think otherwise.

Nicco ripped off his shirt, moving my hands out of the way as he pressed it to the wound. Wells coughed, some blood spurting out of his lips, and I moved closer to his head.

"Surly, stay with me."

"What happened?" Nicco asked, but I shook my head.

"I don't know. I was in the car. He stepped out for a second. It was so quick, I wasn't even sure I heard it correctly."

"Waiting," Wells whispered. I tensed. Did he know who?

"Who?" I gasped, clutching his hand. "Who was it?"

His eyes started to close, so I shook him, begging him to stay with me. "No, don't close your eyes."

I was so focused on him, I didn't notice the ambulance screeching to a stop near us. When hands grabbed me, I shook them off until I heard Atticus. "Lore, it's okay. They're going to take care of him."

I looked up, meeting his eyes, seeing the fire burning there. Atticus was pissed, and he'd kill whoever had dared touch his family. The look should've scared me, but it calmed that part of me that wanted justice, that needed revenge. Slowly, I released his hand, standing as they started to hook him up to an IV and oxygen. Wells reached out, and I grabbed it again, following along with the gurney as they rushed to the truck.

He squeezed it right before they lifted him, and he said the name that made me see red.

Releasing his fingers, I watched as the gurney was shoved into the back, the paramedics jumping up into the bay. The doors slammed shut, and within seconds, they were racing off. It made me feel better knowing they'd been so quick, leaving me with the hope he'd be okay.

He had to be.

A jacket was draped over my arms, and I tensed, looking up to find Atticus. He'd taken off his suit coat and laid it over me. I pulled it tightly around me, needing the warmth. My body was in shock, and cold was setting in.

"Come on. We'll follow. You need to be checked out too."

I followed along numbly, nodding to whatever he said. I didn't remember anything from the moment he guided me to the door or the drive there. I barely acknowledged the walk into the hospital, and the doctor, as he looked me over, telling whoever was with me, I was in shock. Something sharp pinched me as a cold liquid filled my veins. Images swirled as red-coated everything. I started to wonder about the oddest things.

Where were the dogs?

Did Jude like pickles?

Would the guys want to go to the beach?

Should I get another tattoo?

Before it went dark, a resounding thought circled.

I had to tell Monroe.

SCREAMS ECHOED AROUND ME, hands clamped down on me, and I fought, thrashing against them. A cry of panic left my throat as I struggled.

"No! He can't die!"

"Ssh, Loren. It's okay. Go to sleep. It's okay."

A prick against my skin sent a cold shiver through me, but I tumbled into the darkness, my hand reaching for anyone to grab me.

And then it was all dark.

VOICES WHISPERED AROUND ME, thoughts jumbled, but all I could think of was the red stickiness of the blood, and how it had felt coated on my hands.

He was gone.

No! Wells!

A whimper escaped, and I rolled, trying to free myself of the restraints, but they held me down. They would take me under again and steal my baby.

"No! You can't have her. Not again," I cried, the tears covering my face. I didn't dare open my eyes, too scared at what reality I would discover.

"She's panicking too much. I hate to say it, but you need to give her something more to sleep. Maybe if she sleeps long enough, she'll wake up without screaming. I can't take hearing her scream his name like that. Please, Atticus."

I recognized the voice, but I was too scared to face them.

"Fine, Goldie, but it's on you."

"*Please*," I whispered, hoping they'd hear my plea for what it was—a cry for help. I didn't want to be here anymore, not if one of them was gone. "I'm not ready."

I didn't know if I whispered it or thought it, but a few seconds later, the familiar prick of the needle and the cold feeling washed through me and this time, I let it take me under.

THIRTY TWO

LOREN

Light broke through the curtains, and I sat up with a gasp. I didn't remember how I'd gotten here, or how long it had been. Visions of tears and screams played in my mind, but I couldn't quite piece them together, the images too fragmented. Looking down, I realized someone had changed me, and my hands were clean, no longer covered in Wells' blood, and a sigh of relief left me. Picking up the shirt, I inhaled, the material smelled faintly of Nicco.

Glancing around, I had no idea where I was. It wasn't familiar, and everything in the room was generic, like a hotel room. But why would I be in a hotel? My body was stiff, and my hair felt heavy, like I hadn't washed it in a few days. A door opened on the far wall, and I tensed, preparing myself for intruders.

"Hey, you're awake."

At his voice, I was instantly off the bed as I ran to him, enclosing my arms around him, clinging to his frame. Monroe held me back just as tightly, his body shaking slightly. I felt tears pricking at my eyes, but I didn't want to break down again. Pulling back, I took in his face. He looked tired, resigned, and I wondered if he'd gotten any sleep. But I couldn't find anything else out from his expression and it scared me.

"Come, see if you can eat something. You've been out for a few days."

"Have you?" I asked, not able to say anything else, but needing to know before I made a move.

Monroe squeezed my hand, not answering. Apprehension filled me as I followed him out of the room. We walked out into a common area that was more active than mine had been. I spotted Atticus and Sax talking to some guards in a corner, and Nicco looked to be reviewing some plans at a table with men I'd never seen before.

A TV played cartoons further back, and I spotted Levi, Jude, and Imogen gathered on the couch off to the side, the dogs at their feet. I relaxed more, realizing they were all safe. Just how much had I missed? Had I dreamed it all?

"What's going on?" I asked, my words coming out scratchy. Monroe gave me a sad look, pulling me over to the kitchen area. Beau noticed me and filled a mug full of coffee, handing it to me when I neared.

"Thank you," I whispered. He nodded, patting my head as he walked by. Monroe looked at the big man, a strange question on his face before he shook it off.

"Do you want any food?"

I shook my head, but my stomach betrayed me, growling loudly. Everyone around us stopped, turning to look at me. My face heated, not wanting to be the center of attention standing in only Nicco's shirt.

"Take five," Atticus barked, and the room cleared out instantly. He walked over, his face stoic, giving no indication of his emotions. No one was, and it made me fear the worst. His eyes took in every inch of me, cataloging my body to make sure I was still in one piece.

"Lore, are you feeling better?" he cupped my cheek, his thumb brushing over the skin gently.

I shrugged. I wouldn't feel better until I knew how Wells was. "Wells?"

Atticus sighed before turning and walking off. My stomach dropped. No one would say anything. It could only mean… he really was dead. It hadn't just been a bad dream.

When I didn't follow, he stopped, looking over my shoulder, raising an eyebrow. "Are you coming?"

A gasp escaped me, and I sat the mug down before hurrying after him. Taking my hand, he led me to the other side from where I'd been. Knocking on a door, he didn't wait for an answer before entering. Inside, Wells lay in a bed, machines beeped and whirled, but he was awake, a smirk lifting at the corner of his mouth when he saw me.

I flew to him, stopping halfway as I remembered he'd been shot. "You were shot," I said like he didn't know.

"Yes, Kitten. I remember."

"But you're here. How?" I tilted my head in confusion, looking over every inch of him. He nodded behind me, and I turned, remembering Atticus.

"You? Again, how?"

Atticus sighed, a smile crossing his lips as he came closer, wrapping his arms around me. "I'm the boss of Chicago's largest crime family, Bellezza. I can make just about anything happen. I have medical staff on hand around the clock."

"Right, *mafia*. Forgive me for not jumping to that answer first," I sassed, relaxing into his arms, looking back at Wells.

"I'm just… I thought you were dead."

"He was close," Atticus grunted. His arms tensed around me, and I knew, though he pretended to not like my guys, they'd grown on him, and if anything, he cared about them out of respect for me. Some days, I almost didn't recognize him as the same man who'd sat down across from me, giving me the third degree to see if I was qualified to treat his sister.

Wells rolled his eyes, but I didn't miss how fatigued he was or how pale his skin was. "It was a gunshot wound. I've taken worse hits."

Rolling my eyes this time, I walked forward, grabbing his hand. "If you weren't lying in this very nice bed, hooked to machines, I might believe you. Actually, no, I'd slap you for saying something dumb. You don't get to dismiss this. I… I was so scared." Tears filled my eyes, and I quickly wiped them.

"I said the same thing," Monroe uttered from the door. "When I got Sax's message, I thought I'd lost you both. It was one of the scariest moments of my life. That's... that's not something I can pretend didn't happen for the sake of your masculine pride. So, don't ask me to. The last two days have been Hell."

"Two days?" I gasped, looking at the men.

Wells nodded, swallowing, and accepted Monroe's plea to not pretend it wasn't serious. When Monroe walked closer, he grabbed Wells' other hand. Atticus took that as his cue, kissing my head before walking out of the room, the door closing quietly behind him, leaving the three of us alone.

"So, two days and Sax texted you?"

"Yeah, he really needs to work on his communication," Monroe grumbled, and for some reason, it struck me as funny, eliciting a laugh from me. The sound set off Monroe, followed by Wells, who grunted out in pain.

"Hey, no fair. Gunshot wound, practically died, remember?"

"Oh, so now you admit it? I see how it's going to be. You know you can only use this to get your way for a limited time, right?"

"I'll milk it for as long as I can."

Grinning, I wiped the tear that fell, leaning forward to kiss him. I rested my head on him, breathing the same air for a moment.

"I've never been more scared in my life. Thank you for keeping your word to not leave me."

"I'd never leave you by choice, Kitten. And even then, I'd fight tooth and nail to get back to you two. I love you. Can I say that now?"

I laughed, the sound watery as my tears mixed with it. "Shut up, you fool. I love you too."

"You hear that, Roe? Kitten said she loved me first. I think that earns me something."

Monroe groaned dramatically, smiling, relieved we could have this conversation. We fell into an easy rhythm, talking about random things, keeping the topic light, until I noticed Wells starting to tire, and my stomach no longer willing to be left without food.

"We should let you get some rest."

"Not yet," he yawned, fighting to keep his eyes open.

"Wells, it's fine. You need sleep."

"I'm not disagreeing, but first, we need to decide what we're going to do about the shooter."

"You saw who shot you?" Monroe asked, causing Wells to look at me in shock.

"You didn't tell him?"

I shook my head. "In my defense, they apparently drugged me to sleep for two days. I only just woke up. I wasn't exactly in the best state right when you told me." Monroe grimaced sheepishly, but I squeezed his hand, not angry they'd done it. From what I could recall, it had been needed.

"So, no one knows?"

"No," I admitted, biting my lip. I looked up, meeting

Monroe's eyes. They were sad, and I think he knew, but he nodded.

"I'll grab the others."

Exhaling, I ducked my head, gathering myself for the confrontation. I didn't know why I was worried. I hadn't kept it from them intentionally. I'd been in shock and then asleep. If anything, they should be upset with themselves. Resolving my guilt, I straightened my spine, pushing my shoulders back. Wells squeezed my hand, and I nodded, kissing him. We were in this together.

Standing, I waited next to the bed, not wanting to sit when we talked. Monroe returned with Nicco, Sax, and Atticus. When the door shut, Atticus looked between Wells and me, his boss mask firmly in place.

"You have something to share?"

Nodding, I looked at Wells. "I saw who shot me, or at least who was in the car."

"Interesting. The cameras had been turned off. The only thing we'd gotten was a black Mercedes."

"Yeah, that's the one. I'd just let the dogs out, walking over to the area where there was some grass. It was away from the road, probably to my benefit, as they didn't get as great of a shot. When I stepped there, lights flicked on, blinding me. I raised my arm to block the light, trying to see who it was. The dogs were doing their business, so I turned when the car moved. It happened so quickly, I'm not sure of the correct sequence. One second I was standing, the next the car approached with the window lowering and I saw her face. It was Fort who saved me, pulling on the leash and causing me to fall forward out of the original pathway."

"Her?" Atticus asked, his jaw tightening.

Wells flicked his eyes at Monroe, then back to Atticus. "Yeah, I didn't see that she had a gun, but it was clearly her in the seat. I've never forgotten her face."

"Say it already," Sax grunted, his need to fix this and make the family safe riding him hard. I longed to go to him, but I needed to stand tall on my own for a moment.

"It was Brittni."

Monroe jerked back, shock registering on his face. "What? How could she?" I saw the moment he wrote her off, knowing there was nothing to save. She'd never been a mother to Levi, only his incubator. She only cared what he would provide her, not him. Monroe realized that right then. There wasn't anything to preserve. If she was willing to kill or be part of killing his boyfriend, the man he loved, she'd already chosen her fate.

Atticus and Sax started to move toward the door, ready to update the guys out there. Nicco had been watching me the whole time, so I wasn't surprised he was the one to ask, stopping the others.

"What else, Beautiful? Who did *you* see?"

I met his gray-blue eyes, the gray swirling, and I found the landing space I needed. "Your father. I saw Dayton Mascro staring back at me. They didn't drive off after but waited, watching. He was there the whole time."

THIRTY THREE

MONROE

The blood pounded in my ears, and I struggled to grab onto the words being spoken. All I could hear was Wells saying her name.

Brittni. Brittni. Brittni.

She'd finally done it; she'd stepped over the line into a place of no return. I'd hoped she'd prove to love Levi enough to change her behavior and be the mother for him that he needed. Instead, she'd shown she was only in it for herself.

And now, nothing would hold back the Komodo side of me.

Resolution at what was to come filled my veins, slowing the pumping blood to a dull roar, bringing the room back into focus. I heard Loren as she said Atticus and Nicco's father had also been there. It should probably surprise me to hear that my ex-wife had teamed up with a sadistic mob boss, but it didn't. It made me question what I'd seen in her. Had she always been that good of an actress, or had I been so deep in denial of my feelings for Wells that I'd grabbed onto something the most opposite from him?

It didn't matter. We were here now, and it was time to end this once and for all.

"Brittni needs to die."

My statement stopped the conversation dead, and everyone in the room turned to look at me. I could see varying expressions on the others' faces, but I needed to see only Wells and Loren's at that moment.

Loren watched me, studying me intensely. She had her therapist face on, the one where she showed none of her own emotion outside of being an empathic and understanding listener. I waited, hoping she'd see my commitment to this. I hadn't come to this decision lightly, or out of anger or revenge. Those were there, but they weren't the emotions pushing me to that course of action.

This was about Levi and us. This was about our future and the need to not look over my shoulder every second, waiting for her to spring her next trap. Brittni was a disease that needed to be eradicated. It was the only option.

The others were quiet, probably watching Loren as well, but I held her eyes. "It will be better for Levi now to mourn his mother as he remembers her than for her to continue to inflict damage on him and us over the next ten years before he's free of her. This is more than revenge. This is a matter of protecting our future and causing the least amount of damage for my son."

"What about when he learns you were the one to do it?" Wells asked, gripping my hand. I dropped my eyes to him, surprised he'd asked. "I don't disagree, she needs to go. The bitch *shot* me. But… if he ever learned the truth, you could lose him."

I swallowed, knowing he was right, but it felt like a better risk. "It's worth it, and I trust in our bond that he'd know I wouldn't make that kind of decision lightly."

"Good thing you won't have to then," Atticus spoke up from behind me. I swung my head, looking at him in shock. The stern-looking man met my eyes, seriousness in his gaze. I expected to find pity, but instead, I found respect. Atticus had once told me that children were to be protected at all costs, and he'd gone above and beyond helping me in that aspect with the court hearing.

"I can't ask that of you." I shook my head, the momentary peace I felt dropping into the pit of my stomach.

"Of course, you can, Sunshine," Nicco said, grinning at me. He walked over closer to Wells and me. "Plus, you didn't ask. We offered. Mas failed to mention that you're family now, and family doesn't kill alone. You gotta share the fun." He smirked, lifting the mood. "Besides," his eyes moved to meet Wells', holding them for a second. I watched as Wells swallowed, squeezing my hand tight before Nicco looked over to Loren. "You hurt one of us. You hurt all of us. I know this relationship is still new for us, and there hasn't been anything officially discussed on what we all are. But I think I speak for my big bro and the grumpy one, when I say you're one of us and we care about you."

"I… I… don't know what to say," I admitted, looking at the others. Loren was beaming, a beautiful smile on her face. Sax grunted but didn't argue. Atticus rolled his eyes, sighing loudly as he rubbed his temples.

"How did I not piece together you were my younger brother before now? You're definitely as annoying as one." He dropped his hand, looking at Wells and me. "But he's not wrong. We don't invite outsiders into our ranks or let them see behind the curtain, so to speak. The moment you stepped into my home, you became protected, whether you knew it or not. You protect our secret. We protect you. It's as simple as that. It seems now that our two worlds have collided if the impersonator is involved. It's not just your problem. It's ours. Now, I've been awake for almost 24 hrs. I suggest we all get some sleep, and then we can strategize on how best to respond."

"Thank you," I choked out, nodding. Atticus turned to leave, Sax following behind him.

"Wait," Loren said before turning to me. "I'm going to check on the kids. I'll be right back." She patted my hand, kissing Wells on the cheek quickly before she got up and met them at the door. I still couldn't tell what she thought, but it didn't seem like she was against it. Nicco took her spot, lying down in the opposite direction, making himself comfortable. I watched him, still trying to figure him out. His earlier jovial mood seemed to change as he picked at something on the comforter.

"I've seen a lot of blood in my life, but I have to say, walking out of that building and seeing Loren on the ground covered in yours, it was one of the scariest moments of my life."

Wells rolled his eyes, missing the point, his asshole wall going up, and I smiled, kind of excited to watch the show. It was nice being on the other side of this for once. "I'll try not to get shot around her next time. I wouldn't want to inconvenience you." He rolled his eyes, sighing.

"Sure, because that's what I meant." Nicco stood up, his movements stiff as he moved toward the door. "When you're done being a scared asshole, maybe reevaluate that sentence, Crash." He moved his gaze to me, winking. I was sure it was merely to stir the pot, but it made my cheeks heat, nonetheless. "Stay golden, Sunshine. I enjoy looking at your beautiful face."

He shut the door, leaving Wells and me alone. I chuckled, shaking my head, looking back at the man I loved. The reality of the situation hit me again, seeing him hooked up to everything and the momentary relief I had fled me. "He's not wrong, though. I thought I lost you, and I didn't know how to deal with it."

"He's a fucking fool. He's only trying to mess with me." Wells rolled his eyes, huffing as he tried to adjust himself. The wires and bandages kept him from being able to move too much.

"Sure, babe, keep telling yourself that." I smiled at

him, hoping he'd see people cared about him. Wells was so used to being the forgotten foster kid, he didn't know how to accept other people liking him without getting something in return. Wells grunted, but his eyes started to close more, so I kissed his cheek, tucking him in.

The nurse would be back later to give him meds. They had her in another room close by if we needed her, but didn't want her to be around everything they were doing. The attention to detail Atticus went through surprised me at times. He thought through every possibility and managed it all, nothing slipping. In a way, I admired him for that. I'd thought I'd never be on this side of things again, having picked a career that helped me fight against the bad guys.

Turned out, the lines on who was good and bad were very blurred, and sometimes, evil stared back at you under the veil of a pretty blonde in designer shoes.

Perhaps it was time I changed my fight and stopped bucking against the parts of me I thought made me less than and grabbed ahold of them instead. I'd always believed the Komodo made me weak, my reliance on a darker section of myself hindering me from being good. In reality, it had been about survival, and blocking traits I deemed unworthy, and hiding them had only made me vulnerable.

But there was no time to lament on my regrets. I had to focus on moving forward, and that started with deciding how to kill Brittni.

"For some reason, I expected discussions of murder to be more… murdery," Loren commented, looking around the table.

Nicco laughed, setting down a plate of cupcakes in front of her. "Who says you can't talk about death while enjoying some cupcakes? I did make sure to get red. I wanted to color-code our theme."

"I worry about you," I joked, laughing as I grabbed one.

"About time someone did," he quipped, smiling.

"I mean, I'm all for a theme, and cupcakes are always a plus, but like, don't we need a murder board, or I don't know blueprints?"

"Bellezza, we're talking about killing a high-class socialite, not a mastermind killer," Atticus said, raising his eyebrows at her. The talk of murder and mayhem had his eyes heating a little. He might talk about manslaughter being their last go-to, but it still seemed to get his blood pumping. I couldn't say the same for myself. I knew it needed to happen, and I felt relief over the decision, but I gained no pleasure in thinking of killing Levi's mom.

Loren squeezed my hand, and I flicked my eyes to her. She had a caring smile on her face, offering me a look that she understood. "For what it's worth," she swallowed, "I think you're making the harder decision. I don't know what's right or wrong, but I know you didn't come to this lightly, and I would never judge you for it. I support you."

"But you wouldn't do the same?"

She shrugged, a slight smile on her lips. "I have no idea what I'd do. I don't have your life experience or your history with her. I trust you to know what's at stake and the cost. I see all of that, and that's why I can support this; because I know you weighed out everything. I don't think it's for me to say it's right or wrong. Only you can make the choice. I won't deny there's a part of me that's happy she'll be gone, especially after what she did to Wells, but I don't know if that's only fleeting. No matter what, though, I'll be here, right beside you the whole way through."

I leaned my head against hers, something in me relaxing at her words. I didn't know how much I needed to hear them. I didn't want her to judge me or think less of me.

"Thank you, Lo. I needed to hear that."

"I know it's not the same, but I'll try to be the best mother I can be to Levi; I just want you to know that. You don't have to raise him on your own."

"You don't have to try, Lo. You already are. Fuck, I love you." I grabbed her face, smashing my lips to hers, kissing her with everything I had. She made all the rough edges smooth; all my past hurt felt worth it if I got to have her in my life.

A loud whistle broke us apart, and I pulled away,

both of us panting. I turned my head, seeing Nicco fanning himself. "Okay, that was hot. You were all, grr, and she was all lovey, and then bam! If we didn't need to finalize some homicide, I'd sweep everything off this table and see where that went. But alas…" he sighed, placing his head in his hand like a lovesick fool.

"I think you've had too much sugar," Atticus barked, looking at Nicco like he'd lost his mind.

"Nah," he waved him off, smiling, "I was just reminded of what's important and that it's okay to be myself. So, here I am, bro, take me as I am."

Atticus shook his head, a smile playing at the corner of his lips, and I saw the affection shining through. Sax sat back, shoving a whole cupcake into his mouth, licking the frosting that spilled out of his lips and into his beard. He missed a spot, and Loren giggled. The big man stopped, looking up to meet her eyes.

"Yes, Spitfire?"

"You got a little…" She motioned to where, and he stuck his tongue out further, slowly licking away the frosting with the tip, and even I had to drop my eyes, shifting in my seat. That, after our intense kiss, had my cock throbbing hard against my zipper. Fucking Hell.

A throat cleared, and we all glanced over to Atticus, who gave us all a look like he was the Sunday School teacher and we'd all disappointed him. "Despite my *brother's* frivolity, he's not wrong. Murder for the Mascros isn't gory. We discuss most of our murders over food and cocktails. Why does one need to debase themselves just because they're killing someone? You don't."

"I swear, you sound so stuck up right now," Nicco said, laughing. "If you were a woman, I'd expect you to be inspecting the dirt under your fingernails."

Atticus gave him a look, but I noticed he dropped his shoulders some, relaxing. "Fine. But it doesn't have to be a wham, bam, you're dead."

"Hmph," Sax grunted, showing he much preferred it that way. Though, his following words surprised me, making me reconsider. "I think she deserves a death where she's humiliated and discovered in the worst possible way. She doesn't deserve decency."

I sat there stunned for a moment as he licked his fingers free of icing, nonplussed by his words as I watched him. Clearing my throat, I nodded.

"Um, yeah, that could work. What did you have in mind?"

Over the next thirty minutes, Atticus, Nicco, and Sax volleyed ideas, giving me the final say. I didn't disagree with much, as it seemed they had it under control and knew what they were doing. I'd lived some dark days, often having to fight for my life, but I'd never taken one before. This was out of my depth, and as willing as I was to end hers, I hadn't thought much past doing it, much less if it would've been messy.

"Very well, then. I think that's taken care of. It's been an eventful few days, so how about we all do something with the kids and leave the murdering of mothers for tomorrow."

"First, who are you? And second, mothers?" I asked.

"What? I enjoy spending time with our youth." Atticus straightened his jacket, bolstering himself, and ignoring the other part.

"He just wants to watch Harry Potter and is hoping that hanging out with them will allow it," Sax muttered, rolling his eyes. "And he means mothers, to include Queen Bitch Hanover."

Atticus glared at the bearded giant but didn't deny it, and the man that Atticus was, became even more muddled in my mind. I guess it was only fair to get to know him instead of assuming things about him. It was such a rudimentary concept that I'd seemed to have forgotten, hindering myself from seeing people as they were instead of who they presented. I guess I'd been doing that longer than I realized, and it had started with myself.

Glancing around the room, I saw the potential for what I could have if I let myself let go of all the carefully controlled restraints I'd unknowingly been holding in place. These were people who'd accepted me, protected Levi, and were now willing to help me kill Brittni. If that didn't say family, well, then it wasn't one I wanted to be part of. This was everything.

Getting up, I followed them into the room the kids were. Some of the guards were playing a game with the three of them, and I was glad Levi hadn't watched TV all day. I'd been so preoccupied with Wells and Loren, I hadn't spent much time with him once we'd arrived here.

"Dad! Check it out. I just learned how to float the river!"

I paused, feeling that sensation of judgment that an eight-year-old shouldn't be playing poker, but I shook it, knowing that he'd been loved on and safer with these men of crime all day. The should's of the world had no place here. So, I smiled, giving the guard who'd frozen a nod that it was okay.

"Oh? You're not losing all your allowance, are you?"

"Nope! We're playing with M&M's."

"Ah, well, that's good. I think we were going to have a Harry Potter Marathon in a bit. Let's get you in a bath and change into your pajamas before it starts."

"Yes!" Levi hopped off the chair, racing to the room I'd put our stuff in. I loved his enthusiasm and acceptance of these people as good, despite society depicting it the other way.

"It's Beau, right?"

"Yes, Mr. Miller."

I smiled, shaking my head. "Just Monroe is fine. Thank you for looking after him" He relaxed, giving me a nod.

"He's a good kid. Super smart. He's cleaned me out of M&M's." I laughed, liking that.

"Oh, I don't doubt it. He has a look where he can practically get you to do anything if you're not careful."

Beau smiled, agreeing. I waved as I walked off to get Levi ready for bed, finding myself oddly excited about watching Harry Potter with three mafia men, two teenagers, and my boyfriend and girlfriend. My life was strange, but it was my life, and I liked it just the way it was—darkness and all.

THIRTY FOUR

LOREN

I smoothed down my dress, nerves skyrocketing as I waited for my father to arrive. Despite hating having to dress a certain way for my mother in the past, I'd taken extra care to pick out my outfit. It was something new I'd gotten with the girls, and as I stood in the white dress, I felt confident and mature. This was a big moment for me, and I wanted to look the part—pearls and all.

I'd been pleased when my father had responded to my request quickly, not even blinking when I asked for him, and only him. Perhaps things were starting to deteriorate in their relationship more than I realized. It made me curious, but only in the sense of how it might play out. This would be a critical move against my mother, and I had high hopes for my dad, despite his previous reluctance in my life. I think I mostly didn't want to have two awful parents.

Looking around the room, I felt pleased with how everything looked in Atticus' formal dining room. We'd come back this morning, feeling it was safe again. All the little details stood out, and I realized it was the first time I felt pride about setting a table.

Atticus had helped me meet with the staff to plan the meal, pick out the linens, and flowers. The lengths he'd gone to make me happy made my breath stop when I thought about it. His care was woven throughout, and I could see the minor effects he made on things in our everyday lives. Even from the very beginning, when I thought he hated me, when he'd pushed me away, he'd been protecting and caring for me.

Atticus and I had both been blind to our feelings, too scared to look at them closely. With the blinders off, I was learning so much about the man behind the suit.

Stepping away from the table, I was surprised when strong arms wrapped around me, and a masculine cologne full of seduction and darkness wafted over me. Sinking into his embrace, my heart sped up when he rubbed his nose along my neck before whispering to me.

"You look beautiful, Bellezza, and this room looks perfect. It's going to go well. But no matter what, you have us; we're here. Don't forget who you are."

"And who is that?" I asked, a smile playing at my lips.

"Lady of the manor, of course." I could feel his lips move against my neck, and I wondered if he was giving me one of his rare smiles. I almost wanted to see it, but it felt too lovely in his arms to move away. So instead, I turned, wrapping my arms around his neck, getting the benefit of both.

He gazed down at me, his face open, and I lost myself staring into his eyes. Remembering I had a question, I whispered, "Oh, and what benefits does the Lady of the manor get exactly?"

"Hmm," he purred, dipping his head lower, his breath fanning against my cheek and setting off my nerves in a new direction. "Well, for starters, she gets to—"

"Sir, your guest has arrived."

The words stilled the air around us, a reminder of what lay ahead for us today, and I watched as Atticus went into Boss mode. His hands flexed on my hips, but he leaned down, brushing his lips delicately against mine. It was a reminder that while he might be cold on the outside, he burned for me, and I realized he didn't lose too much of himself with me there. When he let go of me, he straightened his tie before grabbing my hand, and together we walked to meet my father.

We approached as a unit, which strengthened me and gave me the clarity I needed. As we drew closer, I tried to look at my dad with different eyes. He looked well, dressed nicely, and no one would know anything was different on the surface. But if I looked closer, I could see the small changes I hadn't ever paid attention to. There were stress lines around his eyes, his skin seemed to have lost some of its glow, and I wondered if perhaps he'd missed his weekly golf game with his club memberships being canceled, as Atticus had stated at the benefit. His hair was thinning, and he looked like he'd lost weight as well. It shocked me. However, more confusing was whether I was finally seeing my dad as a person and not an extension of Jaqueline, or if the past year really had taken a toll on him.

Maybe money really did buy youth, and now that they didn't have any to buy the things that kept him looking young, it made all the cracks in his appearance visible? It was a lot to ponder and not something I wanted to think about at the moment.

"Dad," I greeted, calling his attention to me. Kenneth Hanover looked up, meeting my eyes, and I saw a genuine smile there. Letting go of Atticus' hand, I walked over and embraced him. It was quick, but for us, it was more than I'd gotten in a while.

"It's good to see you, Loren. I was pleased you reached out."

"It's good to see you too, Dad. Come on, let's chat over some food." We walked together, Atticus waiting for me ahead, dropping next to me as I neared. I had my dad's arm in mine, but it felt nice to have Atticus close if I needed him.

"How did you manage to get out of the house?" I asked curiously.

He grunted, displeasure in his tone. "Not as difficult as you might think." I could hear the dissension in his words, and I peeked over at Atticus. He grimaced, hearing it too.

"Well, that's kind of what I wanted to talk to you about," I said as we entered the dining room where the rest of the guys were waiting, quieting as we walked in. "But first, I want to introduce you to some people." I watched as my dad took in the men who'd become my world, watching for any sign of disgust. He seemed shocked, but didn't look at me the way my mother would have, giving me some hope again.

"Welcome to our home, Mr. Hanover. I'm Atticus. Please, have a seat." My father nodded, doing as he was told. As I sat next to Atticus, I nodded at Monroe, who introduced himself.

"I'm Monroe Miller. It's nice to meet you, Mr. Hanover." My dad smiled, but seemed overwhelmed as the others went around. Wells and Sax basically grunted out their names, leaving Nicco to finish. Despite his tattoos on display, I wasn't shocked when he displayed manners.

"I'm Nicolai. It's a pleasure to make the acquaintance of the father of such an amazing woman."

"Show off," Wells muttered, Sax agreeing with a grunt. Nicco just smiled wider, not disturbed. I'd seen him emerge over the past few days in a way I hadn't known he'd needed, and it had been beautiful to watch. Smiling, I turned back to my dad, assessing him again. I wondered what he thought about all these men here. Did he think I was a slut? The fear he would think less of me wanted to rise, but I kicked it away. I hoped my dad would be able to accept me, but I didn't need his approval to be happy.

Kenneth nodded at my guys, swallowing as he looked around the table. They were an intimidating bunch, excluding Monroe, but I'd learned not to discount him. "It's an honor to meet you all as well, but I'm afraid I can't take credit for the woman Loren has become. She's done all of that on her own."

It was the first compliment I could remember my father giving me that wasn't connected to something my mother had forced me to do. I swallowed, willing the burning behind my eyes to go away. The door swung open, offering me a moment to collect myself as the food was placed down in front of us. The silver trays were lifted almost in unison, and wonderful smells greeted us. I breathed it in, smiling.

"That never gets old," Monroe chuckled, making me smile.

"Shall we eat?" Atticus asked, picking up his fork. The other guys waited, but my father wasn't privy to mafia boss etiquette and picked up his own, nodding as he took a bite. He greedily ate the meal, and I worried things were worse than we'd known.

"This is fabulous. I haven't had anything this nice in a while." It made my heart hurt a little, but I had to remind myself he'd made his own choices. He was a grown man and capable of getting himself out of the situation if he needed to.

It was quiet as we all ate the perfect crepes, eggs

Benedict, and home fries. It all tasted divine, but it was hard to enjoy it, knowing the questions I'd need to ask my father.

When my father cleared his plate, Atticus nodded for the waiter to bring him more, and I smiled at his notice. I watched as he looked embarrassed for about a millisecond, but then took it, trading the server. Atticus sat his fork down when he was done, and the staff quietly left. It was time to get to it.

I cleared my throat, feeling Atticus' hand on my thigh for support. How I'd love to give him the reins here, but I knew I needed to do it. It was important. They were all here to support me through this, and that was what mattered. I could do this because of that.

"Dad, I've recently discovered Jaqueline's schemes with Brian, and I just have to ask, did you know?"

His fork froze halfway to his mouth, and he turned, looking at me. He set it down, and I saw the sadness in his eyes. "No, well, not at first."

It hurt, the tears wanting to return for a different reason this time, but I held them back, wanting to give him the chance to explain before I wrote him off.

"It's not an excuse, but I've been on autopilot for the past fifteen years, give or take. Your mother, she's not an easy woman to live with, not that I have to convince you of that. Somewhere around the time you became a teenager, I, um, I had an affair." He dropped his eyes, and my heart sped up. I hadn't expected him to say that. While I could understand how difficult my mother was, it hurt to hear him admit it, never expecting my father to do something like that, something that had been done to me.

"I hadn't meant for it to happen, and honestly, it came out of nowhere. Of course, your mother discovered it, but she didn't confront me about it. She waited, plotted. Do you remember how you wanted to quit that Jr. Pageant and go on the art trip instead?"

I nodded, still stunned.

"I wanted to let you go, and I told Jacqueline I would give you permission. She put her foot down, though, and brought up my indiscretion. She threatened to use it against me, ruining my name and taking you and everything from me. If I wanted my life to stay how it was, I had to back off and let her raise you as she saw fit. I never thought how selfish it was of me to agree to her demands, or the lengths of manipulation she'd go to with you. I'm sorry, Loren. I convinced myself you were happy, so it was okay. I got to keep my secret, and you flourished."

"You were a coward," Sax gritted out, and I looked over, smiling at him. He acknowledged the pain I couldn't, his fierce protectiveness shining through.

My father flinched but didn't deny it. His eyes brimmed at the edges with tears, his regret showing. I remember the trip and how things did seem to change after that. My mother became more overbearing, and my dad had checked out, letting her deal with me. I thought it was because I wasn't good enough, his disinterest in me a sign, so I worked harder to make him proud, to be good enough for him.

Funny how it had all been a lie. All of it.

My mother used me to correct her mistakes, and my father hid his ignorance to cover his sins. They'd both been so busy perfecting their image, they'd neglected to see how miserable and lost I was. A few summers later, I met Brian, and my mother encouraged me to date him. My whole life had been orchestrated to fit their needs. While I'd always felt that way, to hear it blatantly laid out broke something in me.

"Who was she?" I asked. It felt like I was missing something still. Why had my father been so scared of my mother revealing his secret? Affairs were almost accessories in the suburbs.

His face paled, and I wondered if he'd tell me. If he couldn't be honest with me, it would be the killing blow in our relationship.

"His name is Marcus."

I blinked, not sure I heard him right. "As in Marcus West, your partner at the firm?"

He nodded, never dropping my eyes. As I tried to grapple with this new revelation, emotions swirled in me —compassion, respect, confusion.

"When did you find out about the trust?" I asked, deciding I needed all the information before determining where we stood.

"A few months ago. After the benefit, I confronted

her on my suspicions." My shoulders relaxed a little at that.

"And the eggs they stole from me?"

My father reared back like I'd slapped him. "What?" Genuine shock covered his face as his eyebrows rose, his mouth opening. He leaned forward, his hand lifting to touch mine, but stopped, dropping it to his lap. "Loren, I have no idea what you're talking about. I promise. What did *she* do?"

It was what I needed to hear, my shoulders dropping the rest of the way, and I shared with my father the things my mother had been up to in the past with Brian and how things had escalated in the past few months. He nodded, rubbing my hand now.

"That tracks. A few years ago, I got a notice from our accountant that there was a lot of money being moved around, so I asked him to look into it. That was the first time I realized how much Jacqueline had mismanaged things. I started separating our accounts, siphoning money into a separate one she couldn't touch, and removing her from assets slowly. I put her on a restricted budget, stating there had been some bad investments, and we needed to be more mindful. Granted, she still had access to all of her cards and memberships. I've found out she started running up tabs, maxing out cards, and carrying debt from one place to the next, opening new accounts when she could. When she lost it all in the scandal, that was when I realized how bad things were. I've been trying to keep things afloat and thankful I'd separated myself when I had, but she'd still done some damage. Everything in our joint account is gone, and most of our possessions have been repossessed. It's been such a shit show. I've been glad you haven't been around for it. I see now that was short-sighted of me. Of course, Jacqueline would be using you for something. I'm sorry, honey."

I squeezed his hand, but had no words to say. He wasn't faultless, but he hadn't been an active participant in her schemes either. I debated with myself if it was enough.

"Would you be willing to testify against Jacqueline and provide the documentation you have?" I asked.

My dad looked at me, focusing on my eyes. He knew what I was asking, so I kept my focus, not wavering. He looked around at the men at the table before landing back on me.

"I'm proud of the woman you've become. I can see you have people who care about you and not because of what you might give them. I wish I'd realized that sooner in my life. I'm sixty-two, and I don't think I've been happy for more than a few days in my life. I think it's time I quit hiding and live the life I want. It's time Jaqueline pays for her crimes. I'll do whatever it takes to help you, at whatever cost it is to me. It's time I was as brave as you. Maybe then I can be the father you've always needed."

"I'd like that." I smiled, seeing the victim he'd been to Jacqueline as well, but not excusing the choices he'd made. I could understand them, but it didn't mean I would so easily forget the impact they had on my life.

Atticus squeezed my thigh, reminding me I wasn't alone in this, and I felt the collective gazes of the men who'd come to mean the world to me, showing me what courage and honor indeed were.

By the time my father left, we'd found out he'd been planning to move out and make things official with his boyfriend, so divorcing her wouldn't be as big of an ask as I'd thought. Things at the house had been bleak, and he realized he'd had nothing else to lose by coming out of the closet. It was sad that it took him that long to step away from Jacqueline, but I was also happy he was finally doing it. He'd even spent some time getting to know Jude and made plans to volunteer at the youth center when he'd be there. It was everything I'd always wanted from my father, and I was glad I'd get to experience it, at least in this new life of mine.

My dad scheduled a time with Atticus and his accountant before he left, and I felt hopeful this was another win in our column.

Sax's hands skated up my arms, and a jittery feeling coursed through me. "You ready, Spitfire?"

"For what?" I asked, looking up at him.

"We didn't get to have our date, twice now. I think it's time we make it happen."

Smiling, I nodded as nervous and excited energy skated up me. It was time for my date with Sax and Atticus.

THIRTY FIVE

LOREN

Tingles raced up my skin as we made our way into the club, the men bracketing my sides. We'd taken a back entrance, which somehow made it more eerie as we walked down the darkened hallways. I'd video called the girls earlier when Sax had told me about our date, and they'd helped me pick out an outfit that was sure to stun the guys.

It'd been great to see Cami and Nat, but I could see the weariness on them both. I yearned to see them in person so I could hug them. Hopefully, I'd be able to talk Atticus into letting me go to the safe house to check in with them soon.

"Spitfire, you have a decision to make," Sax said, stopping me. His eyes heated as he stared down at me. Both of the men were in their black suits, and I wondered if we'd even have to step out onto the floor. I didn't know if I wanted other women to be able to gawk at them. Actually, no, I definitely didn't.

"What do you mean?"

"Which room do you want to venture to?" Atticus grabbed my hand, running his fingers over the top of my palm delicately before flipping it. Cami had thought it would be a good idea to wear a trench coat over my lingerie to bring the fantasy to life, but as Atticus trailed his hand up my arm, I wished I wasn't wearing it at all. My breath caught, and I swallowed.

"Um, I didn't get to see three of them."

"So you have Masterful, Admiration, or Obsession left," Atticus purred, moving behind me. He pushed the hair off my neck and breathed his words into my skin. I started to list the names of the rooms from the first time, Sensation, Captivate, and Reality.

That was when it hit me, and I realized how right under my nose it had been the whole time. *Mascro.* It was clever, even if I hated being on the side of not knowing.

"Do I get any indication of what might be behind those doors?"

"Nope." Sax smiled, enjoying being in on the know.

"Hmm." I thought about it, trying to find the connection between the name of the previous ones and what lay behind them. A part of me was curious what Masterful might hold, but the more I considered them, the more one word stood out. "Obsession," I said with no hesitation.

Shock flashed briefly behind Sax's eyes before a huge grin filled his face. "Very good, Spitfire."

"Yes, very good," Atticus added, purring.

A warm blush started to spread over my body at their

praise, and I wondered for a second if I'd gone too far. The heat in Sax's eyes, though, had me wanting to see it through.

"Right this way." Sax took my hand, leading me down another pathway before turning and stopping in front of a door.

"How do you know it's empty?" I asked, worried we might walk in on someone.

"They're all empty, Bellezza. Do you really think we'd let anyone else see you?" Atticus asked, possession in his tone.

"You closed?" I asked, stuck on that part.

"Just opening later. Illusion is open for now; Verity will open when we're done. Now, are you ready?"

I nodded, hoping I was. I couldn't deny my nerves, but there was that hint of exhilaration as well, the feeling you got before opening a present on Christmas morning. A million possibilities lay behind that door. I just had to be brave enough to step through.

Loosening the belt on the coat, I let it slip from my shoulders, the smooth material sliding off and hitting the floor. I kept my face forward and turned the knob. I heard their inhales of breath as they took in my outfit, and it emboldened me. A smile spread over my lips, and a sexy vixen emerged. Turning my head, I took in their hungry stares and winked, finishing my entrance into the room.

It wasn't what I'd expected, but I instantly loved it. It was larger than the Sensation room. The back wall was a half stage with a stripper pole in the center. There were soft round couches covered in velvet, and I briefly wondered how hard they were to clean. A bed took up one corner, and a large glass mirror ran along the back of the room with thick curtains on its sides.

I stopped in the middle of the room, and soft music started to play through hidden speakers. Biting my lip, I tried to figure out what made this room an obsession, but nothing was coming to mind unless people became addicted to pole dancing. I supposed that could be a thing. It seemed interesting, but I didn't know if I had the guts, or the coordination, to do it.

Warm hands landed on my hips, the rough texture letting me know it was Sax. He bent down, breathing onto my neck. "Shit, Spitfire. You're a fucking fantasy come to life." I smiled, my confidence returning.

I'd been worried the outfit I chose would make me look too much like all the hatred my mother had spewed at me for years.

Common Whore. Tramp. Prostitute. Slut.

It was what had made me put it on in the end. I needed to replace her hate with my own truths. The vow to believe in myself and the best of me was holding firm, and each day I felt pieces of the past falling away.

The black lace bra, crotchless panties, and thigh-high stockings kissed my skin as I moved, lighting up all my nerve endings. Confidence surged, and I tilted my head up, catching his gaze. "Hopefully, I'll be better than the fantasy, Mr. Sax."

He growled, eliminating the space between us, crashing his lips to mine. He tasted of masculine sensuality, his own confidence spurring on mine and helping me see the woman he saw me as, the woman I was.

"You say the dirtiest things with the sweetest mouth."

I smiled, nipping his lip as I turned fully. "So, tell me, what makes this room an obsession?" Atticus took that moment to trap me between them, his body pressing into my back.

"It's not the room that's an obsession, Bellezza, but the *woman* in it. Some people come to be worshiped, men or women watching and praising their every move and adoring them. Others want to be admired but don't need the praise. The obsession lies in the person and those who willingly worship at her feet. In here, you're in charge."

"And you just watch?" My skin erupted in goosebumps at his words. I licked my lips, absorbing it all.

"At first, usually, yes. It's based on exhibitionism, and the power one gets from being free to be who they want and allowing others to witness it. There's one other feature of this room, and you can choose if you want to use it or not."

I looked up at Sax, and my breath caught. His eyes swirled with need, and I could feel him pressed up against me already. He was waiting, though, waiting for me to make a move.

"What is it?" I asked in a breathy whisper.

He clicked a remote, and the mirror wall in the back lit up, and I could see through it. He clicked it again, and it went dark, and then a third time, it was back to being a mirror.

"You can have it off, and no one but this room can see you. You can have it on, and they see you, but you don't see them. Or," he paused, clicking it again, and this time when it revealed a room, I saw who was reflected on the other side, like a screen.

Wells. Monroe. Nicco.

My breath caught, and I knew if I could share this with them, this would be how Atticus would prefer it for now. He bent down, running his nose up my neck, stopping as he cupped my jaw from behind with his hand. "Only them." I couldn't tell if it was an assurance for me, that only they'd be the ones on the other side of the glass, or if it was all he'd allow.

Either way, it set my heart galloping and my body heated. I rubbed my legs together, the need burning through me now.

"Let them watch," I said, finally managing to get the order out. I wasn't used to having control, and perhaps that was the point of this room, like he'd said.

Attie kissed my neck. "Good girl."

A moan threatened to escape, but I bit my lip, keeping it contained. Why did I like it so much when he said that? His hand left my throat, grabbing my lip and pulling it free. "No."

It was all he said before releasing it, moving away as

he and Sax took a seat side by side on one of the round couches. I instantly got his message and felt the difference between pleasing and displeasing him, and I knew which one I preferred.

Music began to play louder, and I felt my hips swaying to the beat. It felt a little uncomfortable with them sitting and me just standing here, but when I looked into their eyes, I saw how much the little sway I did affected them.

Taking a deep breath, I shook off the insecurities that lingered, wondering if I was doing it right and if they'd seen someone else do it better before. I didn't need to think like that here. It didn't matter. Their eyes told me how sexy they found me. So I grabbed it and took it as my own.

Trailing a hand down, I traced over the outline of my breast, my fingers lightly grazing the skin. I began to move more, taking a few steps toward them on my heels. I sashayed my hips, doing what felt natural. I danced a little, swaying and turning, touching myself in the process. I closed my eyes, getting lost in the music and movements.

"Open your eyes, Spitfire."

I did, locking them on his, and I approached, needing him. He was the siren, calling to me. Sax reached out a hand, and I took it, placing it on my hip, and danced in between his legs. When his hands moved over me, I got lost in the sensation, no longer having to think about what I was doing and just going along with what my body felt.

Sitting down on his lap, I leaned back into his chest and ran my fingers through his beard as I made my way to the back of his head. Pulling him toward me, I met his lips, stealing a kiss before I let go. Rolling over, I sat on Atticus' lap, his hands falling to my hips and holding me still. His dark eyes bored into me, and I stopped, caught in the storm I saw there.

My hand slowly lifted to cup his jaw, and he closed his eyes, leaning into it. Straddling his hips, I ran my fingertips along the back of his head, digging them deep into his scalp. Atticus moaned, and I kept going. Sax moved to my neck, no longer wanting to be left out. A strap fell down my shoulder, and he started to kiss the skin.

Slowly, he slipped the straps off, leaving my cups to fall open and my breasts to spill forth. It was the shot I needed, and I rocked myself on Atticus' lap, leaning my head back to Sax. Each time I took a step, it seemed like it gave them permission as they waited for me to move, and then they would follow. They both worshiped me with kisses, soft touches, and praises.

"You feel so amazing, Bellezza. I love feeling your heat on me."

"What do you need, Spitfire? Tell me."

"More. Touch me."

The second the command left my lips, they both obliged,

and I became lost in ecstasy. Sax's hands found my breasts, tweaking my nipples as he rolled them over his thumbs. His large palms engulfed my flesh, the roughness adding to the sensitivity I felt. I couldn't concentrate too long on what he was doing, though, as Atticus began to trace the lace of my panties. Gently, he grazed back and forth, and I tried to rock into him more, needing the pressure.

When he finally breached them, I whimpered as he ghosted along my lips. He was doing the same slight touch to me, and I'd had enough. Grabbing his face. I held eye contact with him. "Touch me. *Now*. I want your fingers in me!"

He smiled, giving me a satisfied look before he plunged them in, almost like he'd been waiting for me to break and demand it. "As you wish, Bellezza."

It was both too much and yet everything I needed, and my head fell back onto Sax's shoulder as I moved to accommodate the intrusion. Slowly, I rocked on them, finding my pace, and I figured out the game they were playing.

I had to ask. I had to demand it. I had to make them *obsess*.

Thinking about it this way, I flipped the script and knew what I needed to do.

"Take out your cock and stroke it for me, Sax." He smiled, sitting back to release his massive erection. I watched greedily as he unzipped his pants, freeing himself. Pulling back, I whimpered when I moved out of Atticus' range, but I needed to prove a point.

"Good. Now, take off your shirt, and you'll get a reward." While he did that, I slipped off my bra, dropping it to the floor. I kicked off my heels, standing only in my stockings, and looked up at the mirrored window, remembering who was there while I waited. My breath caught as I saw the three of them. Wells looked rough still, the day being long for him, but I knew he wouldn't have wanted to be left out. He sat up on a bed, Monroe next to him, and Nicco in a chair toward the foot of it. They all watched hungrily, my breath catching in my throat.

Part of me wanted them here with me. The other part knew I wasn't ready for that many dicks at once.

Not yet, at least. I would be.

Nicco winked, rubbing himself outside of his pants. It made me smile and helped me focus back on the room. Looking down at Sax, I smiled when he sat waiting for me to tell him what to do next, his large cock straining in his hand.

Kneeling on either side of his thick thighs, I braced myself on his shoulders as I bent down to whisper. "Want to teach Atticus a lesson with me?"

"Always," he grumbled, liquid heat in his words.

I started to lower myself, placing his hands to help guide me. I felt the tip of his thick head, and I stopped, rubbing myself over it. It touched my clit, and I moaned at the slight sensation. Sucking in a breath, I lowered more, stretching to accommodate Sax's size.

"Kiss me," I purred. Sax caught my lips in his, kissing

me as if I was the light to his shadows. It helped distract me from the mild discomfort until I was fully seated, taking a few minutes to adjust. Once I was ready, I started to move, my breath hitching as I felt him hit me in a new spot.

"Shit," I moaned. "Show me how good I make you feel."

Sax grinned. "Good girl. You got it now."

Smiling back, I almost forgot about Atticus as everything felt so amazing with Sax, but he grunted, reminding me of his presence. When I looked over, he arched an eyebrow, waiting for me to direct him.

"Watch." His eyes narrowed, but he didn't take his eyes off me. "Tell me what you see, what you like."

Atticus grunted but leaned forward. "I see a woman taking ownership of her body and sex. I see a goddess making five men worship her. I like watching you come undone. I like watching you receive pleasure from Sax, and I really can't wait until I can show you how good it can be. I love your freedom, and I love how sexy it is when you tell me what to do. You're the only person on this planet who can."

My breath caught at that, and I leaned forward, kissing him. I couldn't not after that. When I pulled back, I held his eyes. "Show me then. I want to know." I'd planned to make him sweat, watching Sax fuck me six ways to Sunday, but when he showed me his vulnerability, I couldn't hold back anymore. I needed them both.

"So sexy, Bellezza. So, fucking, sexy." He kissed me

quickly before his clothes started to come off at record speed. "Sax, turn some and hand me the lube."

"Wait, what? I'm—"

"Trust me, Lore." I swallowed, nodding.

Sax turned us a little to the side, and I lost my view of Atticus as he came up behind me. Sax laid down flat on the couch and moved me, so I was rocking on him. I fell into the movement as Atticus prepared himself. My eyes briefly flicked over to the window, and I saw Nicco was no longer content to rub himself outside his pants, and had pulled his dick free, stroking it as he watched me. It made me curious how the other two felt, but I couldn't think about it too long.

Pleasure coursed through me, and I rocked faster, timing it with Nicco's strokes. Sax twisted my nipple with one hand and thumbed my clit with the other. When I felt Atticus' warmth behind me, I wanted to stop, but I was close, so I didn't. He trailed kisses down my neck and touched my back and ass with his hands. I heard something, but with the slapping of my skin against Sax's and our moans, I couldn't hear much else.

Atticus pushed me a little, and I felt his thumb near my backside. Sax pulled my face to his and kissed me, twirling his tongue around mine. Hands cupped the globes of my ass, massaging them as they dipped down to my core, and I felt a finger next to Sax's cock in me. Atticus trailed it back to my rosette, swirling it around, and I clenched around his finger.

"Ssh, relax. I'm not going to do anything tonight. I'm

just going to start prepping you, Bellezza. Relax and trust me. I got you, Lore."

I breathed out, trying to focus on everything else instead of the fear. Sax moved his hands and began to rock me again, our rhythm and pace increasing, and I soon found myself getting closer to that edge. This time, when he breached my pucker, I didn't fear it. Atticus pushed his thumb in and out, and I found the fullness pleasant, and I soon fell over the edge, spiraling into oblivion. Sax grunted, spilling his release into me, kissing me hard as he came.

When I could breathe again, it didn't last long before I was lifted and placed on my knees. Atticus speared into me quickly, gripping my hips as he pounded into me, fucking me so hard, I would've fallen if he hadn't been holding me up. He must've been close because, within a few seconds, we came together, both of us screaming out our releases. This time, I did fall forward, landing on the soft cushion of the round couch. Sax laid across from me, moving my hair out of my face. He looked at me, his thumb caressing my skin.

"I love you, Loren Carter. You're my spitfire, and you give me a light I never thought I'd see again. I'll spend my life protecting you and giving you whatever you want."

"I already have everything I want—you. I love you, Saxon." I kissed him, feeling everything he said in his embrace, and I wrapped it around my heart, fortifying myself even more against the lies. Each new encounter reinforced the vow I made, and soon I wouldn't even remember them.

Atticus pulled me back, reminding me he was there too. It hadn't felt weird for me and Sax to profess our feelings with him privy; it was just the way our relationship worked. I wasn't there yet with him, and I knew he understood that. I laid between them for a while, content to have this moment of silence. When I remembered the others, I peeked up at the screen, but it was black again.

"You ready to get dressed? I thought we could grab a drink over at Illusion for old times' sake," Atticus murmured into my ear, tickling the skin there. I mumbled something back but rolled over, taking Sax's hand to get off the couch. I looked back at it, the question coming to mind again about cleaning. Sax chuckled, understanding my look.

"They're cleaned. Don't worry, Spitfire." I rolled my eyes, not feeling convinced, but moved over to my bra. But when I looked down at my panties, I cringed. They'd been nice to be crotchless for the sexy, fun times, but the thought of wearing them out made me shudder.

"Um, maybe getting a drink isn't the best idea." I looked back up and found Atticus standing with a garment bag.

"Everything you need is inside per Cami's instructions." He gave me a look, and my cheeks heated. Would I ever get over how he thought of everything?

"Thank you."

"Of course, Bellezza. There's a room over there to

wash up if you need to. We'll be out here waiting when you're ready."

I walked over to the door he'd pointed out and quickly freshened up, changing into the red dress inside. There was a matching mask as well, and I put it all on, feeling confident as I slipped on the heels. I noticed this mask wasn't illuminated, and I wondered if that detail had been Cami or Atticus. I had no need for more men in my life; it was just that his little possessiveness at times made my insides quiver. He was an odd balance of freedom and possession, and it made me want to push the limits of where that boundary lay. But secretly, I loved it.

Stepping out, they stopped talking when they saw me, making my hips sway a little as I walked toward them. They were decked out in black suits again, their masks matching, also not lit, making me smile with confidence.

"Ready?" I asked.

"I don't know," Sax said, "I'm reconsidering now."

"Same."

I rolled my eyes, my cheeks heating. "Come on, I know a good corner where we can have some fun if things heat up. But it would be fun to sit with you both and have a drink. Please?"

"Ask, and you shall receive, Bellezza." Atticus hooked his arm out, and I took it, and then Sax's too. He looked down at me, surprised, always used to having to fall to the back or to the shadows.

"You belong in the light, too. No one knows us here. That's what the masks are for, right? So, embrace it. I need both of you on my arms."

He smiled, and it was so precious and light that I wanted to bottle it up to keep with me. This silly man thought he was all darkness, but there light was, shining out of him, regardless.

We walked out and crossed behind some more hallways. I was glad they knew where they were going because it was all a maze in the dark. A few corners later, we stepped out through a door, and I expected to hear music and people. But instead, it was eerily quiet. I felt the men tense next to me at the realization.

"What time was it opening?" I asked, hoping we were just early.

"An hour ago," Atticus said, his jaw tensed. "Something isn't right. Sax."

He dropped my arm, kissed me on the head, and walked off to see what was going on. Atticus stood sentry next to me, pulling his phone out to see if he had any messages. Sax returned within moments, a grim look on his face.

"Mas, you need to see this."

Atticus took my hand, assuming it was safe since Sax hadn't said anything, and led me out with him. When we stepped out onto the floor, I could feel the difference, noting how cold and empty it felt. It was eerie. Atticus and I walked over to the bar where a bottle of scotch sat, a note under it.

He lifted the bottle, pulled it out, his face turning up in a scowl and crushing it between his fingers before I could read it.

His breaths came out heavy, his eyes shooting fire, as he tried to calm himself. "This ends *now*. Sax, call the lab. I need those results *tonight*."

Fear skyrocketed through me, and I didn't know what I wanted those labs to say. I believed Dayton was alive, but was it better for him to stay dead now?

I didn't know, and that scared me the most.

THIRTY SIX

ATTICUS

I slammed the phone down on the desk, and a splintering sound met my ears. "Fuck," I swore, knowing I'd broken it. It wouldn't do well to have a broken phone right now. But all I could see were his words, making the fury rise in me.

You always were so easy to distract with pussy. While you've been busy with the cat, the mice have played and they don't like the home you're creating. It's time for a new boss.

Get ready.

D

Cursing under my breath, I picked up the desk phone and punched the line for Sax, relieved when he picked up on the second ring.

"I broke my screen."

"Hmm."

"That's all you have to say?" I tiffed.

"I'll send Nicco to grab another."

"No, I mean, thank you, but never mind."

"You're spiraling, Mas, so I have to remain grounded. So, yes, all you get is a 'hmm' because otherwise you might want to punch me, and that wouldn't help either of us at the moment."

"Fine," I grumbled, hating he was right.

"You know I'm right."

"Hmm." I smiled, glad he couldn't see it, but knowing him, he could hear it.

"I'd ask if there was an update, but I'm taking by the state of your phone there isn't."

"You'd be correct. Somehow, my 'guy' has mysteriously vanished. I think it's time we call the Sirens."

Silence met me before a dial tone rang in my ear. Sighing, I set the phone in the cradle and counted as I leaned back in my chair. Under thirty seconds, Sax stormed through my door.

"Are you sure about this? It would mean…"

I nodded, understanding the implication, but I didn't know what else to do at this point. Rawles knew something but wasn't in the sharing mood and was only allied because Delgado was a bigger asshole. The O'Sullivans were still too new to trust fully, and this was too big an ask. I was under no pretense that either of them were friends. There wasn't anyone in Chicago I could trust, which meant it was time to activate the pull string I'd been sitting on.

Pops had given Sax everything we needed to uncover for my mother's history, and after that, it hadn't been hard tracking down her family. The Costas' were legendary, and how my father had kept them hidden from me had to have taken tremendous debt and time. Not to mention, if they'd known one of their own was murdered, I didn't think any of us would've been left alive. Which meant pulling this string came with significant risk—it could backfire as easily as it helped.

I trusted the mother I remembered and hoped her family would honor our war against Delgado and possibly Dayton, if he was indeed alive.

"I know what it means, but we're running out of time. We both know that not only are they hidden players to help us, but they have the tech and resources to do this. We need their help."

"Then I think you should talk with Nicco. He should be given a chance to weigh in on this. Have you spoken with Cami? Did she allude to anything since she's more connected to the Costa last name?"

I thought about what he said and knew he was right, but I didn't want to bring Nicco into this. He wasn't vulnerable like Imogen, but the minute I learned he was my younger brother, the protective streak in me for him doubled. I'd always watched over my younger cousin, but this had morphed into something more. There were too many things I wanted to talk to him about and no words to say.

Sighing, I rubbed my hand along my face, leaning back. "I know you're right. It's just hard to not protect him."

"He can take care of himself, Mas. You know this."

"Who can?" the brother in question asked, strolling into my office in such a different mood than Sax had. He was calm and collected. I'd daresay that Nicco even seemed settled into this way of life now. It was such a contrast from the man I'd basically threatened to become my second a few months ago.

"You."

He lifted an eyebrow, waiting for me to expand. Exhaling, I stood up and walked over to a picture I'd found, handing it to him.

"This is Shayna Costa, my mother." Nicco took it, looking over every inch, taking in each little detail. I couldn't fault him. I'd done the same. It somehow made her different knowing this information about her, more than I'd ever had before. I understood how it had been a ploy by Dayton to keep me from looking further. I hated how easily it had worked. He made me forget her, and she'd become nothing to me in the process, just a name rarely uttered.

Leaning against the desk, I crossed my arms. "Dayton made me believe she was a nobody outside of good family lines to pass down. Turns out he left a lot out. The Costas are a female-led family, having a matriarchal system instead of a patriarchal one. They have their toes in espionage, technology, and are what some would call Femme Fatales. Many older families looked down on them and saw them as lesser because they excelled in the softer aspects of the criminal underground. But while the men bickered, the women worked, and the Costas soon became legendary, gaining respect among their peers. Now, they're one of the top crime syndicates in the south. They call themselves the Sirens because they lure men into traps, taking what they want and using what men see as weaknesses to their advantage."

"So, um, your mom, she was one of these Siren women?"

"That, I don't know. Just that she's connected to them and possibly could've been sent here undercover for all I know. There's so much Dayton covered up. It's hard to make sense of all the lies. I mean, the fact we're brothers just shows the lengths he went to. This was all part of a scheme, and I don't know if pulling one card will make the whole house fall."

"Such as if we alert them to knowing who they are and that Shayna is dead, they could potentially retaliate?"

"Yes. Though, I'm hoping they'll hear us out and go up against the real enemy with us, or at least lend us a hand. They have the technology and resources to test the bones, since our lab technician seems to have disappeared."

"Then I think we should do it. It sounds like there's more to gain than lose, and we're already losing, so what's the downside?"

I assessed him, rolling his question over in my head. "You're good at this, you know." I stood, walking back around to my desk. I picked up the phone and pressed another number, and the line rang. This time it took a little longer for someone to answer, but it was 4 am.

"Hello?" a tired, feminine voice answered.

"Camila?"

"No, this is Nat. One sec." Shuffling could be heard in the background, and then footsteps as Nat carried the phone with her. A door creaked open a moment later before I could hear her attempting to rouse my cousin.

"Cams, phone."

"I'm asleep," she mumbled.

"It's the boss man."

More covers moved before I heard the phone taken and placed against her ear. "Mr. Mascro?"

"Camila, I have a very important question for you that I need you to answer honestly."

"Of course, anything."

"Are you part of the Sirens?"

She sucked in a breath, and a moment of silence passed before I heard her swallow. "No."

"But you know who they are?"

"Yes."

"Can you get in touch with someone?"

More silence and then sounds of the sheets again. "Are you sure about this?" she asked in a whisper. "My mother was one at one time, and she tried to train me, but I didn't really have the stomach for some of it. I went to a boot camp of sorts when I was younger and met some of my cousins then. Our cousins, I guess. They're all intense and hard-core. I didn't really fit in with that, you know. But I did make some friends. In fact, I'd reached out to one with the information I found on Darren before I was, you know. I, uh, I can send her another message, but..." She trailed off, her rambling running out of steam. Once she'd allowed herself to speak of them, it was like she couldn't get it out fast enough. I heard her swallow, and I wanted to hit myself for not thinking about her mental state, but this was important.

"I didn't understand half of what you said, but I'm sure this is the right move. It's life or death, and I think they could be what turns the tide, especially if my father isn't dead like he's supposed to be."

Camila sucked in a breath, and I realized I'd inadvertently let something slip. Shit. I needed some sleep if I was making mistakes already.

"That kinda makes sense," she mumbled. "I'll reach out to Cleo. Do you want them to get back with you or me?"

"Me. It's urgent. The sooner we can verify, the better."

"Understood."

"Thank you. Consider your school debt paid. I'm sorry you got pulled into this."

"You don't have to do that. I made my own choices. Stupid ones, but it had nothing to do with you. I thought... well, it doesn't matter what I thought."

"That's where you're wrong, Cami. I'm sorry, but it

had everything to do with me. I don't know what Darren told you, but you were a ploy."

"I… well, um, I'll let you know, okay. Tell Lor to be safe."

She hung up, and I wondered if I'd said that too insensitively. I didn't want to sugarcoat things for her, though, and Camila had always seemed to be tough as nails. Shaking my head, I ignored my awareness at the end, knowing now wasn't the time to get sentimental, and looked back at the guys.

"It's done. Now, we wait. Preferably, while we sleep."

They both nodded, leaving, and I sat back, leaning my head against the headrest. I'd just shut my eyes for a second.

A LOUD RINGING sound woke me, and I was startled, jumping awake, slamming my knee into the underside of my desk in the process.

"Fuck." Picking up the phone, I muttered a few other expletives when I realized the person on the other end was laughing. "Who the fuck is this?" The laughter stopped, and a thick southern accent filled the line.

"My poor dear nephew, is that any way to greet your elder? Tsk tsk, and here I thought you needed our help. I would've assumed my dear sister taught you better manners, but since I haven't heard from her in ages, I'm going to go with the assumption she's dead. Now that the unpleasant business is out of the way, do I have your attention?"

I swallowed, my pulse racing. "Apologies, Aunt. I was just startled. Of course, my mother taught me manners, even if she is dead."

"At least you're not tiptoeing around it, boy. I admire that. I hear you've finally decided to look into us."

"More like recently discovered."

"Ah, and you thought, what better way to introduce myself to my family than by asking for help?"

"Well," I sputtered. I was practically forty, and yet this woman had me feeling like a young schoolboy needing to bend over backward with every move I made. Taking a deep breath, I counted to twenty, and when I was still feeling out of sorts, I counted to twenty again. By the time I got to two hundred, my pulse was back to normal, and I was surprised to find she'd waited.

"Apologies, ma'am."

"I see your mother did teach you something. Good. I'll be sending your cousin to you. If you're worthy, we'll help, but if you're not, then we'd like to sever all ties with the Mascros, and we'd like Camila to come and stay with us."

My hand tensed against the chair, and I squeezed tight. "I accept whatever test you want to put me through, and I can guarantee you my family is worthy. But this is where I disagree with your request. Listen closely Aunt, who still hasn't told me her name, I don't bargain with my family's lives, nor do I make them stay somewhere they wish not to be. I'm bringing a new order to our city, and it starts with stopping Delgado. If you help us, then great. But if your cost is to make someone join you against their will, I cannot accept that. I am not my father. I am my own person, and you need to respect that. Do you understand, Aunt?"

"Very good, Atticus. I'll be in touch." She paused, almost like she was debating something. "And it's Ophelia. You may call me Aunt Phea." The phone clicked, and I sat, a little stunned, but hope filled me for the briefest seconds as I considered this might actually work out for us.

A knock at the door had me looking up to find Loren standing there. She instantly made me feel better. Loren walked in carrying a mug of coffee and a cellphone. She set the coffee down on the desk and handed me the phone, both without saying a word. I watched, always curious about what was going through her mind. She pushed my chair back slightly, climbing into my lap, and wrapped her arms around my neck.

"Hi," she finally said, looking up at me with her big brown eyes. She casually played with the hair at the base of my nape, her fingertips brushing over the skin softly. I leaned my forehead down, touching her temple.

"Bellezza, you're a sight for sore eyes."

"Oh? Did you get any sleep at all?"

"A few hours. Not enough. It never feels like enough."

"That sounds like you mean more than just sleep."

She was right, and I knew I shouldn't burden her, but in this little cocoon, it felt safe and like maybe we could hide away from all of our problems.

"Attie?"

"I'm scared and feel like I'm failing everyone."

"It is scary, Attie. I think it's smart to be afraid. It helps you not make impulsive decisions because you weigh the odds and understand the risks. Being afraid doesn't make you weak; if anything, it makes you stronger. You carry so much on your shoulders, though. I think it's time you let some of us help and utilize the family you have. You care so much about them; let them show you how much that means to them."

"How did someone so smart, beautiful, and compassionate fall for someone so dangerous and messed up like me?" I looked up, cupping her face. "You make me want things I don't feel I deserve, and you make me feel like I can have the life I felt was too out of reach. I worried it would make me weak, make me fall prey too easily. Sax was right, though. You strengthen us and glue us together. Nicco is a different person now. He's more sure of himself and isn't hiding things. Imogen is coming out of her shell. Sax talks on purpose and jokes with the other men. And while I don't have the history with the other two, I know you've changed their lives too. I know you don't believe me, but I hope someday you see the woman we've all fallen in love with and are willing to share just to be with you."

She sucked in a breath, and I realized what I'd said. "Not just to be with you. I didn't mean it that way."

"Shut up, you stupid man. Somehow, I've fallen in love with you, too."

"Somehow? Geez, thanks." I rolled my eyes but smiled, my heart lifting. "I love you, Bellezza."

"I love you, Attie." I kissed her softly, wanting to cherish this moment, as it might be the last good one I got for a while.

"Just out of curiosity, what number down the line am I? You know that you've said the L word to."

"Hmm," she said, scrunching up her eyebrows in almost an exact replica of Sax. I couldn't stop the laugh.

"Fuck. You've been hanging out with Sax too much. I swear, he just did that same move a few hours ago."

Loren kissed my nose, still refusing to answer, and reached around to hand me the coffee she'd brought in, a soft smile on her lips. I took the cup and brought it to my mouth for a sip when I realized she was watching me.

"Did you put ex-lax in this or something? Why are you watching me so closely?"

Loren slapped my arm, shaking her head. "Nothing like that, I promise. I made it. That's all, and I don't know. I guess I wanted to watch you enjoy it. I've never had that before."

It was such a sweet and sad thing, I couldn't help but oblige. I took a long sip, savoring the flavor as it rolled over my tongue. "Mmm, that's amazing. Damn,

Bellezza, you're definitely earning your title. Maybe we should make it official."

She blushed, looking at me. "Um, what?" She shook her head, dislodging the thought. "Here, Nicco said it's programmed with everything."

"Thank you. For the coffee and the phone, and just listening. I needed it more than I knew. You've helped me prioritize what needs to happen."

"I'm glad. It feels nice to be useful." She laid her head on my chest. "I hate to be a dash and go girlfriend, but I need to head back to my place. I return to work today, and Imogen is starting school."

"Do you really think that's the best idea?" I asked, some tension returning.

"I do. We need to live our lives and not let him take anything else. You have guards in place, and you've covered every detail a million times. The kids will go to school with Beau and afterward to the youth center. I'll go to work with Topher and then meet them there, where we'll come back here. Monroe is keeping Levi home until the Brittni thing is done, but the rest of our family is good. We're ready for this. You do your job, and we'll do ours. Trust, right?"

"I hate that you're right. Fine. But I want check-ins every hour. No exceptions."

"Fine, you overprotective, grump."

"Mm, you better watch it, or I'll make your number 4." She sucked in a breath, heat filling her eyes. Thoughts of making her late to work so I could have her on my desk were dashed away when Sax walked in with a woman I'd never seen before. Her bright purple hair stood out, making me wonder just who she was.

"We have a situation," he growled, his eyes flicking briefly over at Loren. She kissed me, slid off my lap, and then walked over to the angry giant and kissed him, too. She smirked as she left, winking at me. I'd watched her the whole way, forgetting momentarily about the intruder.

"And you are?" I asked, my eyes landing on the purple-haired pixie.

"Impressed."

I rolled my eyes. "Sounds like an odd name." The woman laughed and then looked down at my phone. When I glanced down, it lit up, ringing through with an unknown number. She jerked herself free from Sax, did some jazz hands, and took a seat, swinging her legs over the arm. The phone kept ringing, and she looked back at me, an eyebrow lifted behind her glasses.

"You're gonna want to get that, Cous. Aunt Phea doesn't like to be kept waiting."

Shit. Looked like my Siren cousin was here.

THIRTY SEVEN

LOREN

Barkley nudged me, and I blinked. The woman in front of me was crying, and I couldn't find the words to comfort her. My mind was scattered, thinking of a million other things, and I struggled to focus on the present. Maybe I shouldn't have come back to work today. Work had always been a distraction from my life in the past, giving me a reprieve. However, now, it didn't seem to matter and I couldn't escape the chaos going on as easily.

"What do you think I should do?" she asked, looking up. She twisted a Kleenex in her hand, but every now and then, I caught her scratching Fort's head. It had been a last-minute decision to bring both of them in today, but so far, they'd done great. The clients seemed to be responding well, too.

Focusing on Sara, I nodded, trying to remember the last thing she said. Fuck. I was failing her. That thought had me sitting up, leaning toward her. She didn't deserve a half-ass therapist. "I think knowing what to do and what you want to do are often in conflict. Especially when grief is part of the equation. You feel like you should be at a certain point by now, yes?"

She nodded, wiping her eyes.

"In my experience, that's the lie our doubt whispers. The truth, no one has it together, and no one knows how to handle death. We're all stumbling about, trying to keep our heads on and make sense of a world with a person we loved no longer in it. There's not a wrong way to grieve. Though, I'll add this caveat, assuming you're not violating laws or hurting others or yourself. But if you want to cry or scream out some angry rock music, go right ahead. You want to take up pottery, run a marathon, adopt five puppies, or even change your hair… It's all valid."

"I guess, when you say it that way, rewatching our favorite show every night isn't too out there."

"No, it's not. Some people need to push the sad feelings away until they can return to them. Others dive right in, wrapping themselves in the grief, barreling their way through. And yet, some clients find they can only take sips of the memories and emotions, only letting themselves grieve for a small part of their day as they try to rebuild. Neither process is right or wrong. Grief is as personal as your fingerprint. So, don't measure yourself against someone else. They just might be better at covering it. In the end, we all have to face the feelings. And when you're ready, I'll be here to help you."

"Thanks, Loren. Some days I feel like I'll never stop crying, but it helps to know that won't last forever."

"It won't." I smiled, glad I'd been able to finally focus. Barkley licked my hand, and it seemed she was happy with me, too. She was too bright sometimes. "Let's get you scheduled for next week."

The rest of the morning passed by quickly, and I stayed present with my clients, not thinking about my life or the guys. When lunch rolled around, I was grateful for the reprieve, though. Emoting today had been more demanding, and I was tired, drained of my energy. I debated closing my door and taking a nap. The dogs were both in their respective spots, having claimed their own corners and snoring. Deciding a quick one would be worth it, I stood and walked to my door to tell Topher. When I didn't spot him, I peeked out further, confused.

"Doris? Where's Topher?"

"Hmm?" she asked, glancing up. "Oh, he stepped out to the restroom."

"Oh, okay. Tell him to knock on my door when he gets back."

"Will do, honey."

I smiled, feeling weird, despite not having a reason to. I shut the door, the dogs picking their heads up to see if I needed anything. When I didn't, almost in sync, they laid them back down, closing their eyes. It was too cute.

I got myself comfortable on the couch and picked up my phone while I waited so I could answer some texts.

Monroe: Have a good day, Lo. Love you

ME: You too, Roe. Love you. Kiss Levi for me.

Nicco: Miss you already, Beautiful. Maybe you should be the family's therapist? I'm sure I could get you clients and then you wouldn't have to leave. I'll be your first. *Winky face*

ME: I think that's a different type of client you're speaking of there, sir

Nicco responded back almost immediately, making me laugh.

Nicco: Oh, I like when you call me sir. Say it in front of Atticus next time. I want to watch his head explode.

ME: You're incorrigible.

Nicco: I'll be whatever you want, Beautiful. How's your day?

ME: Weird. But getting better. It's strange not being there, and I was only there a week.

Nicco: We Mascros have a way of seeping into your skin.

ME: You do something.

Nicco: I'm going to pretend that's a compliment

ME: Do what you must. Lol. How's your day?

Nicco: We're getting ready for a family meeting. We should be home by dinner.

ME: Good luck. Let me know when you have the

results.

Nicco: Of course, Beautiful.

My phone started to ring, Sax's name flashing up, and I clicked over, a smile on my face.

"Hey, sexy."

"I'm going to kill this girl. She's Cami x100. *Save me.* Tell Atticus you need a rescue. I beg of you, Spitfire. *Please.*"

I could hear a woman's voice in the background, chatting a mile a minute, some pop music on in the background.

"I'm sure it's not *that* bad." I could practically hear his eyes roll at that.

"It is. It's worse. She acts like I'm her personal slave."

"Oh, Saxy. I need your big muscles to move this."

"Wait, did she just call you—"

"See what I'm dealing with! She's insufferable. Move this, don't touch that. Stand here. I thought Immy was bad, but nope, she's a fucking angel."

"Babe, she's messing with you. She's flirting, and you're not even aware of it." I laughed, no longer feeling possessive.

"You've got to be kidding. She's like 12."

"I'm 24, asshole. That your woman? Are you complaining about me? Here, give me the phone."

"No, don't touch—"

"Hello? Is this the badass woman who kissed the scary giant and mafia boss this morning?"

I laughed, never being described that way before. "Um, yes."

"Girl! So, I need some pointers. Like, how does that work? Do you like to switch off, or is it a free for all? I'm truly—"

"Enough of that," Sax said, taking the phone back. "Thank you, Spitfire. I know how to handle her now. I'll see you later. Love you."

"Love—" he hung up before I could finish, and I laughed. A knock on the door had the dogs popping up, barking as I stood to answer it. Topher stood on the other side, and I exhaled.

"You need something, Mrs. Carter?"

"Loren, Topher. And no, I just wanted to make sure you were okay. Did you get something for lunch?"

"I did, thank you."

"Ah, good. Okay, well, I was going to take a nap, but my break is almost over, so I guess we'll power through the last sessions."

"Sounds good, Mrs. Carter." I rolled my eyes, and he chuckled, knowing he frustrated me with the formality. I got it somehow, but it also made me feel weird. Atticus insisted I was the lady of the manor, but I still struggled to understand what that meant.

The rest of my sessions went by quickly, and I was on my last one before I even realized it. Jill had been making progress, and it was good to see her stepping out of her comfort zone and trying new things. I smiled, happy she'd taken my advice about looking into going back to school and had even checked out the youth center. I wanted to ask if she'd met Jude yet, but I was already toeing the line, suggesting a place I was connected to, so I kept it to myself.

"What about skating? Where are you with that?"

"I was thinking of going just for a fun skate and see how it feels. I dunno, that probably sounds dumb."

"Not at all. I think it's smart to take the pressure off and remind yourself what you loved about it to begin with."

"Yeah? Okay, good." She took a deep breath. "I'm just worried he tainted everything good in my life. I don't want his voice in my head when I skate. That was where he… would give me special training and, um, you know, started grooming me."

I nodded, smiling softly. "It's going to be hard, but you're strong, Jill. You can do it. Just remember the steps we practiced, and take it one thing at a time. Maybe if you were to do something completely outside of what you did. What if you skated on an outside rink?"

She thought about it for a second, nodding, the wheels turning. "Yeah, you know what, that might work. There's the one downtown I could try, but it might be too warm for it. Or maybe even a hockey rink. My dad has some connections with the Ice Devils. I might be able to skate there. It's definitely worth a shot. Thanks, Loren."

"Hey, you thought of the idea. I just helped you get there. Don't dismiss your own work."

"Okay." She smiled, the grin covering her whole face.

It lit up her entire person, and I saw what had attracted that predator to her. She was a gorgeous girl, but she had a sparkle about her that made you want to know her secret. She'd been vulnerable, and he'd preyed on that.

"I love that you have these two here. It's the best." She said, kneeling down to the ground to pet both dogs. They'd both been by her side the whole session. Their uncanny ability to know when someone needed them more was what made them perfect for this. Smiling, I finished up with Jill, and we scheduled for the following week.

Topher poked his head into my door when I was writing her note and asked if I wanted him to take the dogs out real quick. Nodding, I handed him the leashes, taking a deep breath as I relaxed a little to get the notes done. When I had everything finalized, I shut everything off and noticed they weren't back yet. Closing everything in my office, I figured they had to be in the lobby.

Stepping into the small foyer, I stopped dead in my tracks at the sight before me. Brian was standing there, pointing a gun at Topher, a cruel sneer on his face. The door clicked behind me, and he whipped it around toward me. It was dumb on his part because the second he took his eyes off Topher, he pounced, knocking the gun from his hands, it clattering loudly against the ground, and kicking it toward me.

The dogs had both been on guard and now growled at Brian, who Topher managed to subdue in a matter of seconds. With shaky hands, I picked up the gun and raised it. The metal felt hot in my hands, and I wondered why. Looking up, I met my ex's eyes, and the darkness in me whispered to pull the trigger. To just end this here and now. He'd be gone, out of our lives.

Topher was saying something to me, his mouth moving, but I couldn't hear what he said. That was when I realized I couldn't hear anything. There was no sound. Just the pounding of my heartbeat in my ears. This realization seemed to be what I needed to snap myself out of my mental fog, and everything came rushing forward. I dropped my arm, the gun's weight feeling too heavy now. Slinking to the floor, I wish I could go back to the quiet.

Everything was too loud now—shouts, barks, and a ringing were all around me, and I couldn't focus on anything.

Barkley whined, pressing her head into me, and I petted her, the motion soothing. The red stickiness there made me stop when I picked my hand up.

"No, no, no." It was happening again. Everything from the night Wells was shot came crashing into me, and I knew my time of ignoring it was over.

Tears fell down my cheeks, and I pulled Barkley into me, wrapping my arms around her as I sobbed. Fort came to my back, leaning his body weight on me. This was too much. I was losing it. I finally found happiness, and he wanted to take it from me. It wasn't fair.

"Life wasn't fair," my subconscious whispered. "Are you going to sit here and cry or boss up?"

Fuck you, subconscious. I could do both.

Wiping my tears, I felt the blood streak against my cheek as I pulled away from my dogs, my guardians. That eerie silence surrounded me again, and I stood, focused on the asshole who kept trying to take more and more from me. I was tired of being his punching bag. He'd taken enough already.

I held my head high as I walked over to where Topher had him restrained on the ground. He was on the phone, probably talking to Sax or Atticus, but I couldn't hear any of it. The only one I focused on was Brian.

"You're such a stupid, bitch," he spat, the sound returning. I smiled, stepping forward. The tip of my heel pressed into his groin, and I watched as he grimaced.

"The only stupid one here, Brian, is you. Clearly, you don't understand who you're up against. You'll never touch me. I'm fucking Kevlar now. I'm indestructible."

"You sure about that, Loren?" he snickered, not understanding the danger he was in. I stepped forward more, raising my foot and bringing the heel down right on his ball sack. Or at least where I assumed it was. His cry of pain at least let me know I struck something.

"I'm sorry, you were saying?" He fell over, groaning, his face turning purple. I kicked him again for good measure. "Yeah, that's what I thought, asshole."

Topher pulled me back, talking to me, but I couldn't understand him. He placed a phone against my ear, and I tried to focus on what the person was saying.

"Spitfire? Fucking answer me, dammit."

"I'm here."

"Fucking Hell. I was about to murder everyone around me on my way to you. Are you okay?"

"I… I think so. There's blood, but I don't know where from."

"Shit. Give the phone back to Topher."

"Okay."

I handed the phone to Topher, who stared at Brian, unsure what to do with him now that he was groaning out in pain. My legs felt heavy, so I sat down in a chair, the room starting to spin now. Fort came to me, licking my hand, and I rested my hands on him.

"You're a good dog," I whispered. The room started to blink out of focus, and I lifted my head, the movement feeling strange, my head weighing a million tons, moving in slow motion.

"Topher," I said, but it felt like it came out in a jumble.

Movement came from the door, and I tried to look, but my head didn't agree. Familiar hands braced my face, his pale green eyes a comfort.

"Roe, you came."

"Of course, Lo. I need to have a talk with you and Wells, though. You're taking years off my life. Come on, we need to get you to see the doctor."

"Doc…tor?"

I blinked once before everything went black. I could've sworn I saw Dayton's smiling face right before I shut my eyes.

THIRTY EIGHT

SAX

I was close to strangling Atticus' cousin. I'd never met a more insufferable human before. For one thing, she never shut up. She was always prattling on about one thing or another as if I cared. The second thing, she asked too many questions and reminded me of a rambunctious child who'd been let outside for the first time and had to ask a question about everything.

"Are you about done?"

"Not yet, Oscar. Like I was saying, I think what the problem is, that, in our town, everyone knows who I am, so no one wants to ask me out. What do you think?"

"For the last time, my name's not Oscar."

"Whatever, you say, Oscar. So?"

"I'm pretty sure no one wants to date you because you're annoying, not because they're scared of you." I glared at her, daring her to retort.

"Interesting. You see, I hadn't considered that angle." She flitted around the room she'd made into a lab, going from one machine to the computer, back to the machine that was running some diagnostic thing. As frustrated as I was, I couldn't deny she was brilliant. Half of the stuff she spouted off, I had no clue what it meant. "So, what you're saying is I should be more mysterious? Did that work with you and your girl? She's hot in that whole sexy librarian kind of way. I dig it for you, Oscar."

Growling, I turned my back on her, ignoring her, and pulled out my phone again, tempted to call Spitfire back, so I didn't have to listen to this insufferable child any longer. Instead, I found a text from Atticus asking how it was going and another one from Monroe updating me on the Brittni situation.

Golden Boy: I've found where she'll be tonight. Are you sure this will work?

ME: It will work. Not having second thoughts are you? And here I was just starting to respect you.

Golden Boy: No. It needs to happen. I see that now.

ME: Good. It will be taken care of. I'll send you proof once it's completed.

Golden Boy: That's not necessary. I trust you.

ME: Suit yourself.

ME: And thank you.

Golden Boy: Shouldn't I be thanking you?

ME: Not for taking out the trash, for trusting me. It means a lot to me.

Golden Boy: Oh, well, I do. I know you love Loren and wouldn't do anything to jeopardize her. She trusts you, so I do. Plus, Levi and Jude like you, so you can't be too bad.

ME: Geez, thanks.

ME: Tell the runt I'll teach him how to win at poker next time.

Golden Boy: I don't know if I should be happy you want to spend time with Levi or scared you're teaching him how to gamble.

ME: This is our life. You're a part of it now, so get used to it.

Golden Boy: He says he's looking forward to it.

Later, Sax

Smiling some, I clicked over to Mas' message, hoping it meant I could leave. We still had the family meeting and Brittni to contend with before I got to see my spitfire again. The sooner those two things happened, the sooner I got to hold her.

MAS: Status?

ME: Still waiting. She talks too much.

MAS: Tell her to speed up. The meeting's starting. I'll send someone to replace you. She's to text you and me as soon as she knows.

ME: Understood.

I sighed, feeling some of the tension leaving me. Turning, I found her watching me, waiting for a response. "What?"

She shrugged, miming zipping her lips, before going back to the computer screen. I knew what she was doing, and I'd asked for it, but now I needed her to talk. Fuck! This woman was going to kill me. I calmed myself by taking a deep breath, remembering I got to leave.

"Atticus would like to know if you have an estimate?"

"Nope," she sang, popping the p.

"Okay, well, the meeting is starting. He's sending someone to switch with me. You're to text him and me as soon as you get it. Understand?"

"Yep," she said again in the same annoying way.

Holding my hands out in front of me, I pretended to strangle the air, wishing it was her in a way. Not really, but at the same time, I did want to shake her.

"I'd say it's been a pleasure, Pixel, but that would be a lie."

"Ah, and here I thought we were bonding, Oscar." She pouted, sticking out her lip. Rolling my eyes, I turned, marching out of the room, deciding I'd prefer to stay outside the door until my replacement came.

Thankfully, a guard appeared within seconds of me leaving, and I gave him some brief instructions before booking it to the meeting room. We'd come to the warehouse, figuring it was the best place to be since we needed to gather everyone. The only thing I didn't like was how far away we were from Spitfire. The warehouse was on the opposite side of town from her office, and if anything happened, it would take us too long to get to her. I knew she had Topher, and Beau was with the kids a few blocks over, but it made me uneasy being away. I'd liked having her with us. It felt right, and this, it just felt wrong.

When I walked into the open meeting room, I was surprised to find it only half full. I nodded to a few guys, making my way to the front with Atticus and Nicco. I could tell Mas was stressed, the look on his face one of paranoia and fear. He was starting to crack, his edges fraying as this ordeal with his father continued to lag. If we didn't get those results today, I feared he'd completely lose it, and I didn't know what that would mean for the family.

Atticus shifted his eyes to me, our silent communication from years of practice zinging between us. I subtly shook my head, and he nodded, understanding. I lifted an eyebrow and looked at the crowd, and he grimaced, the lack of family members not slipping his attention either. I wondered if the letter at Climax had anything to do with it. We'd found out later from one of the bartenders that all the staff had been sent a text stating that they were given the night off and to not return until the next day, as the club was undergoing new management.

Whether it was Darren or Dayton, it didn't look good. However, if it was Darren, he had bigger balls than I thought after we'd cut him out of the crime scene. It was almost like he'd deliberately bated us to see if we'd follow through with our threat. Thankfully, Atticus didn't play when it came to safety and had sent the information on. Darren would be the laughingstock of the community by this evening, and his misdeeds at the dock had been sent anonymously to our detective friend.

Darren was about to find himself so tied up in red tape from every direction, he wouldn't be able to make a play at us. We'd taken his criminal empire, his family, and now his reputation. Darren was no more, and the Delgados were barely a blip on the radar.

Which meant, it was time to see if there was a bigger dog in the race—Dayton. It was time he stepped forward if he was indeed alive. Either way, the true boss behind the Delgados would be revealed.

Atticus had a plan, one we'd stayed up all night discussing, but it was solid and would work with only minimal casualties to ourselves. We just needed the proof first.

But looking around the room, I wondered if we already had our answer.

"Family, thank you for coming on short notice. Though, it seems not everyone was able to make it. They will be docked an extra 2% this month for their insubordination." Murmurs went around, but no one dared say anything. "The reason I've asked everyone here is to discuss the direction of the family. It's come to my attention that some rumblings are going around, and I want to dispel any misgiving you may have. This is your opportunity to bring forth any dissension you may feel."

Atticus sat back, his chair almost like a throne, as he

crossed his ankle over his knee and waited. It was quiet for a few minutes, everyone shifting on their feet. When someone stepped forward, it was as if all the air in the room left it.

"I've been hearing rumors that 'The Reaper' isn't really dead and that you're in violation of the code."

"I assure you, I shot my father after he betrayed our family, selling us out to the Delgados and promising my underage sister as a bargaining chip. He was the one in violation. But to dispel these rumors, I have the bones left at the site, being tested to verify their authenticity. They should be completed any moment, and then we can put these rumors to rest."

More mumblings went out through the crowd, and I shifted, not liking the energy on our own grounds. This felt more like a trial than a family meeting. It didn't bode well for Mas. My pocket vibrated, and I pulled it out, exhaling as I saw the text from the Siren. Opening it, I blinked, not believing it. I glanced over at Atticus and Nicco. Both of their faces were ashen as they read the results.

100% match to Benny Mascro.

If the bones were Benny's, then did that mean... a low chuckle caused shivers to travel up my spine, goosebumps dotting my skin as I searched the crowd that now seemed bigger, for the source. Where had all of these people come from? They weren't here a moment ago.

Atticus stood, having heard the same sound, scanning the area.

"Show yourself! Stop being a coward and step forward, *Dayton*. If you're really alive, then prove it."

The chuckle sounded again, this time from the other direction. "You finally figured it out, huh? I always thought you were more clever, but it seems I'd overestimated your intelligence. It's been such an enjoyment playing with you these past few months."

Dayton Mascro, The Grim Reaper himself, stepped out from behind some guards I didn't recognize, looking very much alive.

"But I shot you…" Atticus trailed off, still trying to make sense of the fact his father was alive.

"You did." He nodded, not denying Atticus' memory of the night in question. "I didn't think you had it in you, to be honest. I was proud of you, taking something for yourself for once. Until you mucked it up, that is. Then I couldn't help but teach you a lesson."

"But how?"

Dayton's lips lifted, a cold sneer gracing his lips. "A conversation for another time. I've come to tell you that you're no longer in charge. I gave you time to make a name for yourself, but you've only made our family a mockery. So, I'm taking it back, and combining it with the Delgado family like I'd originally planned. Though, I have to thank you for taking care of Darren. Now with him out of the way, it's a prime opportunity to swoop in and lay claim to all of Chicago. So, thank you, son."

He turned to the men gathered, addressing them, "This is your one chance to leave with me if you want to join the *true* Mascro family. After I leave this place, you will be my enemy if you're not with me. You can decide for yourself which boss you want to serve, but I think we all know which one is the correct choice."

He strutted out, men and women following him as he did, and we stood there, too shocked to do anything. Dayton stopped before he walked out the door, looking at his sons one last time. "Nicolai, this is your chance to prove to me I made the wrong choice in which son to raise as my successor." When Nicco didn't budge, Dayton sighed, hanging his head. "Very well. As a parting gift, you may keep this shithole, and I can't touch your place in the city, but the estate is mine. Hope you didn't have anything of value left there. Tell that sister of yours that I'll be seeing her shortly."

Atticus jumped off the stage, rage coursing through him now. "You'll stay away from Imogen if you know what's good for you," he seethed.

"Oh, son, haven't you learned yet? I *always* win. You can't win here. You better enjoy the time you have left before I take everything." He grinned, the smile making my insides boil and freeze over at the same time.

Nicco seemed to realize the threat first and pulled out his phone, calling someone. "Topher, is Loren okay?" When he relaxed his shoulders, Atticus and I exhaled with him.

"Check on Immy. Tell Beau it's Rapunzel time. We

need to retreat and reconvene before going off on a half-built plan. Tell everyone to meet back in the hotel. I don't trust the mansion." Atticus turned, looking out at the men still gathered. They looked weary but had stayed; that counted for something.

"Thank you all for staying. I won't let my father take everything we've earned away. We'll fight against him, but we have to be smarter. He's been ahead of us this whole time, playing from the shadows, but now he's out in the open, no longer hidden. It's time we remind him who we are and not the mimicry he's made our family into. If you're with me, you're with me."

"We're with you. We are Mascros." The words filled the space, stealing my spine with some confidence that we weren't screwed.

Picking up my phone, I dialed Imogen, remembering my tasks. "Hey, Sax. Are you coming to the center? I have something I can't wait to show you all."

"Imogen, listen closely. I hate to tell you this way, but I don't trust him not to bombard you to try to take you by surprise. Your father, he's not dead. He's here, and he's taking over the family. I need you to stay put until we get you. Do you understand?"

"I'm ready for this, Sax. You don't have to baby me." Her voice was filled with determination.

I closed my eyes, biting my knuckles as I tried to keep my scream controlled. "Imogen. *No.* This isn't the time to run off acting like a hero. We need to take cover, so we don't give him the advantage right now. *Please.*" When she didn't say anything, I held my breath, knowing it was a choice I wouldn't be able to make—to go after her or Spitfire.

"Fine," she huffed. "But I want in on everything. I'm not a wilting flower, and I deserve to be part of this."

"Absolutely, princess. Put Beau on the line."

After going over what went down with Beau, he understood the plan. I'd given him all of two seconds to decide if he wanted out, praying he wasn't going to stab us in the back. As I glanced around the room, I counted twenty men and five women. If we assumed the family that hadn't shown up were already on Dayton's side, we'd lost over three hundred members tonight. It wasn't good for us.

"Climax is ironclad in my name, so he can't take it, no matter what he tries. Evolve he may try to reclaim. It's Upswing I'm the most worried about," Atticus said when I walked over to where he was. "Imogen?" he asked, and I nodded, indicating she was good and I understood our situation.

"The princess is secure. She's not going to make this easy, though."

"I didn't think she would. I'm just glad she's not in a corner rocking herself."

"Definitely not."

Pixel walked out a minute later, skipping as she entered the room. "Hello, Cous. Did you get my text? Good. So, now what? I never get to travel, so know of any good places we can go?" She danced on her feet, her body moving in every direction as she watched Mas.

"This isn't the best time, my non-dead father just staged a coup, and we're scrambling."

"Fuck. I still need to go and take out the trash. I promised the golden one," I sighed, rubbing my head.

"Oh, that sounds like fun," she sang, lifting up on her toes in excitement and clapping.

"No!" Nicco, Mas, and I all said at the same time.

"Geez, touchy. Fine. Order my guard to take me somewhere then."

"What part of 'we are under attack' makes you think it's the perfect time to go clubbing?"

"Um, the under attack part?" She screwed up her face, looking at us like we were the dumb ones. "If you're gonna die in the morning, might as well fuck someone good the night before."

"Just, ew, gross. I can't take you."

Pixel rolled her eyes, not impressed with us. "Fine. What can I do to help then? I'm trained in Jiu Jitsu, Krav Maga, a whiz with the tech, and science." She cracked her knuckles. "Give me something to do."

An idea popped into my head, and I looked at her, smiling genuinely for once. "How good are you at making a chemical to kill someone that can't be traced?"

"Only the best," she beamed.

"If you can make her shit for days before she dies, you'd be my hero," Nicco added, understanding what I was getting at.

"Fine, she can help with the trash. Meet back at the rendezvous. I'm going to meet Topher and head to pick up the kids with Loren. We need to all be together. Text the boy next door to tell him to meet us there."

"Now, I don't want to take out the trash. I want to go with you to meet Spitfire," I whined.

"Oof, Oscar, not a good look for you, man. Come on, I'll be quick with my chemical formula, and then you can go and make goo-goo eyes at your sexy librarian."

I lifted my eyebrow at the other two, but they didn't do anything to help me. "Be good, *Oscar*," Nicco said, chuckling.

"My name's not fucking, Oscar." I stomped out of the room, fully prepared to kill the bitch and then go fuck my woman. The brat had a good point, at least about that. Pulling out my phone, I almost dropped it when it rang.

"Topher."

"Her ex showed up, he had a gun..." he started, as panic filled my veins.

"Let me talk to her, now." There was some rumbling before I heard breathing.

"Spitfire? Fucking answer me, dammit."

"I'm here."

"Fucking Hell. I was about to murder everyone around me on my way to you. Are you okay?" I sighed, rubbing my temple.

"I... I think so. There's blood, but I don't know where

from." Her voice sounded weak, almost like she was far off in the distance.

"Shit. Give the phone back to Topher." The time it took for her to transfer the phone felt like eons.

"Boss?"

"Go to Doc's and then report back to the hotel. We're under Rapunzel protocol."

"Understood."

"Topher?'

"Yes?" he asked, his voice a little shaky.

"If anything happens to her…"

I heard him swallow. "Got it."

Hanging up, I sent off a text, needing to not focus on the fact my woman could be bleeding out at the moment, and sending up a prayer to whoever would listen that I'd get to hold her again. First, I needed to kill someone and make them pay for hurting her.

THIRTY NINE

MONROE

I couldn't get comfortable. My insides were quivering, and I felt like I was about to crawl out of my skin. I'd joked with Loren that we needed to talk about her and Wells finding ways to stop bullets, but if my current predicament was any indication, I wouldn't fare well if this continued. I was barely keeping it together, and it felt like at any second, I could lose everything.

"I can't sit here anymore. I need to do something."

Topher looked over at me, his eyes a little vacant, and I wondered what he was thinking. It didn't matter though, even if he felt bad, it didn't compare to what I felt. That might be selfish of me, it might be narcissistic of me, but I didn't care. Not right this second, anyway.

"Where are the others?" I asked, standing as I started to pace. The sterile waiting room we'd been sequestered to for the past hour felt like a different kind of prison.

"I don't know. It's like my messages don't go through. No one is answering. They haven't since I spoke with Sax on the phone."

"Isn't there some type of protocol for these types of situations, then? I mean, you're the fucking mafia, shouldn't there be a chain of command?"

He looked at me, nonplussed by my outburst, probably because he was the *fucking mafia.*

"That's what we're doing. We go to Doc's, avoid the hospital, and meet up at a safe location. We're on step two. How did you know to come there?"

He looked at me suspiciously for the first time, and I didn't like it. "I got a message to meet at Loren's office that something had gone down at the meeting. It was vague and short, like most of Sax's text messages."

"Interesting you showed up when you did."

"Are you seriously asking me if I had anything to do with shooting my girlfriend? Are you insane?" I screamed, finally losing it.

The noise startled the dogs and our hostage, who was duct-taped together sitting in a chair. Topher had been relieved when I showed up, struggling to know what to do with Loren's bleeding and the asshole responsible for it writhing on the floor in pain. It had been a cluster, but we'd worked together to secure everyone and came here. But now he was questioning me? I shook my head, screwing up my face as I looked at him.

"Deal with your feelings and quit pushing the blame on me. As far as I'm concerned, we're on the same side. So quit pointing fingers, and let's figure out how to deal with this. Shit, why am I always having to be the parent? My girlfriend—"

"Is fine," a voice said behind me, and I whipped around so fast, I almost fell over. Loren stood in a doorway, an elderly man behind her. He gave me a soft smile and nodded, patting her on the shoulder.

"Rest. I'll see you next week for a follow-up, dear. Atticus knows where to send the money."

Loren smiled, though her eyes were tired, and her arm was in a sling. I ran toward her, stopping before I crushed her in my arms, gently patting her.

"I'm not breakable, Roe. You can hug me. Besides, right now, I'm on such major pain pills, I doubt I'd feel a truck hitting me."

"Let's not test it to find out, okay?"

She gave me a crooked smile, and I knew she was putting on a good front. I could see the exhaustion on her face and the effort it took for her to stand. Placing my arm around her shoulders, I led her over to a chair. Topher had stood as well, looking her over carefully. I wanted to punch him for putting his eyes on her, but even I could tell it was all clinical. I didn't know if it was out of genuine concern for her wellbeing or if he just didn't want to be the one to tell Atticus or Sax she'd been shot on his watch.

"It's just a graze, Topher. When you knocked the gun, I suppose it went wide. I can't believe the fucker had actually tried to shoot me." Loren shook her head, sighing in exasperation. "I'm so glad I squashed his balls." She chuckled to herself, her eyes closing as she let herself relax.

"Now, do we head to that safe place?" I asked, ready to get out of the back alley doctor's office we were in.

"Yes. Can you get her and the dogs? I'll get the asshat."

"Yeah." Together, we managed to get the passengers into the SUV. My phone buzzed as I buckled Loren in, and I pulled it out, happy to see messages coming through finally. I'd given Topher a hard time, but I'd also noticed a severe lack of messages in the past hour.

Wells: I'm bored. Entertain me dammit
Wells: Tell Kitten to send me a sexy pic

Sax: Status update?
Sax: Fucking hell, dude. What's going on?
Sax: I'm going to kick your ass if you don't report in.
Sax: That's it. You're grounded.

I rolled my eyes. Someone was not having a good day. I skimmed through the rest, but nothing of importance. Deciding it was better to call, I hit the dial button for the overgrown lumberjack.

"I swear to God, if you don't tell me what the fuck is going on, I'll kill you myself and not even feel bad about it," Sax growled into the phone. Oddly enough, as it sounded, it was the comfort I needed, to not be solely responsible in making decisions, and knowing that someone else cared about Loren as much as I did. It was the only reason I could think of for my response.

A sob broke free, and I sucked it in, trying to stop myself from falling over that edge of panic. It went quiet on the phone, and I took a second to gather myself.

"Is she..." he said, his voice small and quiet.

"No." I sucked in another breath, wiping the few tears that had escaped. "He shot her, but she's okay. But I... I was so scared. I'm sorry, our phones..."

I heard crashing in the background, and the sound helped ground me even more. I wasn't alone in this. I hated to share the panic, but it felt nice to not be the only one having to solve the problem.

"And is he still alive?" he growled.

"He's currently gagged and taped up in the back of the SUV."

I heard him take a few deep breaths. "I need confirmation that Spitfire's okay. I believe you, but I need to see her. The past few hours have been a shitshow. Daddy Mascro rose from the dead, and I thought...."

"You thought he went after Loren."

"Yeah. When we didn't hear back, I assumed the worst."

"It felt like it when I got there and saw all the blood. We really need to have a talk about people getting shot. I can't handle much more of it."

"I'll back you up. Thank you... thank you for taking care of her when we couldn't."

"I didn't do much, but I did feel an odd sense of relief

when I heard your concern. It wasn't something I expected from this type of relationship, but I can't say I hate it."

"Well, yeah, same. Though, to be honest, it's what the family was always supposed to be like. It's just strayed so far from that, it no longer resembled a family." He paused, taking another deep breath. "Meet us back at the hotel. Bring the dipshit with you. I think it's time both of your exes leave this world. I'm done with their bullshit."

"Okay, I'll—"

"Jude," Loren mumbled into the phone. She leaned against me, the phone perched between us, so I could still hear the conversation.

"Spitfire. *Fuck.*" A sharp inhale of breath was taken as we waited for him to get himself together. I understood, so I didn't mind waiting. "Listen here, woman. You will go nowhere, do nothing, or speak to anyone else until you're back in the suite. Do you understand? We have Jude and Imogen covered. Atticus was headed to New Horizons, but when he got to the office, there wasn't anything but blood and an absence of you. I think the only reason there isn't a slew of dead bodies currently is that he trusted you, so don't mess it up. He'll pick up the kids and will head to the suite. I'm on my way to grab the bitch. If you're not back in the hotel in twenty minutes, then I'll do something stupid. Just please..." he growled, but I could hear the panic. He wasn't fairing well.

"All you had to say was you were getting Jude. I'm

drugged up. I'm not going to try to run into danger. Geesh. I'm not some heroine in a romance novel running into danger every chance I get, needing you to save me."

"And yet, danger keeps finding you."

"Well, that's different." She sniffed, snuggling her head back down on my shoulder.

"Sure, Spitfire." There was a pause again, a deep breath released before he spoke. "I love you, Loren. You're my whole world, please be safe, or I'll have to kill everyone to get to you, and that's a lot of work and missed opportunities. So, think of all the other things you could be doing."

She giggled, the sound soothing a part of me, and I sighed, tugging on her hand. "I'll be safe. I love you, you big oaf."

"Sweeter words have never been spoken. Put Golden boy on the phone."

"I'm still here, you big lug."

"Ah, look, we have our own pet names." I rolled my eyes, but actually didn't mind it. "Repeat anything you heard me say that was sweet, though, and I'll make you think your name is Bertha. Understand?"

"Just pay me a dollar next time you see me, and we'll call it a lawyer-client privilege."

"That actually works? Shit. I'll pay you a million."

"You have that type of money?"

The phone was silent, and I could imagine him lifting his brow. "Never mind. We're headed back, no detours. I will keep her safe and bring the douchebag."

"Hope you feel like getting a little dirty."

I laughed, but he hung up before I could say anything else. I took a picture of Loren asleep on my shoulder, kissing her forehead, and sent it to him for his visual.

He sent back a puking emoji, but it only made me laugh and hold her closer. This could've been so much worse, but it wasn't. Threats kept coming at the people I loved, and it wasn't from the mafia but our own lives; that was the ironic part of it. In fact, it was because of the mafia we were still alive. So, while the world might see them as the bad guys, I knew differently. To me, these men had become my family, and even more so, heroes.

I just wouldn't tell Sax that. His head was already too big.

Forty

LOREN

When I woke up a few hours later, my arm was a dull throbbing ache, but outside of being stiff, it wasn't too bad. I still couldn't believe that Brian had tried to shoot me. I didn't know what it meant for him, but I'd hit my expiration date for dealing with his crap.

Sitting up, I found Wells asleep next to me, his breathing heavy, letting me know he was in a deep sleep. A dog slept between our legs, and when I reached down to pet them, I found Fort. His fur was coarse and not the soft, tight curls of Barkley. This was twice now that they'd saved someone. They really deserved the best treatment. I'd need to schedule them a doggy day spa or something or get them steak. Maybe I'd ask Wells what would be the best.

Throwing off the covers, I realized we were back at the hotel. Our return to the mansion hadn't lasted long. It could only mean we were under attack. Scooting out of bed, I softly padded my way toward the door. It opened easily, and I stepped out into the quiet hallway. I didn't know what time it was, but I found it strange that the place we'd been at a few days ago was this silent. It had been bustling with people at all hours of the day prior, so what was different?

A soft light peaked out from under a door, and I pushed it open. A gasp left me when I found Brian sitting bloody and bruised in a chair. When I looked over, I found Sax standing against the wall. His face was a blank mask, and I didn't like it. His eyes flicked to me for the barest of seconds before returning to my ex-husband. The most jaw-dropping thing, though, was the man I found behind Brian, the one with his own bloody knuckles.

He looked up at me, his eyes swirling with an immense amount of emotion. I covered my mouth with one hand, not sure what to do. Sweat dripped off his forehead, his hair hanging down in his face. He wrenched Brian's head back, holding my gaze before a sneer formed on his face, and he looked down at my despicable ex-husband.

"What's it going to be, Brian? Ready to spill, or are you going to continue to play dumb? Maybe I should have Beautiful step on your balls again. She did a real number on them. I'm surprised your voice can come out at the same octave." Nicco flicked his eyes up, a smirk growing on his face in pride. "That was fucking magnificent, babe. If I didn't have to take care of this sad sack of shit, I would've come and rewarded you right then."

I blushed, my cheeks reddening at the heated

comment. I didn't know if I wanted to be attracted to him going ape-shit on my ex, but I was. It was a side of Nicco I'd never seen before. He'd unleashed his darker urges, letting himself be free, and I realized that was what I found attractive. His authenticity.

I walked over to the wall where Sax was, and the instant I was in reach, he snatched his hand out, pulling me to him. He held me tight, pinching my arm some, but I took it, knowing he needed to feel me. I'd been hurt at first when he hadn't shown any emotion, but I got it now. He couldn't let himself yet, or he would've fallen apart, and he still had a job to do.

His hand smoothed down my hair, and I felt him breathe in my smell. His lips pressed into my scalp, and his body shuddered. When he released me, he spun me, pulling my back to him, not letting me go now I was here.

"Fine," Brian hissed, his eyes glaring into me. "Some scary dude gave me half a million to walk into Loren's office and keep her occupied. I didn't know the gun was loaded. I didn't want to kill her. That was an accident and all that brute's fault for knocking it out of my hand."

I stiffened, not liking where it was headed. The door opened again, and Atticus walked in with Monroe. Monroe ran over when he saw me, hugging both Sax and me, since the giant refused to let me go.

"You get a hug, too, then." I chuckled, not minding the sandwich. Atticus walked over, impatiently waiting for Monroe to let me go.

"You already got to hold her. It's my turn, goody-two-shoes."

"Call me names all you want, boss man. I'll still hold my girlfriend as long as I want."

Atticus growled, and I smiled at him over Roe's shoulder. I raised my non-injured arm, beckoning him. "There's room, Attie."

"Fucking disgusting," Brian murmured before I heard the sound of flesh hitting flesh. I didn't have to look to know Nicco had hit him. Monroe stepped back, letting Atticus pull me from Sax. The big man growled, but let me go for Atticus. He held me close to him, kissing my cheek.

"I'm glad you're okay, Bellezza."

"The kids?" I asked. I trusted him to have taken care of them, but I still needed to know.

"Asleep. Jude's been a worried mess. You might want to stop by his room and wake him when you get a chance."

"Thank you."

"Of course. We're all family. There's been a few things I need to discuss with you." His eyes lifted above me to Sax. "Are we done here?" I didn't hear Sax answer, but he must've responded enough for Attie to know, pulling me toward the door. "Wrap it up, Nicolai. It's time we lay all the cards on the table."

"Sure thing, big bro. Though, I was just starting to have fun."

"It's like he decided to go back through puberty," Atticus muttered to me.

"I like it. He's being his authentic self." I giggled, feeling high on the relief of being in a room together.

Atticus rolled his eyes, but I think he agreed. He was just too keyed up at the moment. When I walked into the formal dining room, I was surprised to find Cami and Nat there. They both squealed, running to me. Atticus stopped them, pushing me behind him. "She was just shot! Caution."

"Grazed," I mumbled, not missing his narrowed eyes.

"Sorry, we just miss her," Cami said, looking apologetic. Atticus relented, letting me move around him. They both smiled, coming over, but with less enthusiasm. They hugged me, being mindful of my sling, not that Atticus would've allowed them to hurt me.

"Oh my God, your hair! I love it," I exclaimed, touching Cami's now lighter locks. It was more strawberry blonde with highlights than the darker red it had been.

"Yeah, well, I needed a change. Nat did it. Isn't it great?" she asked, but I caught some of the anxiety and realized it must've been needed to move past Darren. Giving them both one more hug, I moved to sit down.

The woman I'd seen in Atticus' office earlier was already sitting at the table, her legs kicked over the arm as she watched us in interest. Her electric purple hair stood out in the bland room, and I instantly wish I could pull something like that off. Her glasses perched on her nose as she looked back and forth between us. All she needed was some popcorn, and she could've been the perfect replica of that meme.

"Hi, I didn't get to meet you earlier. I'm Loren." Her face showed surprise, and she hopped up, wiping her hands on her plaid skirt. Her whole look was eclectic. She was a little punk, a little grunge, and a little sexy. Somehow, it worked for her, and she pulled off this sexy, nerdy vibe.

"Oh my goodness, it's so nice to meet the infamous girlfriend of Oscar. That man, he would not shut up about you." She laughed, and I found myself smiling at her. I could see why Sax had gotten so annoyed, but I found her charming.

"I'm sure he did. He's such a chatterbox, that one. This is Cami and Nat. And you are?"

"Oh, apologies, I feel like I already know everyone from my internet stalking." She peered around me, waving at Cami. "Hey, Enigma, long time no see."

Cami rolled her eyes, sitting down, and I noticed she kept her hand with her finger missing cradled to her, and I wondered how she was doing with it all. I needed to reach out more and check in. She ignored the girl, waving her off. "Don't mind, Cleo. They hardly ever let her out around others."

"You blow up something one time, and it's like you can't be trusted with explosives. But who do they all come to when they need help with their computers and phones? That's right, me! *Pixel, fix this; Pixel, work faster.* I swear, it's been a freaking holiday coming here. I get to actually do the shit I've been trained for. So, Enigma, what's your game? How did that project I helped you on turn out?" She leaned on the table, her chin resting in her hands.

"It's just Cami here. I'm not a Siren."

"Hmm, sure." Her bright purple hair swished back and forth, her face showing she didn't believe anything Cami said.

"I'm sorry, Sirens?" I asked, feeling lost. Those drugs were affecting me more than I realized.

"It's the Costa women's mafia name, and each recruit gets a code name. Cleo here is Pixel because she's so good with the tech stuff. I was Enigma because I excelled in the brains part, and I could be mysterious. I was on the seduction track before I decided it wasn't for me," Cami explained, shrugging her shoulders like it wasn't a big deal.

Nat and I looked at her, blinking as she revealed this part of her life we hadn't known. She looked between us, some guilt on her face. "It's not a part of my life I like to remember. After my dad died, I went a little off the rails and my mom sent me to camp. I tried it out, but it wasn't what I wanted. End of story. Now, can we focus on something else? So, is it true? Is Dayton alive?"

Atticus cleared his throat, drawing attention to him. The others had filed into the room, sitting down at the table while we'd been talking. Even Wells leaned against Monroe, along with Topher and Beau. I noticed that Nat kept averting her eyes from looking in his direction, and his only seared into her, not even trying to hide who he was staring down. I'd need to get the story behind that.

"It's true. Pixel's test showed that the bones were actually Benny's. Somehow, Dayton managed to escape after I shot him and put the decoy bones in his place. It was probably Uncle Seth, but it's hard to know since one of them is dead, and the other isn't really being forthcoming."

"What was his intention of keeping himself hidden? Is he working with Darren?" I asked, not seeing how it all measured up. What was the purpose of him coming to therapy? Was it just to unnerve me, or had there been a plan to get information from me? Was he that deluded to think it would be a head game? Actually, I wouldn't put it past Dayton to not play with his food.

"It seems that Darren was a means to an end, and we inadvertently helped him get Darren out of the picture, leaving the Delgado family for him to take over, along with swaying most of our family members as well to his new one."

"Fuck," Nat swore, her fingers beginning to tap nervously on the table.

"He's taken over the house in the suburbs, and he's tried to take over several of our businesses. Climax was bought with my own money and is untouchable, despite his attempts to have all my staff leave. The others, they will be a battle to show who has the claim—him or me. I worry the most about Upswing. Rawles took the Masked Kingpin when we dethroned Darren, and I could see Dayton wanting it. While I've done all the legwork for it, it was initially his idea. He might try to poach it, stating he has more stake in it. A lot of my money is tied up in that place. It was to be our family's new future, and I could see him wanting to attack that to prove a point, especially after losing the other one."

"I might have something to add," Cami stated, lifting her head. She looked at Pixel and then Atticus. "Before I was, um, captured, I'd taken some files from Darren's computer and had Pixel help decode them. When I was trying to figure out what they connected to, that was when he caught me."

"What did the information you found say?" Atticus asked, his jaw tensing. I could practically hear him grinding his molars together from here. I reached over, grabbing Cami's arm in support. She took a deep breath, giving me a watery smile. I knew it couldn't be easy to share this with us.

"It was blueprints, mostly and some plans to operate some type of club underneath it. I couldn't piece it all together, which was why I had Pixel looking into it for me. If I had to guess based on the information I've learned in my stay… it looked like a full-blown operation, effectively cutting out Rawles and, well, you."

"Fuck," Sax said. I watched Atticus as he mulled it over.

"So the question is, why hasn't our dear friend Ethan told us what he's found?"

We all sat quietly, thinking it over, not sure what this meant for their alliance.

"And our captives?" I asked. It had been quiet too long, and I could feel myself wanting to fall asleep.

"Oh, let me," Pixel started, excitement entering her voice. "So, I was able to formulate this chemical compound that will enter their system and kill them later. It's got a delayed function, giving you the perfect alibi, plus you know, it's untraceable. I'm calling it the *Filibuster* because it fills you with gas until you bust, and it's delayed. Get it?" She mimed brushing her fingernails on her sleeve. "Yeah, I'm that good."

"While that's all creepy in a way I never thought about before, where does that leave us?" Nat asked, eyeing Pixel, who still seemed impressed with her killer agent. Atticus answered, pulling our focus back on him.

"I don't know. About fifty people have chosen our way of life within the family, but it's not enough. He has the numbers and the capital now. He's also been planning and scheming for months. I... I don't know what he's going to do next."

I watched as Atticus admitted his uncertainty, showing his vulnerability to the people who'd chosen to stay. It made me love him even more.

"We got some information from the bag of shit. Once brat here fills him up with the gas, we can let him loose. Bitch #1 has already taken the bait. She won't be found for months, I hope, and it won't be pretty when she is. I doubt even the rats will want to feast on her." Sax filled in, smiling at his words.

"What did you do?" I asked, but then shook my head. "Never mind, not an image I need in my mind."

"Just know she's leaving the world the way she lived it. Alone, entitled, and full of shit." He grinned, and it had a manic edge to it. Again, something inside me said I shouldn't find that hot, but I was tired of listening to that voice tell me what I should and shouldn't like. I loved Sax, even the crazy killer parts of him, and that was that.

Feeling pleased with sorting out my moral compass, I looked around the room while they all spoke, laying out some plans and options. I didn't have anything else to offer, so I stood up and slipped out of the room, wanting to check on Jude.

Nicco caught my hand, a little fear in his eyes I wouldn't accept him. Lacing our hands together, I pulled him with me down the hall to the room Jude had stayed in last time. I knocked softly, but when I didn't hear anything, I peeked in slowly, not wanting to wake him if he was asleep.

Except the room was empty, his bed unmade, like he'd climbed out to get something. I walked over, touched it, and found it cold. But that meant… dread started to pool in me, and I looked over at Nicco. He tugged me out, going toward the room with Brian. My eyes swept every possible place Jude could be, but I already knew as well as Nicco. He wasn't in the hotel suite.

"Where is he?" Nicco bellowed, slapping Brian awake.

He started laughing, the sound chilling me to my bones. Fuck. I dropped Nicco's hand, running back through the rooms, opening and closing every door, hoping and praying he was here, just out of sight. Again, I knew this wasn't the case, but my thoughts wouldn't let me believe it until I checked. When I opened Imogen's room, she peeked up, squinting against the light.

I sighed in relief that she was still there. "Lor, is that you?" She started to get out of bed to come to me. "We were so worried."

I stopped her when she got to me, holding her arms. "Immy, do you know where Jude is?"

"Of course."

I relaxed, pulling her into my arms. "Thank God. I was worried. Where is he?"

"What do you mean? Elijah woke us and said there was some emergency at the center." Her face heated at the mention of them being asleep, but I didn't care.

"Tell me exactly what happened."

"We fell asleep watching a movie in Jude's room. Elijah came in, said you told him to take Jude to the center." She rubbed her head. "Um, something to do with his brother. Jude didn't want to, but Elijah insisted. So he changed and left with him, and I came back to my room. Jude only went because he thought you told him to. What's going on, Lor? I'm scared."

I shook my head, my hair swishing. *No, no, no, no.* I backed away, my hand going to my mouth as I tried to hold it together. This couldn't be happening. *No. No. No.*

Imogen started to panic, coming after me, asking me questions, but I couldn't hear her. I ran back into the meeting room, the door slamming against the wall. Atticus turned, a glare forming until he saw it was me and the state I was in. He leaped up, running to me, along with the others.

"He's gone. He took him. He's gone, Attie. You promised to keep him safe. *You promised.*" My voice was one notch above hysteria as panic overwhelmed me.

I hadn't meant to say that last part. I knew this wasn't his fault, and I watched as something in him cracked, but I couldn't take the words back. I could only move forward and show Atticus I trusted him, despite what my panic was saying.

"Tell me everything." His face went hard as granite, mimicking my heart.

I pointed at Imogen, unable to say anything else until I had a handle on my emotions. Someone grabbed my arm, pulling me to a chair, and I sat down, a plan forming in my head. Dayton had taken my son. He was sending *me* a message. So, what was it?

Thinking back over our sessions and everything I knew about narcissism, I tried to put the pieces together, a puzzle beginning to form in my mind. I could do this. I could be smarter than the cold-blooded psychopath. It was no longer okay for me to just stand on the sidelines. This was my life, and I needed to embrace it. It was time I stepped across the line, and made the vow I made to myself count.

It might be the only thing that saved us.

EPILOGUE

Unlocking the door to the center, I reached for the light, but nothing happened. Pulling out my phone, I used it to light my way, trying to remember if Mitzi had shown me where the breaker box was on my tour. Stepping around a corner, a figure jumped out, grabbing me.

Panic clawed up my throat, and I fought against them, trying to escape. Blackness seeped in, and I slid to the ground, falling to the cold concrete beneath me.

When I woke up later, the air was thick with smoke, and I started to cough. The room felt warmer than it should and as I sat up, I realized I was sweating. The room was cloudy, the smoke making it difficult to see, and I watched as flames licked up the walls around me.

Pulling out my phone, I prayed I could send one text before I met my end.

Loren: I love you

Do you kind of hate me? It's okay if you do. I'm expecting the shouting. If you want some sneak peeks into things that happened in this book with Cami and Nat, then you'll want to grab their novellas releasing in March and April before Dangerous Love.

Not only will they give you some insight into their stories, but there are also some clues to that ending. So, if you can't wait until May/June, then be sure to read their books. I think you'll love their stories. I know I did writing them.

I can't believe we're at the end of the series and Loren's story is almost over. Loren has been extra special to me in so many ways, and her story is my story in a lot of ways. Though, not in the fun ones.

This book was my favorite so far as I loved seeing Loren grow so much and the men coming together. Now that Dayton has revealed himself, it will be interesting to see how these characters rise together to take back what is theirs.

I couldn't have written this book without the help of a lot of people. Emma Henn, you're my light in the darkness. Kayla and Amber, you give me life with your comments. Cat you're always there to help me and I couldn't ever thank you enough.

To my amazing beta team: Megan, Shawna, Michelle, Marla. Thank you for reading and loving this characters. I didn't give you much time this book, but you pulled through and made it shine.

To my ARC readers and anyone who picks up this series, thank you for taking a chance and reading my book. I hoped it brought you some laughs, and you don't hate me too much. I promise to deliver an amazing final book for Loren and her guys. In the meantime, make sure to subscribe to my newsletter and stay up to date on the bonus material for this series.

You can help me out by leaving a review, or sending me a message to tell me your thoughts on this book. If you spot an error, please send to me or my PA at authorkrisbutler@gmail.com

Thank you. Now, time to have some murder cupcakes.

Tattooed Hearts Duet

Tattooed Hearts Completed Duet

Riddled Deceit (Part 1)

Smudged Lines (Part 2)

Sinners Fairytales (standalone)

Pride

ABOUT THE AUTHOR

Kris Butler writes under a pen name to have some separation from her everyday life. Never expecting to write a book, she was surprised when an author friend encouraged her to give it a try and how much she enjoyed it. Having an extensive background in mental health, Kris hopes to normalize mental health issues and the importance of talking about them with her characters and books. Kris is a southern girl at heart but lives with her husband and adorable furbaby somewhere in the Midwest. Kris is an avid fan of Reverse Harem and hopes to add a quirky and new perspective to the emerging genre. If you enjoyed her book, please consider leaving a review. You can contact her the following ways and follow Kris's journey as a new author on social media.

Join the newsletter

Join KB's Mavens of Mayhem